ALIX JAMES

NO SUCH THING AS LUCK

A SWEET VICTORIAN ROMANCE

Print ISBN: 978-1-957082-15-8

Cover Artwork by GetCovers.com

Cover Images licensed by Shutterstock.com

- Blog and newsletter: https://nicoleclarkston.com/
- Facebook: https://www.facebook.com/NicoleClarkstonAuthor
- Twitter: https://twitter.com/N_Clarkston
- Amazon: https://www.amazon.com/Nicole-Clarkston
- Austen Variations: https://austenvariations.com

To my father and my husband-
two men who taught me how a real man loves.

Contents

One

Hannah Thornton looked up from her needlework when she heard her son's quick step at the door. She did not smile, but her eyes acknowledged her affection in a slight crinkling around the corners; a miniscule softening of her expression which none but he would recognize. He did not look at her directly but passed by her chair in the dining parlor with a brief touch on her shoulder. Reaching for the pot of tea she had kept hot for him the last hour, he poured silently.

Mrs Thornton dropped her eyes back to her point work. She had made little progress today. The black stitching was wearing on her eyes, but that was not the real reason for her lack of success. For weeks now, her son had been laboring late hours, even for him, trying to singlehandedly make up for the disastrous blow to the mill caused by last year's strike. Mrs Thornton considered it a point of honour to never take her ease when he was in distress. As a consequence, they were both tired and worn.

She knew that business with the bank had called him out most of the afternoon. He had tried to make up for lost time all evening, poring over his ledgers. Over the rim of her sewing glasses, she arched an eyebrow- a silent invitation for him to reveal what he would of his latest conversation with Mr Dalton from the bank. He fingered the smooth rim of his teacup as he tried to form the words he must speak.

"Mother, we have few options left." She let go the breath she had been holding. She was as relieved to hear him finally speak as she was when she comprehended what he had *not* said- he did not say they had no options at all. She set her needlework aside and folded her hands in her lap, waiting for him to continue.

"The bank has extended the loan on the equipment I purchased last year. Twice, in fact. They will not do so again. I have little enough real property- all my assets are already leveraged and they do not like the risk. The banks are being very careful, as most of the mills are in a bad way. Cotton from the Americas is going up in price and our buyers are not paying for product on time. The weather has not warmed this summer as we had depended upon, and we have little hope of a good season at this point. It is a time of bad trade in general.

"That speculation of Watson's paid off handsomely last week. Most of the other mill owners invested in it, and will now have ample capital to ride out the lean times. Marlborough Mills will be seen as a liability in comparison, so it will be difficult for us to attract new orders." He took a long, pensive swallow of his tea. The lukewarm liquid swirled tastelessly in his mouth. He set it down impatiently and went to the sideboard to pour himself a drink.

Mrs Thornton watched him silently, waiting for him to continue. "We had so much bad product from the Irish workers all those months ago that we had to discard much of our material and got even further behind on the orders. We never have caught up, and I have no idea how we ever shall. We are going to exhaust our supplies before our buyers finally pay up. By summer's end, I will either not be able to purchase more cotton, not be able to pay the hands, or the bank will collect on the equipment."

He finished the contents of his glass and dropped it with a loud *clink* on the table. Mrs Thornton cringed as much at the abuse of her furniture as the words he had said. All of these things she knew already. John was clearly trying to persuade himself to something radical.

"But," probed she cautiously, "you believe we do have options? Do you mean selling and giving up the lease on Marlborough Mills?"

"Possibly," he murmured. Steepling his fingers, he continued, "However, there may be an alternative. An investor.... A partner, really," he amended.

Her surprise was evident. John had gotten his start in the mill through the aid of a partner, who had been a trusted business associate of his father's. Since then, however, he had assiduously avoided such entanglements. He preferred to do business according to the strictest moral standards, and no one was ever deemed trustworthy enough.

In addition to that, he had simply never needed another partner. His success had been rapid and very great. By the age of four and twenty he had been Master of the most modern and promising cotton mill in the region. Other men, older business men, looked to him for advice. He was quickly known for his keen business sense, his disciplined management, and his unimpeachable honour.

A year ago, all of that had changed. Mrs Thornton recalled bitterly the labor strike which had begun the pendulum swing in Milton. John's actions had ended the strike, but the damage to Marlborough Mills and the others affected by it was already done. It had been a large financial blow, one more easily absorbed by the older tradesmen who had been building their capital reserves.

John, however, had foreseen the potential boon in newer equipment which could handle massive orders. The possibilities had been tremendous, but to lose such ground when all of his capital was invested in equipment meant that recovery now was all but impossible. Additionally, he alone had carried the financial burden of the Irish workers, whose arrival had precipitated the rioting. The strike ended to the benefit of all, but John bore the cost.

"There *was* another alternative, you know, Mother," he went on. "Watson, he's been gloating all week about how that scheme of his paid out. He was right, and now he has proof that I was wrong. Despite all, Mother, I cannot bring myself to regret not joining him in the venture. I would have had to invest all the capital I have left, much of it not rightfully mine. Still, it is true, all of our worries would now be at an end." John bit his lip and blinked rapidly as his mind again reviewed the week's events.

"John, you must not look back with regrets. You were right to refuse. What if it had failed?"

"I would not be able to pay my debts, leaving my creditors without hope of recovery. The mill would fail, and all the men would be out of work immediately. I would have injured others for my own selfish gain."

"I would not have you compromise your honour and dignity. I will stand proud knowing my son is a man who would not yield to the temptation of an easy fix at the price of his integrity." Mrs Thornton's eyes flashed, her square chin raised emphatically.

Despite himself, he could not help a small smile. He clasped her wrinkled fingers in grateful recognition of her unswerving support. "Mr Dalton knows of a fellow in Spain who has been making inquiries, a Señor Barbour. Apparently, he owns a large shipping business, having contacts throughout the Continent as well as Africa and South America.

"In addition, he appears to have recently acquired an interest in an estate which grows cotton in the Andalucía province. The province does not grow the quantity of cotton there that the Americas or Egypt do, but they do have the right climate and have become a reckonable source on the Continent. Apparently, his estate is rather large- exceedingly so- and he claims the soil is excellent.

"He has taken on a young English partner, a Mr Marshall, who is by all accounts resident in the country now. He speaks glowingly to this Señor Barbour of the opportunities for industry here in the North. It seems this partner had an occasion recently to see what we have built here, and Barbour wishes to forge an alliance. He believes there is money to be made in eliminating a few middlemen and dealing directly with the mill owners. He proposes a partnership with an English mill to refine his product which he will then sell at a better margin."

Mrs Thornton considered. "What about your profits? Would you be losing a great deal?"

"I believe not, no." Agitated, he poured himself another cup of the tasteless tea, wisely deciding not to return to the sideboard for another drink. "Dalton had a financial proposal drawn up from the fellow. Interestingly enough, Señor Barbour contracts to supply me exclusively at a fixed price. I may buy elsewhere, of course, since he will not be able to meet all of our demands, but he proposes to ship all of his raw product to me. The contract dictates that he will place orders of his own for a fixed percentage of the finished product. The rest I would sell to other buyers for cash up front.

"In effect, I would be paying for my raw material with finished orders, rather than ready cash. The tradeoff is favorable for me, in terms of our usual profit margin. If the cotton is the quality he claims it is, the proposal has merit. It solves our immediate supply problem, at any rate, and might buy us the time we need.

"There is the additional advantage of having a steady supply outside of the American cotton. I fear for the political instability there. However..." he looked up from his cup, "I will have to go myself."

"Go? To Spain?" She tried to conceal her distress, but was only partially successful.

"It is the only way to work out the details of what he proposes, as it is a rather radical shift from the way we usually do business. Also, I need to see for myself what manner of man he is. I would rather sell out this minute than become irrevocably involved with an unscrupulous partner, no matter how deep his pockets or intriguing his ideas. Yes, I will have to go to Spain- to Cádiz. And I will have to leave soon if I am to make a go of it."

She slowly blew air through her clenched teeth, seeking control of her words. "How soon?"

"I hope to leave in three days. There is a steamer, the *Esperanza,* to set sail from London on Monday. I just missed the Liverpool packet. The next ships are not until much later in the week. I asked Mr Dalton to send word to his contact in Cádiz to expect me."

"How long will you be away?"

"I am not sure, exactly. It should take three or four days to sail each way, and of course I will have to spend some days viewing this Barbour's operation. I hope I should return inside a fortnight, but it may well take longer to settle matters. I hate to leave with things the way they are here, but I believe I must. You will not be worried to stay alone?"

"Nay, John, I shall manage. You will do as you must, as you always do." Her firm conviction reassured him. He had spent many years caring for his mother's every need and concern. He felt derelict in his duty leaving her to her own devices. Of course, she would be cared for in every physical comfort and certainly would be safe, but he knew her days would be consumed with lonely worry while he was gone.

"Thank you, Mother," he replied with sincere feeling, truly appreciating the brave sacrifices she made to support him. "Perhaps you may wish to stay some days with Fanny and Watson while I am away?"

She made a derisive noise. "I should be much more comfortable here."

He smiled with only his eyes, fully understanding her meaning. Fiercely loyal to him as she was, she would not be able to bear the company of his triumphant business rival at a time when his own affairs were so uncertain. Of all people, his mother would manage on her own.

Still, he disliked that she would be kept in anxious suspense these many days, waiting alone without word of his fate. As he intended to depart again as soon as matters were settled, one way or another, it was not likely that a letter from Spain to apprise her of his findings would reach her any earlier than he himself could.

He stared into the fire a moment. He had never been a man given to fear, but the oppressive weight of his immediate future bore down upon him like a leaden blanket. For years he had been sole provider, slavishly devoting every waking breath, every striving energy to lift his family's burden. Gradually he had seen all his labors come to fruition, and his ambitions had bought him a place of honour out of shame.

Now, standing at the brink of ruin once more, his heart lamented at the futility of all he had borne. It seemed that every work, every achievement, was melting away as straw before the flames. The one thing which could have remained his own through any trial-the loyal heart of a partner to his life - had been destined to never be his to claim. The hope and fire that had kindled briefly in him had been entirely doused, leaving behind a broken shell with only a failing business to satisfy his hungry soul.

Mrs Thornton watched him unobserved. The etched lines of worry deepened on his face as he let his guard down to his own private thoughts. Fortune was a capricious thing. It tore her heart to see her precious son, a man above other men, forged out of the fires of adversity, brought low at the whims of fate. He deserved all the fine things this world had to offer, and yet all slipped through his fingers as sand through the cracks.

He scrubbed his face roughly with his hands, raking his fingers through his hair. He blew out an exhausted sigh. "I must begin making preparations. Do not wait up for me, Mother."

She nodded, and he rose to go. No more words were needed between mother and son. Their conversations had always been concise and to the point, but lately they spoke even less. He had become withdrawn from the one person to whom he had always gone for advice. He was always gentle when he spoke with her, but never revealed his deeper feelings.

Never, since... since *her*. Mrs Thornton pursed her lips in irritation as the image of a queenly young woman with a proud demeanor came to memory. Margaret Hale had left Milton over four months ago, bereft of family and destitute in grief, but a mother's sense knew that the young woman could still count her brave son's heart among her few possessions.

With a rush of anger she did not understand, she picked up her work and stabbed her needle through. She blamed Margaret for the distance between herself and her favorite child. She had seen him often, when he thought she wasn't looking, slip into a state of anguished loneliness. His haunted eyes spoke of the great yawning chasm of emptiness slowly devouring him.

She had been his sole confidante and partner for over seventeen years, and he hers. Selfishly, the widow had wished to keep her son all to herself, but the soul of a mother could not dwell perpetually in selfishness. She ached to see her son well matched, and to see finally a happy contentment grace his beloved features.

In sudden mortification, the widow admonished herself for ever believing she could satisfy all of her son's needs. A heart as generous as his needed the love of a woman and the hope of a future. None had ever caught his eye, much less held his interest, until the displaced beauty from the southern countryside. *The one woman*, she reflected grimly, *who failed to see all that he was.*

The foolish lass had rashly thrown away a good and noble man, preferring instead to keep her own questionable company. Mrs Thornton grit her teeth. And after all of that, when confronted with her folly, the girl had acted like an offended princess instead of the contrite, malleable young woman Mrs Thornton decided she ought to be. Proud and haughty was Margaret Hale. So unlike her meek father and docile mother!

At the time, Mrs Thornton had been well pleased to discover that her son had escaped the grasp of such a headstrong woman. She did not deserve him. For his part, he ought to have a wife who could honour and respect him, not a foolish lass who subverted his authority at every turn. Miss Hale had too much fire and spirit to ever make a respectable wife for one such as her son.

Despite all the very sound reasons he should put her out of his mind, it was clear that thus far, at least, he had been unsuccessful at banishing her from his heart. Mrs Thornton could almost find it within her to regret that Miss Hale had failed to see her son's finer qualities. Margaret had salt and pluck- Mrs Thornton wished she could have liked her. Particularly now, when John most needed a staunch supporter, she would have been comforted to know that he at least had the woman he loved by his side.

Would pampered Miss Hale have remained loyal through his struggles? Inwardly she doubted. The girl was a puzzle of discrepancies she did not understand. At once so regally distant, and yet so warmly caring for those she loved, Margaret Hale was an enigma. Could the young woman have ever renounced her Southern prejudices in favor of the virtuous and tender-hearted man who loved her?

No, she decided, *that is not likely. She does not even realize what she rejected.* She had her fashionable airs and graces and, Mrs Thornton admitted, a lovely face, yet with all of that Margaret would never find a truer heart than her own son's. *Let her be happy in London*, she thought sourly. *Where she can torment him no longer.*

She sighed heavily. *I suppose it is too late for that.* She could not reasonably blame Margaret Hale for John's business troubles, but his state of mind could most certainly be laid at her door. *At least she is gone to London for good,* Mrs Thornton thought. *Back with her* own *kind in Harley Street, wherever that is. He never has to see her again.*

Two

MR THORNTON ROSE EARLY the next morning to set into motion everything he must do before his departure. His overseer, Williams, arrived soon after, and Mr Thornton pulled him aside for an hour's conference on the status of the mill. Williams would be stretched to the full during his absence, trying to cover the tasks of two men, but Thornton had no doubt of his competence. Though he ought to be nearing retirement, Williams had always been loyal and honest, as well as keen work master. The mill would be in good hands.

Behind two stacks of papers, they reviewed the next week's orders. The Brighton order was complete, but the New York order was behind schedule. Biting back whatever scalding remarks he would once have made to his overseer, he resolved to speak to some of the hands. A few of the older machines had proven difficult to adjust to the finer cotton fibers they had been receiving of late. He knew specifically the man to ask about that.

As the steam whistle sounded and the men filed in, Thornton's attention was diverted. He watched as one man after another shuffled to his work station. Most ducked their heads, avoiding his scrutiny, but one looked up at him on the scaffolding and met his gaze with a twinkle in his eye and a friendly smirk. Higgins.

His look was impertinent- many masters would have instantly put him in his place for such bold familiarity. Hamper had thought his former employee to be a dangerous loose cannon. He was disrespectful to authority, incorrigibly opinionated, and an instigator among the men whom Hamper fought to keep subdued. Thornton liked him immensely.

Once, he would have agreed with Hamper. Every common sense rebelled against hiring a troublemaker like Higgins. He had never expected anything should occur to change that opinion. Then, *she.* Still, after all of these months, he could not see Higgins without that familiar warmth stealing through him. *Margaret.* In his thoughts he always called her by her Christian name, but he kept that tender secret locked away in his heart. His hopes for the right to speak thus openly were turned to ash, but he could never again use the formal appellation when he thought of her privately.

His gaze followed Higgins as he sauntered to his machine. He was a hothead, he admitted to himself. He was passionate in his opinions and fiery in his speech. He held sway with the other men, who looked to him for his intelligent leadership. He was indeed informed, having been well read, but only on one side of matters.

Their association had brought more advantages to both of them than he had at first thought possible. Both had begun to understand the difficulties the other faced. Thornton had been forced to concede that Higgins spoke out of the deep needs and dismal poverty surrounding him, while Higgins had come to respect the Master's formidable responsibility to keep solvent the dynamic business which employed them all.

Whether or not their newfound understanding would be enough to forestall future strikes remained to be seen. He felt the experiment should be tried, and was grateful for the chance to do so. His thoughts turned once again to the woman whose quiet insistence had made it all possible.

Margaret had looked at the roughened union leader and seen the loyal heart and kind soul which he had not. In her profound loneliness, she had befriended the man and his family, despite their vast differences in society. Thornton was still a little baffled about how they had begun, but the regal clergyman's daughter and the careworn old weaver had formed an unusual attachment.

It was for her that he had given Higgins a chance. At the time he had rationalized that he owed it to his own sense of honour, setting right a wrong. He knew he had judged the man prematurely and could not rest knowing he had been unjust. The truth of it was, though, he had also hoped somehow to make Margaret think a little better of him.

He'd fully expected to prove her faith in the man wrong. Instead, he had been most pleasantly surprised to find an impeccably honest, hardworking, intelligent, and highly skilled craftsman had come to him. The fellow was a wizard with the machinery- he could fix any breakdown quickly and even spot flaws in the cloth which many others did not until it was too late. Coupled with the knowledge that Higgins had taken in the orphaned children of a man he had not even liked, Thornton had found a new respect growing for the man.

A new idea pricked him. Had his staid overseer also come to appreciate the quirky Union leader? It would be of value to know how the man was relating to others already in his employ. "Williams? How has that man Higgins been working out?"

Williams started with a grunt. "Better 'n I ever thought, sir. He's a hard worker. Never had any trouble with him. Did you know he and some others stayed over their time without pay last week to finish the order that was to ship to Bath? I found out about it a few days later. I know it was him what led them on to do it. I had my doubts sir," Williams turned back to the tally sheet for the day's orders, "but I think he'll keep."

Thornton felt a slow smile spreading across his face. "Williams, could you use an extra hand while I am gone? Someone to watch the carding and sorting rooms while you handle invoices? You cannot cover it all at once."

Williams looked up, frowned, and pulled his glasses off. Wiping them thoughtfully on his handkerchief, he replied slowly, "You're thinking of Higgins, sir?"

"I am asking what you think. Do you think it would cause trouble?"

Williams replaced his glasses. "If you mean union trouble, I don't think so, sir. The men respect him and he knows the mill better than you or I. As long as you rate his pay higher for the extra work, sir. They get mighty touchy about wage differences."

Thornton nodded. "I will speak with him. He is to be under your authority while I am away, though. If it doesn't work out, you will need to move him back." With a last imperious glance over his domain, the Master turned his back on the even thrumming of the machines and stepped back toward his office.

Williams gaped as Thornton walked away. A year- no, even six months ago, the Master never would have asked his opinion on the management of any of the men. Thornton had always been the undisputed ruler of his little kingdom. He certainly was not known to place men above their stations or take chances on those with dubious backgrounds. That last conversation had sounded positively revolutionary. *What's come over the Master?* Williams marveled.

WHEN THE WHISTLE SOUNDED for the dinner break, Nicholas Higgins pulled the lever to disengage his machine from the overhead drive belt. Adjusting his battered old cap, he ambled off toward the little soup kitchen behind the shipping yard. His Mary would have a plate set aside for him, so he didn't hurry to beat the rush of others crowding for a seat at the narrow benches. He preferred to stand near the window, where he could easily shift into any one of several conversations as well as watch the goings on in the yard.

Mary dashed over with his plate, and then returned just as quickly to her stove. She hurried to dish out the brothy stew to the line still growing behind her. Two or three of the young men teased her to notice them as she handed them their plates, but her cheeks just reddened as she flew to her work even faster. The old weaver nearly forgot to swallow his food. When had his Mary grown up?

The young woman he saw now had grown taller in the last year and her figure was formed. Her complexion was more delicate and little tendrils of curls fell over her softly rounded cheeks as she worked. The very image of her mother, she was.

It was clear that her appearance was not lost on the young bucks from the shipping yard. They leaned a little closer, spoke a little more softly when she was near. With a sigh, he mopped up the remains of his stew with a bread crust.

Barely more than a girl herself, Mary had been thrust into the demands of motherhood to Boucher's six children- starving for care as well as food- soon after losing her closest friend and beloved sister. Now she had taken on the entirely new role of kitchen maid at the mill, more than doubling her work load.

She had matured into her new responsibilities with a graceful aplomb previously unknown to her character. Mary had come into her own since Bess had passed on, that was for sure. It was a pity that her mother and older sister were not around to guide the girl standing at the cusp of womanhood.

Not for the first time, Higgins missed the old parson's daughter. "Miss Marget" had a grace and a kindness about her. She would have been a fine friend to his Mary now. And he suspected, with a glance out the window at the shape flashing by, that he was not the only one who sorely regretted the loss of Miss Hale.

Higgins turned out of the door just in time to catch the retreating back of the Master. He was walking quickly, his head down, as always. Knowing Thornton would not have eaten probably all day, Higgins had snatched a full plate that Mary was about to hand to another admiring young worker then ran after the Master.

Thornton had barked out his orders to a dock worker in the yard and was turning back when Higgins nearly collided with him. The full plate of stew sloshed appetizingly as he held it out. "Yo' favorite, isn't it Master?"

Thornton smiled in surprised acknowledgement, taking the plate. "Thank you, Higgins." He took a few hasty bites. This had become a regular ritual with them. Thornton often worked right through the dinner break, but Higgins had made it his personal mission to see that the Master did not starve himself completely to death. Usually he ate a few bites in grateful silence, then handed the plate back, going on his way. Today he lingered, seemingly savouring each morsel.

"Higgins, there is something I need to talk to you about. Would you join me in my office after the break is over?"

The weaver's active curiosity was piqued. Thornton's manner was thoughtful rather than irritated, so he felt no cause for alarm. He nodded, "Aye, sir." Thornton ate a few more mouthfuls, then handed him back the nearly finished plate. A bare ghost of a smile touched his eyes, then he strode quickly off. *Master's go' a deal to potter him,* Higgins thought to himself.

A QUARTER HOUR LATER found Thornton buried behind a stack of invoices. The fingers of his left hand drummed out a quick staccato on the pile of papers as his right hastily recorded figures into his ledger. His mind consumed with accomplishing his task as quickly as possible, he was taken by surprise at Higgins' knock. "Come in," his authoritative voice summoned.

Higgins stepped inside, doffing his cap out of respect for the mill master's domain. "Yo' wanted to speak wi' me, sir?" he reminded the younger man.

Thornton rose, both annoyed at the interruption to his work and grateful for a brief respite. He had come to see this plucky fellow as something of an ally, if he was not quite willing to call him a friend.

"Yes, thank you for coming, Higgins. I have something I would like to ask of you. I will be leaving the country on Monday and I shan't be back for perhaps a couple of weeks."

Higgins let out a low whistle, a mischievous twinkle in his eye, "Fine time o' year for a v'cation, Master." Higgins knew the man had probably never even considered a day of liberty away from the mill in the several years he had been Master, but with loyal determination he sought to lighten his employer's somber mood by whatever means he could.

Thornton rather liked the man's casual friendliness, but he went on as if he hadn't heard. "I have to go to Spain to see about a source of raw cotton. I would like you to give Williams a hand supervising the men while I am gone. Will you do it?"

Higgins looked surprised. "Me, sir?"

Thornton came round the massive desk to face him. "You, indeed. You know the equipment, you know the workings of the mill, the men respect you, and I trust you. Williams will have his hands full. You're to be under his complete authority and assist him with whatever he requires. Your pay will, of course, be adjusted to suit your extra responsibilities. Agreed?"

Higgins was flattered beyond measure, but his old pride would not allow him to show it. He nodded smartly, his hands twisting his cap. "Aye, Master." Then the idea of Mr Thornton's destination struck him. Thornton was about to step away when Higgins boldly stopped him. "Master, ha' yo' heard aught of Miss Marget lately?"

"Miss –who?" replied Thornton. His mind was already returning to his ledgers.

"Miss Marget- Miss Hale- th'oud parson's daughter? Me and my Mary, and the children, you know we're right fond o' her. I was wond'ring, were she doing well?"

"Oh, yes!" and suddenly the deep melancholy etched into Mr Thornton's face had been replaced by a warmer expression. "Yes," here a long pause, "Sadly, I cannot satisfy you. I have heard nothing since her maid left Milton some three or four months ago, after the last of the family's affairs were settled."

His voice was so soft, his eyes smiling distantly, that the suspicion which had already taken seed bloomed in the old weaver's mind. Higgins decided to follow to where it might lead. "And she's na' go' married, Master?"

"Not yet, I believe." Thornton's face closed once more into his customary mask. "There was some talk of it, I heard once, with some connection to the family- some attorney."

"Then she'll na' be for coming to Milton again, I reckon."

"No!" Thornton shook his head, and the astute Higgins caught a glimmer in the younger man's eye.

Higgins leaned closer and whispered confidentially, "Is the young gentleman cleared?" He enforced the depth of his intelligence by a wink, which only made things more mysterious to Thornton. The Master narrowed his eyes curiously.

Higgins was about to clarify his question when an altercation broke out between an angry drayer and two of the dock hands unloading cotton bales. Rough shouting and coarse epithets ensued until Thornton, his expression stormy, opened the window of his office and bellowed commands for the lead workers to secure order once more among their inferiors.

He turned back and sank down heavily in his chair. The clawed feet of the furniture clattered against the floor as he adjusted his seat to resume his work. His mind weighed ponderously with other matters. He seemed to have forgotten that Higgins was even there.

Higgins chewed his lip. It was obvious the Master considered their business over, but he did not feel right about walking out just yet. He was a man too familiar with pain to fail to recognize it in another.

Higgins was no simpleton. He knew that business was poor all over Milton, and he was not fool enough to think that if Thornton failed, another mill would ever take him on. It was still a miracle to him that Thornton had handed him this one opportunity. He had a deep interest not only in his own livelihood, but also in that of the one man who had given him a chance against his better judgment.

"Master," he began slowly.

Thornton looked up, surprised. He had come to value the man too highly to snap at him, but he was impatient at finding him still there and demanding his attention. "Yes?"

Higgins looked down, fingering his cap. He wasn't entirely sure what he wished to say. Something jogged his memory. "If yo'd forgive me sir, I was jest thinkin' tha' I wish our ou'd friend Hale were here. Jest Master, tha' you seem a knot o' worry. Th' ou'd parson, 'e knew how to ease a man's soul."

Though Higgins had no business speaking to his employer thus, Thornton's eyes grew misty as he stilled for a moment. "He was a good friend to me," he sighed softly.

"When my Bessie passed, it was th'ou'd parson wha' brought me comfort." Higgins decided to carefully avoid mentioning the man's daughter again. "'E was a man wha' knew sorrow." Higgins chuckled ruefully to himself. "E'en go' me to pray with him once. I 'adn' done that since 'fore my dear Jenny passed."

Thornton smiled wistfully, trying to picture the scene. "I would imagine it was not he who suggested it."

Higgins did not reply, but his face confessed the truth. It was Margaret who had brought him to her father after Bessie's death, keeping a promise to her departed friend to drag him away from the bottle. In her sweet determination she had insisted they offer him whatever comfort they could. With a dying wife and a crumbling future, the gentle old man had done as his daughter asked.

"They were kind folk, the Hales. Bro' me a deal o' good, though they was suffering theyselves."

Thornton glanced away, suddenly blinking rapidly. "Thank you, Higgins," he murmured in a low, lingering tone. His face schooled carefully back into that of the Master, he nodded curtly to dismiss his worker. Whatever pain the man was feeling was ruthlessly bottled back up.

Pity for his wealthy employer filled him as Higgins confirmed in his mind that he was quite certain now of the source of that pain. "'Tis a sorrow," he murmured to himself. Still, 'Miss Marget' had embodied to Higgins everything that a lady ought to be. She was as lovely as the most beautiful of her class Higgins had ever laid eyes on, but her tender compassion and genuine kindness won his old heart. There could be none finer, and knowing that his employer had cared for her, even in vain, elevated that man in his estimation. It made him seem almost human.

He closed the door and shook his head, wishing once again that matters had settled differently for the young lass. Whistling tunelessly, the old weaver shoved his hands in his pockets and walked slowly back to his post.

Thornton struggled valiantly to return to his task, but Higgins' words had effectively disrupted any coherent train of thought. Sighing deeply, he sat back and tugged open his desk drawer. Inside was a musty old book with a worn leather cover.

Gently caressing the gold leaf lettering, he let the book fall open in his hands. Plato. He treasured the book as his old friend's possession, but he cherished the note inside even more. It was brief, written in a graceful feminine hand which his heart had memorized. The edges of the note were frayed with reverent caresses, but the writing was still crisp and clear as the day it had been penned some months ago. The words were thoughtful, but carefully chosen to convey no real feeling from the author. His fingers stroked the edges of the paper as he once again tried to imagine what she was doing, far away.

Three

"MARGARET, DARLING, YOU HAVE scarcely touched your dinner!" Edith Lennox's blonde curls bounced perfectly as she shook her head in mock consternation. "You know Mamma will be calling the doctor again if you do not eat more."

Margaret Hale drew her gaze back to the young woman sitting across from her. Mentally she chided herself. It was not like her to be so distracted. "I am sorry, Edith. I was just... thinking about Mr Bell." Margaret's eyes dropped to her plate as she tried to quell her emotions. The excellent braised poultry could not spark her interest any more than last night's delicious veal had.

Edith pursed her lips in understanding. She was annoyed on Margaret's behalf with the old Oxford fellow. He had dropped a hint about taking Margaret to Spain to see her brother Frederick, in hopes of lifting her spirits. Instead, Margaret had received word from France some weeks ago that he had business affairs on the continent to settle, and had gone alone. He had not been specific about his travel plans, but Edith had loudly declared him to be an unfeeling brute, to have pointedly neglected Margaret so.

Margaret's disappointment was indeed bitter, but she could not roundly condemn him as Edith had. She had always known her father's old friend had ties all through the continent, and even in the Americas, and that a young lady could hardly expect to accompany an old bachelor on a business tour.

Still, he had been so very kind to her since her father had passed away- even taking her on a journey to Helstone to see her old home. She knew she could not monopolize all of his time, but she had allowed herself to hope that he might take her with him and that she might once again see Frederick.

His note had spoken of dealing with urgent business affairs, requiring his personal attention, so she knew better than to think she could do other than be in his way. Still... she worried about him traveling alone. He had seemed more frail on his last visit. He was several years older than her father, and his usual boundless energy had seemed somewhat subdued. He had looked to her quite worn, although Edith, who did not know him as well, claimed to notice no difference.

Making an effort to eat a little of her meal, Margaret focused her attention back on the dinner conversation between her aunt Shaw and her cousin. They were discussing tomorrow night's dinner party at the Whites,' which interested Margaret not a whit. Pleading a headache, Margaret excused herself and withdrew to her room. She had never liked London society with all the swirling events, and found its demands to be exhausting to her quieter disposition. Her heart longed for deep, sincere connection with dear friends, not endless chatter among bare acquaintances.

Edith, on the other hand, had blossomed into the ideal young London wife during the last two years. After her marriage to Captain Lennox, she had spent well over a year stationed with him in Corfu. She had easily become the leading officer's wife in social circles. Now that she was returned home, her popularity as a London socialite was firmly fixed.

Margaret had grown up with Edith, shared her lessons and her confidences, but was not a sharer in the wealth and status to which Edith had been born. Though never treated as such, Margaret was the poor relation and had always sensed her differences. Their connection had brought Margaret many material advantages, but at her heart Margaret had always craved the peace of Helstone over the finery of London. Since her visit with Mr Bell, however, her feelings had undergone a remarkable change.

She still loved the open, rolling country, the clean air, the beautiful walks and groves, but it had been hollow. Her disappointment with what she had anticipated to be a wonderful escape had not been lost on Mr Bell. She had tried to hide her unhappiness, but the shrewd old gentleman had not been fooled.

She had spent a lot of time thinking since her return last month, and had concluded that it was the people who made the place. Nothing she loved remained in her old home. All that was left were the shattered remains of her idealized memories. The people she loved were here... some of them, anyway.

She and Edith had grown apart somewhat in two years. Edith's marriage and motherhood, her status in London, and her more frivolous nature served in part to place more distance between them than had ever existed.

Margaret knew that her time in Milton had changed her in her cousin's eyes as well. She had eschewed the traditional socially correct topics, and could not stop herself from speaking out of the cares of her heart. She knew she had raised a few eyebrows among Edith's friends, but she could not help herself. Her concerns were deeper now. She spent hours in thought and prayer, unable to forget the people she would probably never see again.

She had been so terribly lonely when she had moved to Milton. Her parents had been poor substitutes for friends. Her mother had been ailing, her father had been distressed, and the relations between them had been strained for years. Forced to look elsewhere for companionship, she had made friends among the working class of Milton.

At first mortified by the vast differences between them, Margaret had come to value the genuine honesty and lack of pretension she found in simple girls like Bessie Higgins and her sister Mary. The men had frightened her at first with their roughness, but she had come to know that most were loyal, dedicated to their families, and carried their own distinctive brand of honour. She had come to understand and respect Nicholas Higgins. Margaret smiled as she thought of how shocked her aunt had been when introduced to the unpolished former union leader.

Her aunt's stiff reaction to another Milton man had also lingered in her memory. Margaret heaved a sigh as she thought of Mr Thornton. Too late she had realized how greatly she had misjudged him. Margaret covered her face with her hands. The feelings of shame *would* come whenever she thought of him. She had treated him with disdain and scorn, but when given the opportunity to treat her in kind, he had instead shielded her.

She had wanted for so long to tell him about Frederick, to explain some part, only, of her actions to him, even if her reasons could not justify her falsehood. She felt like he deserved the entire truth- she trusted him with the entire truth. She wanted for him at least to know of her gratitude, but she would never force her communication on him.

He had lost all respect for her; he had told her as much. Any attempt at explanation now would seem only like a vain attempt to justify her wrongdoing and he would be well within his rights to refuse to hear her out. She would never again have a chance to right her wrongs.

She swallowed hard. At least she did have that comfort; she would never have to face him again. Time, though, had done little to ease the familiar ache whenever she thought of him.

"I don't know what's to be done with her, Mamma," Edith pouted after Margaret hastily left the table. "She is still wearing black and she barely eats."

Mrs Shaw thoughtfully sipped her port, pondering the problem of her niece. "Well, if you want my opinion, she needs to be getting out in Society more. It would do her good; she only sees us and Sholto. Has Henry Lennox called lately?"

"He was here last week, but he did not stay long. Mamma, I really think he does fancy her. Do you think he could lift her spirits?"

"I do not see why not. They always got on well enough, and he is family now. We ought to be inviting him more to be in her company. "

"It would be so wonderful if they were to marry! Then she would never have to leave us. Why, I know Henry has little enough of his own money, but he is sure to do well in his profession in time. And Mamma, I do so dote on Margaret, and she is so helpful with Sholto, that I would wish them to remain with us after they marry!"

"Then, my dear, you must try to create opportunities for them to see more of each other. If Margaret will not go to dinner parties with you, you must have more here and invite Henry. Having him here will also give you the advantage of arranging the seating as you like." Mrs Shaw smiled into her glass as she finished the last of her port.

"Excuse me Ma'am," Nancy, the housemaid, bobbed a curtsy as she entered the dining parlor. "The post has arrived."

"It is so late today!" Edith exclaimed. She took the tray and her eyes scanned her invitations. Indeed, it was about time for another dinner party of her own, and after her meal she would sit down directly to issue invitations. "Oh, Nancy," she called to the retreating maid. "Here is one addressed to Miss Hale. Would you take it to her, please?"

"Yes, Ma'am," Nancy retrieved the tray with the remaining letter and went to find Margaret.

Edith and her mother withdrew to the downstairs sitting room. With much enjoyment, she thumbed through the rest of her correspondence and decided which to answer first. She looked up in surprise when Margaret appeared suddenly in the doorway, holding a letter in trembling hands, her face white as a sheet.

"Why, dear Margaret, what is wrong?" Edith did not rise, but anticipated that Margaret would come to sit near her. She did not.

Margaret was clearly fighting back tears. "It is a letter from Frederick. He writes me about Mr Bell! Oh!" She covered her face with a sob and could not continue.

Edith did go to her then, draping an arm around her cousin's shoulders and drawing her to the sofa. As girls the two had shared many confidences, many heartaches, and Edith instinctively knew there was nothing she could say until Margaret was ready to speak.

Margaret wiped at her eyes with a handkerchief, her free hand kneading her skirt. Mrs Shaw wanted to chide her about making her eyes puffy or wrinkling her gown, but she decided in favor of silence.

Margaret sniffled a little as she composed herself. "Frederick says that Mr Bell did indeed come to stay with him, and that he's fallen deathly ill. He does not expect him to live long!" Margaret hid her sobs in her handkerchief. Her initial reaction of shock and dismay that Mr Bell had gone to see Frederick without her had worn off, to be replaced with overwhelming grief. Mr Bell was the last remaining friend of her father's- with whom she was on good terms- and she had come to care a great deal for the old codger. If she never saw him again, was never able to say goodbye to him as she had not been able with her father... her heart rebelled violently at the probability.

"There, there, Dearest," Edith crooned, drawing Margaret's head onto her own shoulder. She stroked her cousin's arm soothingly. Edith had never known what to make of Mr Bell. He was far too sardonic for her taste, and she did not understand him. She knew, however, that Margaret would be plunged back into grief at his passing, and for that she was very sorry. Her mother was quite silent.

"Does Frederick say what the matter is?" asked Edith gently.

Margaret drew away and attempted to calm her shattered nerves. "He thinks it is an illness that has been coming on for some time. The doctor's been, and he thinks the heart is weak. Frederick says they have no hope he will live more than a few more days, a week or two at most!"

Edith clucked comfortingly over Margaret, but knew there was little she could do to console the young woman who was more like a sister than a cousin. With a plaintive look, she begged her mother to ring for Dixon, Margaret's loyal ladies' maid.

Dixon eventually hobbled into the room. Her gout was acting up again, but she would not relinquish her care of Margaret to one of the younger maids. Miss Beresford's daughter held a special place in the older woman's heart. Her face red and puffy, she shooed her young Miss upstairs. It would not do for Margaret to be seen so by her aunt and cousin, but once safely upstairs she would comfort the girl as if she were her very own.

Mrs Shaw watched with a frown. She did not quite think it fitting that Dixon should take charge of Margaret so fiercely as she did. The woman had been practically nanny to her niece, as well as nurse to her own sister, and had been given far too much authority as far as Mrs Shaw was concerned.

It was a power Dixon was loath to give up easily. Too many demands had been placed upon her in Milton- she had been the family's only permanent servant, but she had slowly come to admit that her position in Milton had allowed her freedoms with the family that London life never would have.

She was glad that her young mistress was safely ensconced in a fashionable household again. It had shocked her to be welcoming all manner of rough folk to their home and to have to rely on the young mistress' help in menial household tasks. Still, she had lost somewhat of her influence and comfortable familiarity that had grown out of their time in Milton.

Dixon firmly but gently escorted Margaret to her room. Thinking it would be helpful to soothe her worries, Dixon ordered hot water to be sent up for a bath. Margaret meekly submitted. She was too preoccupied with the contents of Frederick's letter to make much objection. She sobbingly wiped her eyes before allowing her servant and friend to lift her gown over her head.

Once her young charge was settled for a good long soak, Dixon betook herself to her own quarters, a comfortable little nook off Margaret's dressing room. About time, too. Her toe felt like it was on fire! Gritting her teeth, she prepared her own soaking solution and eased her foot into the salt bath. Her aging bones sighed in relief as she lowered her ponderous weight into a battered old chair.

There was much Margaret hadn't told her aunt and cousin about Frederick's letter. Languishing in the bath, she re-read the letter, careful to protect it from the water.

8 July 1856

My dearest Margaret,

I am sorry to have to write you thus. I have sad news. Our Mr Bell is currently staying in my house. He did not want you to know of his visit right away, but now he begs me to write and tell something of his circumstances.

He told me he was settling some affairs, and has indeed been visiting quite a number of local agents. I do not know all of the details of his transactions, but during one such visit with a broker he collapsed. He was brought back here, and has not been able to rise from his bed.

We summoned the doctor, a friend of Dolores' family who studied medicine abroad. He is the very best in the city. He believes Mr Bell has been suffering for some time from water on the heart. He has done all that he can, but I am sorry to report that he does not expect our dear friend will live more than a fortnight, more probably less.

Now, dear sister, I know you will want to see him, but I fear the journey may be impossible. Mr Bell has been asking for you, saying I must tell you something as soon as may be, but he has yet to tell me what that is. At times he is not quite reasonable, I think due to the remedies employed by the doctor.

He mentioned that he would like to have brought you with him but that he had feared his health may fail for some time now, and did not want to trouble you with an ailing companion. That was the most we have been able to coax out of him.

Dearest, you know how Dolores and I would love for you to come to us. I know Edith's husband is a retired captain, perhaps you can persuade him to accompany you here. If not he, perhaps his brother Henry could see to your safety. He seems very fond of you, little Sister. I trust the Lennoxes, and I know you would be in good care if one of them can ensure your safety.

I would not wish you to travel without an escort, so please, dear Margaret, do not attempt to travel alone. You see, I know you, my little sister! The voyage is not arduous, but the company aboard ship is not something a lady should face alone.

I am eager to see you again, and I truly hope it possible that you may be able to come before Mr Bell is no longer with us, but I beg you to only travel if you can do it safely. Give Dixon my love, and please send your reply soon.

Yours,

Frederick

Margaret again wiped the tears from her face. The letter was dated five days ago. She may already be too late! Still, if there was a chance.... She set the letter down on a little desk near the tub and got out without calling for Dixon. She dressed herself and lay on the bed, deep in thought.

Four

NOW, NOW, MISS," DIXON used her firmest authoritative tone, chasing Margaret's bobbing head the best she could with her pins. "Ye can't go." Dixon stabbed an errant curl with a pin for emphasis. "Ye know 'tis not proper for a lady to travel alone! Yer mother would never have allowed it."

Margaret hastily snatched a bite of toast from a plate by her dressing table. She had convinced one of the kitchen maids to bring it up so she could breakfast before the rest of the family were awake.

"Dixon, I must! Mr Bell and Frederick are all I have left of my family." Margaret could not contain her agitation, and she was sure she gave Dixon no end of trouble finishing her hair.

"And what of yer aunt and cousin? They took y'in, didn't they? Is not the Beresford line yer own family?" Dixon finally finished with the last pin and stepped back in relief. She sat down as quickly as she could to take the weight off her feet.

Margaret demurred. She could not bring herself to admit out loud what she had come to know in her heart. Her aunt and cousin were indeed dear to her, and undeniably were cherished family, but there was a distance in her own mind that she could not cross.

This posh London life had ill suited her before her time in Milton. She had always treasured her escape to Helstone each summer and the freer way of life it brought. After living a year and a half in Milton though, she had come to nearly despise the artificiality of this life. She was continually making social missteps and would never make a proper London lady.

She ached to see Frederick again; she knew he would understand her feelings. And Mr Bell... dear Mr Bell who had done so much for her father and so kindly looked after her since his death! She lifted her chin. "Dixon, I must go. Alone if I must, but Mr Bell has been asking for me!"

Dixon harrumphed her disapproval. "Well, then I'm goin' with ye, Miss! It's a papist country, after all; I won't see ye go there alone. Why, they might convert ye! Don't know what Master Frederick was thinking of, settling among those heathen! It's not fit for decent folk, that's what. I'll not see ye traipsing off by yerself! Miss Beresford's daughter, no less." Dixon continued grumbling in that line while Margaret shuffled through her drawers.

Margaret knew it was impossible to take Dixon. She had begged her to take her ease while she was unwell, but Dixon always stoutly refused. Negotiating the large London house in her condition was painful enough, and it broke Margaret's heart to see it. She could not let her old friend risk traveling, where she might fall aboard ship. There would be no relief from her agony, and it was quite possible her condition would worsen in the Spanish summer heat.

Setting her jaw, she told Dixon as much. They argued for a long while, neither accustomed to yielding- although, in Dixon's case, she kept it up more out of a sense of duty than any expectation she might prevail over her stubborn young mistress.

Margaret intended to approach the captain of the vessel and ask to sail under his protection. Dixon was firmly against her plan, but could not stop her. Margaret hoped she could change the woman's mind- it truly did frighten her to think of sailing all alone and she did esteem Dixon's good opinion.

A male escort was out of the question. Captain Lennox was an indolent as his wife could be- heaven bless her- and Margaret would not have liked to travel long in his company anyway. His brother, Henry... well, it would not be proper for two unmarried people to travel together, and what Frederick had implied on more than one occasion regarding Henry was simply inconceivable. She knew Henry would be glad to make the journey with her. What other sentiments he would read into the request, she did not wish to consider.

She knew that it was not at all uncommon for a lady to be placed under the protection of the captain, but it *was* rather unseemly. Circumstances, she decided, warranted the risk. Surely if he was a man of honour, as English captains ought to be, he would watch out for her dignity and safety.

Margaret had already sent one of the household servants off to find out when the next ship was leaving port. She was awaiting the return news with some anxiety. She hoped there was one leaving that very day, and she intended to steal away without giving her aunt a chance to object. It was not like her to be secretive and rebellious, but she was finding herself at odds every way she turned of late. It seemed she was not at all the girl she had been a year ago, and she knew she could never find a way to explain to her aunt without loss of precious time.

A soft knock sounded at the door. Dixon answered it to let in one of the serving maids. At a look from Margaret she frowned, then turned and began to fold linens at a discreet distance. The maid placed a paper in her hand, bobbed a curtsy, and left. Margaret unfolded the paper with shaking fingers. The paper held the departure times and dates of three ships.

Quickly scanning the list, she noted that only one was leaving today. The others were four and six days out, respectively. The one leaving today… "Dixon! Quickly please, I must be packed and on my way within the hour!"

Margaret clutched her small valise tightly and glanced uncertainly up and down the dock. She checked the slip of paper she held in her hand- The *Esperanza*. Her larger trunk would be sent aboard by the porters, but she had wished to keep at least a hand bag with her, in case it proved difficult to retrieve her trunk right away. It contained two of her father's books, a few handkerchiefs, and a light shawl. There was also a small but precious gift for Frederick's sweet Dolores.

She was having some trouble making her way. Everyone was rushing and shouting, giving her no opportunity to ask directions. She decided to follow the crush of human traffic which led primarily to one of two steamers moored on the row of docks to her left.

The dock workers shouted orders and retorts as ropes and luggage were swung about with careless grace. Once she would have been utterly appalled at their roughness. These men were still a different lot than she had become accustomed to in Milton, but she had learned to look for more essential qualities. A person's speech and dress branded them forever in the class to which they had been born, but Margaret had learned that gems could be found anywhere, and she had begun finally to look for them.

Looking for gems was not what preoccupied her at the moment, however. Biting her lip, she strained to see over the hats of the taller men in front of her. She was hoping to ascertain the name of the ship she was approaching as soon as possible, to make sure she was not wasting her time struggling toward it.

There was a slight gap in the sea of humanity before her, and she took a few quick steps forward and to the side. The shouting grew louder with each step she took closer to the vessel. Porters bustled all around her, carting heavy barrels, trunks, luggage carts, and other last minute provisions. Some of them were lucky enough to have a hand truck of some kind.

Others were obliged to hoist their burdens on their shoulders, which, in addition to the fatigue and discomfort, made it awkward for them to maneuver in the crowd. Two or three of these were behind her. One young boy, no more than thirteen, was struggling with a trunk much too large for him to carry. He was tiring, and could scarcely see around the edges of the trunk when he lifted his head.

Margaret only heard a grunt, then a voice raised in alarm, "Watch it, laddy!"

Something hard and blunt struck her from behind, propelling her forward. She landed heavily against the back of the tall man in front of her.

The man turned in surprise and then their eyes met. Margaret was still trying to regain her footing when her mind registered the additional shock of recognition. "Mr Thor-," but the name was cut off.

Neither she nor the lad carrying the trunk were yet recovered from the first blow when he accidentally struck her again. This time the poor boy tripped in her skirts, causing trunk, boy, and Margaret with her valise to tumble into a painful heap.

MR THORNTON AT FIRST thought he must have been hallucinating. Margaret? Here on the dock? His mind saw the boy stumble over her while she was trying to recover her own footing, and slowly, too slowly, he tried to reach out and catch her. He was too late.

Finally, his body obeyed him. Dropping his own case, he rushed to her side. The trunk and her own body had landed on her right arm, which was twisted above her head at a grotesque angle. He heaved the trunk off of her, and saw that beneath it she had been carrying a bag, which had certainly wrenched her arm further. Others were crowding around now, some proffering assistance to the fallen woman, some chastising the poor boy for his clumsiness, but most simply gawking at the scene.

Instinctively he wanted to protect her from the trampling feet and the prying eyes. As a gentleman, he would have done the same for any woman, but perhaps with less vehemence than for the woman who had captured his being with a glance. Lifting his head, he began barking out orders in his best Master's voice. "Back up! Give way! You, sir, are you taking passage aboard this vessel? Get word to the captain to send a doctor down immediately!"

He had not taken his gaze from her face for more than an instant, and he was relieved to see that, though confused, her eyes were open and watching him. She seemed to be experiencing some kind of a shock, because she was having some trouble commanding herself. She tried once or twice to speak his name but no sound came.

Every tender feeling he had ever held for her came rushing back. Without even conscious thought, one hand went to her side to steady her, and the other affectionately stroked her forehead as he tried to ascertain how badly she was hurt. "Margaret? Can you speak?" he queried gently.

She took two more shaky breaths, then managed a hesitant "Y-yes." His eyes encouraged her to try for more. "M-my arm... ah!" The last utterance came as a small gasp when she tried to move her arm down to her side. He could tell easily that the shoulder had been dislocated, and imagined she was in a great deal of pain. Fortunately, or unfortunately, depending upon how one looked at it, he had seen this type of injury again and again in the mill.

Knowing that at least her condition was stable, he turned his attention to what must be done next. Her skirt and petticoats were in disarray, and with a stammered apology he attempted to drape them in such a way as to protect her modesty. Glancing around, he could see there was a fish warehouse not two hundred feet away. It was the nearest structure that could afford her some protection from the crowd, distasteful as it surely must smell.

"Margaret, I must turn you. Can you be brave for a moment? This will likely hurt very much." She nodded, biting her lip. Whatever opinion she had of him, she at least was willing to accept his help. She had little alternative at the moment, he thought ruefully.

Slowly and carefully, he hooked his left hand under her spine and rolled her to rest on her back. From there he would be able to reposition her and hopefully lift her. As much as it would pain her, he had to bring her right arm down in front of her in order to carry her. "Hold on, love," he whispered under his breath.

The words came before he could think better of them. Wincing, he hoped she had not heard, or at least under the circumstances would not take offense. He certainly had no right to speak to her in such an intimate way.

There was no time for such niceties now, though. The crowd was still pressing, and at any moment he feared a careless passerby would step on her. As gently and slowly as he could, he drew her arm downward. Experience had taught him that he could not bring the injured limb back toward her body in the most direct way- he had to work it slowly round until he could angle it better.

She screwed her eyes shut and clamped her little white teeth into her bottom lip to keep from crying out. A small whimper leaked past her guard, but she fought for self-control. He knew he must be hurting her terribly, but he admired how courageous she was. He had seen grown men, strong and rough, brought to tears by the very same injury.

"Margaret, you must open your eyes. Look at me!" His voice became insistent. Wincing from pain was understandable, but he could not risk letting her slip into shock. He had seen it all too often. She did not relax her jaw, but her eyes squinted open again. He waited until he was sure they were focused on him before giving directions. "Now, can you put your left arm around my neck? I am going to carry you. That's right, do not be afraid."

He murmured encouragement as he drew her upper body close to his. He wrapped his other arm under her knees, too concerned for her welfare to be discomfited by the close contact. As soon as he had a fair grip on her body, he rolled her closer yet to protect her injured arm from dropping away from him and causing her more pain. Then, he grimly stood and made his way to the nearby fish house.

With her head draped on his shoulder, her perfectly curled ear tantalizingly close to his mouth, he did not wish to raise his voice again to clear his path. Fortunately he did not have to. The crowd had begun to thin somewhat, and the remaining passersby grudgingly parted to let him through.

"Wha's this then!" a loud voice demanded as he stepped inside the warehouse. "Nay, ye canna bring yer wenches in here! Out wit ye!" A sturdy fishwife wielding a broom guarded the doorway and glared at him.

Thornton's eyes narrowed and his temper rose. "Madam! You are speaking of a lady! This woman was injured just outside. Someone has gone for a doctor and we must wait within. Kindly allow me to enter!"

The woman sneered, but lowered her broom. She continued to glare at him, as if daring him to make further demands. He spied a stack of crates in the corner but saw no better place to let her rest. With a curt nod to the proprietor of the noble establishment, he turned Margaret's body in his arms so that he could gently set her down. The woman crossed her arms and pursed her lips. She could see that Margaret was truly in pain, but she was affronted by this haughty fellow who strode commandingly into her place of business and took over.

Thornton did not care in the slightest. He knelt in front of Margaret and tried to get her attention back on him. She was looking very faint indeed. "Margaret, you must use your left arm to support your right... like so... Margaret?"

Her face had broken out in a cold sweat. She opened her eyes blearily, blinked them several times, but still her gaze did not focus. Her face was pale, her skin clammy, her lips parted as if she wanted to speak and could not. He feared she was slipping into the early stages of shock. "Margaret! Can you hear me?"

She was shaking her head, the expression on her face a strange combination between alarm and lethargy. Finally, words came, "...can't... see... can't...." Her eyes rolled back in her head and she slumped forward onto his chest. She recovered with a jerk even before he could reposition himself to support her, and tried to sit upright again. Still he could tell she could not see. She kept trying to open her eyes wider, but after a few more seconds she slumped forward again.

Thornton tried to fight the panic growing in him. He had seen shock many times, but in his concern for Margaret, his experience failed him. All he could think of was protecting her, helping her, easing her pain... something! Anything!

"Oh, fer the love o' Saint Peter an' a' the apostles!" He had nearly forgotten about the beefy woman with the large stick in her hand and the hostile expression in her eyes. Before he could even turn to her, she had pulled him back roughly and taken charge. He guessed she was used to throwing around things that weighed nearly as much as Margaret, because she pulled the younger woman forward and expertly rolled her onto her back, directly on the soiled floor.

"Hold hard, Madam! You cannot..." but his words were cut short when Margaret's eyes almost immediately flew open. She gasped a few short, sharp breaths, and her clear gaze shot around the room until it rested on him.

Quickly he knelt at her head, finally realizing what the woman had done. Of course Margaret would feel faint and light headed if she were sitting upright! Inwardly he cursed his own stupidity. He had acted like a foolish novice, setting her upright to preserve her dignity when she should have been lying flat to preserve her health.

He cradled her head in his hands and encouraged her to respond to simple questions; her name, what day it was, and what colour her gown was- distantly noting that she still wore her black mourning. He was curious when he saw the fishwife draw a short crate over and immodestly prop Margaret's feet on it. He decided not to argue, as her alertness was improving almost with every second. "Madam, I believe we owe you our gratitude. I apologize if I was rude before."

She crossed her arms and harrumphed. The door opened again, but this time she did not threaten the man who entered with bodily harm. A head stuck inquisitively around the corner. "Ah, I see I am in the right place. Dr. Grayson, at your service."

Thornton introduced himself and shook the doctor's hand. The doctor was a slight man, somewhat past middle age with graying sideburns. The rest of his hair was still dark, but his weathered skin stood testament to many years at sea.

The doctor wasted no time examining his patient. Thornton appreciated the man's direct and professional manner, but was disconcerted by the reassuring chatter he carried on between himself and... well, himself. "Hmm hmm... yes... ah, very good... yes.... Hmm. Oh, I see." Dr. Grayson straightened and looked Margaret in the eye. "Young lady, I understand you have had quite a blow. Can you see me well enough?" She nodded, her eyes drifting from him to Thornton's face as if she desired his reassurance.

The doctor proceeded to check Margaret for signs of head trauma or shock, but he was apparently satisfied with what he found. Next, he addressed himself to Thornton. "We will need to set her shoulder. It will cause her a great deal of pain, I am afraid. I have laudanum, which I will administer directly, but it will take at least a quarter of an hour to have proper effect. As I understand it, you were intending to take passage on the *Esperanza*?"

"Yes!" Margaret sat bolt upright, then cried out in pain, clutching her right arm.

Until that moment Thornton had not considered why she would have been on the dock. The miracle of seeing her again and the urgency of the moment had taken precedence. He frowned down at her now. Surely, she could not be meaning to sail! And alone! He could not be mistaken; there had been no one with her. Her eyes had been clenched against the pain of her movement, but she opened them again and gazed imploringly at both him and Dr. Grayson.

Thornton sighed. "A moment alone, if I may, Doctor?"

Dr. Grayson nodded understandingly, but he continued to prepare a dose of pain medication for her. Clearly, he was a determined doctor. "Now, my dear, if you please." He tipped her head up to administer the vile spoonful.

Margaret shuddered at the bitter taste of the medication but swallowed dutifully. Dr. Grayson stood and excused himself back through the front door. Thornton glanced pointedly at the sullen woman in the corner. Scrunching her face in challenge, she finally stated that she had crates to sort behind the building.

Five

"Mar... Miss Hale. Forgive me." He realized he had been calling her by her Christian name throughout their encounter, just as he was wont to do in his private thoughts. He wondered what she would make of that later, when her head had cleared from the pain-induced haze. He forged on. "You cannot seriously be intending to sail on a boat bound for Spain. What possible call can there be for you to do so?"

Gripping her arm, she stiffened her neck, squared her jaw, and leveled her gaze at him. Thornton knew that expression. She was steeling herself for a fight, and he knew already that he had lost. For a woman reclining on a greasy floor with an injured arm, she was frighteningly imposing.

"Mr Thornton, I beg you not to try to stop me. I must... I... I cannot tell you everything now. Please, I...." She stopped. Slowly she rolled herself to a sitting position, this time jostling her arm as little as possible. He braced an arm behind her shoulders for support, drawing himself very close to her. Proper or not, he could not stop himself from trying to help her.

He shook his head as he endeavored to speak with some measure of authority. "Miss Hale, there can be no reason for you to endanger yourself by sailing like this. You must not consider it. The risks are too great. I cannot allow you to...."

"It is a matter regarding Mr Bell!" she interrupted. Beseeching eyes looked up at him again from her somewhat more dignified posture. "He is traveling in Spain and Fre- I mean a mutual acquaintance wrote me that he is dying and wishes me to come to him. I must see him!" she pleaded.

Mr Bell dying! Certainly, after losing nearly everyone else she had cared about, there would be no stopping her from trying to attend the old gentleman in his last hours. Thornton knew he would never win the argument by insisting she not travel. He clenched his teeth and tried a different tactic. "But alone? Surely someone from your family in

London can travel with you. It is too dangerous to go alone. Your reputation- your very safety! You must not attempt it!"

Margaret looked down. She did not want to go into a detailed explanation of why she found no one from her aunt's household a suitable traveling companion. "I must," she insisted softly. "I was going to speak with the captain. I know ladies sometimes travel under a captain's protection...."

Tears glistened on her eyelashes, and he wasn't sure if they were from the pain of her shoulder or her anguish over Mr Bell or her frustration with her circumstances. It didn't matter. He knew he could never win against the tears of the woman whose sweet voice and gentle smiles arrested his very heart pulse. What man could?

Thornton raked his free hand through his hair. His mind was churning. So highly improper! But then, he mused, it would certainly not be the first time he had seen her rashly compromise herself for someone else. Somehow, hopefully he could find a way to protect her without allowing her to court disgrace.

In his heart, he could not help but rejoice at the possibility of sailing with her himself, though he knew his own feelings clouded his better judgement. Closing his eyes, and not believing his own voice, he began to present her options, trying to make them sound as dire as possible. He had one last faint hope of discouraging her.

"The ship sails almost immediately. The other passengers have already boarded. If you wish to be able to board, we must set your arm without delay. I fear that settling you on the ship without first seeing to your injury could make matters worse. I have seen it before- the muscles can be torn and the damage to your shoulder cannot be undone. Ordinary movement should be no concern, but aboard a rocking ship, with cramped quarters and crowding where you may fall again, you cannot take the chance. Think me a tyrant if you will, but I will not allow you to do permanent harm to yourself for the sake making a passage.

"If, however, you choose to stay, perhaps at least wait for another ship, we can give you time for the laudanum to take effect. You would not feel the pain of the doctor's ministrations and you would have time to rest and recover some before sailing."

He had avoided looking at her directly, but now he did. Her answer was clear. Icy determination glinted from her eyes, her lips pressed together. She gave a firm nod.

"Are you quite sure?"

"Yes." She swallowed. "Please call the doctor back in. Let us proceed."

Shaking his head, he went to the door. The two men had a quiet conversation about what needed to be done. They decided that they would build a rude sort of surgery table for her to rest upon out of the fish crates. Thornton would brace her left arm and torso, and they would apply to the fisherman's wife to hold her legs steady, so that Margaret might not topple off the makeshift table. She grumblingly agreed.

Bending beside Margaret's head, Dr. Grayson explained to her what he intended. Then, pulling a pair of scissors from his medical bag, he moved toward her shoulder.

Margaret jerked away in alarm. "Doctor! You cannot mean to cut my gown!"

He smiled understandingly, but was firm. "It is the only way, my dear. Your gown is too restrictive for me to set your arm properly, and I fear that trying to remove it will only cause you further injury."

Her cheeks flushed scarlet. Glancing at Mr Thornton, she could tell he was excruciatingly embarrassed. He turned his face away, closing his eyes and biting his upper lip. Margaret continued to protest weakly, but Dr. Grayson was firm. Tears of mortification slipped down her cheeks as he snipped away the sleeve of her gown.

To her surprise, he did not pull the sleeve all the way down her arm. She looked down at his handiwork and saw that the doctor indeed had done a singular job. He had managed to snip only the seams of the sleeve, loosening it so he had free access to her shoulder but no more. The dress was not ruined beyond the ability of a good seamstress to repair, and her shawl could even preserve her modesty for the short trip between the fish house and the ship.

"Now, then everyone. Are we ready, my dear?" the doctor asked kindly. She clenched her teeth and nodded in painful determination.

The fisherman's wife wrapped Margaret's knees gracelessly in a bear grip. Thornton braced his shoulder and upper arm against her ribs and pinned her left arm tightly to her body, trying to ignore the delicate scent he detected by her neck. Margaret's heart rattled in her throat- even through her pain, the shock of his nearness jolted her.

The doctor took her hand and began to move her arm. He slowly pulled down and out, gradually rotating her hand as he went. Margaret winced against the pain. Dr. Grayson continued to pull, and the stabbing pressure was building. Thornton watched her carefully. Once she glanced at him for reassurance, then shut her eyes again.

The searing pain intensified, and she could not help crying out. Suddenly, she felt a shift in her shoulder and the pain lessened dramatically. Thornton was watching for this, and jumped away from her as quickly as a man could possibly move. Still at her side and reaching to steady her on the wobbling crates, he struggled to school his bounding pulse.

Dr. Grayson gently brought her hand to rest on her stomach and helped her to sit up. "Now, my dear, we will have to keep your arm stable while you heal. I have just the thing aboard ship. If I'm not mistaken, we should hurry, because Captain Carter will not wait even for me!" he added, with a twinkle in his eye.

Thornton leaned near her and asked in a low voice if she felt she could walk. He would not be averse to carrying her, but he felt at the moment it would not be good for his equanimity. She was still gasping in shock, but nodded determinedly.

He reached down to help her to her feet with her good arm. She leaned on him heavily and swayed very slightly when she stood. He saw her struggle to steady herself, then with a grateful nod, she released his arm and stood on her own.

With a start, he realized they had a problem. "My luggage... your.... we left them."

Her face registered her dawning dismay. Would this day ever improve? They both knew the likelihood was slim that their possessions had remained safe, sitting unguarded on the dock.

"Oh, I wouldn't worry about that!" chuckled Dr. Grayson. "There's a very enterprising young lad out front who would like to speak with you!"

Stepping quickly to the door and opening it, Thornton encountered a grimy-faced boy of perhaps seven or eight, with the brightest blue eyes he had ever seen. Possibly, he thought, the brightness of his eyes only seemed so intense because they contrasted so with his sooty face. "'S'cuse me Guvnah! You and the laydee needin yo' bags?" He stood proudly beside Thornton's case, with Margaret's smaller valise in front of him.

Smiling and shaking his head, Thornton wondered how the small boy had possibly carried both bags, but he reached in his pocket and counted out several shillings. The boy's eyes widened. The amount Thornton had given him would allow an urchin like this boy to live like a king for weeks- or keep a family of four in rare comforts for one.

Remembering another debt, he turned to the fisherman's wife and counted out more change. "Thank you kindly, madam, for your trouble." She grunted inarticulately, but seemed well pleased.

Margaret's disconcerting gaze never left him, but he could not read her expression. If he were not mistaken, her eyes were taking on a glassiness already. It was hardly surprising, of course; the pain medication always took effect more quickly on women because of their smaller frames, and she could not be expected to be accustomed to such narcotics.

Between Thornton and Dr. Grayson, they managed to carry the luggage and support Margaret to the ship. She was largely able to hold her right arm herself, but Thornton kept his own arm hovering protectively around her, barely touching her small frame. He could not help reveling in her very nearness and her dependence upon his care. Her steps were becoming heavier, but she was still alert enough to walk herself without danger. Both men watched her carefully, but she made it to the ship without incident.

When they arrived at the ship, Dr. Grayson took over. Being familiar with the faces and workings of the ship, he was just the friend one could need at such a time. After settling a few things with the men on board, he returned to them.

"Mr Thornton, we are in luck. It is a very full passenger list, as the accountants are known sometimes to oversell the cabins at the last moment. There is, however, one cabin remaining where you and your wife can stay in comfort. It is not large, only one bunk, but perhaps..." the doctor stopped abruptly at the look of alarm on both faces.

Thornton recovered first. "My apologies, Doctor, but there has been a misunderstanding. This is..." with a quick glance at Margaret, "...my sister."

It was fortunate, perhaps, that Grayson's eyes were fixed on Thornton's face. It was also likely fortunate that Margaret was beginning to feel rather dazed. The scandalized expression Thornton would have expected from her went unnoticed.

"Ah, forgive me. Of course, I will see about another berth for you, but there is very little room. It seems we were all a little late boarding," the doctor's eyes twinkled again.

As the doctor strode off, Margaret tightened her grip on his arm. "*Why did you say that?*" she whispered fiercely.

Thornton turned to her with a fire he scarcely felt, determined to win at least this round. In her drugged and pain-fogged state, he had a chance.

He answered her quietly through clenched teeth, "If you are determined to do this foolish thing, the least I can do is protect you! I owe your father's memory that much. You know we cannot decently travel together! You should never have attempted it alone, and certainly cannot do so injured! If I travel as a brother, I can watch out for your safety without censure. Unless," he could not resist leaning close to her ear with a small smirk on his face, "you would *prefer* to travel as my wife!"

His mischievous final comment had the desired effect. Her eyes widened, her mouth snapped closed, and she drew back fractionally.

The good doctor chose that moment to return. "I'm afraid, Mr Thornton, there is no other cabin, but there is a berth in steerage. Of course, you will be free to move about the first class cabins with Miss Thornton. Will that do? The other option would be to set up a cot for you in Miss Thornton's cabin. She may well need additional care during the first day or two of the voyage."

With a sigh, he accepted the steerage berth. It would be further away from Margaret, but he did not dare expose himself to the temptation of constant proximity to the object of his fondest affections. The distance between their sleeping quarters would be a necessary barrier for propriety. He could still protect her as he had purposed; as her "brother" he would be able to watch over her most of the time, at least. Surely, no one would trouble her knowing she was not unescorted.

Their bags were sent ahead while the two men helped Margaret to her cabin. She was fading quickly. She stumbled at the steps, but made it to the door without incident. Here the doctor produced a long strip of linen and began to bind her arm closely to her body. She was relieved to be able to let go of her injured arm.

She sagged wearily and found Thornton close behind her, steadying her against his firm chest by wrapping an arm protectively around her waist. She felt oddly relieved to have him so near. Whatever their history and his opinions of her, she knew that she could trust him utterly.

"All right, my dear, let's lie down. That's it... mm-hmmm, yes. There we go, and let's just place this... yes, that will do nicely...."

Margaret was beyond noticing he doctor's chatter as the heavenly relief of her bunk reached out to encompass her. The doctor expertly fluffed a poor excuse for a pillow behind her to support her body comfortably on her left side, then stood.

"She'll need supervision for a while. She'll be far too relaxed for a few hours to support herself in her sleep. There's a possibility she will roll off the pillow and perhaps even off the bunk when we hit the open sea. I will have a rice sack sent up from the galley to help hold her.

"I can also see if there are any women on board who would be willing to help her... ah... change her garments when she wakes, but I imagine the larger share of her care will fall to you, sir. I will check on her as often as I am able. I advise for her comfort that she take another dose of the laudanum when she awakes. The first couple of days are the worst."

Thornton sighed. "Thank you, Doctor. We appreciate your help." He shook the man's hand, then reached for his pocketbook.

"No, no, sir. As you are passengers, I cannot accept any remuneration without first apprising the captain. If you'll excuse me, I must go make my report." He turned and left.

The door latched shut and Mr Thornton turned back to the bed. Margaret was already deeply asleep. *Now what do I do?* Thornton sat on the floor and leaned heavily back against her bunk.

Six

HE HAD NOT SAT more than ten minutes when there was a brief knock at the door of the cabin. Rising, he answered it and discovered a matronly woman of middle years and ample girth. She smiled winningly and introduced herself with a boldness he found refreshing.

"Begging your pardon sir, I'm Mrs Carter, the Captain's wife, and this here," she gestured to a young woman just behind her, approximately the same age as Margaret, "is my daughter Melanie. We're traveling with my husband this trip, and it's a rare treat it is sir."

Her eyes smiled with genuine warmth. She was a gentlewoman, but her speech was laced with a familiar Northern accent. Thornton smiled. He couldn't help but wonder what her story was, a woman from the north married to a southern sea captain, but he liked her immediately. He introduced himself and she turned quickly to the bed.

"Ach, the poor lass," she clucked. "She'll be down for a good spell. Dr. Grayson is never one to skimp on the laudanum! He says she'll be needing some help with her gown?"

Thornton nodded. "He had to cut it to set her shoulder. Can you help? I don't imagine she'll be able to mend it herself. I've no idea how she is to..." he stopped, embarrassed at what he had been thinking.

Mrs Carter grinned comfortably. "Not to worry, sir. We'll have the young miss all settled. I see they brought her trunk in, that's fine. A dressing gown would be the easiest," she spoke this to her daughter, "but if the men will be tending to her we should find something more decent."

Thornton swallowed hard. A dressing gown? Dear heavens, he hoped not! His sanity was already clinging by a thread.

"Now, go on with ye, sir." Mrs Carter's voice interrupted his brief reverie. She and Melanie maneuvered past him in the small room. Mrs Carter stood next to Margaret's bunk and tilted her head expectantly at him.

He stared blankly at her. Realization dawned slowly. "You mean... you will change her now? While she is asleep?"

"Aye, it's the best way, sir. Less pain for the poor lass to feel. We two can handle matters. Why, my Mellie has a fine hand at nursing, and I raised three young'uns myself while my husband was away at sea. Fear not, we'll take good care of your sister."

Firmly she propelled him toward the door. He needed no further encouragement. Making a hasty grab for his hat, he stepped out and closed the door firmly behind him.

More quickly than he would have thought possible, the ship had cleared the Thames and was pulling out to sea. Thornton stood on the deck, relishing the fresh salt breeze. Such a treat was a rarity in the North, where factory smoke had obscured the landscape and tainted the air since he was a small boy.

He took the chance to glance around the deck. The sailors knew their jobs well. Captain Carter had not made an appearance on deck, but his crew were a well-oiled machine. Each task was completed with only the necessary amount of chatter between the mates, their movements fluid and efficient.

Suddenly he snorted at himself. Even here on what could nearly be called a vacation from the mill, he was thinking of efficiency and labor management. Margaret had more than once accused him of seeing his men only as working hands, and himself only as a master of business whose sole purpose was to conduct trade.

He had tried to change his perspective, and had even had some success at it. Here in a new place, however, his old habits re-emerged. They had served him well for many years, but he knew his singular focus meant he missed some other details. He wondered- if Margaret were above deck, what would she be noticing?

Gazing up the starboard side, he saw two or three men in nearly the same posture as himself. Travelers, all playing a waiting game, and deciding to make the most of the fair weather. Several couples wandered about, arm in arm. There were even a few children. Some were passengers and tagged along behind their parents, but a few of the older ones were employed about the ship doing odd jobs.

His gaze settled on a lad of perhaps two or three who clung to his father's hand as they strolled the deck. The boy was wholly enamored with the expanse of sea before him, and kept trying to drag his father closer to the rail. The boy's dark curls glistened with salt water. He had apparently already been close to the rail, and it was clear the father did not want any more close calls.

The father said something to catch the boy's attention. What it was, Thornton could not hear over the roar of the ocean, but the child abandoned his quest to plummet over the side of the ship and reached up for his father. The man picked him up and the pair walked in the opposite direction.

Thornton felt a small ache in his soul. For most of his life, he had put the idea of having his own family off to the side. He had his mother and sister to care for, a business to run, and little time or desire for anything else. When he had met Margaret Hale, he had not been able to help himself. The dream of holding her- and perhaps even their children- had been shattered, but never forgotten.

She excited ideas and hopes in him that had long lain dormant. Never had he met a woman so easily capable of inspiring him. She wasn't intimidated by him, and she carried an elegant grace, sorely lacking in his busy life. He had been like a moth to the flame. She drew him unconsciously yet inexorably. She was the answer to his lonely heart, the partner and lover he had never dreamed could really exist- yet she hadn't even liked him.

His eyes turned to the water churning below the prow of the ship. What was this mysterious voyage she was on? Who was it who had written her and urged her to come? She'd caught herself, but the fact was not lost on Thornton that there was someone she was not telling him about. A man? Possibly even the same man from the train station last year?

His face dropped into a scowl. What manner of man would compromise her yet again? He had no right to demand she sail alone, even if Mr Bell was on his death bed! No right to....

No. He bit his lip. It was *he* who had no right. She had not given it to him. He had assumed responsibility for her safety, but that did not give him rights over her life. He could not stop her from giving her heart to a fool and a blackguard.

She would be forced to speak to him on this trip, at least enough to be civil. She would be expected to appear as the "sister" of an obviously concerned "brother," but would she forgive his presumption? When she had left Milton, she had seemed to never want more to do with him.

How many times had he wished for an excuse to travel to London? Some made up errand- an impromptu visit with Mr. Bell, or perhaps a package from Higgins and the children who were so fond of her. Some chance, only to see her again! So often in his dreams he had seen himself knocking at her door, then welcomed by her smile, but always the door was closed firmly in his face again.

His brow clouded darkly. He had his chance to see her again, but he doubted she would be glad of it when the drug and the pain of her shoulder dissipated. At best, she might view him as a helpful old friend of her father's. At worst? A meddling and officious rejected suitor who insisted she travel as his sister. A lie!

His conscience was in utter turmoil. Margaret's falsehood last year had been a tremendous blow to his respect for her. How could the woman he admired so easily slip? Now he knew.

Whatever her reasons, it had been clear even then that she was protecting the man. He ground his teeth. An undeserving cad, in his opinion, but she so obviously cared for him. She had sacrificed her honour and dignity to shield him, sullying herself with that falsehood... but it was no more than he had just done for her. Groaning, he dropped his face in his hands, elbows braced on the deck.

"Mr Thornton?" At the sound of a deep bass voice, he turned. A thick-barreled man with silver sideburns and a glittering uniform approached, his beefy hand extended.

"Captain Carter," Thornton greeted him. They shook hands. The captain had the grip of a bear. Thornton turned to glance at the crew, Captain Carter following his lead. "Your men know their work. My compliments."

The captain was obviously pleased. "Spoken like a man of business. You're the Mr Thornton of Milton, are you not? We do a deal of shipping, despite being a smaller steamer, and your reputation precedes you."

"Thank you Captain, as does yours. My shipping agent in Liverpool recommended me to your ship. How long do you expect before we reach Spain?"

"About four days, hopefully a little less if we have good tides. We should have smooth sailing this time of year, but we have to put in at Le Havre. It will be a quick stop, nonetheless it costs us about half a day's sailing. I understand," he said, changing the subject, "that you are traveling with your sister and she met with an unfortunate injury on the dock. My apologies sir, it can be a rough place."

"It was quite accidental, I assure you. Your doctor was a great help. As were Mrs and Miss Carter, I thank you for allowing them to attend Margaret." He felt it was safer somehow to refer to her first name, rather than calling her "my sister."

The captain beamed. "It's right delighted I am to have them traveling with me! It's a rare pleasure for a sea captain to have his family close, that it is. Mellie is my youngest, you see, and she was living with her brother in London until he married earlier this year.

"My dear Connie thought the voyage would be a fine thing for her, and I was glad we could make it work this trip. Though, I suppose," he added, "having her along means we've one less cabin for the passengers such as yourself. I understand you'll be having to bunk in steerage. Those cots are the devil's bane, and no mistake!"

Thornton shook his head. "Do not worry on my behalf. I have been accustomed to worse, and the trip will be a short one."

"Aye, that it will. 'Tis a fast ship! If only my grandpappy could have seen her! It used to take us weeks to reach Spain." The man's eyes gleamed with pride in his vessel. Glancing out at the rolling waves, he recalled the reason he had come to speak to this man.

"Dr. Grayson and my wife tell me that your sister will need some extra attending while we are at sea. It seems they worry she will roll out of the bunk, being sedated, do you see. They've bolstered her the best they can, but they believe she should be watched closely. Mellie would be able to help some, I believe she has remained in there for now. I would prefer, though, that she not spend all of her time so employed. Forgive a selfish old man, but I see my daughter rarely enough as it is."

"Of course, Captain, and I thank you again for all your family is doing. I will care for her most of the time myself," he assured the captain, though hardly knowing how he was to do it.

The captain extended his hand again. "Very good, Mr Thornton. Now if you'll excuse me, I had best see to my crew. The galley opens in a quarter of an hour, and since the supplies are all fresh, you may even find something edible!" Laughing heartily to himself, the captain turned to go.

Margaret was in a fog. She could hear voices in the distance, but could not follow their words. Her mind simply would not exert itself. Her arms were leaden, and she did not even remember her feet. She felt herself rise and fall, over and over again, and she couldn't catch herself. Pain... she remembered pain, but she could not tell where it was from, or even bring herself to care about it.

Some while later, she began to moan in her sleep. She had vague memories of strong arms raising her up, then of tea being held to her lips. Another bitter swallow followed it. The fog claimed her once more.

Some time later- was it minutes or hours?- she was awakened by voices again. She could decipher a woman's voice and a man's. Her name... were they saying her name? She tried to turn toward the voices but only managed a strangled groan.

There was a loud thump, like a door closing. After a few moments, a rich baritone voice echoed in her scattered dreamlike state. The words were comfortingly familiar, though in her stupor she did not make any tangible response to them. Her mind caught snatches of the deep voice.

"*...The point of it surely is that anger is sometimes in conflict with appetite.... Do we not often find a man whose desires would force him to go against his reason, reviling himself and indignant with this part of his nature which is trying to put constraint on him?.... Take a man who feels he is in the wrong. The more generous his nature, the less he can big indignant at any suffering... inflicted by the man he has injured. He recognizes such treatment as just....*"

Margaret was still struggling to regain control of her body. She willed her neck to move, but her eyes would not respond. The voice, low and gentle, spoke her name. It was like a rope cast to her in the darkness.

She grabbed it and fumbled toward where it led. She knew that voice. Mentally she grasped for a name to go with it. Where was she? Oh, yes, Frederick's letter! It must be he! Mr Bell... was she too late? No!

The voice had stopped speaking, but it had done its magic. Slowly, she forced her eyes to open. Rough-hewn wood paneling surrounded her. She seemed to be facing a wall, and could see nothing else but a coarse woolen blanket thrown over her. She blinked several times, trying to focus her eyes and her mind. "Margaret?" the voice sounded more hesitant now.

She turned toward it, more alert than before but still blinking rapidly to clear her blurred vision. The voice now had an owner, and she could never forget that face. "Mr... Th...thorn...?"

He smiled tightly. "How are you feeling?"

"S...sit up..." Her tongue felt thick and dry. She tried to push herself up, but her arm was pinned to her side. In irritation, she tried to push with the other arm but she was lying on it, with a pillow and something heavy holding her wedged into a tight corner of the bunk. Her movements became frantic but Mr Thornton's hand reached out to still her. She stared at it for a moment, still not fully registering her surroundings.

"Here, let me help you." His voice was so gentle, his tone so commiserating, she would have trusted him if he had been a total stranger. Stranger he was not, however, and she felt an odd fluttering in her stomach when he braced an arm behind her.

He drew her to a sitting position then sidled closer to her so that his shoulder supported her weight. He reached down with a long arm and picked up a heavy, rough-shaped seaman's mug he had set on the floor near her. "Can you drink something? I brought you some tea. I did not think you should eat anything solid until you wake more."

"Hmmm," she tried to answer, but she was nodding, so he brought the mug to her lips. He did not trust her to hold it herself, so he carefully tipped it toward her mouth. She managed to swallow the first sip but not the second. It sloshed over his hand.

Her eyes widened, registering her embarrassment. "I'm so- sorry!" she stammered.

Setting the mug down, he deftly reached his breast pocket, under her shoulder and brought out a handkerchief. "It is my fault. I tipped it too fast for you. Do you want more?"

She shook her head. "I should wake up more. Head hurts." She leaned back against him and closed her eyes.

For one brief moment, he tasted heaven. Margaret was nestled close to his heart, her hair tickling his neck. He could feel her soft breathing as her body rose and fell next to his. The delicate scent of rosewater he had detected when they were setting her shoulder still clung to her. Rebellious curls, loosened in her sleep, spilled just at the edge of her hairline. He could almost imagine that she really belonged there, by his side. She fit so perfectly!

The moment could not last. *What was that name she had said a moment ago in her sleep? Fred?* He must be the one she was rushing off to meet, who seemed to be such good friends with her Mr Bell. He grimaced. He was a fool, losing his heart again to a woman who would never have him. Carefully he tried to extricate himself. "Can you sit up if I prop the rice sack beside you?"

Her eyes opened again, more focused this time. "Rice sack? Why is there a rice sack?"

"We feared you would not be able to prevent yourself rolling out of the bed while we are at sea, so we propped you up with this."

Clarity returned to her face in an instant. "Sea? We are really on our way?" She looked down at her hands, then over to him, gathering her thoughts.

He was seated close to her on her trunk, a book lying next to him. Looking more closely, she recognized her father's copy of Plato. The rich, compelling voice in her dreams, she realized, had been his. He had brought the book she had given him, and then he had kindly read to her in her sleep to help her rouse herself. Once again she had underestimated him, and she blushed in humiliation.

He saw her eyes resting on the book. With a small smile, he held it up for her inspection. "I never was able to thank you for this. It was very thoughtful of you." He spoke softly, his eyes shining with affection for the gift.

She smiled back at him for the first time, a spark of good will. She was glad to see how he valued what had once belonged to her father. "Mr Thornton?"

"I think you had best call me 'John,' as everyone on board believes you are my sister." If he admitted it to himself, he would very much enjoy hearing his name on her lips. He knew it would increase his torment, but he was helpless to resist thrilling in it. In his dreams she had whispered his name, the single syllable that had always defined him coming as a caress from her lips. With a pang of self-pity, he reminded himself that the reality could not be so exquisite.

She looked him full in the face for the first time. "So I do remember that correctly. Why?" Her eyes seemed to ask so many questions, he did not know which to answer first.

"You seemed determined to travel," he shrugged. "I know you well enough to know that if I had tried to bundle you in a coach and take you back to your home in London, you would have merely found another ship and would have sailed alone. Alone and injured! At least this way I can keep an eye on you." His cheek tightened, nearly a smile.

She gave a small, embarrassed laugh and looked down at her hands again. It was a full minute before she spoke again. "You seem to be developing a habit of getting me out of scrapes. Thank you." She looked back to him then, her eyes full of meaning. He stiffened and did not make any response.

Discouraged, she looked back down. "I would not have expected to find you here," she added softly.

"I promised to watch over you, and the doctor said you should have someone with you for now," he answered curtly.

"I- I meant to find you sailing. I did not think you often left Milton."

"I am investigating a new source of cotton from Spain," he replied shortly.

"Oh." She hesitated. He clearly felt little inclined to bandy small talk. An awkward silence ensued.

His lips thinned and he looked down. "I must ask you, Margaret; why was it so important for you to travel? I believe you owe me that much."

She drew a deep breath. "Yes, I do," she agreed softly. "How much did I tell you about Mr Bell?"

"You said he was dying in Spain, and that... someone... had written to you to come quickly." He let out a long sigh, watching her face carefully.

She nodded. "Yes." A stab of fear pierced her. She was about to reveal a family secret which had kept Frederick safe for years.

She trusted Mr Thornton's discretion, but she expected her revelation would displease him. His sense of honour loomed large to her- she knew he was the kind of man who would sacrifice for duty and integrity. Would he have made the same choices as Frederick? He was a magistrate in Milton, sworn to uphold the law, but she had also seen remarkable compassion in him.

She feared that he was not likely to sympathize with Frederick's situation, but she had decided to trust him. Trying to quell her fears, she gestured for the mug of tea, and he gave it to her. She swallowed slowly, thinking of how best to tell him.

"Mr... John," she corrected. She smiled a little nervously as she said his name. It was new, but not unpleasant to speak so familiarly with him. "There is something I have wished to tell you for a very long time, but for... many reasons... I was never able to."

A sense of foreboding filled him. *Now she is going to tell me about this man she loves, who holds first place in her heart and is the reason nothing can ever exist between us.* He fought to stay still but failed. He jumped to his feet and began to pace the length of the tiny cabin. When he thought he could handle her silence no more, he asked, a little more testily than he would have liked, "What is it?"

She gazed at him steadily, her eyes sad. *He is still angry with me. I owe him the truth, but he already despises me! He has been so kind just now, I thought, perhaps, he could forgive me. He will see it as a weak excuse for my past behavior, but I must bear his censure. It is too late for anything else now.*

Her voice shaky, she began, "Mr... John, I have a b..."

She stopped when someone banged on the door, then opened it suddenly. Dr. Grayson strode in, filling the tense little chamber with his sunny demeanor. "Well, my dear, I see you are awake! Good, that's very good. How does the shoulder feel?"

Thornton turned away sharply in furious vexation. He had not wanted to hear the truth, but being denied it stabbed him painfully.

"Uh..." she faltered. Oddly enough, she hadn't given a thought to her shoulder. Now that she did, she identified a throbbing ache. She imagined it would be worse if she tried to move it. Dr. Grayson leaned over and gently probed the injured joint, checking for swelling.

The door opened again to reveal Melanie Carter with a tray of warm broth and bread. "Miss Thornton, you're awake!" She seemed genuinely delighted. Margaret looked curiously between her and the two men.

The cabin was not large, and John found himself pinned in the corner. Moving slowly, he squeezed past the doctor. Melanie ducked decently out of his way.

"Excuse me, Margaret. I will return later." She caught his eye and he did not miss her look of regret as she saw him go.

Seven

Dr Grayson finished examining Margaret's shoulder and pronounced that she would likely heal well in a few weeks' time. "Now, my dear, I'm going to leave you the laudanum. Be sure to only take a small spoonful at a time, no more! I recommend you take some soon after you eat," he winked at Melanie.

"Being at sea is not terribly comfortable for ladies as it is, and you may find it difficult to rest if you have pain. The shoulder will probably begin to hurt more as the medication I gave you earlier continues to wear off. Now, I must insist on one thing; if you wish to walk the decks above, you wait until tomorrow in the daylight and you only do so with your brother's help at first. You will find it difficult to balance yourself with one arm hobbled so, but he is a stout enough fellow and can support you. Well, is that all?"

After his long-winded speech he looked from one young woman to the other and stood. "Send for me if you need anything Miss Thornton!" he cheerily excused himself.

The door closed behind him and the girls looked at each other. Melanie giggled. "You probably don't remember me, do you?"

Margaret shook her head. "I assume you were helping me earlier? I was not wearing this dress before."

"Mamma and I got you changed," she confirmed. "Your other gown had seen the effects of Dr. Grayson's ministrations. He's a good doctor but terribly hard on clothing, Miss Thornton!" Her face fairly sparkled with good humour.

Margaret chuckled and extended her left hand, as her right was still tightly bound. "Please, call me Margaret." How was she to make it through the next few days with everyone calling her "Miss Thornton"?

"Melanie Carter, I'm the captain's daughter," the young woman took Margaret's hand in both of hers. "I'm so glad to have someone to talk to on this trip! I've only sailed with Papa twice before, and there is not usually someone my age."

"I am pleased to meet you as well." Margaret smiled. She liked this bright young woman already. She had spent so much of her life with so few friends, she was glad of the chance to meet a new one.

Melanie set the tray on her lap and helped Margaret with the broth and bread. It was wonderful to her hungry stomach, and she indulged with enthusiasm. The two began to chatter amiably.

Melanie had thick reddish-brown hair, nearly auburn, coiled into a plain knot. Her cheeks were sprinkled with a fine dusting of freckles, and her rich chocolate eyes matched her hair. Her clothes were of good quality and were fitted nicely to her trim figure, but not so fine as those Margaret's aunt had had made up for her.

Margaret found that Melanie had spent a great deal of time in London and they discovered that they both enjoyed walking in the same parks and museums. Melanie had kept house for her brother, a solicitor, until he had married two months prior. "I do hope they have children soon!" she enthused. "I adore the little ones."

"Perhaps you will just have to have your own," Margaret smiled, quickly at ease with Melanie's humour.

Melanie blushed prettily. "Mamma has tried introducing me to so many gentlemen! She is from Scarborough, you see, and since Papa is away so much, she would like me to marry and settle near her. Your brother," she brightened, suddenly changing the subject, "Papa tells me he is from Milton. Yet you sound as if you are from the South?"

Margaret blanched a little. "I... I have lived some in Milton, but I have spent much of my life in London with my aunt," she answered truthfully.

"I do love London," she sighed. "If I could find love and a home there, I would be well pleased."

Margaret smiled wistfully. She could almost have shared that sentiment not so very long ago. "What is it you love about London? Besides the parks?" she probed gently. It was a pleasure to find someone with whom she seemed to have much in common.

"I love the culture, all the education available. I cannot seem to learn enough. Most of the people in the North," she frowned, "they live to work, work, work. Books do not interest them a whit. I would so wish to be able to share ideas with someone I can respect..." She stopped, blushing once more. "I'm afraid it all sounds silly."

"Not at all. My father..." Margaret tried to decide how much she could share. She was not comfortable deceiving anyone about her identity, but she recognized Mr Thornton's efforts at protecting her as honourable in intent, if not perfectly honest. Knowing his scrupulous character as she did, she felt the full force of the sacrifice he was making for her.

Still, how could she share her history with her new friend without either weaving a web of lies or revealing too much? Melanie thought she was John Thornton's sister, daughter of a tradesman, not the daughter of a former Southern parson turned Classics teacher.

"My father set great store by learning and fine ideas," she managed at last. "He was forever reading the Classics. He taught me so much." Her eyes became misty and her voice trailed off.

"And, from the way you speak of him," Melanie said slowly, "he is gone now?" Margaret nodded.

"I am so sorry. I cannot imagine losing my dear Papa, though I do see him so little. And your mother?"

Margaret inhaled sharply and realization dawned on Melanie. "I'm so sorry Margaret, I have no right to pry!"

Margaret blinked away the unwanted tears before they could be shed. "No, it is all right." Seeing Melanie's look of apprehension, she sought to reassure her. "I'm so glad to have someone to talk to. I have had few enough good friends, and I am glad to meet you. You are easy to talk to." Margaret smiled with her eyes, a genuine, deep smile that Melanie immediately trusted.

Melanie looked relieved. "So... your brother...."

Margaret's interest was piqued. "Yes?"

"He seems very good to you. He was so worried when he brought you on board."

"He was?"

Melanie giggled again. "I thought Mamma was going to have to throw him out when we came to see to you! He stationed himself by you like a bulldog and looked like he would eat up anyone who came near! He says little enough, but I can see that he is very devoted to you." The girl sighed, then, in a small voice, offered, "He is very handsome, too. I imagine your father was proud of him."

Margaret gazed at her in silence for a moment, uncertain how to respond. A growing warmth spread through her when she heard how Mr Thornton- John- had cared for her after her injury. After all that has passed between us, he is still so good! And yes, my father was indeed very proud of him, but I cannot explain that to her. But what can she mean by telling me he is handsome? Surely she cannot have formed designs on him so quickly!

With that idea, a sick feeling gnawed at her stomach. *Could it already be too late to ask his forgiveness?*

Melanie became uncomfortable with Margaret's long silence. "Are you feeling ill?" she asked. "The doctor said the pain might increase. Do you want some more Laudanum?"

Margaret shook herself out of her reverie. "Yes, er, no. I am not ill. My arm is beginning to ache more though." It was not a lie. All through their conversation Margaret's arm had been throbbing painfully, and it was becoming a powerful distraction. She did not doubt the doctor's words when he cautioned her that she would have trouble sleeping without pain relief.

"Only a little, please. I do not like that sick feeling when I cannot even think properly." Melanie nodded sympathetically. "Do you know what time it is?"

Melanie carefully poured half a spoonful of the vile liquid. "It is dark out, I believe it is nigh on ten o'clock."

Margaret's eyes widened. "So late? Oh, dear, I truly have slept all day." Repressing a shudder, she swallowed the bitter spoonful Melanie offered.

"Do you want me to stay with you tonight? Papa wishes me to read to him in the evenings, but I will defy him if you need help!" Melanie winked conspiratorially.

"That is kind of you, but I probably will not even know you are here. You must rest too. If I could just ask you to help me lie back down? This rice sack makes it difficult." Melanie helped brace her so she could rest comfortably and then straightened. Margaret was truly beginning to appreciate her new friend. "Thank you Melanie," she murmured wholeheartedly.

"Of course, Margaret. You know, my cabin is just next door. It is a lucky thing, is it not? Just rap on this wall here and I can come help you if you need anything. I hope you will feel up to walking on the deck tomorrow. I think you will like the coastline of France, we'll be able to see a good bit of it."

Margaret smiled. "I'm sure I will," she assured her. "Good night, Melanie."

"Good night Margaret." Melanie gave her a friendly squeeze on the left hand and closed the door behind herself.

MR THORNTON HAD SPENT an hour pacing briskly up and down the deck. As he did when he was working, he walked with his arms hanging heavily at his sides, his shoulders bent, and his tall frame stooped forward slightly as if he were perpetually at a task. His eyes were fixed unseeingly before him, as though he could make out the problems he faced written on the very planks of the ship.

He noticed other passengers only enough to avoid bumping into them. His mind was churning as he tried to rule his heart. He never had found much success at controlling his feelings for Margaret. Why he thought he might now be able to rein in that willful organ, when she was so near and needed his help, was something of a mystery to him.

He shook his head vehemently to himself. *She loves this Fred fellow. Get her out of your head, man! She never even liked you and yet you cannot leave her be. Let her go, fool! Aye, she will never find a heart as true as yours, but she has made her choice!*

The stricken look on her face when he had indirectly asked about the person who wrote her from Spain told the story. This was the man she'd been protecting. The coward! Depending on an innocent woman to conceal him... from what? He pounded his own hand with his fist in his frustration.

He could not help but remember a conversation they had had long ago at his dinner party at Marlborough Mills. They had talked about the differences between a "man" and a "gentleman." In her mind, a "gentleman" had been a more civilized, refined version of the whole man.

He, however, had always felt that society's definition lacked something valuable. To him, the word "man" was a truer, finer form of maleness. A real man was one who could depend on his own honour, dignity, ingenuity, and worth, independent of what others thought of him. A real man was a gentleman, as society dictated, but he was much more than that.

John had always hoped to become such a man himself. He had tried every day since his father's death to make up for that man's shortcomings. He had striven to be a firm but fair master, a man of business not easily shaken by the tide of opinions. He had worked to be a gentle and dependable son to his mother, and had become more like a father to his younger sister. He had singlehandedly drudged his family out of poverty and shame, and his labors and sacrifices had purchased them the comforts and respectability they had for the last several years enjoyed.

He had dared to believe he had succeeded at making himself into his own idealized version of manhood, until he glimpsed the unattainable. He could never measure up in the eyes of a woman who expected a refined gentleman, schooled from birth in the ways of superior society. Hard as he might try, he would always fall short of the hope she had ignited within him. Those years spent slaving in self-denial and hard labour had scarred him indelibly, losing him the precious opportunity for refinement and education.

He stopped near the stern and looked over the rail at the water churning in the ship's wake. A full moon hung low in the sky, glinting harshly off the waves as they rolled ever further away from him. *Like her. Like everything else in my life. I am losing control and it is all slipping away.*

He covered his face with his hands. The discipline for which he had fought so hard all his life finally broke. For the first time since his father's death, he sobbed like a child. Mercifully, he was alone on the deck, the others all having gone below for the night. He could not bear knowing anyone had witnessed his weakness.

Somehow, this moment was worse than the day Margaret had left Milton for good. That ache had been nearly unbearable! He'd believed then that he would never see her again. The one woman he had ever loved would never come back to his life and he had simply to let her go.

Now, though, she *had* come back into his life, and she still did not want him. He would have to spend the next few days in tantalizingly close quarters with her, watching for her safety and comfort because his honour would not let him do otherwise. Then he would have to watch her walk away again, into the arms of another man while he would be left to piece together the empty, meaningless shell of his crumbling business. Alone, as always.

How he longed to pull her to him, to beg her once again to stand by him through the rest of his days! With her by his side, he would never want for inspiration or hope, regardless of life's trials. He spent several minutes more berating himself.

Margaret deserved better than an uncivilized oaf of a traveling companion who growled possessively over her. She had not asked for his love, and had never consciously led him on. Any hope she had ever cast his way had been quite inadvertent, as she had wrestled with her notions of right and wrong where they conflicted with society's expectations. He could not blame his feelings on her, and he would not burden her with them again.

The only thing he could think to do was what he should have done long ago. What would his old friend Hale have advised? His head still in his hands, he offered up a humble prayer. He confessed his vain efforts and inadequacies. He prayed desperately for guidance and moral strength to do what he must. He then prayed for Margaret, that she would find what she sought- what she needed, though it could not be him.

He continued for some minutes more, pouring his feelings out inarticulately. When at last he wiped his eyes and raised his head, his heart felt lighter. There had been no thunderclap, no shining moment of revelation, but he had released his heavy burdens. It was a beginning. With a deep, shuddering sigh, he breathed a silent, "Thank You."

He realized he should check on Margaret for the night before it got much later. Whether she desired his company or not, he was responsible for her for now. If he hurried she might still be awake, for it would be even more improper for him to look in on her while she slept.

MARGARET FELT TERRIBLE. SHE had never been to sea before and had not known what to expect. The effects of the laudanum, the rolling sea, the close cabin, the pain in her shoulder and her head, and the hasty meal she had eaten all conspired to churn her stomach most unpleasantly.

She wanted to sit up, hoping the upright posture would ease her discomfort, but she was tucked very tightly against the wall. She would manage to rise a little, but in her dizziness and weakness she could not support herself.

With a groan, she fell back again. The medication was muddling her head. She had taken enough to dull the ache, but not enough to bring immediate blissful rest. The room spun crazily. She shook her head, trying to clear it, but only earned a throbbing pain behind her eyes and another tightening in her stomach.

She started at a soft knock on the door. That familiar deep voice sent shivers through her. "Margaret? It's John."

"Come in!" she called hopefully. She was not resting anyway, and she was glad he had come to see her. She had been sadly disappointed at the interruptions earlier when she had finally found the courage to tell him about Frederick. Would he still be willing to hear her?

He opened the door and stepped partially inside. She greeted him with a timid smile that she hoped did not look too dazed. She tried to appear cheerful, but her stomach lurched treacherously.

He saw the nausea cross her features, and his expression turned to one of concern. "Are you ill? Can I help?"

"I was trying to sit up. I keep falling."

"Here. Let me help you." His traitorous heart fluttered when her grateful eyes met his. He looked quickly away, savagely schooling his emotions into some semblance of order.

He crossed the tiny room, pulled the rice sack out of the way, then gently drew her to a sitting posture. He fluffed the pillow behind her, frowned, and tried fluffing it again. The pathetic little wafer was wholly inadequate to the task of supporting her entire upper body. "There," he finished. "That's about as good as it's going to get."

She breathed deeply with relief. "That is much better. Thank you so much." Her dark eyes studied his face. "Is something wrong?"

Can she really read me that easily? He blinked, stalling for an answer. "I... it's nothing. Can I get you anything? Another pillow? Something to eat?"

Margaret was not easily diverted. She gazed carefully into his eyes, as though willing him to reveal what he would not. Finally she relented. "I believe I ate too fast before," she admitted. "I think that's part of why my stomach is upset."

He bolted to his feet. "I will find you some mint tea." He was out the door before she could even reply.

Why is he suddenly jumpy? Margaret chewed her lip wonderingly. She had seen him in many attitudes; thoughtful, masterful, studious, professional, rough, gentle, unyielding, political, spiritual, passionate, and even on rare occasions humourous. She had never once seen him behave nervously. He was perhaps the only person she had ever known who always seemed controlled, determined, and certain of himself. It was a trait she had at first disliked, then grudgingly come to admire.

He must still be angry with me. I doubt he will want to hear what I must tell him! I cannot justify my wrongdoing, I know that, but if he at least knows my reasons... can he look past my grievous error? I know I have lost his respect, and I refuse to try to gain his pity or sympathy, but I owe him the truth. He has asked now, and I must be brave enough to tell him all!

An old passage memorized in childhood came back to her. *"Ye shall know the truth, and the truth shall make you free."* Margaret's head spun. She hoped he would return soon, so that she would be alert enough to talk. Her stomach grumbled and lurched, reminding her that speech was not her only priority.

A few moments later the latch turned, and he entered carrying a tray like an ordinary domestic. The thought of the proud Master of Marlborough Mills waiting on her brought an amused little smile to her face. "I could not find another pillow," he apologized. "My own berth in steerage does not even have one for me to rob." He stood for a moment, uncertain what to do with his tall frame or the tray he carried.

She tried to reassure him of her gratitude and that another pillow was not necessary. He set the tray before her, and she eagerly gulped the soothing liquid. The first sip helped ease the lurching in her stomach. She feared she did not appear very ladylike, but it would be far less desirable for her to become sick right in front of him. Would she forever be embarrassing herself before this man?

He watched her with some amusement. Never had he seen Margaret as anything but perfectly elegant, even when shaking with passion for her opinions. *She must be positively queasy*, he thought, as he watched her desperately fighting for equanimity. Her hands trembled as she visibly struggled to control her nausea and continue sipping the mint tea.

Margaret glanced up at him. He smiled strangely, but stood warily by the door, his hand hovering near the latch. *I must speak now, before he tries to go! And this time I cannot risk interruptions.* Steeling her resolve, she took a final sip of tea and, swallowing, asked, "Is there a bolt on the door?"

His eyebrows shot up nearly to his hairline. Glancing down, he replied hesitantly that there was. Her voice shaking, she asked him to lock the door. He did so, then turned to her, his eyes narrowed.

"Will you sit down? Please?" Her luminous eyes implored him to settle himself near her. He glanced around the small room for an appropriate seat, finally easing himself again on top of the trunk near her bed.

She sought to straighten herself and took a few deep breaths. "Mr... John... earlier you asked me... that is, I had started to tell you..." she faltered. Did he really want to hear her pitiful story? She looked back at his face and saw that he was, in fact, intensely interested in what she had to say. His face bore the look of a martyr, but his eyes fastened unblinking on her. *The truth shall make you free,* she echoed to herself. Setting her jaw, she forged ahead, avoiding his eyes.

"Did my father ever tell you about Frederick?"

There it was. The name he had dreaded. He closed his eyes. "No, I have never heard of him," he replied, his voice thick with resignation. *Except for when you cried out his name in your sleep.*

"H-he is my brother."

Eight

THE CABIN WAS SWATHED in silence, except for the gentle creak of steel on wooden planking as the ship rolled slowly on the waves. She dared to look at his face and what she saw there warmed her right to her toes.

His mouth gaped in wonder. His breath came shallow and fast, his eyes widened then narrowed again and again. His gaze wandered aimlessly from the floor to her hands, the wall, and back again. Had he heard her properly? A brother?

She could not look away. She had never seen such an expression on his face. It was as though he had been holding his breath for a week and had suddenly taken a great gulp of fresh air. His features were suffused with shock, glad surprise, and sudden understanding.

He finally managed a soft response. "Your brother? I never knew...." His eyes finally met hers. He leaned closer, aching to touch her.

Deep shivers ran through her. She was feeling dizzy from the medication, but her heightened pulse helped her fight for alertness. What was it that had altered him so? She had not imagined he would be so affected, but realization began to glimmer.

Was it possible that he had been jealous of the man she had lied to protect? After his assurances so many months ago that he no longer thought of her, she had only sought to explain her motivations- not to clear herself of wrongdoing, but to make him understand the nature of her urgency. Why, then, would he react so powerfully to the revelation of Frederick's identity?

"Why would your father- and you- never mention him?" His words were choked with emotion.

She couldn't answer when he was looking at her in that tender, desperate way. At last she tore her gaze away from him and focused on the floor by his feet. "Frederick joined the navy. He left when I was very young, while I was living with my Aunt Shaw in London. I cried when I heard he had left, and I know Mother did too. He wrote me often; he was so full of hope! Father knew he was determined to go, and believed it would turn out for the best. He had such ambitions!"

She risked a glance up at him, but he only gazed back in rapt attention. "His very first post was with a Captain Reid, on the *Russell*. As soon as they left port, the captain began abusing his crew. Frederick hated him, and he wrote that the feeling was mutual. He was glad for another post soon after, but a few years later he found himself under Reid again on the *Avenger*. He beat the children, and needlessly endangered the ship. He mercilessly ran the crew to rebellion and exhaustion- he was utterly mad! Frederick and some of the others tried to protect the ship and the men from him, but it was no use."

"Captain Reid?" His brow creased thoughtfully. "I remember reading about him. They say he went insane. And... your brother... he was involved in the mutiny?"

She hesitated. "That is what the navy called it. They called him the ringleader, branded him a traitor." She shook her head forlornly. "My poor mother and father! Frederick, he... well he was always trying to protect people, even when we were children.

"You may believe he acted foolishly, but he only did what he thought was right. I know he was angry at injustice, and he could not stop himself from acting, not caring what it would cost him." Despite her desire- her deep need- for his sympathy, her eyes flashed in defensive passion for her brother.

He smirked wryly. "A bit like someone else I know." At her quizzical expression, he continued gently, "Were you not protecting an unworthy soul when you took that blow that was meant for me during the rioting?" His eyes trailed to the side of her face where the horrifying blood had once trickled. "You never would allow me to thank you for that. Every breath I draw, I owe to your goodness. You have given me life in every way possible."

She looked steadily at his face. "I put you in danger. I should not have... It all seemed so unfair, but I should never have encouraged you to go down there. They were so many, and they were so desperately angry... I was wrong." Her lower lip trembled with feeling.

"No, you were right." His voice was gentle, but it was laced with deeper tones that made her shiver. "Had I attempted to reason with them sooner, perhaps some of the ugliness could have been avoided. Things... well, things are not perfect, but my men and I understand each other better these days. I owe much of that to you." Her heart fluttered queerly at his revelation.

He reached for her hand, lightly tracing the tops of her fingers. Margaret's heart thrummed in her throat. It was such a simple touch, but it was like fire tingling through her limbs.

Margaret had never considered such a touch from a man before. How could she know how it would make her pulse race and her hands tremble? Every rational thought fled her grasping mind. The feelings were so intense; she did not know how to respond. She commanded herself to remain still, but her body fairly quivered.

His long fingers traced up to her wrist, circling the small bones gently. She bit her lip. The hairs along the back of her neck pricked with electricity. Her breath came in shallow, silent little gasps and she felt her face burning. She did not want him to pull away, but she had to stop this feeling that threatened to drown her.

Turning her hand, she trapped his fingers, stilling their delicious wandering. They each raised their eyes to the other's face. Their gaze held for a moment; his intense and inscrutable, hers uncertain and searching. She looked back down to their intertwined fingers, knowing not how to answer the question his eyes asked.

He had frightened her. Inwardly he cursed himself. Brash fool! The very moment she had cast him a shred of hope he had acted like a boor, trying to claim affections he was not sure were his.

Hesitantly he began to withdraw his hand, but she would not release it. *Slowly,* he schooled himself. *I can wait as long as it takes for her. If I have one chance in a thousand, I will wait!* He relaxed his hand into what he hoped she would perceive as a friendly and companionable grasp, and attempted to urge her to speak more.

"That night, at the station... it was Frederick? He came to see your mother, didn't he?" He watched with concern as a faint dazed look cross her face. Perhaps he had judged wrongly in asking her to continue. She needed rest.

She nodded in response to his question, fighting back the looming lightheadedness. "We did not tell anyone he had come, even Mr Bell. We were so worried for his safety! Then one day, just after Mother passed, Dixon met Leonards in the street. He and Frederick had been in school together as boys, and never cared much for each other. He asked her directly about Frederick. We feared that word had gotten out that Fred was in the country, and Father insisted he sail immediately." The room spun. Margaret shut her eyes briefly against another wave of nausea.

"Leonards knew of him from Helstone? Of course! We knew the worthless fellow was not from Milton." He chided himself for not seeing it sooner. It all made sense now. There would have been a reward for a traitor, and Leonards was just the sort to wish to cash in on it. He had drunkenly attacked, and Frederick had fought him off.

And then- brave woman! She had walked home alone! After grieving the death of her mother, facing a brutal attack, then bidding perhaps a permanent farewell to a beloved brother, she had made her way home to her worried father while Leonards was still nearby.

He looked tenderly to her again, tightening his grip on her hand slightly. "Would that I had come by only a moment later! I could have at least seen you safely home. Had I only known!" *And all those months I spent consumed by envy of another man might have been avoided!*

She smiled gratefully. Her eyelids were beginning to droop powerfully, but she struggled for alertness. It felt so good to finally be open with him! He had proven far more understanding than she had ever hoped.

"The worst was the inspector. I did not know what to do or say, I was so worried about Frederick! You see, he did not sail directly, and I had not received word yet that he was safely out of the country when the inspector came to the house. We had him go to London to speak with my cousin Edith's brother-in-law, Henry Lennox."

"Lennox...." he mused thoughtfully. "I believe Mr Bell has mentioned that name to me before." He pressed his lips together firmly. What Bell had said about Lennox, he did not like to remember.

Margaret's eyes flashed to his, and she continued more hesitantly. "He is an attorney, and we had hoped..." her voice broke. "Well, that is at an end now. We had hoped he could clear his name, live in safety and honour. While we thought there was a chance he might return, we were afraid to let anyone know he had been. However, since then, no witnesses could be found to corroborate his story, and we gradually gave up hope. Oh! I wanted to tell you then!" she looked up to him earnestly. "I was so sorry to have caused you to despise me!"

He gave her a heartfelt smile and squeezed her hand reassuringly. "Margaret, I believe I could never despise you. I was wrong to have thought the worst of you, please forgive me for my lack of faith in you. It was clear to me from the beginning that you were protecting someone, and I know you well enough to know to what lengths you will go. My anger can be traced to simple and despicable jealousy. I believed," he intoned softly, "that you had given him the love that I had so desperately coveted for myself."

Her eyes widened. Her body flushed anew at his admission, but she did not feel equal to addressing it. Fear of the unknown crawled through her. Thrilling at his confession, but still unable to wholly believe it, she doggedly turned the conversation back to her own failure. "But I lied! I broke faith, grasping at the temptation to save myself. I should have trusted that God could protect Frederick. Instead I brought shame on myself." She shook her head wearily.

He stroked his thumb gently over the back of her hand. "And what do you consider my tale about you being my sister?" he chided warmly. "You were faced with the option of betraying an innocent brother or concealing him. I believe your heart was faithful. Life is rarely clear-cut as I once thought. We make choices and make the best of it, trusting that our honest intentions will not be in vain. I would consider it a greater wrong *not* to attempt to protect another under such circumstances if it were within my power."

She gazed at him wonderingly. Such an idea had not occurred to her. She closed her eyes briefly and then offered him a conciliatory smile. His deep blue eyes twinkled freely back at her. She laid her head back in relief against the rude pillow he had carefully arranged for her.

John could see her fighting to stay awake so she could continue their conversation. His heart warmed immeasurably. Margaret wanted to talk to him! It was a first. He could be selfish no longer, however. He sensed there was more she wanted to tell him, but there would be tomorrow. "Margaret, you must rest. We can talk more when you feel up for it."

She sighed and he could virtually watch her deflate. It was clear she had been struggling even harder than he realized to remain alert enough to speak to him.

The ship rolled on a particularly large swell, pitching her uncomfortably to the right, and she gasped in pain. Quickly he reached an arm around her to steady her. In a sudden flash of insight, he realized that her profound drowsiness was likely due to more of Dr. Grayson's narcotics, and she would be rapidly and soundly asleep.

"This will not do," his voice was warm in her ear. "You must lie back; I worry that you will fall."

She shook her head vigorously. "My stomach... I- I'm still a little queasy. I am afraid to lie down." She blushed at having to admit such a personal thing to him.

He considered for a moment. He believed her nausea would likely pass after she submitted in slumber to the medication, but for now she must be allowed to sit up securely.

Margaret wondered if he realized his thumb was tracing reassuring little circles around her upper arm. Secretly she hoped he would not stop. She was amazed how comforting his presence suddenly was to her.

"I am afraid to leave you as you are. You cannot sit up on your own while you are asleep. If you fall..." The only solution he could think of was wildly improper. He could not stay with her! She would never consent, and his own scruples forbade it.

Her head drooped onto his arm. "Don't go then," she murmured sleepily. "Stay, as you did earlier."

His eyes widened in shock at hearing her voice his very own desire. "Margaret, you know I must not stay the night here! It is not right for me to do so."

She smiled up into his face, a glint of humour surfacing through her fatigue. "Why ever not? I thought you were my brother."

He could not help laughing a little. Whatever she was, or could ever become to him, his feelings for her were far from brotherly.

He did not condemn her natural need for assistance. Of the people available to provide it, he was the most willingly attached to her, but he did not entirely trust himself. Could he remain with her, rendering support while keeping his honour as a gentleman intact?

The bounding desires surging in him with her every glance, every touch, threatened to quite undo him. He was certain that any length of time with her supple body pressed against his, even in sleep, would prove more than his unraveling self-control could possibly handle. He would never forgive himself if he compromised her.

Even now, if events were publicly known, her reputation would be in tatters. He groaned inwardly. She deserved better, an untarnished future- hopefully with him in it.

His eyes searched her face. She gazed back at him in an open, honest need, utterly devoid of impropriety or impurity. She, in her innocence, could not be expected to conceive what she was asking of him! Impatiently he raked his fingers through his hair, his breath hissing between clenched teeth. He turned his face away from her briefly, deliberating.

Margaret looked away. His reluctance was plain. She regretted the awkward position she had put him in, the necessity which demanded she depend upon his forbearance. "I ask too much. Forgive me, I do not wish to impose upon you any further."

He turned back sharply. "You do not impose," he returned, his tones as soft as before. "I want nothing more than to be of assistance to you, but I would not dishonour you. I fear... I do not wish any offense against you."

She smiled weakly, but with genuine warmth. Something inside him melted. He knew he would be powerless to resist anything she could desire. Her expression fluttered again as she fought another ripple of queasiness.

"I would... I would very much appreciate if you could stay," she asked humbly. "I know it is improper, but our circumstances are rather unusual. I believe I need your help, if you are willing." Her voice was barely above a whisper, and her lash-shaded eyes betrayed her uncertainty.

A wry expression quirked his mouth. "Are you quite certain? You will not awaken in the morning and strike me soundly as I deserve when you find me in your bedchamber?"

"Hmm, possibly," she mumbled drowsily, a small smile playing at her lips. Then her face grew more serious as her eyes dropped to the floor. "I trust you, John," she murmured.

She had never spoken more beautiful words to him. He nodded, and she released a deep breath in relief. Crooking his arm more intimately around her shoulders, he inclined her body slightly more forward. He slid behind her on her bunk so that he was sitting against the back wall, his legs dangling over the side. Reaching with his free arm, he dragged her trunk at an angle so he could prop his feet upon it more comfortably.

"Here," he whispered. He drew her beautiful head onto his chest, supporting her by wrapping strong arms around her slim waist. Her thick curls, tugged loose from her plait, tumbled about him intoxicatingly. He sighed in deepest contentment as she burrowed her face near his shoulder. In moments, her breathing was steady and regular. She was asleep in his arms.

Nine

JOHN DOZED INTERMITTENTLY. IN his waking moments, he was floating in rapturous delight. Her sweet form pressed deliciously against his chest and outer thigh. Mercilessly he dug his fingernails into his palms, determined he would not take advantage of her slumber to caress her beautiful features. He knew that one small permission granted himself would lead to greater compromise. She trusted him, and he would sooner cut off his own hands than violate her trust.

He fought the good battle for self-denial over and over, all through the blissful hours of holding her. Each time, to stave off the nearly painful desires she aroused in him, he would turn his thoughts to the sheer ecstasy of her companionable nearness, and his budding hopes for the future. He had been living and struggling alone for far too long!

Margaret's beauty and grace had sparked his interest, but it was her unusual likeness to his own private character which had fueled the flame of his passion for her. He recognized in her a similar soul, with the same deep needs and aching loneliness he himself faced. There was not, could never be, a partner more suited to him with whom he would gladly share the rest of his life.

Did he dare hope again? He could not help the euphoric satisfaction that filled him when he thought of how she had suddenly opened her heart to share her fears and secrets with him. The full knowledge of her trust in him came as a sublime thrill. How differently he saw the world this night than only a few hours earlier!

He resolved that once off the ship, he would court her, as he had failed so miserably to do before. He would pay her the proper gentlemanly attentions she so richly deserved, and had no doubt been taught to expect. His own education in such matters had been so sorely lacking, but he was convinced that he need only look to her for guidance.

He loved her self-assured confidence, so utterly unique to herself alone. No other young woman of his acquaintance had ever demonstrated half her fortitude, though it caused whispers and raised eyebrows among the gossips. He was determined that their newfound understanding of each other would not be allowed to wither.

He expected it would be difficult to invite their friendship to blossom under the scrutiny of others who believed her to be his sister. It would be tricky, but not impossible. He had every faith in her discretion, and with their new familiarity she was certainly perceptive enough to read his heart.

It was a thing worth doing, he thought with satisfaction. It only wanted time. Convincing himself that winning her heart was within his grasp, he would slip into a light, contented slumber, only to wake again to the throbbing pleasure of cradling her in his arms.

Sometime near dawn, he reluctantly admitted to himself that he should leave her. He could not justify his continued presence any longer, as surely the nausea which had threatened her would have abated in her sleep. There was still the greater need to protect her reputation. It was risky enough to pass himself off as a concerned brother. If he wished to avoid attracting attention to their unusual circumstances, he needed to withdraw himself whenever reasonably possible.

Still unwilling to detach himself from her, he allowed himself just once the profound pleasure of burying his face in her luscious hair. He inhaled her feminine scent deeply, afraid to lose the magical time and space where they had at last set aside their misunderstandings.

With regret to be leaving her warm presence, he pressed a chaste kiss on her temple, lingering over the softness of her skin. Temptation loomed, but miraculously his self-control won out. He gently disentangled himself from her, tucking the pillow beneath her sleeping face as he laid her down. She stretched uncomfortably in her sleep.

He pondered for a moment the problem of how to make her more comfortable. After making a few extemporaneous arrangements and deciding her injured shoulder would be well supported in her sleep, he straightened. He felt his heart swell as he looked down at her slumbering form.

The privilege of seeing her thus thrilled him with a warmth that stole through his entire body. How was it that he, a rough manufacturer without knowledge of refinement, had been granted the supreme honour of becoming a trusted one to so divine a creature? Trust him she did, however unworthy he might feel, and he would not prove her trust unfounded. With great effort, he bade himself to go.

He lurched to his feet precariously. He had long endured the numbness in his legs in favor of the delightful closeness of her, but now his body screamed in protest as he tried to make it do his bidding. He held on to the frame of the bunk for support, gritting his teeth as the painful surges in his muscles tingled to life.

At last he felt he could walk safely. With a final long look of silent devotion, he forced himself to step out of the door and to close it firmly behind him. *Soon,* he promised himself, *perhaps I will earn the right to remain with her always.*

In the chill gray morning light, he pulled out his battered pocket watch, one of the few remaining mementos of his father. He considered returning to his own bunk for another hour or two. He was at his leisure, with nothing to do for a change but enjoy the ride.

It would be wise, perhaps, to catch up on some of the sleep he had lost this night. A shave would be desirable too, he thought, ruefully scraping his fingers over his fresh stubble. While he gazed thoughtfully at the mute face of his watch, he heard a whistle from the men on deck. Feet scuffled overhead, and he presumed they were nearing the port of Le Havre. His curiosity won out- he went up on the deck.

Upon arrival, he saw that they were, in fact, drawing away from the coast. So drowsily distracted had he been by his alluring companion that he had been utterly unaware of the ship putting in. He shook his head, a little shocked at himself. If this was how oblivious he could become when Margaret was around, he was indeed in a perilous position!

A few groggy seamen were still wrestling the last of the cargo below deck, but he could see that any new passengers would have already been settled. Wondering if there were any new cabins opened up from London passengers decamping, he decided to seek out the captain.

He found Captain Carter pacing the quarterdeck with another officer. The younger man was showing his captain a weathered pad of paper, whereupon could be found a confusing jumble of figures. The captain traced a thick finger down the page as the two men conferred.

John knew in principle how the seas were navigated, but he had never himself had opportunity to ponder the calculations necessary for a safe passage. Curiosity got the better of him, and he found himself craning his neck to try to glimpse what was written. The busy junior officer nodded jerkily to his captain's commands. Not wishing to interrupt a conversation between the captain and his subordinate, he hung back, but kept his ear trained on the navigator's descriptions.

At long last the young officer walked away, and Captain Carter met his eye. The robust silver-haired man greeted him genially. He wore a large smile, the result of fine weather and a remarkably efficient performance by his crew at the port of Le Havre. He clapped his hands together enthusiastically. "Well, Mr Thornton, what can I do for you this morning?"

Thornton smiled and extended his hand in reply. "Good morning, Captain. I was wondering if any cabins had opened up after last night's passengers disembarked."

A cloud crossed the man's face. "I'm sorry, Mr Thornton. We took on a few new passengers, and I'm afraid every cabin was filled again. I sent a man to look for you last night to verify whether you wanted a cabin before we docked, but he reported he could not find you. We presumed you may have needed to attend Miss Thornton, and would perhaps continue to do so for the rest of the journey. I apologize for any inconvenience."

Thornton tried to keep his face neutral upon hearing the captain's assumptions. He had not considered that he might have been missed. He mentally reaffirmed his resolve to keep Margaret's true identity private. There would certainly be no sympathy for his actual position as a friend of her family if it were reported abroad that he had stayed most of the night in her room! He would have to be extremely careful of his behavior regarding her.

"I understand. Thank, you, I will make myself comfortable in the third-class."

"If I may, how does Miss Thornton this morning?"

He grimaced inwardly at the name. His honest scruples chafed at having to deceive anyone, but he had given his word to protect Margaret. He knew of no better way to do that at this point. "I believe she had some trouble with nausea last night, but she was resting comfortably when I left her."

The captain nodded. "I'm glad to hear it. My daughter has taken quite a liking to your young sister. I know she was hoping the two of them could spend some time together; that is, if Miss Thornton feels well enough later."

"I am sure Margaret will like that." His thoughts warmed suddenly to the bright young woman he had met the day before. He knew how bitterly Margaret had struggled with loneliness, and his heart had ached for her as much as for his own empty life. If Melanie Carter could become a friend to her, he would do everything in his power to foster that bond.

Their private conversation was interrupted by the approach of a stranger. One of the new passengers, he guessed. He stood to one side as the man approached. "Monsieur Giraud," the captain greeted him with a slight bow. He proceeded to introduce the two, seemingly glad to have found a way to extricate himself from conversation so he could return to his duties. He walked away as soon as decently possible, leaving Thornton with his new acquaintance.

MARGARET AWOKE EARLY THAT morning, cold and alert. She had not been so groggy last night that she did not remember Mr Thornton- John- staying with her while she slept. At the time, overcome with nausea, pain, natural fatigue and the effects of the narcotic, she had heartily appreciated the comfort his nearness offered.

In that light, the impropriety of the act had seemed of little importance. With the morning, however, came new perspective. Her body flushed with humiliation. What would he think of her, asking him to stay with her in her room? If he had thought her behavior improper during the riots, or while walking the unknown Frederick to the rail station, or when insisting upon sailing alone, he surely would think her an utter wanton now!

She was grateful he had arisen earlier and that she did not have to face him immediately upon awakening. Her brow furrowed. Had he been seen leaving her cabin? Of course, if everyone on the ship thought he was merely being a helpful brother to an injured sister, they would think little enough of it.

A wistful, rebellious part of her heart wished she had been able to awaken to the comforting warmth of his chest cradling her, but her reason argued it was better to find him gone. Their situation had become awkward enough without the further disadvantage of an early morning encounter!

She lay still a moment, taking a mental inventory of her physical self. The pain in her shoulder had dulled to a distant ache. She was still wedged very carefully between the wall and a rice sack, but her upper body was propped up on the pillow and something else, something thicker... what was it? She was able to sit up a little, thanks to the added padding beneath her, and discovered to her surprised delight a man's thick woolen overcoat. It had been carefully folded and positioned behind her shoulders to best support her.

Experimentally she pressed her face into the wool. His scent lingered- masculine and fresh, the natural aroma of his body unenhanced by colognes such as the Londoners of her acquaintance would wear. A small smile crept across her face. How differently she felt about him than she once had!

The man she had once scorned as a great rough fellow, uncaring and cruel, had proven to be tender and honourable. They had done naught but disagree during the early part of their acquaintance. She had found little to admire in him but his great force of will, and even that she had disdained because she did not care for his direction.

No, she admitted to herself, *that is not quite true. From our earliest conversations, I quite liked his smile*. It was rare enough, but brilliant in its purity. Unlike most gentlemen and nearly every lady of Margaret's acquaintance, John had always been clear and forthright in his opinions, and guileless in his enjoyments. The raw honesty of their discussions had frightened her until she began comparing them favorably with the stilted and scripted conversations of men of Edith's circle. Men like Henry.

She pursed her lips. Henry was a good sort, and a kind friend, but she never could feel more for him. Odd, that her cordial, platonic feelings for a man more suited to her original expectations should never improve, while her violent dislike of a man so unlike what she had once desired should undergo a complete reversal.

Perhaps, she mused, that would be an important matter to consider in the very near future. She was perfectly aware that, under present circumstances, propriety would dictate specific expectations of both of them. It was possible, of course, for her reputation to be preserved without a marriage. She had no doubts of his discretion, and as for the other passengers, none knew of her or her true identity. She chuckled at the very idea of being confused with Fanny Thornton.

She expected, however, that he would feel obliged to her. She could even believe he still had genuine feelings for her, judging from his behavior last evening. Could she really be considering marriage to the man? Her pulse beat loud and quick at the concept.

He had always challenged her. He was a veritable thunderstorm rolling through her life. By his own force of will he had carved out a formidable niche in the world from nothingness and debt and shame. By that same power of command, he had held on to his position through the rough seas of more than one labor strike and had drawn the admiration of his equals.

Yet she knew he was just and fair, nearly to a fault. She remembered how he had given Higgins a chance, after the older man had virtually roused the strike singlehandedly. Higgins had told her once of their conversation. After Thornton had initially refused to have anything to do with him, he had seen the unfairness of his position and had come of his own accord to admit the wrongness of his actions.

She had often wondered if her connection to Higgins had had any influence upon him. He had at one time harbored tender feelings for her, but she also knew he kept them severely in check, jealously guarding them from discovery. So well, in fact, had he suppressed his feelings that any slight against them was met with even more dignity and fairness than was deserved. He had shown the greatest kindness and consideration for her own poor mother, almost as though he were deliberately trying to prove his control over himself.

He had even buried his own jealousy at seeing her walking with Frederick, and begged his mother to come to her to offer womanly counsel. Margaret heaved a deep sigh when she thought of Mrs Thornton.

The older woman had been terribly bitter for her son's sake. The mother's resentful words had revealed, perhaps more than the son's ever had, how deeply and truly Mr Thornton had cared for her. She had shunned and scorned him mercilessly and unfairly. Mrs Thornton had been fully correct in her acrid judgement- Margaret had not known what sort of man she had rejected. How much abuse could a man's feelings withstand?

As she pondered these things, she had begun to sit up. Her stomach still lurched, but not as threateningly as the night before. Her head felt clearer this morning, as well. She felt safe enough to stand, despite the gentle rocking of the floor.

She did so, and suddenly realized something was amiss. She wore no corset under her gown! The full petticoat was missing as well! Good Mrs Carter and Melanie had dressed her in another gown for decency's sake, but had omitted the proper undergarments for the sake of her comfort. She gasped in mortification. And last night he had held her!

At least, she thought ruefully, *the women had been able to fasten her gown completely, even without the corset. Oh, foolish, wicked, wanton woman I am! Yet, I did not realize at the time how it might tempt him. In intention I am blameless, but in deed... I may as well have thrown myself at him!*

Margaret's attention was diverted by a soft knock on the door. "Yes?" she called, hesitantly. If it were *he*, how was she to face him?

"Margaret, it's Melanie," the muffled voice replied.

Relief washed through her. "Please come in!"

Melanie's smiling face bounced through the door. "I heard you moving, I thought you might need help. Why didn't you knock on the wall, silly goose?"

Margaret couldn't help liking this effervescent girl. She smiled back. "I am sorry, I forgot you were so near. I've only been awake a moment."

"Mamma mended your other gown; would you like to change?"

Margaret thanked her but glanced at her trunk. "I would like to change, but I did bring a third gown, my gray silk. I think I will just wear that for now and we can retrieve the other later."

"Oh, let me help you. You cannot possibly do on your own." Melanie moved to the truck, efficiently locating the remaining gown, and helping Margaret slip the rumpled one off her shoulders.

"I am so grateful to you and your mother for all your help," Margaret offered softly. "I truly do appreciate... I could not have managed on my own."

"I do not believe in accidents," her ruddy-haired companion replied stoutly. "You and I, we were meant to be good friends. I am very happy to be able to help you, Margaret." The sincere smile she flashed her new friend reached her eyes, and Margaret could not help replying in kind.

Melanie's nimble fingers had Margaret properly dressed in no time. She was amazingly skilled at maneuvering Margaret's wounded shoulder with minimal discomfort. After she had the gown properly fastened and arrayed, she fashioned a sling out of the doctor's linen strips. "There," she finished, "That should be fine support for the day. We needn't fasten it so tightly when you are not lying down. Now, sit on the trunk," she ordered.

Margaret cocked her head questioningly.

"I must do your hair, silly! You must be properly coiffed to welcome all the new French travelers!" Melanie teased, her eyes sparkling. "My, but you have lovely hair. How thick and dark it is! Mine is not thin at all, but you have nearly twice as much!"

Margaret smiled as Melanie chattered comfortingly. After berating herself so severely, Melanie's charm and brightness was a much-welcomed relief from her worries.

"There! It's not as fancy as the 'do you had when your brother brought you on board, but you have such a becoming face, anything looks lovely."

Margaret blushed and thanked her for the compliment. "I am sure you are too modest about your abilities though," she added seriously. "You have a gift of caring for people. Truly," she assured her, placing her good hand on Melanie's arm.

"Oh, thank you! I..." she dropped her eyes, flushing modestly, "I do so love helping people. I'm meaning to stay on with my brother, help with his children someday... that is, you know, as long as I can."

Margaret assured her she would be very good at it. Melanie glanced back at the bed and noticed the folded overcoat. "Now, where did that come from?"

"I believe... John left it," Margaret stammered. She could feel her cheeks warming, but she forced herself to behave casually. "He... he looked in on me last night after you left."

"Oh, of course! He is so kind to you. So much more than my own brother is to me! If I didn't know better, I'd say he had a *tèndre* for you, but of course that's silly." She sighed wistfully, not noticing her companion's shocked expression.

"I saw him walking the deck with my father and one of the new passengers this morning. He is very handsome you know! I guess," she giggled, "this would explain why your brother did not have a coat when the others did! Perhaps we should take it up to him before we go to the galley to see about some breakfast?"

During this little speech of Melanie's, Margaret had gone from embarrassed to thrilled to mortified to hopeful. Melanie bent to gather up the coat, but Margaret halted her with a quick objection. "No, I- I should take it to him."

"How will you carry it, dear Margaret? I must hold your left arm, you know, for support, and you cannot possibly carry it with your right."

"I will manage," replied Margaret obstinately. She was not willing to allow the other woman the honour of returning John's coat.

Could it be, she wondered, a twinge of jealous behavior on her own part? She would not dwell on that now. She felt she owed him the return of his coat in person, and secretly hoped she would soon have a chance to thank him properly for his noble friendship. Hopefully, he would forgive her scandalous behavior.

Ten

MELANIE DRAPED MARGARET'S OWN cloak over her shoulders and they set out. The two women mounted the few steps to the upper deck with little enough difficulty. Margaret saw Dr. Grayson standing near the captain on the main deck, and she hoped to escape his notice. She remembered his admonishments regarding walking about on the rolling deck with her injured arm. She could see already that he was quite correct; it was more difficult to balance herself on the rocking ship, but she did not want the doctor's interference.

"There he is," chirped Melanie. Margaret followed her friend's gaze and saw John walking near the rail with a blond stranger in expensively tailored clothes. She could tell by the set of John's shoulders that he was not entirely delighted with his companion's presence. She frowned to herself. *When did I come to know him so well?*

The gentlemen drew near and Margaret found herself eagerly searching his face. She had never seen him other than close-shaven. His cheeks were bristling with two days' growth of beard, making him seem somehow more mysterious and imposing, and, perhaps, a little less the meticulously disciplined master of machinery she had once disdained.

His eyes lit upon her and his entire face fairly blossomed. He stepped quickly to her side; the other gentleman momentarily forgotten. He surveyed her appearance with appreciation. Her cheeks were flushed prettily, rather than pale and wan as of yesterday. She had changed out of her black mourning gown to a light silvery gray dress which became her well.

Despite his altered appearance, his welcoming smile immediately eased her uncertainty. She drew the bundle out from beneath her own cloak and extended it. "I thought you might like to have this back," she told him shyly, her eyes downward, her lashes brushing her cheeks.

He grinned broadly, and with a warm murmur of thanks, took the coat and put it on. Then, extending his elbow, he tucked her left hand under his arm and held it gently with his other hand. "How are you feeling this morning?" he inquired, in a voice too low for the others to hear.

"Much better, thank you. I- I thank you for... all your help." She blushed again, darting her eyes to the side to glance at his face. It was a study in composure, but she could read a small twinkle in his eyes.

He cleared his throat and turned back to the gentleman with whom he had been walking. "Monsieur Giraud, may I present my sister, Margaret, and Miss Melanie Carter, daughter of the captain."

The Frenchman bowed with a flourish, drawing a giggle from Melanie and a smile from Margaret. "Enchanté!" he beamed. "We were just about to take a déjeuner! May I 'ave the honour of escorting you, Mademoiselle Carter?"

Melanie curtseyed playfully and took the man's arm. The pair walked on ahead toward the ship's galley. Giraud was loudly and verbosely wondering at the ship, the weather, and obviously working very hard to delight his companion. Margaret glanced questioningly at John's face. She had always known John to have little patience with frivolous people, and she wondered at finding him with such a companion.

As if in answer to her question, he began explaining himself. "Monsieur Giraud boarded very early this morning and he apparently has some family connection to a linen mill. The captain introduced us this morning and he has had... many questions," he finished with a sigh. She could see the tension behind his eyes and she knew immediately that her arrival had been a pleasant relief from the man's conversation.

He stopped her fractionally, just enough so as not to be overheard by the couple ahead of them. "How are you this morning, really?" he whispered.

She bashfully met his eyes. She found only concern there, without condemnation for her behavior. "I am well enough. Truly. Last night..." she faltered, not sure how to express herself. "You were most kind," she finally managed. "I am sorry if- if I put you in an awkward position. I fear I was not myself."

His smile returned, this time with a humourous spark behind it. He leaned close to her ear, and in a low voice rumbled, "You need not apologize, Margaret. Indeed, I believe I have never spent a more pleasant evening in my life."

Her mouth fell open, scandalized, and the heat crawled into her neck. She felt both thrilled and embarrassed that he should think of her in that way. She searched to make some proper response, but he laughed merrily. Her eyes flashed to his. His face was so becoming, so carefree and happy for the moment, that she could not help joining him.

The entire incident was ridiculous, and perhaps he was right. It might do both of them good to laugh at themselves.

They stepped into the small galley, both still chuckling lightly, and found a seat at a bench near Melanie and Monsieur Giraud. John would have liked to sit elsewhere, keeping Margaret to himself, but they could not do so without offending.

Margaret studied the new arrival. He had dark blond hair, styled fashionably at chin length. Ice blue eyes gazed out from his sculpted features. He had a habit of grinning widely, showing off his neat white teeth. Margaret found something about him disconcerting. He was too perfect, somehow.

Giraud introduced himself to the ladies and it became clear that he liked talking about himself. He was from a bourgeois family who had risen to prominence in his grandfather's day. He was well connected, and apparently affluent. Margaret thought wryly that he was now everything that the French peasants had despised and bled to abolish only half a century ago.

Giraud wasted no time acquainting the ladies with their conversation from earlier that morning. "Your brozer was just telling me," he informed Margaret in his heavy accent, "zat zere was a razer bad strike in Milton last year. We in France," he leaned back proudly, "we deal wit' zese things most severely. It is against ze law to strike, you know. Zose fellows of yours," he glanced back at Thornton, "would have seen ze Bastille!" he jabbed his teaspoon in the air for emphasis. "Ze workers in France, you see, 'ave been known to cause much damage to machinery in protest. We give no quarter to such rabble. Arrest ze lot, I say!"

John tensed, his eyes upon Margaret. "A strike *is* a devastating thing to trade. However, I have come to know something of the other side of the coin. I as a master I try to pay a fair wage, but when times are lean for trade, the workers do struggle more. Unfortunately, not all masters are fair, and that puts us all in a bad light. If I lose the confidence of my men due to the games others play, we all suffer."

"Ah, oui! But you must see, Monsieur T'ornton, zat 'arsher measures would discourage ze strikers in any case. Zey may be angry all zey wish, but if zey fear imprisonment, zey will t'ink twice before turning out, nôn?"

John considered his next words carefully. Inwardly he cursed the Frenchman for bringing up a sore subject in Margaret's presence. They had just reached an easiness between them which had taken many anguished months and even more painful misunderstandings. He would have much preferred to discuss his business matters with her in private before being forced to air his opinions publicly.

"I value my men, Mr Giraud. They may be simple mill workers in your mind, but my best can out-do two to three scab workers. They make a quality product I am proud to sell to my buyers, and they have a peculiar kind of honour among them. I have found that, when treated fairly and honestly, most work harder. A man who can respect his employer and who is treated as a man will give a better effort than a poor brute who is always threatened with the law."

"Bien sûr, but you cannot deny you 'ave employed ze law! You said yourself you 'ad to call ze troops to quell a riot. Why not call zem when ze trouble first begins? Arrest ze 'ole lot of zem! You seem to believe zat leniency 'as a place when dealing wit' zese rebels."

John steepled his fingers and fought a discouraged sigh. This fellow lacked the quiet, thoughtful dignity of Mr Hale or the quick caustic wit of Mr Bell. He had enjoyed debating trade practices with them, but this man simply irked him. He wished to shut down the conversation, but his inner businessman could not help wishing to enlighten the other. Before he could begin, however, Margaret's sweet voice spoke up. He listened in awe as she gently expressed herself.

"John *has* had to employ the law to quell riots." She risked a quick glance at him, begging him with her eyes to trust her enough to continue without interrupting. "The men were desperate, you see, driven mad with hunger. But that, of course, cannot excuse their more harmful actions. There were those among them, their leaders, who pled ardently against violence, but some of the rabble would not be made to listen. These men could not be brought to reason, though John tried himself to speak to them."

At this point in her speech, he noticed the pink tinge to the tips of her ears. His own stomach lurched at the memory of Margaret's pale face, the blood flowing as she lay lifeless at his feet. She bit her lip, deciding what parts of the incident to share. "They became violent and destructive, but when the officers of the law arrived, they had already begun to disband out of shock at what they had done.

"John," here she raised her eyes to his face, "did not prosecute the leaders of the riots. Members of the union have a peculiar way of punishing their own. They will completely shun a man, and in its way, their punishment is far more cruel and harsh than the law.

"The police and magistrates were able to identify the ringleaders, but prosecuting was unnecessary. The union leaders who had urged against violence were actually angry about this, because there were some who continued to stir up controversy and strife for many days afterward. The troublemakers hurt the union's cause in the eyes of the public.

"The union was put out with the mill owners in general, and John in particular in the first place, but they were quick enough to demand he settle a score with one of their own. John did not, because to do more than he had would have been to seek vain revenge. He forced them to deal with their own, and the town settled down the more quickly for it."

John's mouth gaped. He had not considered that she could have understood his reasoning and actions immediately involving the strike. He thought she had willfully misconstrued every action he had ever taken in his dealings with the unions. Gratitude warmed his face, and when her eyes shyly met his, she offered a small contrite smile.

Giraud watched them through narrowed eyes, his fingers thoughtfully stroking his small goatee. "Mademoiselle T'ornton, forgive me but you sound a bit revolutionary! A mill owner's sister, yet you manage to defend everyone involved on bot' sides of ze strike but ze men who commit ze violence. 'Ow is it zat you know so much about ze unions? It does not seem a proper diversion for young ladies."

John was quick to defend her. "Margaret has a tender heart, Monsieur Giraud. She is well known to many of Milton's working families for her charity and justice. I was doubtful at first of the friendships she forged, but I must say that through her, I learned a great deal more about my own men. I have begun to believe that open relations and a more... shall I say "democratic" approach to managing the hands has served Marlborough Mills well since the riots.

"Not all is quiet and smooth, of course, but when I have allowed them leeway for certain decision making, they have actually taken greater pride in their work and in a job well done. It is an experiment, of course. No one can say how it can turn out, but after what I have begun to learn, I think it wrong not to attempt." He finished with a hopeful glance at her face and was rewarded with a dazzling smile.

"Indeed," the Frenchman sipped his tea thoughtfully. He had picked Thornton's brain as much as he cared to for the moment. Thornton's opinions were sensible, and he expressed himself well. It was easy to see how he had gained such a reputation in trade circles.

He would have liked to argue his politics, but it was clear that he would not win any debate with the man as long as his sister was there to defend him. Giraud watched them narrowly. *If she is Thornton's sister, I am an Englishman*. He certainly never looked at his own sister as tenderly as Thornton was looking at his Margaret. And a beautiful creature she was!

Giraud mused a little at his good fortune. Finding Mr Thornton of Milton on his ship had been a boon, but the company of two lovely ladies was positively icing on the cake. They were different creatures, however. Melanie Carter was a young woman of substance and intelligence, possessing greater wit than he normally encountered. She was a diverting companion, certainly, but she was simple and naive in the ways of the world.

Margaret Thornton, if that was really her name, was a singular creature. He had met few women who could hold their own in a man's conversation, and none who did so with such graceful aplomb. Her bearing was regal and humble at the same time. He sensed that she was well-read from the way she expressed herself and could easily see that she had been educated in finer circles than would normally be available to a tradesman's sister.

Giraud considered himself something of a ladies' man. He could see their vulnerabilities as easily as other men saw strategic weaknesses on a battlefield. French women were different than English women, as well he knew, but he enjoyed a challenge. This English beauty would certainly prove a challenge! He would enjoy very much a chance to divert the lovely "Miss Thornton." And whatever her relationship with the man sitting across from him, Giraud relished the chance to flaunt his victory.

Eleven

"HENRY! THANK GOODNESS YOU are come!" Edith hurried into the parlor to greet her brother-in-law. Henry Lennox rose quickly, taking her outstretched hand and greeting his sister-in-law. Maxwell trailed less frantically behind his wife and greeted his brother with a cheerful grin.

"What is this all about, Edith? I got your note only late last night; I was assisting my partner in chambers all day yesterday."

"It's Margaret!" Edith sobbed, dabbing her eyes fashionably with a lace handkerchief.

At the mention of Margaret's name, Henry stiffened visibly. "Margaret?" His eyes darted around the room, as if suddenly noting her absence. "What has happened? Is she unwell?"

Edith broke down into helpless sobs. Her mother had isolated herself in her room. Her own constitution, she fancied, was no more equal to the task of describing Margaret's desertion and betrayal- for in her mind, it was very little less. Her dearest friend and cousin had vanished with only a note, placing herself in the gravest danger and without a proper escort. Margaret was lost to her!

Even should she return in safety, the rumours of indiscretions of all kinds would abound, and that she could not bear. Edith crumpled, but carefully, so that she landed in the sofa rather than in a scandalous heap upon the floor. Her husband sat near her and put his arm around her in awkward sympathy.

Henry looked anxiously to his brother for some explanation. After ensuring that his wife would not collapse into further hysterics, Maxwell began. "Margaret had word from her brother- you remember him, the one from Spain."

Henry nodded blankly. He had tried to assist Frederick Hale in his legal defense some months back. He had thought it a vain endeavor at the time, and had told his client as much, but for Margaret he would make every effort. Had the fool at last been captured?

Such an unfortunate event could certainly precipitate sudden desperation on her part. She was utterly devoted to her brother.

Henry had thought Frederick an amiable enough fellow, but rather simplistic, like old Mr Hale. Both had gotten themselves into a situation beyond their control by their impulsive and slavish devotion to their notions of morality. A little foresight and common sense, he had always thought, would have made all the difference. Both could even now be living in peace and relative prosperity, had they but modulated their emphatic principles. He leaned forward eagerly, waiting for Maxwell to continue.

"It seems that old Mr Bell, you know, that queer old fellow from Oxford, is presently in Spain with Margaret's brother, and the poor old chap is failing. Apparently, he had been asking for her. Margaret set out yesterday morning for Cádiz without telling anyone. She left a note by Dixon, but she swore the woman to silence until after she had been well gone."

Henry felt the hair on his neck standing up in alarm. His eyes rounded and his jaw fell slack. Margaret would never do such a thing! The Margaret Hale he knew had spirit, that was true, but she would never stoop to such blatant impropriety or walk boldly into such danger. "What has been done to recover her?" he nearly shouted.

Maxwell shrugged helplessly. "There is little we can do, Brother. She left very early, and we knew nothing of it until late morning when Dixon finally gave us the note. She was likely already out on the open sea by then. We cannot exactly chase after her in a rowboat."

Henry sat silent a moment, gripping the arms of his chair as if they were, in fact, a sturdy set of oars. "Do you have the note?" He watched as Edith sniffled, composing herself a little, and withdrew a rumpled paper from the pockets of her gown. She handed it to her husband, then returned to the task of mopping her sodden eyes. Maxwell wordlessly passed the note to Henry.

14 July 1856

My Dearest Aunt Shaw and Edith,

By the time you receive this, I will be aboard a ship bound for Cádiz. I am exceedingly sorry that I have had to depart in such haste and without properly discussing matters with you, but I could not afford any such delay. I fear already that it may be too late by the time I arrive, but I must try.

I know you will be shocked at my behavior, and I deeply regret any pain I will cause you. Please know it was not done with any malice and I dearly hope that one day you can come to forgive me.

I must see Mr Bell if at all I am able. Frederick wrote that Mr Bell desired me to come to him. He was the only one to be with my father in his last hours, and I wish to perform for him that same service if God grants me the ability to do so.

Please do not fear for my safety. We English have been masters of the great seas for a good many years, and I intend to appeal to the captain's protection. You know as well as I that even merchant sea captains are under the Queen's authority and must discharge their duties with honour.

I beg you would not attempt to follow me or even to write; Frederick's security is a very delicate thing, as you know, and even in our regular correspondence all mail is sent very carefully through an intermediary so that he cannot be traced. He took a great risk in sending his last letter to me directly because haste was vital, but it would be far too dangerous to do so again.

I will send word once I have safely arrived so that you may not worry on my account. It may take some days to reach you, though. You may depend that Frederick will see to my safety from there, and he will be looking out for my arrival.

I am most truly sorry again for all the trouble I know I have caused, but this is a thing I must do. I have lived for too long under the shadow of fear and grief, and it is time for me to take control of my life. Where it may lead, I cannot say, but I must finally leave my doubts and worries in the past where they belong. I am trusting myself to Providence. I dearly hope to see you again soon.

I remain yours most faithfully and affectionately,

Margaret

Henry let the missive fall to his lap. His fingers were white and trembling. He tried to imagine fragile, docile Margaret, alone and unprotected on the open sea aboard a ship full of any number of ruffians. What could have possessed her to so heedlessly fling away all propriety? Why would she be so desperate to go that she would knowingly take such wild risks with her safety and her reputation?

After a moment he had recovered his voice enough to speak. "Do you know the name of the ship she boarded?" he ventured, a quaver in his words.

Maxwell nodded. "One of the chamber maids revealed later that Margaret had requested her to inquire after any vessels departing soon for Spain. James, our footman took the errand, and the first ship on the list was the *Esperanza*. It sailed yesterday morning, as she said. She would have had to wait some days for another passage, which explains her urgency to depart early yesterday."

Henry's face began to redden. "They must be terminated immediately for such insubordination! Your own staff went behind your back to enable a lone woman to sail abroad? You cannot let them remain longer in your employ! And Dixon! When I have words with her...."

Maxwell interrupted, shaking his head. "Think, Henry," he suggested reasonably. "Dixon is Margaret's personal maid; she does not answer to Edith or Mrs Shaw or myself. We have no authority over her whatsoever, and Margaret pays for the woman's wages and board out of her own pocket.

"As for the maid and footman, they are not complicit in some heinous scheme. We have always allowed Margaret free authority with the staff, which she has never once abused. They are well acquainted with her somewhat nontraditional ways, and every one of them adores her. They had no reason to deny her requests, and in fact had every reason to believe they would face censure for doing so."

Henry clamped his mouth shut in frustration. Maxwell was perfectly right of course, but it did nothing to alleviate his wild concern for Margaret. He leapt from his chair, beginning to pace briskly. Margaret, his dainty Hampshire flower, was off on a perilous journey and he was helpless to forestall her. She ought to have known that any of them, he especially, would have gone along with her if she had only asked!

His pride stung more than a little when he considered that, perhaps, she did not want his company. She had been cool and distant ever since her return from Milton... well, in truth, ever since his failed proposal two years ago. She had tearfully begged off, declaring that she thought of him as only a friend.

Much as he could have desired more from her, she could not give him what he had wished for. He had tried desperately to backpedal, hoping to pull his amicable friendship with her back from the brink of something which had terrified her. Once the words had left his mouth, he had been helpless to draw her back or to reestablish their comfortable familiarity. Then, she simply left.

Margaret's removal to the dirty stinking streets of industrial Milton had cemented the rift between them. He had not ceased thinking of her, but he had to resign himself to the hopelessness of it all. She had been beyond his reach there, he had thought. Her firm devotion to her aimless father drew the final veil over their former friendship.

Why could she not have chosen to remain in London? Certainly, if she had wished it her cousin would have left the house open to her while they were stationed overseas! Even as the thought ran through his mind, he rejected it as ridiculous. Of course, loyal Margaret would choose the company of her parents over a barren house, even if the house were a posh Harley Street residence.

Once or twice, he had thought of visiting her as the old friend he was but had never been certain of his welcome. Better, he had decided, to immerse himself in his career. It had really been too soon for him to think of supporting a wife, but if Margaret would have had him, he would have indeed been a blessed man.

Henry fisted his hands over his eyes, dragging his careening thoughts to a screeching halt. What good was it to think of the past? What they needed now was damage control.

"Maxwell, who else knows of this?"

His brother shook his head, his hand resting lightly on his wife's shoulders. "We have kept it quiet. The staff are all loyal to Margaret, and Edith forbade anyone to speak of it for her sake. She has very few friends here in Town, and it will be easy to make her excuses at dinner parties, since she rarely goes into company anyway. I think we can conceal her absence for the immediately foreseeable future."

Henry nodded thoughtfully. "That may prove vital. You know how people talk. One can only imagine what will be said of her! We can at least act to preserve her reputation in Town."

"Unless she was seen boarding the ship," Maxwell pointed out. "That could prove difficult to contend with."

Henry had not thought of that. Margaret was a striking woman, and an unescorted lady traveling abroad might well raise interest. "We can only hope not. I know those docks, so do you. They are chaotic at that time of day; it is possible that her presence went unremarked. We cannot very well go inquiring about it, for if we do, what might have been forgotten as incidental would certainly become fixed in memories."

"Yes, exactly what I thought. I expect it will be eight to ten days at least before we can reasonably have any word from her- longer, possibly if they must use that intermediary of which she wrote. I do have an old comrade, retired from the navy, who is a merchant captain now. You remember Captain Harper, do you not? He was rather helpful when you were asking questions about Frederick Hale. He may be able to find out something for us, and the old salt knows how to be discreet. I will keep you apprised, but for now that is all we can do."

Henry nodded sullenly and began to take his leave. He made his slow way back to his office, dully heeding the flow of traffic on the walkways but observing nothing. His thoughts were for the dark-haired beauty who had marched alone into peril.

How could such a gently bred, proper young lady have taken on such a daunting and foolish journey? There must be some iron will in her that he had never detected. How else would she have found such determination and such immodest, careless disregard for discretion? He had never thought of her as impetuous or headstrong. Was it possible that he had never really known her?

He shook his head silently as he pondered these new ideas. Perhaps reckless behavior ran in the Hale family. He sighed. He had hoped to reestablish their friendship, with the desire that it might finally blossom into more. He began to think he had been wrong all along about her. Perhaps... perhaps they did not really suit. He still worried for her, and in truth he would have dashed off to find her, bring her back to safety if he could have.

He longed to understand her actions, to have the answer to her rash impulsiveness. Only Margaret herself could explain her motives, and he was forced to wait for that- if, that is, she decided to come back at all once in Frederick's home. On the other hand, if this sudden unpredictability were an indicator of a deep restlessness in the woman, Heaven only knew what she might determine to do next.

Twelve

AFTER BREAKING THEIR FAST, Margaret and John wished to walk about the deck. The foursome kept together, taking in the beauty of the new day at sea. Thornton insisted on keeping Margaret's arm tucked in the crook of his elbow. He would not risk her safety on board the rolling deck, and he quite delighted in his right to escort her. The pink tinge of her cheeks and the sparkle in her eyes assured him that she had no complaints about the arrangement.

Giraud and Melanie walked behind them, and the Frenchman was inquiring about Melanie's upbringing and her time in London. She chattered expressively, drawing hearty laughter from her companion as she told various anecdotes about her brother and his new bride. It seemed that the younger Mr Carter had been led on a merry chase to win his love's hand.

Melanie spoke in glowing terms of her new sister-in-law but claimed she had had little opportunity of late to enjoy her company. John could not help but listen with longing as the young woman described, blushingly, the long mornings she had spent alone downstairs immediately after the couple's marriage.

Their conversation was interrupted by the arrival of the captain. He quirked his eyebrow at his daughter, and diplomatically invited the pair to tour the quarterdeck with him. Thornton believed privately that the offer of a tour had more to do with guarding his daughter than any special liking for the Frenchman. Giraud cast a regretful glance over his shoulder at them as he followed the captain and Melanie.

They continued on in companionable silence for a short while. It was the first episode in the memory of either in which they had been content simply to be in the other's company without argument. Thornton was admiring the glow of fresh air on her face and the stirring of the little tendrils of her hair loosened under the brim of her bonnet in the breeze. They stopped by the rail and she closed her eyes, inhaling the salt air deeply.

She opened her eyes and looked up to find his eloquent gaze on her. Wondering what he could be thinking, she hazarded a topic of conversation intended to ease the flutterings in her stomach. "How does your mother?"

"She is quite well enough. Her health is sound, and I believe she is satisfied to have Fanny well married."

"Is Fanny happy, then?"

He gave a short laugh. "Watson allows her free rein with whatever fancy comes into her head. She has spent a small fortune redecorating his house... their house. She has some notion for the latest fashions from the Continent. I can only be glad," he gave a little sigh, "that she is no longer spending from my purse."

Margaret wondered privately what the marriage of the two in question could be like. Fanny had not married for love and had not been shy about that fact. Fanny was not a woman given to sentiment; Margaret knew. Still, she shuddered a little considering the implications, the requirements made of a wife. She could not fathom marriage to a man whom she could barely esteem.

Sensing her shiver, John turned to her in concern. "Are you cold? Perhaps we should return to your cabin."

"No!" She reacted more energetically than she had intended. "That is, I am enjoying the exercise. I imagine I will have time enough to spend there."

His face relaxed into a happy smile. "How does your shoulder feel? Are you in any pain?"

Glancing down self-consciously, she admitted that her shoulder throbbed a little, but that the pain was tolerable. She repeated her desire to remain outdoors. Pleasure shone on his face as he guided her away from the rail to avoid a spray of steam from the paddles.

They walked the decks a little longer, conversation lurching in fits and starts as they attempted to find an easy rhythm to their discourse. Margaret once wistfully admired a passing family with two young children. The father bounced a toddler with dark curls on his shoulders, while the mother lightly clasped the hand of a girl, perhaps four years old. The couple laughed easily with each other as they enjoyed observing the wonders of the ship through the eyes of their children.

Catching herself, she glanced guiltily to John to find his warm, penetrating gaze lingering on her. Her cheeks burning, she looked uncomfortably away. Living with Edith and her spunky child of one year had taught Margaret how dear little ones were. She had given over the notion of ever having her own family, relegating herself to the position of loving "aunt." The idea had begun to flutter again in her heart, but she was not yet comfortable acknowledging the budding hope.

John smiled to himself. Margaret was always the perfect lady, discreet and prudent, but she had let herself slip there. The longing in her eyes as she looked at the young family had buoyed his own hopes. He rested his free hand atop the small one nestled in his elbow. He felt her stiffen slightly in response, but she flashed a quick nervous smile to him instead of a frown of castigation.

"Miss Thornton, Mr Thornton!" A voice raised in greeting roused their attention. They turned together to see Dr. Grayson striding in their direction. He acknowledged one or two others who saluted him but made his way assiduously toward his targets.

"Miss Thornton, how do you do today?" The good doctor inquired. "I can see taking the air has benefitted you today, your countenance is much improved! What a lovely young lady your sister is, Mr Thornton. Were I twenty years younger I would be asking permission to walk with her myself! Now, truly Miss Thornton, how do you do today?"

Margaret thanked him bashfully and assured him that she felt well. She was a little unsettled by the familiar, casual way in which the Doctor spoke. She supposed that years at sea, away from typical society might have dulled his more polished manners. Surely a naval doctor's daily struggles against life and death in the grit and squalor of a sailor's life would refine the dross out of anyone's conduct.

He chatted amiably with them a few moments. He wanted to know how Margaret had fared in her rest aboard ship and if she had experienced any queasiness. She felt her ears burning and from the corner of her eye she saw John tense a little. Quietly, and with as much dignity as she could muster, she assured the doctor that she had managed well enough.

"Excellent, excellent. I worried, Mr Thornton, when I could not find you last evening that perhaps Miss Thornton was feeling poorly. I ought to have looked in on you, I apologize."

Margaret felt her stomach knot. It was known to others that John had been in her room? She darted a quick glance to his face. His jaw was set and he met her eyes with a silent remorse.

Dr. Grayson had not noticed their exchange, bent as he was on atoning for his lack of attentiveness to his patient. "You see, as a smaller steamer, the *Esperanza* hardly merits a full-time doctor. Carter and I go back a good long way, and he will not do without a doctor on board. Still, there is little enough space and each crew member must pull his own weight, so I tend to oversee the passenger accommodations and ship stores as well. It suits me, but I was very busy last night."

Mr Thornton thanked the doctor, hoping to assure him that all was truly well and they required little looking after. The less close conversation they carried on with the doctor, or anyone, he reasoned, the safer they were.

Dr. Grayson cheerfully took his leave, admonishing Margaret to send for him at any need. John arched an eyebrow and extended his elbow to Margaret.

Once he was certain they were not to be overheard, he murmured to her in a low voice. "Perhaps it would be best if I see you to your cabin now. I do not wish to excite any talk by spending... too much time together." He glanced significantly over her shoulder at a few other passengers. A brother might be expected to escort his sister about, but not to gaze raptly into her eyes as he was inclined to do.

She nodded reluctantly, her countenance falling. Guilt washed over her features. "I think that is wise," she whispered.

"Margaret- Margaret, look at me please."

She did so, chewing her upper lip and blinking rapidly. His eyes caught and mirrored the sterling blue of sea and sky. He smiled hesitantly, his expression pleading her to return in kind. He cupped her hand in both of his, caressing her fingers gently.

"All will be well, Margaret. I promise. I beg you would not blame yourself. You have done nothing wrong; you must believe me."

She released a long quivering breath of relief. He tugged her hand playfully until she finally smiled a little and nodded her acquiescence.

"We only have a few days. When we reach Spain we can start again, properly this time. I hope you will still be speaking to me by then," he teased, his eyes twinkling. In spite of herself, she chuckled a little and he watched her face flush.

"I am glad. Will you promise to introduce me to your real brother? I feel he might know something of my troubles in keeping pace with you. Tell me; were you as spirited and headstrong as a child as you are today?" His words were provoking, but his face cracked with humour.

She drew her hand back and playfully cocked it on her hip. "Now Mr Thornton, you are trying to vex me! I was a perfect lady, or if I was not, you cannot find evidence to the contrary."

"Can I not? I imagine Frederick knows a few things. If he is reluctant to share your childhood indiscretions, I am certain I can persuade your Miss Dixon to divulge what I want to know. Did you know, she has a weakness for chocolate sweeties?"

Margaret's mouth flew open in mock horror. "You would not dare! How did you find this out?"

He grinned like a Cheshire Cat. "I did not, until you confirmed it for me just now."

Margaret pursed her lips in an affectation of displeasure. "What you can possibly hope to learn, I am sure I cannot fathom. Dixon would never betray my involvement in the disappearance of Mrs Cargill's cat. Most certainly she would never breathe a word of her suspicions regarding a certain broken window in the chapel, or the half-eaten apple from Mr Drake's orchard that was found inside."

He laughed, his eyes dancing. "I had better escort you to your cabin before you inadvertently confess to more youthful crimes!"

She arched her eyebrows and lifted her chin in challenge. "And you were always a paragon of puerile virtue, I suppose?"

"According to my mother, yes. However, my own memory tends to err." He leaned closer confidentially. "I could be persuaded to confess my crimes if the inducement were sufficiently intriguing. Until such time," he winked, "I will have to keep you in suspense."

Her cheeks burned, delight tingling through her nerves when he winked at her. Boldly she slipped her arm through his and he gently steered her toward her cabin. "I cannot imagine what sway I might hold, or why a lady would wish to hear of a young man's folly," she returned with a saucy toss of her head.

He grinned hugely, his chest swelling in joy. Margaret was teasing him! Never before had she spoken with such levity in his presence. Was she habitually so easy with those she cared for? If so, was she welcoming him into that coveted place? His face beamed with rapt enjoyment. He bent to speak again, but another voice interrupted.

"Oh Margaret, there you are!" Melanie Carter caught their attention from across the deck. Sun glinting from her hatless auburn hair, she expertly wove her way to them, scarcely troubled at all by the motion of the sea or the working sailors in her path.

"Margaret, I came to ask if you would like to take tea with Mamma and myself in Papa's quarters. It is so much more comfortable than our own cabins, you know, and Mamma thought you might enjoy a visit if you are feeling up to it."

Margaret smiled and accepted the invitation, her eyes dwelling on John's face for a brief second. He nodded encouragingly; glad that she would have an opportunity for a pleasant way of spending her time on this voyage, though still regretting that not all of it could be with him.

"Good!" enthused Melanie. "I am glad you agreed so readily, for now I will not have to employ Dr. Grayson's orders to demand that you rest quietly." She linked her arm through Margaret's. Turning to John, Melanie gave a very modest curtsey and Margaret favored him with a secretive smile.

Thirteen

"So, Miss Thornton," Mrs Carter tipped the shining seaman's kettle into Margaret's cup, "What takes you and Mr Thornton to Spain?" The captain's matronly wife settled back in her husband's chair, taking up her own saucer and tipping her head conversationally toward her guest.

Margaret hesitated. "My godfather went there on business, and I received word two days ago that he has fallen gravely ill. I... We are hoping to be in time...."

Mrs Carter's motherly face fell into an expression of tender concern. "Oh, my dear, I am sorry to hear that, truly I am. Still," her cup hovered skeptically before her, "'tis a very long way to go. One does not often hear of making such a journey for a godfather. Now a father, perhaps, or a mother, that I have heard of."

Melanie interrupted her mother with a quiet look of alarm, and an apologetic glance toward Margaret. "Mamma," she spoke in a low respectful tone, "Margaret has lost most of her family, except for her brother."

"Oh!" Mrs Carter set her cup back on its saucer, her expression contrite. "Do forgive me, my dear. I did not mean to sound so critical, and I certainly understand your concern for your godfather. It is only unusual, that is all. You must have a very strong attachment to the gentleman?"

Margaret swallowed a sip of her delicious mint tea and nodded. "He was my father's dearest friend. He was always such a great comfort to Father, and then to me when... when I was alone."

"But you are not alone, Margaret dear!" Melanie chided. "You have a very fine brother, and I can see he is very good to you."

Margaret's face froze in momentary shock. "Yes... yes, he is very good." Flustered, her eyes dropped to the floor and she hid behind her teacup to gather herself.

"Are you unwell, Miss Thornton? Does your shoulder pain you?" Mrs Carter asked gently.

"No!" Her eyes flashed to the older woman's face. "That is... Yes, I suppose it does ache some, but no more so than one might expect," she faltered.

Melanie leaned closer, resting her hand upon Margaret's arm. "Margaret dear, do you wish to rest, or to have some more medicine for the pain?"

Margaret smiled gratefully. "No, I thank you. I could not rest better in my cabin, and I prefer not to take more laudanum just now. You are very kind, Melanie."

"Well, Miss Thornton," Mrs Carter passed a tray of small sandwiches, "you must tell me all the news from Milton. I have not been home in a long while, and I feel we may know some of the same people."

Margaret flushed. "I- I beg you would call me Margaret, please, Mrs Carter."

"Oh! Why certainly, my dear. Now, how are things settling down in Milton after all those dreadful strikes last year? I heard it affected the whole of the city, not just the mills. You know, my sister wrote that even some of the businesses in my own hometown suffered. Think of that, one hundred miles away! Caused a deal of backup with the shipping, it did, being shut down for a month like that. Quite a nasty deal."

Margaret steeled herself, pausing a moment to decently swallow her bite of sandwich. It turned unpleasantly tasteless in her mouth, likely for more reasons than one. "I feel I am not the proper person to ask, Mrs Carter. I have been living in London for the past several months with my cousin. When last I was in Milton, the mills were all operating once again, but I believe they had taken quite a blow."

Mrs Carter tilted her head curiously. "Forgive me, Margaret. You struck me as a rather outspoken and intelligent young woman. I assumed you would follow your brother's business affairs more closely. You must excuse my Northern ways, my dear. We forget that in some circles it is considered indelicate to discuss such matters."

Margaret could not help a warm smile. This woman was beginning to remind her of Mrs Thornton, without the prickles. "You need not apologize, Mrs Carter. I do not consider it at all indelicate, not after having lived in Milton. I am very fond of that town, and the people there. I... suppose I have not had much opportunity of late to discuss business matters with... with John." Margaret hastily lifted her cup for another sip of tea. As she did so, her eyes came to rest on Melanie, who was regarding her with an inscrutable expression.

The rest of the visit passed quietly. Melanie sensed that her injured friend would wish to be a listener rather than a speaker for the time being, so she began telling Margaret more of her stay in London. Margaret listened politely, growing more and more at ease with her new friend's gentle and unassuming ways.

As Margaret began to feel it was time to take her leave, Captain Carter strode into the cabin for his meal. Margaret began to rise hastily. "Do not get up for me, Lass!" he laughed. The captain stepped to his wife, planting an affectionate kiss on her cheek, then another on Melanie's. Margaret could not hide her shock. Such overt displays of tenderness were utterly unknown to her. Even without a guest present, her own father would never have presumed so much.

Captain Carter finally turned to her. "I do not think we have been introduced properly, Miss."

Margaret blushed uncomfortably and curtseyed as Mrs Carter made the introductions. The captain bowed handsomely. "Pleasure to meet you, Miss Thornton. I was just speaking with your brother a while ago. Very sensible fellow, I must say. I am glad to see you are doing better today. Now, I do beg your pardon, but I must be back to my duties soon." The captain then turned to his wife, who served him his luncheon on a shining tray near a sturdy desk.

"Margaret, let me see you back to your cabin." Melanie took her friend's arm and the two of them made their way to the main deck. They carefully negotiated the stairs, and on the landing, they were spotted by Mr Thornton and Monsieur Giraud.

"Ah, Mesdemoiselles!" Giraud drew near and bowed graciously. Melanie curtseyed in return, but Margaret only offered a grave inclination of her head.

Margaret quirked a skeptical eyebrow at John. His lips thinned ever so slightly, acknowledging her unspoken question. She could read his dissatisfaction plainly. She also could easily surmise that he had been watching for her to depart from the Carters' cabin so he could see her safely to her own. Had he not been so determined to wait, he would most assuredly have already been on his own bunk with a book rather than walking the decks with the Frenchman.

A sweet smile of gratitude warmed her face. She watched a tense breath escape him as he relaxed and smiled himself under her gaze. *Melanie is right... he is so very handsome! How is it I spent so long never noticing?*

"Margaret, are you listening?" Melanie threaded her arm back through Margaret's and gave a gentle tug.

"Excuse me? I did not hear you." Margaret's attention snapped back to her friend.

"I said you were looking rather pale, and I was just telling Monsieur Giraud that I was taking you to your cabin to rest a while."

"Oh..." Margaret nodded hesitantly, "...yes, I do need to lie down. Thank you, Melanie. Please excuse us Monsieur Giraud, John." Her eyes lingered on his for another second, wishing him to sense that she was truly well. The worry in his eyes faded, and he gave a quick nod.

A moment later, Melanie held open the door of Margaret's cabin for her, then closed it firmly behind herself. She stood in the doorway, her arms crossed and a serious look turned upon her friend. "Margaret, you are a terrible liar."

Margaret's eyes widened in shock. "Excuse me?" Her own guilt and worry over discovery washed plainly over her features, confirming Melanie's suspicions.

"John Thornton is no more *your* brother than he is mine! That man looks at you like you hung the moon, and *you* are almost as obviously smitten as he is."

Margaret sat heavily upon her bunk. Her face drained of colour and her mouth felt suddenly parched. She hid her eyes behind her hand, unable to meet Melanie's unyielding gaze. A tear of mortification began to slip down her cheek and she wiped it savagely, afraid to shame herself further in Melanie's presence.

"You are perfectly right," she whispered. "He is no relation of mine. My real name is Margaret Hale. I am so sorry, Melanie... what you must think of me! I know how it must appear. He was only trying to protect me. I beg you to believe there were no improper motives!" She drew her lips into a taut little frown, too humiliated to say more.

Melanie came to sit by her, looping her arm over Margaret's good shoulder in companionable ease. "Suppose you tell me?" she suggested kindly.

Margaret raised her eyes, disbelief written over her face. By all rights, Melanie should have left the cabin that instant and never returned. Moreover, she should quite naturally have informed her father the captain of Margaret's dishonour. Margaret did not like to think of the fallout from that revelation. "Why would you wish to remain, Melanie? What can I possibly say to justify the fact that I am an unmarried woman travelling with a man who is not my brother?"

Melanie's determined expression never wavered. "Margaret, I try to study people. Call it a hobby. I can see that you are a real lady, and that Mr Thornton treats you with every respect. You are not the kind of woman to act dishonourably. Are you in some trouble, Margaret?"

Margaret sighed. "No… not I. Mr Thornton was a dear friend of my father's, before he passed away. I moved back to London after that. I had not even seen Mr Thornton these many months. He was there yesterday, quite by accident, when I was injured on the docks. He is a kind friend and wished to see to my protection." Margaret stopped there, her eyes on Melanie's face. Her friend's reaction would determine how much she really could dare to reveal.

Melanie narrowed her eyes, not satisfied. "He is something more than just a kind friend, is he not? That man cannot take his eyes off you for a second."

Margaret swallowed. "He proposed once, about a year ago. It was just before my mother passed away. We argued, and I refused him."

"What? Margaret!" Melanie's hand fluttered near her breast. "Why ever would you do so?"

Margaret shook her head sadly. "Oh, Melanie! It was so complicated. I think neither of us really understood the other. I thought at the time that he spoke only out of obligation and a misguided sense of my true intentions… oh, dear, it would take a great deal of time to explain all!"

"Well, I have no better place to go," Melanie smiled, a spark of mischief returning to her eyes. "There is nothing like a good story to pass a slow afternoon at sea, is there?"

With a shuddering exhale, Margaret nodded. She told her friend about the riots, about her indignation with what she had perceived as John's callousness toward his workers. She related their heated exchange and how John had faced the rioters alone and at her bidding, and how she had felt subsequently responsible for his safety.

"So, you dashed out there to save him?" Melanie shook her head, clucking her tongue with a chastising smile. "I might have expected as much of you. You are honourable almost to a fault Margaret, but you are an impulsive one, aren't you? I take it that Mr Thornton assumed you came to save him because you cared for him?"

"Yes… and then I was struck by a heavy shoe flung by one of the rioters." She paused as Melanie gasped, her eyes wide. "I was unconscious for a little while, it hurt a great deal, but I was able to go home a short time later. I feared alarming my mother, but I feared him even more, and what I knew people would say. John came the next day to offer his name, but I was affronted that he could think…. I know now that he spoke not only out of obligation, but out of real feeling, which I could not credit and would not heed at the time. Poor John! I spoke so harshly to him!"

"Margaret, you were almost killed! Why, even in a single day I can see the gentleman wholly adores you. He must have nearly died of fright when you were hurt! At *his* mill, no less. I should be righteously angry if he did *not* offer marriage after all that had passed. Yet you refused him? Was he very heartbroken?"

Margaret sighed softly. "I am beginning to understand... yes, I believe he was. I am heartily ashamed of the pain I have caused him. He had many an opportunity later to lash out in bitterness at me, yet he did so much for my family- for me. He was kind- so very kind, Melanie, and I did not deserve it."

Melanie straightened, leaning back a little on the bunk. She fixed her friend with a look of deep contemplation. "There is a good deal more behind that statement. Something rather drastic happened to change your opinion of him, did it not? Whatever it was, I can see that you think of him very differently now."

Margaret studied her hands. "Yes, I do," she whispered at length.

Melanie grinned. "Then do not keep the man in suspense! Promise me, Margaret!"

Margaret chuckled a little, relieved and entirely surprised at Melanie's easy acceptance. "I promise."

"I would only suggest you wait a day or two... you know, get somewhere where people do not believe you are his sister. I always thought it would be romantic to have a honeymoon in Spain!" she winked.

Margaret shook her head, still smiling lightly but sorrow returning to the slope of her shoulders. "What I told you about my godfather is quite true. I am greatly worried about him, and I expect that even if I am in time to see him, it will not be for long. This is unfortunately not a pleasure trip.

"John happened to be traveling at the same time to find out about a source of raw cotton, he told me. He will undoubtedly need to return to the mill quickly, whereas my plans are wholly dependent upon Mr Bell's condition. It is possible we may not even be able to travel home together."

Melanie tilted her head with a skeptical frown. "Do be serious, Margaret. Mr Thornton is the kind of man who would arrange heaven and earth to remain by your side, if you will but allow it. He will most decidedly *not* stand for you to travel home alone. Now," she shook her auburn head seriously, "You really do need to rest, Margaret. I fear I will have to answer to that bear of a "brother" of yours if you do not lie down a while. I will help you settle in, then I will come back just before teatime to help you freshen up again."

With a murmured thanks, Margaret accepted her friend's assistance. She declined more laudanum, though her shoulder still ached some. She did not feel it wise to become once again incoherent under the influence of the medication. She curled on her side, still fully dressed, then eventually slid into peaceful slumber. Her dreams tended to revolve around a tall, dark-haired gentleman with a rich baritone voice and the smile of an angel.

Fourteen

MELANIE CLAIMED MARGARET FOR tea, escorting her again to her mother's table. To Margaret's infinite relief, Mrs Carter had apparently decided not to query her guest further about her life in Milton. Margaret suspicioned that Melanie had related the main points of their earlier conversation to her mother, and that she had gained a second ally in Mrs Carter.

Later, the two young women walked the decks together. Melanie introduced Margaret to a few of the other passengers whose acquaintance had escaped her as she had lain recovering from her injury in her cabin. With great pleasure she greeted the couple she had seen earlier in the day while walking with John.

Mr and Mrs Stanley Sheffield were traveling on to Italy for a much belated wedding tour. Mr Sheffield was a gentleman farmer, and immediately upon his marriage he had inherited his father's estate, which had been in some disarray. Finally, their affairs had been brought under control, and they were embarking upon their dream voyage. Margaret bent down to smile at the little girl, Emily. The child cooed and grasped for the brooch on Margaret's shawl, and she allowed her to touch. Mrs Sheffield drew the toddler back, apologizing, but Margaret would not hear it.

"I am surprised, Madam, that you bring your children with you. Most do not. I think it is wonderful," Margaret's voice was soft as she reached to gently accept the little girl's hand.

"It was Stanley's idea," the young wife's face shone with pride in her husband. "He knew he would have a much harder time convincing me to leave the children behind with my aunt, and he so desired for me to see Florence."

"Both a wise and thoughtful husband then," Margaret complimented her with a smile. "You are very blessed!"

"Do not sound so wistful, my dear Margaret," Melanie met her glance with an impish sparkle in her eyes. "I have it on good authority that a certain gentleman waits with bated breath to worship the very ground you walk upon."

Margaret widened her eyes in shock and appeal, but Melanie only laughed lightly. Mrs Sheffield chuckled at the two single ladies, then her energetic toddler claimed her full attention. With apologies she took her leave. Margaret and Melanie spent the time until the dinner hour strolling along the rail, admiring the occasional glimpses of the shoreline over the clear seas.

Dinner was a noisy affair, with most of the steamer's first-class passengers crowding into the narrow galley. John helped Margaret into a seat as a crew member began to serve her. Giraud had once again attached himself to Melanie, who would not stray far from Margaret. The four chatted good-naturedly, though Giraud and Melanie did most of the talking. Melanie was curious about Paris, and he was more than willing to share his expertise on that city. Melanie listened raptly as he described the Seine, the Louvre Museum and L'Arch de Triomphe.

"I had heard that there is currently in Paris an undertaking to improve the living conditions of the very poor." Margaret softly interjected. "Is that true, Monsieur Giraud?" Her quiet steady gaze bored into the man across the table from her. Beside her, John chewed silently with a tiny smirk on his face.

"Ze poor?" Giraud asked, mystified at her interest. "I know little about it. Is it zat you speak of zat Le Play fellow? Oh, Lá! 'E has caused some trouble. Very 'igh wit' ze President they say. I know little of what 'e plans, zough I do not expect 'e will meet wit' much success."

"Why is that, Monsieur?" Margaret queried sweetly. "You do not think it possible?"

Giraud leaned back in his chair, fingering the rim of his glass and fixing Margaret with a thoughtful expression. "I t'ink ze poor will always be ze poor, Mademoiselle T'ornton. Giving a man a better 'ouse does not change 'is character, n'est pas? T'ornton, what is it zat you t'ink?"

John tapped his finger meditatively on the table as he composed his thoughts. He still felt much as he always had- the experiences of a lifetime were brutal and effective teachers. From Margaret, however, he had learned to unlock a hearty dose of his native compassion.

"Much as one might wish to simply fund a solution, it will not be that simple. You are correct, of course, that more than a man's living situation must alter to improve his life. I believe much indolence and hopelessness has been learnt from one generation after another, and it would take years to have an appreciable impact.

"There is no perfect answer. Some men are capable of bettering themselves if only granted the opportunity; others will have none of it, wishing instead to take it from others who *would* make the necessary sacrifices. I speak with some authority on this point.

"There are things that can be done, however. I have been following the efforts made in my own country- whole towns are beginning to spring up around factories of various kinds. Owners build safe housing and sanitary facilities during the initial planning of the town, making later retrofitting for such concerns unnecessary. The entire community is essentially employed by the factory. Cities are cleaner, maintenance is attended to, and the workers are naturally closer to their homes so it is easier on families.

"The housing is not free to the workers, but the rates are fair and affordable, and the quality of life is greatly improved. It is not condescension or charity. Both employer and employee can hold their heads high. There are numerous advantages to such a system. It actually makes very good business sense, for many reasons. Unfortunately, such an idealized scheme is out of the reach of most businessmen, for one must have- and be willing to risk- substantial capital to begin such an undertaking."

Giraud waved a hand dismissively. "Ze 'ousing would all be destroyed in a 'andful of years. *Croyez-moi*, T'ornton, most of zem know no better way to live."

"I cannot agree with you, Monsieur," Margaret gently replied. "It is not Christian to leave our fellow man to live in squalor. How is a family to manage to problem of clean water, for an example? I have seen a number of children succumb to illnesses. It is not their fault, nor is it directly the fault of the other wealthier residents of the city. No specific blame can be assigned, but something must be done. It is a problem too large for an individual; it must be addressed as a community. I do not absolve the workers of the responsibility to take the opportunity to better themselves where they can, but if they have no resources with which to make a beginning, must not others help to bear the responsibility as well?"

Giraud laughed. "I can see, T'ornton, zat you must 'ave your 'ands full! Oh, lá, I do not envy you 'aving to argue every business decision wit' your sister!"

John beamed proudly at Margaret, but out of the corner of her eye she caught a warning glance from Melanie. Quickly she looked down, breaking his hold on her attention. She heard him clear his throat.

"It is not that challenging, Monsieur. You might be surprised to find her charitable concerns masquerading as sound business sense. In truth, I might say she played a part in inspiring us to begin a kitchen at the mill. I purchase the food at a wholesale price and employ a cook. The men pay a fair price for their lunch; thus, I am reimbursed. The savings on the food are passed on to them, and I have men with full bellies. A fed man is a happy man, Monsieur Giraud, and one who can perform his duties."

Margaret gazed at him in some wonder. It was the first she had heard of this, but now Dixon's cryptic statement some months ago about Mary Higgins learning to cook at the mill made sense. Reminding herself to school her emotions, she snatched her gaze back to her plate, forcing herself not to reveal more.

The conversation turned to the quality of raw cotton that had lately been available on the market, then to concerns over the political stability of the countries most involved in the cotton trade. Margaret found herself quite out of her depth, so she listened with interest but made no comments.

Once again, John impressed her with the breadth of his knowledge and his carefully reasoned opinions. She learned that there was real cause for concern in the supply over the next several years. The Americans, it seemed, were experiencing a great deal of unrest and the cotton trade was at the center of it all. Little wonder, she realized, that John had undertaken a long journey to investigate another source.

Dessert came, a surprisingly delectable treat for such an environment. Margaret savoured the tart, the first food all day which had really appealed to her struggling appetite. Melanie informed her that her father's galley cook was one of the finest to be found. Giraud teased lightly that the chef was nothing to the cooks of France, but Melanie only laughed gaily without making dispute.

Margaret set her fork down as the meal ended and made eye contact with John. She hoped he would walk with her, but she recognized Melanie's admonition to caution. Still, she ached to stretch her legs, and longed for some more time with him alone.

Fifteen

The opportunity for privacy came more easily than she might have thought. Giraud intended to try his luck at cards that evening with some of the other gentlemen on board and invited John to join him. John, of course, politely declined. He had never had a great deal of interest in cards, and never less than now when the alternative was spending time with Margaret. Melanie claimed her father wished her to pass the evening with him at a game of chess.

So it was that she enjoyed the waning hours of evening basking in the glow of the hazy sunset over the water, her arm looped through John's. The dimming light took the heat of the day with it, and she was grateful for his nearby warmth permeating even through her woolen cloak. They had spoken little. The beauty of the glowing waters had captured much of their attention, and they were still becoming accustomed to their new closeness. Margaret no longer minded the long lapses in discourse with him, and she discovered a new easiness in his presence.

John was less certain of her. His feelings prodded him to find something to induce her to speak, to begin to deepen their knowledge of one another. "I was wondering how you have found London," he offered by way of opening a conversation.

She had not expected him to ask about London. "Oh- I have been well. My aunt and cousin have been very kind."

"I am glad," said he. His eyes studied her. "I was hoping you would be able to rest. You have been through enough trial."

She considered before answering immediately. "Edith is very dear to me...." she broke off, chewing her lip.

"But?" he arched an eyebrow challengingly.

She glanced up quickly, knowing he had sensed her hesitation. "I- I suppose I have never cared much for London Society."

He was surprised at first to hear this confession. When he considered what he knew of her character, he found that he should not have been. She was far too forthright and outspoken to willingly submit to the social constraints of high society. Truly, it was one of the qualities that had always drawn him to her. She was willing to eschew social propriety when she felt herself in the right. Her heart was pure and untainted by the strictures of upper-class superficiality, and she would not be willing to bend herself to suit their fancy.

"I would have assumed that you would enjoy the finer scenery available in London. You were fond of walking, as I remember, and I'm afraid Milton's parks are nothing to compare."

Her smile warmed as she recalled past conversations with her father, Mr Thornton, and Mr Bell about Milton's rough-hewn appearances. She did not reply to his comment directly. "London does have its charms, but Milton has possibilities." He raised an eyebrow in interest.

She did not seem to know how to make further reply. How could she make him understand that, as she had seldom if ever had someone to share her walks with her, the exercise had become its own reward? The scenery of either place had mattered little after a time. It simply was.

Milton's harshness had certainly come as a shock to her sensibilities, but after those dreadful first months it had become home. It had taken her much longer to admit it, but she had come to see Milton for its potential just as anywhere else she had been. Her main sorrow had a great deal less to do with the place than with the people, and in retrospect it had been essentially the same everywhere. She could have wished in each place for true companionship. How often she had tried to persuade her father to join her on her walks, but to no avail?

Her hesitation had become an awkward silence. He looked at her with some apprehension. "I have made you uncomfortable," he apologized.

She looked back to his face quickly. "No, I was just- thinking of something. Did you know, it was on one of my walks when I first met Nicholas Higgins?"

John broke into a hearty laugh. "Higgins is a bit of a diamond in the rough, I'll admit, but he is a regular brick. I am remiss in thanking you for sending him my way. I left him as second-in-command to Williams. I have a good deal of respect for the man."

Margaret's eyes were touched with grateful tears. "I am so glad of it!"

"He asks about you, you know. Just the other day, in fact, he..." he stopped, struck with a sudden revelation. "He tried to ask me if your brother was cleared, and I was too preoccupied with other affairs to realize what he was asking! How is it he came to know of the matter?"

Margaret blanched. "Mary, you remember, she used to help us when Mother was... was dying. We trusted her silence. I suppose she must have told her father, though I now would trust him as well. She is so very quiet; I admit I am surprised to find she mentioned anything even to him." She looked quickly to him, realizing at once how she would have sounded. "Oh! I did not mean that we did not trust you. I am quite sure Father would have spoken to you above anyone...."

"You needn't apologize," he interrupted. "It was right that you should protect him with close secrecy. I didn't need to know," he reasoned, "and it is best in such circumstances to not disclose anything."

"Of anyone you had a right to know. You acted to save him! What must you have thought?" She blushed furiously. "You did not know he was my brother when you saw me with him. And yet, after... after everything you protected him."

"It was you I wished to protect, Margaret." He hesitated, unsure if he should add what he wished. "I could not see you brought to harm." His voice softened as he spoke. He was gratified to see her eyes mist slightly and a gentle smile appear on her face. He could have stayed to gaze at her sweet countenance endlessly. Sensing her discomfiture, however, he began walking again, tugging her ever so slightly closer.

After a moment, he spoke again. "You never told your father about the incident at the station, did you?"

Her eyes fastened on the deck before her feet. "No," she answered quietly. "I did not wish to worry him more than he already was. He had so much to bear after Mother..." her voice broke, "...after Mother passed."

He turned to her abruptly. She tried to hide the troubled expression on her face, but he lifted her chin with his fingers, causing her to tremble. "And what of you?" he demanded tenderly. "You have had no one to turn to this long while. I have wished so many times- more often than you can imagine- that I had been gentler to you in the beginning! Had I not been so rough and abrupt, perhaps I would not have frightened or affronted you so. Perhaps we could have forged some manner of friendship. I could have offered some comfort...." he broke off as she began to shake her head.

"No, John, you did nothing wrong. It was I. I was too quick to judge Milton, and you, and I fear nothing could have pleased me. I am heartily ashamed of my prejudices. You humble me with your generosity. You have been too good! Any regrets must be mine alone."

He was not satisfied with her response but was uncertain how to counter it without offending her. He could not look on his own behavior and motivation with complete equanimity, but he was delighted beyond measure to hear her contrition. *Perhaps*, he hoped, *she has had a true change of heart since that terrible day.*

They walked on in some silence, the memory of that dark time pressing on them both. The light mood of a few moments before seemed out of place. She had carried so much grief, faced so much trial and worry! He wished fervently to carry her away and use any means at his disposal to bring her some measure of joy. *Patience*, he cautioned himself.

After several minutes, Margaret paused in her stride, causing him to stop and turn to face her. "George. Your father's name was George, was it not?"

He paled a little. "How...?"

She looked down, flexed her fingers thoughtfully as they rested in the crook of his elbow. "You mentioned my walks before. I was most often alone, and I sometimes amused myself by wandering through the graveyard bordering the park. Some of the stones seemed to tell their own story and I used to wonder at them. More than once, I saw..." she faltered.

His mouth set into a grim line. His arms dropped, releasing their contact, and he reached to clasp the deck rail. He leaned over it, his head low.

She approached, resting a gentle hand on his shoulder. "John, I am so sorry. I did not mean to hurt you."

He did not move from the rail but turned his head toward her. "You could not have known. There are things about that time I never told you."

She bit her lip. "Father told me," she confessed softly. "It must have been dreadful for you. You were truly only a child yourself, were you not?"

"Fourteen, just barely." His voice was husky. "Old enough to work, and old enough to fully feel the shame it brought to my family." His face turned to the sea again, but his eyes did not seem to focus on the water. "My father was a good man, and I remember that he did truly love my mother. He never had her strength, though. What he did... he was weak and selfish! He could not have thought of what would become of anyone he left behind. What my mother had to endure...." His voice trailed off as his jaw tensed and locked.

"You are still angry with him," she observed.

He heaved a deep sigh. "Yes, I own that I am. What he should have done, could have done, I was forced to do- a mere boy! Rather than face the consequences of his disgrace, he chose a coward's way out. In addition to the shame and hardship of his debts, we bore the grief and betrayal of his death. I have tried for years to reconcile the man I thought I knew with his final act. He could not have been himself that day! He could not have thought that his own family would have to...to..." his voice broke and he stifled a gasp with his fist.

A cold realization crept upon her. "You found him?" she asked slowly.

He nodded; his eyes clenched against the pinpricks of emotion working their way to the fore. "He hung himself. Right there in his study, just below my own room." His voice trembled. "I heard a crash- I learned later it was his feet sweeping the things off his desk as he fell. I had to cut him down, hoped I was not too late. But I was. All I could do was to cover him with a sheet before Mother saw him." He balled his fists, doing his best to block out the horrid memory. The vision clung to him- of his father's purpled and blotched face staring into his own as he, but a boy, had sawn madly at the rope in vain hope.

Margaret sucked in her breath. The horror he had been forced to endure! With full force of conviction, she finally understood how joyless the last decade and a half had been for this man. How bitter and friendless had been his days! Yet despite all, he was at his core a generous, kind man, determined to prove himself better than the shadows which haunted him. Her father's deep respect for his friend's character and resolve even seemed inadequate. How could she ever have thought him anything but the very best of men?

He shook with emotion, striving desperately to regain his composure. Little as he desired to crumble entirely in her company, it would be even worse under public scrutiny. His heart screamed at him to seek her warm embrace, drawing strength from the woman who could peer into the depths of his soul. Such a risk to her reputation he would not take, however, no matter what it cost him in terms of his own peace of mind.

Margaret had only once before heard his voice waver so. She was overwhelmed with the need to offer some comfort, but here on the ship's deck, anything she might offer seemed inadequate. She settled for weaving her arm through his and hugging it perhaps more tightly than was considered usual, resting her head on his shoulder.

At length, he opened his eyes and took a long shuddering breath. "I was glad- still am glad- that I could spare my mother that discovery. She had been sorely tested already. I had another sister you know. Sarah- she was born before Fanny but lived only a few months before the fever took her. I was only eight, but I remember.

"Mother changed after that. She clung to Father a good deal more, needing his assurances, I suppose. When he was gone as well- by his own hand!- something inside her hardened. She closed down, trusted none but me."

He turned his head slightly to look at her for the first time in many long minutes. "I would not have you think my mother was always distant and cold as she seems. She used to laugh. She had a wonderful sense of humour."

She could not help a small amount of surprise creeping into her voice. "She did? I thought she was always so...."

"Bitter?"

"I was not going to say that, exactly."

"It is true, you know. She was merry and joyful when I was a boy. She used to sing to us. She taught me to dance," he smiled ruefully at the memory. "I stepped on her toes more than once! Father used to take us to the seaside once a year, for their anniversary, and I remember her teaching me to fly a kite."

"Forgive me," she whispered. "I never knew she had... a softer side. I have always seen her as so strong, like she were made of iron."

He turned slowly to face her fully once more. "She is, but she is more than that. She used to be a great deal like you."

Margaret's surprise was difficult to conceal.

His eyes crinkled and the corners of his mouth crept upward wryly. "Is it truly any wonder I should have loved you? I had learned from a young age what sort of a woman I would admire. Until you so blithely put me in my place, I had never encountered another woman with the same force of character. You and she have the same sort of spirit and strength, but you were untainted by years of grief and bitterness."

He studied her reaction carefully, willing her to understand. "That is why I was so worried about you after your father died. I wanted to comfort you, longed for the right to go to you, but it was more than that. I could not bear to think of you hardening your heart as she had."

He stroked a stray wisp of hair fluttering before her face, tucking it behind her ear. She blinked away the tears that had begun and wordlessly nodded her understanding. He dropped his hand without touching her further but aching to be able to crush her to his chest. He had never opened his heart so deeply to anyone, not even his mother. He sighed, a long, shaking, restorative breath, and together they turned to the length of the deck.

They walked in silence for some while afterward, each deep in thought. She was profoundly sorry she had mentioned his father, but she admired him even more greatly for his vulnerability. At length, a thought came to her. "John, did you ever talk to Father about all of this?"

He blinked at her in some surprise. "I have never spoken to anyone at all. I cannot imagine many who would wish to hear, nor whom I could trust enough to tell. It seems, Margaret, that you are something of a magnet for all of the worst in me." Some warmth came back to his eyes.

She smiled in return but would not be dissuaded from her thought. "I ask because I believe he would have counseled you to forgive your father."

His brow furrowed. "Why? He is no longer here to make amends with. What good can come of it?"

The delicate space between her eyes pinched in thought. "That is true, but it is not necessary for you to speak with him in order to forgive."

"Be that as it may, I do not believe he deserves my forgiveness. I should have liked him to come to me and beg it, and in my darker moments, I confess I relished the thought of denying him. And then..." he gazed into the distance, a sardonic curve turning his mouth, "a sound punch in the stomach would do nicely."

"That would make you feel better?" In spite of herself, Margaret could not help a small chuckle.

"Aye, it would. At least, for a moment." His hand covered hers as it rested on his elbow. "I am curious to hear your thoughts on forgiveness, since you evidently think me lacking in proper feelings."

She bit her lip, trying to remember what her father had once told her. "It is not about *feeling*. It is an act, a deliberate putting off of your thoughts of betrayal." Seeing his puzzled expression, she went on. "Of course, your father does not *deserve* forgiveness- that is what makes the thing so profound. If he deserved it, it would not be necessary.

"You have spent many years burying your feelings. That will not do, John. You must acknowledge them fully. Whatever his situation, deep as was his despair, your father wronged your family terribly. It is only natural you should feel as you do, but Father used to say that 'what is natural is not always what is right.'"

Her words only confused him more. "If I am not to bury my feelings, and yet they are so improper, how am I to put them aright?"

"You are a man of action and deeds, are you not? This is something you can *do*. You must not prevent your thoughts and memories from surfacing, but when they do you must choose to distance yourself from your bitterness. Decide you will not dwell on it; break the hold it has on you. It does not happen at once, but over time you will become... practiced I suppose."

He arched a brow. "You speak as though you have some experience with this."

She smiled impishly. "How do you think it was I learned to endure our removal to Milton? You would not believe the ilk with whom my father kept company!"

He laughed outright, completely caught unawares by her sudden delightful shift in mood. "Snobbery!" he cried. "I will have you know Milton boasts the finest of England, all gathered into one place for your social enjoyment."

She lifted her chin haughtily, smiling in arch challenge. "Do enlighten me, Mr Thornton. I have met your manufacturers. They are a stuffy set, particularly that master of Marlborough Mills. A bulldog, they call him, both in looks and character!" The sparkle in her violet eyes belied her harsh words, and he laughed easily.

His hand slid down to capture hers, and he bowed over it in exaggerated respect. "I regret, the manufacturers are a rough lot. What of the architecture though? We have many fine cobblestones and smokestacks for your enjoyment. And for the more discerning tourists, Milton boasts a fine public house and any number of shipping yards."

"Indeed? And what of museums, has Milton any which you recommend?"

"Oh, quite so. Why, I myself have quite a collection of artifacts, as do many of Milton's private citizens."

"Pray, tell me where I might find such a display, for I would dearly love to partake of Milton's delights." She tilted her head with a provocative flare.

He nodded sagely, adopting the air of a curator. "Why certainly, *Miss Thornton*," his eyebrows waggled playfully, drawing a light snicker from her. "I would be happy to show you at your earliest convenience. But for now, a description will suffice. I have rows upon rows of a precious material. It is white, quite soft, and has many fine properties. The natives call it 'White Gold.' Should you like to see it?"

"In truth, I have already had the pleasure, on many occasions," she dipped her head in acknowledgement. "I must confess, however, that my attendance upon that particular delight was often diverted by that aforementioned bulldog, as I often found the one exhibit in the company of the other. I have found him a most confounding figure, quite contrary and difficult to comprehend."

"Indeed? Well, that will not do, not at all. If you like, I can arrange for a more private tour, to allow you time to fully experience and become truly familiar with both 'exhibits'." He lowered his head to murmur the words suggestively close to her ear.

Margaret flushed and giggled. Her daring eyes met his, then dropped again quickly in embarrassment. Sensing she would appreciate a few moments of silence to compose her feelings once again, he gently took her elbow once more to guide her to the stern of the ship. They stood close, their heads bowed as they watched the glorious sparkle of the rising moon on the rolling waters below.

Sixteen

HOW LONG THEY STOOD thus, neither could have told. They were content merely to be near one another. At length, Margaret spoke with regret in her voice, "I am growing a little weary. I feel I ought to retire."

He looked down to her with concern. "I am so selfish! Of course. Does your shoulder pain you?"

She shook her head, wishing to allay his self-chastisement. "Only a little. It has begun to feel a great deal better."

"You are not being fully truthful, Margaret," he chided.

She smiled, amused that he could see through her fabrication so easily. "No, not fully. It does ache, but it is not your fault that I have stayed out so late, nor would I find relief merely by returning to my cabin. I should go now though, as the cold does not help." He nodded, tucking her hand firmly into the crook of his elbow as they stepped from the rail and strolled toward her cabin.

He opened her door for her and stood hesitantly in the planked corridor. He was hoping she would invite him in, improper though it was. Despite Margaret's strategic levity to draw him from his pain, he was still rolling in turmoil. John had ever been one to carefully analyze every thought, every word, over and again to exhaustion. Their long talk had rattled him to his core, stirred up feelings and memories long buried. He had bared his soul, and she had bravely faced the ugliness of his darkest hour.

The last thing he cared to do was to leave her side, but he had no right to enter in a lady's cabin when he was trying with all his might to protect her reputation. He also was not certain how fatigued and sore she really was. He watched her hungrily for any sign, any hint that she wished for his continued presence. She turned and smiled warmly at him- it was decided. He stepped inside with her.

They stared at each other a moment, each uncertain what to say. Finally, he began awkwardly, "Is there anything I can do to make you more comfortable?"

She glanced about her, as though now she had reached her cabin, she did not quite know what to do once she was there. "I shall need this sling repositioned somehow," she offered. "I am not sure what the doctor did with it while I was to lie down. I kept it on before, but I would prefer to have it loosened at least for the night."

"Perhaps you do not need it now when you lie down," he suggested. "I think his primary concern in the beginning was for the reason that you were heavily sedated. He was afraid you would not be able to keep yourself from re-injury on the rolling ship while you slept."

She nodded, agreeing with his reasoning and grateful for a chance to rid herself of the restraining cloth. "Can you help unbind me? Melanie apparently wanted to be sure I didn't wiggle my way out!" she smiled.

He returned her smile and stepped behind her to loosen Melanie's knots. Margaret felt a deep tingling thrill in her belly at his nearness from this new angle. She could feel his fingers graze the nape of her neck as he slowly worked the knot free.

John could not tear his eyes from her beautiful profile. She stood before him, trusting and still. Her head tipped to the side just enough for him to see her lashes fluttering over her downcast eyes, the lips parted ever so slightly. He would have had more success freeing her from the encumbrance of the sling had he been looking at the knots.

But why, he reasoned *would I wish to hurry?* And if his fingers spent more time entangling themselves in the thick dark curls at the base of her hairline than performing their appointed task, who was he to condemn them? Soon the sling was utterly forgotten as his fingers trailed along the lines where it had creased her perfect skin.

Margaret gasped in surprise. The tortuous ecstasy of the sensations he created flooded through her. She arched her neck, allowing him freer access to the creamy expanse of skin below her earlobe. His thumbs began describing little circles at the base of her neck. How delicious it was! The muscles were sore and aching from her injury and from the weight of the sling around her neck.

His ministrations went beyond physical relief, however. He enticed and excited her, causing flutterings and shivers she had never known. She did not know how she could bear the torment much longer when she felt his warm breath tickle her ear and a new flood of sensations burst upon her.

"Margaret," he whispered hoarsely. Her breathing grew ragged as she leaned toward him fractionally, closing her eyes. She gasped and shivered deeply as his lips briefly brushed her ear lobe. “Margaret, take care. If I must go, send me away now. I promise you, if you do not, I will do something rash to claim you forever as my own.”

She tilted her chin up and around to face him. His eyes burned darkly. “I do not wish you to go,” she whispered.

Something broke inside him. He wanted to sob for joy. Lowering his head, he touched his forehead to hers, steadying himself. He could not bear to frighten her! His fingertips found her chin, her cheeks, and he guided his lips to hers. A shared breath, the barest touch, the lightest caress. She responded hesitantly; her lips only scarcely parted.

He cupped her delicate jaw and drew her more firmly. She came willingly, tipping her face to meet him. He brushed her lower lip with his, tasting her sweetness. Her hand lifted timidly, then came up and around to rest on his cheek, fingers teasing the stubble of beard growing along his jaw.

She opened her eyes, drawing back only enough for their eyes to meet. The hopefulness he found mirrored there answered every question, every doubt. Joyfully he claimed her mouth again. As if of the same mind, they moved to face each other fully, their lips never parting. He shivered involuntarily, his chin trembling ever so slightly. She had felt so in his dreams!

Groaning in pleasure, he wrapped his arms around her slim waist, pulling her even closer. How small she was! She roused his deepest feelings of protectiveness, and yet she was no helpless waif. She was vibrant and piquant, full of liveliness and spirit, and she was content to make her home in *his* arms. His expressive hands stroked her back. His lips teased and played with hers, encouraging her to open them more, deepening their kisses.

Margaret’s courage rose and she found herself responding with an ardor she had not known herself to possess. Once, there had been a time when she would have been scandalized and affronted by the mere hint of such advances. Now she felt she could not possibly draw away. Trusting fully in him, she allowed him to entice her more deeply. There would be no turning back. Somewhere in those few blissful caresses, Margaret irrevocably gave over the care and keeping of her heart to the man who had long ago surrendered his to her.

With a shuddering sigh, he at last pulled away from her intoxicating lips. Neither spoke, both breathing heavily. Her hand fell from his neck to his side, and boldly she slid her arm around his body. She pressed her forehead to his chest, and he twined his fingers into her hair. He buried his face in the curls mounded atop her head, and they both stayed in silence for several delicious moments.

"Margaret," he murmured dreamily, her name spoken as a caress. She could hear his strong heartbeat rating itself, as though her very presence was a balm to his tormented soul. She sighed in contentment. He pressed a kiss into her hair and straightened, stepping away from her at last. She felt suddenly bereft as though she had lost something that she had never known how to be without.

"I should not be here." His fingers stroked her cheek, her neck. She closed her eyes, leaning into his hand and curling her own fingers over his. He groaned. How was he to walk away from her, even for a moment? Honour, if not his own feelings, compelled him to speak, and to do so immediately.

"Margaret, I..." She shushed him, pressing gentle fingers to his lips. *She will not hear me out... Again, and after what has just passed?* Cold dread spread to his limbs. Could she really still be refusing him? What would it take to win her?

His stricken look did not go unnoticed. Margaret sought to reassure him but words were inadequate. Instead, she smiled softly and stood on her tiptoes. She could only just reach his jawline but it was enough. He shivered and pulled her close again while her delicious velvet touch trailed from his chin to his throat.

"Margaret!" he whispered in desperation. "Please allow me to say what I must!"

"I will, John," she promised in his ear. "Only wait. Our situation right now... I do not wish you to be under the shadow of obligation or shame. I want to be able to accept you freely and openly." She gasped as his lips hungrily tickled low on her neck, nibbling, and savouring her skin. How could she maintain her resolve under such an assault? "John!" she panted frantically, clinging to him lest she lose her balance entirely, "I am traveling as your sister- surely we must do our best to behave as such!"

He pushed a little and held her at arm's length, gazing steadily into her eyes. "I love you, Margaret. I always have. No sense of obligation compels me." His hands slid down to capture hers, and he brought it to his chest. "Please, my love." He began to kiss each daintily tipped finger. "I need to know your feelings, to hear them from your own lips!"

Her heart hammered; her breath caught in her throat. Then without warning the words came tumbling from her, lighting his countenance with such transports of euphoria as it had never known. "I- I have known for some time that I cared for you- since before Father died. I don't know when or how I first realized it, but I was afraid to speak. You had every just reason to despise me. When I left Milton, I never even hoped to see you again, but there has never been any other, John, nor would there have been. I love only you, John."

Her chest heaved, the words she had just uttered pounding in her head and echoing in her heart.

He stood almost transfixed, his face suffused with a growing exhilaration. Gently he brought his hand back to her cheek, stroking her soft skin. He was blinking rapidly, his mouth quivering- he could scarcely form the words he longed to repeat back to her.

Finally, with a deep trembling sob, he pulled her against his chest, his work-hardened hands carefully cradling her delicate form. He bent to rain gentle kisses on her brow. "My Margaret, oh, my Margaret. My dearest love!" He tilted her jaw with his thumb and began to tenderly explore her mouth once more.

Margaret found herself responding to him eagerly- too eagerly. His touch satisfied her yet made her yearn for more. Recognizing the looming peril, she purposely lowered her chin from his grasp, turning her mouth to kiss his palm.

"Have I frightened you?" his low voice, tinged with regret, tingled in her ear.

"No! If anything, I have frightened myself. I could never fear you." She took a deep breath, turning to look into his eyes. "John, there is something I must tell you."

His tender expression became at once serious. "What is it, my darling?"

She trembled slightly. "Melanie saw... she saw that we are not brother and sister. She confronted me earlier today."

His hands fell to his side, as he gazed in wide-eyed surprise. "She did! It is my fault! I should not have allowed myself to be near you so often Margaret. I wished to protect you and I have brought you shame...."

"No, John!" She placed her fingertips upon his lips, silencing him again. "I am just as much to blame. Melanie is very astute, and I am not practiced at concealing my feelings. We have nothing to fear from her, but I am afraid that if she could see through me so easily, after only a day's acquaintance, that others will be able to do so as well!"

His thoughtful and distressed expression began to blossom into a mischievous smile. "Do you mean, my precious Margaret, that you were displaying a fondness for me that you were not conscious of and could not repress?" At the crimson staining of her cheeks, he gave a short cry of triumph. "I think, my love, that I can bear the consequences of others seeing clearly my affections for you if they are to be so beautifully reciprocated!"

She raised an eyebrow at his jesting remark. She was beginning to quite like his sense of humour. In part, she suddenly realized, she enjoyed his quips because beneath it all, she knew him to be as serious as she herself was in her concerns. She could trust him with her deepest fears, for he was not frivolous or careless. It was simply that he had begun at last to see a lighter side to weighty matters, and his rising spirits encouraged her to join with him.

"You will not crow so loudly, sir, when my brother challenges you to pistols at dawn for besmirching my virtue," she informed him archly. "Frederick was in the Navy too, and I have no doubt he could best the likes of you." She smirked and turned away slightly in mock disdain.

His strong arms wrapped around her suddenly and drew her close, his breath hot against her ear. "Perhaps so, as I am, after all, only a lowly tradesman who has no skills of the kind. With the memory of your sweet kisses though, I would cheerfully face sword or bullet and declare with my last breath 'What a way to go!'"

Margaret burst into surprised laughter, making only a pitiful effort at escape. Seeing that he meant to retain his hold on her, she turned in his arms and drowned her giggles in his kiss. After a moment she rested her head upon his chest, once again wrapping her good arm around his body. "John... what do you think we should do? You know as well as I that after tonight we will have even less success at hiding our feelings for each other."

He sighed and kissed her forehead one last time. "Speak for yourself, my beloved. I spent a good long while learning how to bottle up my feelings for you. After so long in the desert, I could feast on the memories of this evening for as long as need be... but hopefully it will not be too long." His fingers traced her jaw, caressing her chin as he smiled contentedly. Finally, his hand dropped and he took a resolute step back from her.

"I think you are right that we must take better precautions. For one, I should not have followed you in here tonight, but you will never force a confession of regret from me on that score." Margaret suppressed a deep smile, flattered at his expressions of pleasure. "Let us try to spend more time apart tomorrow. If Miss Carter is willing, perhaps she could be of assistance in our endeavors."

Margaret nodded. A part of her already ached at the thought of not being near him much the next day. She felt an irrational tear begin to well within her eye. *It is only for a couple of days!* She chided herself. *It will not do to behave shamefully; we have done enough already.*

Those seemingly interminable hours would at long last see them safely delivered to Cádiz, where John could properly address himself to Frederick, and they could commence a bona fide courtship. "Will you see me to breakfast tomorrow?" she asked hopefully. "It would look odd if we suddenly avoided each other, particularly since-" she held her slung right arm aloft a little with her left hand.

"Of course. By the by, I seem to recall some while ago that you asked for my help with that. I will remove those knots for you, but you must promise not to ensnare me again, you enchantress."

A sly smile curved her lips. "In that case, my dear John, I would recommend you withdraw immediately! I can promise no such thing. Perhaps I can call the good doctor, as I am certain *he* at least is quite capable of gentlemanly behavior."

"Well, now, let us not be too hasty! I suppose I can find it within myself to exert some measure of self-control. May I?"

Grinning, Margaret turned to present him with the snug knots of her sling. True to his word, he deftly worked them free, and soon her arm hung loosely supported only by her left hand.

He stepped back, eyeing the rest of her vestments appraisingly. "How do ladies ever manage to dress themselves? I fear, my love, that you have a very serious problem. Miss Carter has no doubt long since retired, and you will never manage to unfasten your gown, injured as you are. I could offer my services...."

Margaret pursed her lips and gave him a playful shove with her good hand. "Mr *Thornton!*" A lady's dress is most certainly *not* your concern!"

He sighed mournfully. "Alas, it is not!" He winked suggestively, enjoying the scandalized flush upon her cheeks. "Good night, Margaret. I will see you in the morning." He leaned close and dropped a delicate kiss on her cheek, then he was gone.

Seventeen

FREDERICK HALE SAT IN his father-in-law's office, riffling through the morning's correspondence. Since marrying Dolores half a year ago, his father-in-law had truly opened his arms and business to his young employee from across the ocean. He had become like the father Frederick had lost, teaching and shepherding him in the ways of his business.

From lowly immigrant clerk, he had risen to the status of partner and son. His new father trusted him utterly in his expansive shipping business, though the older man still regarded some of Frederick's ideas as somewhat revolutionary.

One letter in the stack, postmarked from his home country, caught his interest. It could well be the lead he had been waiting for, and none too soon. His warehouse was fit to burst with unmarketed material, and Barbour had been growing antsy.

Drawing out his letter knife, he carefully broke the seal and read the missive from the chief loan officer of the Sterling Bank and Trust. His eyes scanned the page quickly, stopping and hovering over the name of the man the banker had referred to him. His gaze narrowed and he frowned thoughtfully.

In quick decision, he rose and left the office, letting the doors clatter loudly shut behind himself. The walk to his home was not far, but the neighborhood where the shipping office was located was situated along the wharfs, in a rougher part of town. Some of the alleys were unsavoury, the smell of overripe fruits of the sea permeating the air as he walked briskly by. The humanity moving thereabouts could be as rancid as the filth lining the street. Frederick never failed to keep a sharp eye out among the denizens of the wharfs.

He kept walking until he reached his own door, gleaming bright red with fresh paint against the white stucco. Dolores heard his step at the door of the parlor and struggled to rise from her needlework. "Stay, *mi querida*," he crooned softly. "You must take your ease now." She fluttered her thick lashes and smiled as he reached to stroke her protruding abdomen.

Only a little over halfway through her pregnancy, already she found it difficult to move about. Her ponderous belly seemed too large for her petite frame. Frederick feared for her, despite her constant assurances that she was well. He was inclined to believe the doctor, that there was possibly more than one child within her.

Dolores stood on her little toes to greet her dashing English husband. She spoke low words to him, an eclectic but beautiful mixture of both their native tongues. Frederick adored how hard she tried to learn his language, though she never had need to speak it to anyone but him- or Margaret when they wrote.

"Please, my dear," he spoke in Spanish, knowing it to be more persuasive on his spirited young wife, "go be seated with your mamá. I wish to check on Señor Bell."

She nodded, then walked away shaking her head. "That poor man," she was murmuring in her native Spanish.

Frederick sighed, climbing the steps to the upper chambers. *Yes, that poor man.* His godfather had been staying with him for over a fortnight. Only a few days after his utterly unexpected arrival, Bell had collapsed in the office of a local land agent. He had been gasping for breath and nearly faint.

Since then, he had been unable to rise, and the medications the doctor administered had at first made him ill and delusional. The doctor had quickly amended the dosage, but it was some days before Mr Bell had begun to improve at all. Still, Frederick feared, the best of the doctor's efforts could only delay the inevitable.

Knocking softly at the door, Frederick waited for the hoarse, "Come" before he entered. His godfather was reclining on a stack of pillows, carefully arranged that morning for him by Dolores and her mamá. He was smiling over an old copy of *The Taming of the Shrew* of which Frederick knew him to be fond. He eyed Frederick with a weak interest before lowering his book.

"And here I thought you were a man of business these days, up and abroad early. What brings you to an old man's sickroom at this hour?" A wry expression curled his lips. Frederick could tell by the way Bell's words caught in his throat that he would have liked to share a merry chuckle but had not now the strength to laugh without triggering a racking coughing fit. *A dreadful end indeed, to have even laughter stolen!*

Frederick sat in the chair nearest the bed with a frown. "I wish you would allow one of the girls to sit with you. You oughtn't to be in here all alone."

Bell waved a dismissive hand. "And have that lovely bride of yours wearing herself out for my sake? Nonsense, I am well used to being alone. What could the poor girl do but worry over a foolish old man, when she ought to be instead caring for her babe? No, Lad, when my time comes, I shall meet it cheerfully whether I have company or no."

Frederick's frown did not fade, but he knew he would not win. It was the same discussion they had had over and over. He drew the letter from his pocket which had brought him home.

"Mr Bell, do you remember that idea I told you of when you first arrived? I was trying to decide how best to manage the plantation you had purchased last year, the one you asked Barbour and myself to oversee for you. We spoke of partnering directly with a foreign cotton mill to sell finished product through the Continent?"

Mr Bell nodded impatiently. "Yes, yes, lad. I still do not see why you think it best to go out of the country. Is there not someone nearer to finish the cotton?"

"None with the most modern machinery, Godfather, and I believe that is what will be required to produce the larger bolts most efficiently and still have material of the best quality. The cost of shipping would be more than compensated." Frederick fingered his letter. "I have sent out a few inquiries, some to France, some to Holland, and some, of course, to our own homeland."

Bell grunted softly. "You had best not tangle with the French," he retorted with a hint of a sneer. Frederick could not help a little tug on the corner of his mouth. Detached academic though Bell was, the old fellow had grown to manhood in the heady days of the Bonaparte wars, and like most of his generation, still nursed a healthy grudge.

"I do not intend to. There was one fellow very interested in talking to me, but his family is heavily invested in linen. I think I should prefer to deal with someone who is already well established and experienced in cotton."

Bell's eyes narrowed acutely. "You have had some news from somewhere, I take it?" Weak as he was, the opportunity for a new object to hold his interest lent him strength. He reached a hand for the letter Frederick produced, never for a moment imagining that he would not be welcome to read his godson's business correspondence. His eyes scanned the letterhead. "Ah, yes, Dalton, there's a good fellow. I have still some accounts with him."

"I know. It was you who gave me his name."

"Did I?" the old gentleman's eyebrows raised innocently. He perused the rest of the letter without comment and a sly smile began to waver upon his lips. Folding the letter, he passed it back to Frederick. His faded blue eyes met the younger man's.

"So, John Thornton is the man old Dalton was able to interest in your scheme? I must say I am surprised." A sudden fit of coughing seized him. His face crumpled in pain- he had neither the strength to cough well enough to clear his airways, nor the ability to stop himself once he had begun to heave.

He hacked pitifully, then finally drooped back on the pillows, exhausted. Frederick offered him some water, which he refused. "Let an old man catch his breath before you try to drown him," he wheezed. After a moment he gestured with a swollen finger to Frederick's letter, wordlessly demanding that Frederick speak his mind.

Frederick struggled to remove the expression of pity from his face. Mr Bell had vehemently declared his dislike for such melancholy displays. He dragged his mind back to the cause of his visit. "Thornton is your tenant, is he not? I had quite forgotten that; you have interests in so many properties." Bell nodded without comment, still striving to moderate his heavy breathing.

"I have never met Mr Thornton," Frederick mused. "I saw him once, in the doorway when he came to pay his respects to Mother, though I stayed out of sight. I saw him once more from a distance at the train station when I left Milton. He struck me as a disagreeable fellow, but Father spoke well of him, said he had been kind to our family. I should like to know for certain- what manner of man is he?"

Bell, his eyes fixed unseeingly on some object above his head, made no answer for a moment. "Thornton is as honourable as they come. If you have dealings with him, you never have need to fear deceit of any kind. He would take ruin upon himself before disgracing himself by defrauding a partner." He paused, gasping a little.

"But?" Frederick prompted gently.

"But... Thornton is exceedingly cautious- he does not take risks. He is also a shrewd businessman and keen to his task. The man will not waste a second or a scrap. Everything he touches, he puts to good use. He will demand a perfect accounting down to the very last half-penny, always on time, and he will hold you to your figures. You had better be accurate with your numbers and absolutely certain of your forecasts, Lad, or Thornton is not the man to meddle with." Bell broke off again, breathing heavily.

"That I am," Frederick smiled. "Between my father's tireless teachings on ethics and Señor Barbour's relentless instruction in all minutiae of business, I feel confident that Thornton will like what he sees when he arrives. He will stand to profit, surely, if his operation is as efficient as you claim. I am curious though- why do you say you are surprised that he would be interested in the prospective partnership?"

Bell's face became reminiscent. "Thornton learned about business partners the hard way, you could say. His father took risks and was swindled, lost everything... more than everything." The last words were spoken softly, and Frederick lowered his gaze. "The son has far more than made up for the father's losses, but he is a careful fellow and strict to the letter in his resolve. I should think he must be in rather dire circumstances to make him consider the notion."

Frederick nodded, digesting this new intelligence. "Margaret told me about the strike, and how it virtually crippled Milton. It had only just ended when I was there last year. She said Mr Thornton's business was likely the hardest hit. I imagine it would take a deal of time to recover from something that shuts down all business for a month."

Bell's eyes flickered in confirmation, then his face changed. "Margaret... did you write to her?" His expression was full of pleading.

"Yes, sir, I did, though I wish you had not asked it of me," he mumbled.

The blue eyes turned on him again. "Why, Lad?"

Frederick hesitated. "It will worry her needlessly. Aunt Shaw will not hear of her traveling so abruptly, and most assuredly she cannot go alone. There is hardly anyone who can escort her, you know. Unmarried women cannot go about as freely as we can. When you recover well enough, she will be most relieved to welcome you back home," he added hopefully.

Bell checked himself once again from a short laugh. "I thought your father taught you about ethics. What did he say about lying to an old man on his death bed, eh Freddy?"

Frederick bit his lip and looked down, deeply uncomfortable with Mr Bell's cavalier attitude regarding his own imminent demise. "You have improved greatly since you were brought here. Can you not have some hope?"

Bell studied him, resignation apparent in the lines of his face. "No, Lad, here I will rest. I thank you for your goodness to take in and look after a doddering old man. I had hoped to make my way to South America once more, but your home is as fine and warm as any I could ask for." He paused to catch his breath.

"I think you underestimate your sister, if you believe she will not attempt to come," he went on in his gravelly voice. "Should she not, I will have full confidence that she shook your aunt's house from bottom to top before admitting defeat."

Frederick pinned him with a curious gaze. "What is it that is so important that you wish to speak to her? I know she is dear to you, and I, too, long for her to see you again, but you spoke of something I could not understand when you were delirious."

Bell shook his head. "That is for Margaret to know when the time comes, Lad. I left a letter for her with my solicitor in London, but I had hoped to speak with her in person."

"I do not know if that will be possible, I am sorry to say. I do not know how she can come to us." He chewed his lip thoughtfully, tapping the folded letter upon his knee. "Thornton is to arrive in a couple more days. You were something of friends with him as I recall. Would you wish for him to see you?"

Bell's face twitched. "'Friends' is hardly the word I would use. His greatest esteem for me was in the fact that I let him alone to do his business. Thornton has little use for the 'idle rich,' as I have heard him describe me. But for your father's sake, he might come. He thought a great deal of Richard."

Bell paused a moment in wistful remembrance, then turned to look at his godson once more. "Yet... how should you explain that, Lad? You always use an alias in business, do you not? That will not do, dragging the poor man back here to find me abed in your house. Neither your father nor I ever told him of your existence. Poor old Richard," the last words escaped as a whisper.

Frederick folded his arms. "If everything you and Father say about the man is true, I tend to think I should like to speak with him frankly. He deserves my thanks for all he did for my poor mother and father- things I ought to have done and could not- and it always pained me that I was never able to render it."

Bell's eyes twinkled approvingly. "I still maintain that your sister will come," he murmured, in a random shift of thought.

Frederick frowned. "I should feel rather awkward for her sake, having her here about at the same time I will be welcoming Mr Thornton to look over business matters."

"Oh?" an amused expression lit the old man's face for the first time in days. "Why is that?"

"Well... she does not like him. Not at all, I am afraid. I am sure she thinks him most objectionable. You know Margaret and her opinions of tradesmen and the North."

Bell narrowed his eyes thoughtfully, letting his head fall back upon his pillow. "Yes, I do," he whispered.

Eighteen

MARGARET WAS UP WITH the sunrise the next day, aching to move out of her stifling cabin. As soon as the sun was up the heat had begun to build in the small chamber. They were most assuredly reaching warmer climes! Fortunately, she had not, in fact, been forced to sleep in her gown. Melanie had looked in on her a short while after John had left, claiming she had only just finished a long evening of chess with her father.

Margaret did not wish to wake her friend so early, so she drew a different gown out of her trunk. It was the one which had been carefully cleaned and mended by Mrs Carter. Though it was a cheerless return to her former black, this particular gown boasted the enviable virtue of having buttons down the front.

Margaret found the undergarments more difficult than the gown itself. Though Melanie had left her corset greatly loosened for the night, she had insisted upon at least keeping it on under her night dress for her convenience, if not her comfort. She tugged awkwardly at the laces until she felt satisfied. It was not laced anything close to as tightly as Dixon usually managed, but it mattered little. She had grown thin from poor appetite during her first two days at sea. Mint tea did little to fill a stomach, and her gown fitted easily.

She was fortunate that her hair had suffered almost no damage from sleep, and a bonnet would do very well to complete her attire. She then sat upon her bunk where she could support her sore arm on her thigh and fumbled with the sling. Her lips kept curling and twitching in delight as she remembered John's dealings with that recalcitrant piece of cloth. At last, she had a solid knot tied, though it would have to be somewhat looser than the previous day's arrangement if she were to slip it over her own head.

Eschewing her shawl, she reached around herself with her strong arm to adjust her self-made sling. She settled her bonnet upon her head, heedless of the fluttering laces, and met the day with an exuberant smile. Somewhere out there, the man she loved was waiting for her.

Margaret made her way up the steps to the main deck. She discovered that she was becoming quite accustomed to the gentle rolling of the sea. Like Melanie, she began to brave the open expanses of the ship without needing to hold a railing. She inhaled deeply of the cool salt breeze, relishing its refreshing tang after the stuffiness of her cabin.

She strolled the deck, searching the stern, even peering toward the dining room, but did not see John. Her brow furrowed. Perhaps he assumed she would not be about so early and had decided to remain in his bunk with a book. She was quite positive that he would be awake, accustomed as he was to rising early. She decided to loiter about the deck, waiting for him to emerge. Only a few passengers were wandering about, like herself, and none she remembered meeting. She would have enjoyed talking again with young Mrs Sheffield, but instead contented herself with temporary solitude.

Monsieur Giraud found her leaning out over the stern, where she had stood with John the previous evening. "Good morning, Mademoiselle T'ornton!" He lifted his ridiculously pompous hat in greeting. Margaret offered him a grave nod but smiled in welcome. Nothing could dampen her mood this glorious morning.

He held out his hand and she gave him hers. He bowed low over her fingers, grazing them with his lips. Had she not been so carefully schooled in proper etiquette, she would have jerked her hand away. After sharing her heart with John, another man's touch- no matter how socially acceptable- felt increasingly wrong. Still, she did not know a polite way to refuse when he offered his arm to escort her.

They walked slowly, Margaret carefully keeping her gaze on the ocean waves, and Giraud craning to study her face. "I understand," said he, "zat we should make Cádiz by tomorrow. Ze captain 'opes to make landfall early in ze day."

She acknowledged that she also had heard as much.

"I was so 'oping to 'ave a chance to enjoy more of your company during zis voyage, but, eh, you 'ave been difficult to find!" he laughed reprovingly.

She nodded sedately. "I have been recovering from my fall, Monsieur. I have found, much to my good fortune, that it has been a restful journey."

"Indeed. Do you travel often zen, Mademoiselle T'ornton?"

"No," she replied blithely, her eyes on the glittering horizon. "I have never been abroad."

"*C'est dommage*!" he declared. "Unt'inkable zat such a divine creature should be denied ze pleasure, ze true joy of traveling ze world! *Alors*, it is one of life's genuine refinements!

Tell me, Mademoiselle T'ornton, what criminal would keep you sequestered away in fair old England?"

She turned a questioning gaze upon him. "Sequestered? No one keeps me there; it is my home. I am afraid my tastes are not the same as yours. I am quite content to remain in the places and with the people I love."

"Mais, mademoiselle, you simply 'ave not been properly introduced to ozer tastes. Eh, it would be mon plaisir to acquaint you wit' ze delights of many places. Shall I tell you of my own 'umble 'ome?"

Margaret inclined her head, acquiescing. Her eyes occasionally drifted to the stairwell which might at any moment admit John to the deck, but so far there appeared to be no tall gallant buffer from the Frenchman's address.

"I come from a little village in ze nort' of France. You know, mademoiselle, zat I share similar interests with your brozer. My family owes much of its wealt' to our flax plantation near Amiens. My grandfazer owned a small farm, but after ze Great Revolution 'e found many of 'is neighbors, eh, destitute. 'E slowly acquired ozer properties until 'e found himself vastly wealt'y. My fazer, *eh bien*, 'e was no farmer! 'E invested some of Grandpere's capital into ze mills 'o bought our flax. After 'e 'ad bought zem out, 'e purchased new machinery and closed all but ze largest of ze mills. *Oh, lá*, 'ow ze workers were angry! Mais, 'e knew what 'e was doing. Now, our mill is ze most profitable in ze region and our own plantations supply all ze flax. And ze profits, *ah*!"

Margaret murmured a detached congratulation. *Where is John?* An unfavorable comparison of the two men sprang up in her mind. John had always been proud of his mill's achievements, but never once had she heard him brag about his wealth. He was proud of his hard work and success, but there was no avarice in him. John strove for the dignity he found in a job well done, and in the progress, he believed industry made possible. This Giraud seemed to glory only in his riches.

"I was quite delighted to find myself sailing wit' your brozer. Ah, I see you will not ask me why?" He stopped her, his beaming smile never leaving her. "As you must know, mademoiselle, cotton is *la chose la plus récente.* It is a foolish man 'o does not keep up wit' ze times, nòn? My fazer is very certain zat linen is ze superior, and zat zis cotton will go away, but I do not agree. I intend to invest in ze cotton aussi. What do you t'ink, Mademoiselle T'ornton? Your brozer is just ze man one could wish to meet if 'e is in the market to buy, n'est pas?"

Margaret nodded vaguely. If he wished to invest in cotton, John was certainly the one he should speak with. Surely, he would have already done so, as they had been at sea for many hours together with little else to do but talk. A nagging thought formed in her mind. If this man had gotten the answer he wanted from John, why would he be apparently courting her opinions? If, in fact, John had refused to satisfy him, was he trying to use her to work on him?

Turning to him with a smile she did not feel, she attempted to beg off. "Monsieur Giraud, I believe you should speak with Mr Thornton. I know very little about the business, you see."

His eyes narrowed. "Ah, but *Miss T'ornton,*" he overemphasized the name, "You know a good deal more zan you will let on. You are a keen observer, I t'ink. I would very much like to 'ear your t'oughts on Monsieur T'ornton's business."

"I am not quite certain what you can mean." She arched an eyebrow and lifted her chin. "Of what value can my opinions be? I have nothing to do with the mill."

Oh la, she is bewitching! He thought to himself. *A perfect lady, but she is hiding something.* "I understand zat ze mill is facing some, eh, financial trouble," he supplied, watching for her reaction.

Margaret's façade cracked a little. She had known that all of Milton was in hardship. Her father had once even mentioned specific concerns about John's business, and how a failure might affect his favorite pupil. She had not considered that even now he might still be holding back the financial tide of ruin. Worry creased her forehead very faintly, despite every effort not to show her distress.

"Your Monsieur T'ornton's reputation is well known, you know," he continued smoothly. "Anyone even vaguely interested in ze cotton 'ears of him before long. I have been following affairs in your country for some while. Word is," he cocked an eyebrow at her, "zat most of ze ozer mills in your area 'ad made some investment in a rail shipping company recently, but your Monsieur T'ornton did not. When zey found zemselves secure in zeir returns, 'is position became more- 'ow do you say it- *precarious*. I was 'oping," he went on, studying his fingernails, "zat in light of zese matters 'e might be interested in a partner."

Margaret began to think herself on dangerous ground. She did not feel qualified to make any comment regarding John's business and would not dare say anything that could put his position at further risk. She had no doubt that what Giraud had said about the investment was perfectly true- she would have been shocked to find out that John had been party to an investment scheme after his father's failure.

Was he truly in danger of losing the mill? She did not trust Giraud, and she felt certain that John would not wish for such a partner in any case. Margaret felt it would be safest to extricate herself. She drew herself up to her full regal height. "You will have to speak to Mr Thornton about that," she informed him firmly. "I believe I will return to my cabin now."

He smirked inwardly. He took her elbow presumptuously, not wishing to allow her a chance to escape just yet. "I will see you to your cabin," he offered gallantly. "It is not fitting, n'est pas, to allow an injured lady to shift for 'erself? I wonder at your brozer for not looking better to you." She held herself stiffly but allowed him to walk with her. She did not feel it would help her cause to create a scene, and only hoped to regain her cabin quickly.

Once there, he opened her door for her. She stepped inside, but then he pushed in after her, closing the door firmly. Margaret recoiled in horror. "Monsieur Giraud, I insist you leave my room this instant!"

"Not until you 'ave 'eard me, *Chèrie*," he crooned. "Zere is much I would 'ave to say to ze sister of Mr T'ornton of Marlborough Mills- if indeed, you truly are 'is sister, which I do not t'ink zat you are."

Margaret's eyes darted to the door. She could not pass by him; the room was too narrow and he was far stronger than she. *Is Melanie still in her cabin next door?* She grasped at that hope. Her eyes searched desperately- she had nothing ready to throw at the wall, but she hoped her raised voice could be heard through the thin planking.

He took a bold step closer, smirking. Margaret shrank against the wall. "Monsieur Giraud, step back! Leave this room *AT ONCE*!" She raised her good hand defensively, her haughty head thrown back.

He grasped her hand, pulling her unwillingly toward himself. "*Miss T'ornton,*" he purred, again over-emphasizing the name. "Surely you can see ze advantage of an alliance between your... 'ouse... and mine." His eyebrows arched suggestively. "Your *broze*r is in dire need of capital, which I 'ave in abundance. And I..." his eyes scanned down her throat, toward her décolletage. "I find many of 'is assets *très interessánt*."

Margaret struggled, finally wresting her hand free of his grasp. She slapped him as hard as she could across the face. His head snapped back sharply with the force of her strike, but he turned back toward her with a sly smile.

Giraud had not intended to treat her roughly, preferring to woo women with his charms, but this alluring woman with her mysterious connection to his business rival stirred his ambition. He *would* have her, willing or not. He roughly grabbed her hand once more in both of his, gripping it so tightly she could not free it again.

"Do not be so missish, Chèrie. Perhaps you do not wish to 'elp 'im, nòn? You see," his tone dropped conspiratorially, "I see 'ow it lies wit' you. You are not truly a sister. 'E 'as everyone else fooled, but I see 'ow 'e looks at you. 'E has devised a clever way to travel, nòn? Ze company of a lovely dâme, without ze 'assle of an attachment. I t'ink, zough, when you 'ave 'eard my proposal you will find I 'ave more to offer to..." his eyes roved her form suggestively, "...one such as yourself."

Rage and indignation surged through her. No one had ever dared such impertinence to her face! Her voice was the only tool she had at her disposal, and she took a great breath to scream, but he clamped a hand over her mouth and the other- still pinching the fingers of her left hand- behind her neck with a vise-like grip.

"Now Chèrie, zat is no way to be. *Nòn!* I only wish a little, eh, professional courtesy. A sample, nòn?" He leaned closer, his mouth hovering near her face, and Margaret could scarcely breathe through the reek of last night's brandy on his breath.

She railed against him with her weak right arm, shooting stabbing pains up through her shoulder. Tears streamed down her cheeks. She shook her head like a wild thing, trying desperately to break his grasp on her mouth.

Her bonnet tumbled to the floor, and she began to truly panic. She clamped down on his fingers with her teeth. He jerked his wounded hand back, tightening his grip behind her head and pinching the cords of her neck even more fiercely. With a growl, he slapped her hard along her jaw, causing an explosion of light in Margaret's head. She began to sag.

The door burst open and strong hands tore Giraud away from her. John's face was bright with rage, his eyes glittering darkly. Margaret staggered back against her bunk, gasping and sobbing. Her body shook with fury and helplessness, the shock of what had occurred and the terror of what might yet have taken place leaving her weak.

John's only thought was to get this blackguard away from her, and he dragged the shorter man, swinging and fighting, back through her cabin door. He pinned him against the opposite wall in the narrow corridor, punishing the Frenchman mercilessly with his fists. Epithets poured from him as he took out his fury on the man who would dare to hurt his beloved Margaret.

Melanie stood by in the door of her own cabin, her face pale, her hands gripping helplessly at her skirts. As soon as she saw a slight opening, she dashed past the struggling men into Margaret's cabin.

In no time the noise and scuffle had drawn a crowd. Sailors, their hands hard from years at sea, tore the men apart. "And wha's this, then?" bellowed a burly fellow.

"He attacked a lady in her cabin!" John spat out. He turned his back, his only thoughts for Margaret. The English sailors would give no quarter to a French dandy who would attempt to violate a woman, and they dragged him away. Two of them went to find the captain for instructions.

Rushing through the door, John found Margaret sitting on her bunk, Melanie's comforting arms around her. Margaret's body shook with sobs, her left hand covering her face in shame. Without even acknowledging Melanie, he fell to his knees before her, then pulled her into his arms. Melanie got up quickly, without a word, and exited. She would check on her friend later.

Margaret's frame was racked with gasping, heaving cries. She buried her face in his chest and clung to him. She was too distraught for articulate words, but she cried his name again and again. He cradled her against his body, stroking her hair and murmuring comfort into her ears.

He longed to know what had happened, how that man had forced his way into her room, but he dared not press her yet. Gently he lifted her chin so he could see her eyes. She tried to duck away from his gaze, but he would not relent. "Look at me, darling," he whispered urgently.

She sobbed, falling once more on his shoulder. "Oh, John! I am so ashamed!"

"No!" he declared, startling her. "You have nothing to be ashamed of, my love. No reproach, you have done nothing wrong. I was a fool to have left you alone within his reach. I will not see you take this blame upon yourself. I must beg you, please forgive me for not protecting you!"

Her head burrowed low, muffling her broken voice into his overcoat. "You did not hear the things he said! The things he implied about me... about us!"

He pushed her upright again and saw her face for the first time. "Margaret, he hurt you!" His voice trembled with agony.

Tenderly he inspected the angry red streak on her jaw, quivering with rage. Had he not been most concerned for Margaret, he would have set after Giraud again with even less restraint than before. He grit his teeth, his face white and livid.

Margaret was shaking her head. "I will be all right, John!" She choked on a sob. "It was his words which cut the worst!"

His breath heaved furiously. Comforting Margaret was all that mattered right then. He reached for his handkerchief and gently he dried her tears as she tried to compose herself. Gradually her breathing slowed, and she took the handkerchief into her own hand. His fingers cupped her cheeks, his thumbs stroking the sides of her face lovingly.

"I do not care what he might have had to say. You and I both know the truth. We walk blameless. Do you hear me, Margaret? Do not listen to the lies of a fool!"

She sniffled. "It was not his lies, so much as what others must also think if our situation were to become known. He saw, John! He could see as well as Melanie that you were not my brother. There must be others! What must everyone think? I am so ashamed!"

"Let them think what they will." He pulled her to himself, searching for her lips. She responded, desperate for reassurance. She poured all her hurts and uncertainties into their embrace, pleading for his strength.

His pulse raced. Never had he seen her so abandoned to her feelings! He could not have restrained himself by any means. He gently encouraged her jaw open further, deepening their contact. Until the night before, he had never held any woman, never known how, but it mattered not. Margaret melded to him as naturally as his own soul. His fingers plied her hair, his other hand fisted behind her back.

"*Mr Thornton!*" Captain Carter's voice boomed in the small cabin.

Nineteen

MARGARET'S EYES FLEW OPEN in horror. She tore her mouth away from John's and gazed in wide-eyed shock at the captain, standing in the open door of her cabin. Saved from violation, from certain ruin and disgrace, only to be caught in a compromising position with another man mere moments later- Margaret's mortification was complete.

John bolted to his feet, striving to compose himself. The captain's steely blue eyes fixed him to the floor. Seldom- almost never in his life- had John Thornton been intimidated by anyone, but this barrel-chested sea captain fuming with indignation positively frightened him.

Carter glared at the younger man coldly. "I think you had better come with me, *sir.*" He flicked his eyes to Margaret. "Miss... whoever you are... you had best stay here."

Bolstered as she had been by John's encouragement, Margaret found her strength and her voice at last. "No, sir, I prefer to come." He rounded on her, his face reddening, but she lifted her chin defiantly, her eyes flashing. Thornton could not help the corners of his mouth twitching slightly. *She has looked at me that way once or twice! I could not win against her iron.* Neither, it seemed, could Captain Carter. He narrowed his eyes. "Very well."

The pair followed meekly behind the seething captain as he made his way to his quarters. John ached to reach for her hand in reassurance, but he dared not under the circumstances. Melanie, hovering just in the door of her cabin, caught Margaret's eye. She ducked in behind her, following her father. She dared to do what John could not, and clasped Margaret's hand tightly. Margaret squeezed back, thankful for her friend's support.

Together they climbed the short steps to the quarterdeck, drawing curious stares from crew members and a few of the passengers. Margaret kept her eyes focused on John's back, her cheeks flushed crimson. Thornton's jaw was set, his resolve fixed. He would not be bullied by the captain, wrong though his behavior had been. He was determined to protect Margaret's reputation and would do whatever it took to defend her honour.

They finally reached the captain's quarters, and as he turned to admit them, his eyes lit on his daughter. "Melanie," his voice was menacing, "go back to your cabin immediately. I will not have you mixed up with this..." he gestured to Margaret "*...woman.*"

John's careful control snapped. He adopted his sternest Master of the Mill voice. "Captain! I will not allow you to disparage her! Enough has been said and done against her today. I insist you hear me out at once!"

The captain's face hardened. "Melanie, go get Dr. Grayson. I imagine I will want a witness to whatever this man has to say."

Melanie's eyes fell imploringly on Margaret, who smiled reassuringly. Some kind of understanding passed between them, and she nodded. She left them to go do her father's bidding.

The captain shut them all in his quarters and began pacing the floor like a tiger. His hands clasped behind his back, his teeth set, his brooding manner proceeded to put the other two in their place.

Thornton was no longer intimidated. He knew the man had every right to call him on the carpet, but he would not stand idly by and allow the captain to insult Margaret, even silently. The looks the captain cast her direction were more than enough indication of what manner of woman he believed her to be.

"Captain Carter, allow me to explain." He kept his voice crisp and controlled, not allowing his true contrition to sneak into his tones.

"Aye, young man, you *will* explain, but you will wait for Dr. Grayson! I will hear nothing until then," the captain snapped.

He set his mouth grimly, deciding to bide his time. In his mind he began formulating what he would say. He reasoned that nothing less than a full explanation, from the beginning, would do to clear her character. The captain was a hard man, but, he sensed, a fair one. He caught Margaret's eye and arched his eyebrow. She took a small inward breath, then gave a barely perceptible nod. She would trust him to speak as he saw fit.

The door opened again to admit Melanie and Dr. Grayson. The younger woman stood inside, shutting the door behind her. She gazed unabashedly at her father with a look which demanded his attention. He pursed his lips and decided to let her remain for the moment.

"What is it I have heard about a man attacking you, Miss Thornton?" The wiry doctor was at her side in a moment. His keen eyes detected a spreading bruise around her jaw. "Did he harm you? What of your shoulder?" She thanked him softly for his concern, assuring him she was well.

"Doctor, it would seem that there is more to... *Miss Thornton* than we originally were led to understand." The captain's clipped tones interrupted the doctor's investigation.

"Oh?" he glanced questioningly to each face in the room in turn.

"It seems," the captain continued, "that after Monsieur Giraud attempted to rough up the young lady, Mr Thornton caught him in her cabin and dealt with him- rather admirably from what I hear. My men hauled Giraud away, but when I came to check on her welfare, it appeared that Mr Thornton was doing a *more* than adequate job of comforting her."

His voice was wry and sardonic as he glanced at Margaret in distaste. "It is a foregone conclusion, Doctor, that she is *not,* in fact, Mr Thornton's sister."

The doctor's brows arched. "I see," he said softly. He glanced between the parties in question, searching for confirmation. He found it in Margaret's vividly coloured countenance and Thornton's closed eyes and abashed expression.

"Captain Carter," Thornton's clear voice resonated in the room. "May I present Miss Margaret Hale. Her father, Richard Hale, formerly rector of Helstone, was a dear friend of mine."

The captain's face was impassive, the doctor's thoughtful. Melanie sidled next to Margaret and took her hand. Her father's sharp eyes bored into her, but she remained in quiet defiance.

John went on. "Miss Hale's family lived in Milton some while, where we became acquainted. Both her parents are now deceased and she had removed to London several months ago.

"I assure you, Captain, there was no improper motive in our sailing together. We had not seen nor even had contact with each other all that while. When Miss Hale was injured on the docks, I happened to be the nearest person at hand. I did not know before that that she was present, nor did she know that I was. My only thoughts were to protect the daughter of my friend. She was determined to sail, and I hoped that I could look to her welfare better if I were known to be escorting her."

The captain glowered. "I do not condone deceit and immorality on my ship!" he snarled. He turned on Margaret. "Why would a proper young lady desire to sail alone, or consent to be presented as the sister of a man to whom she is not related?" he demanded.

"Captain...." John's tone carried a heavy warning note.

"It is all right John," Margaret interrupted. She stepped nearer, her courage never wavering. "The captain believes I have been unwise and wanton in my behavior. I well know the risk I took in sailing." Her sincere, earnest gaze divided between the doctor and the captain.

She continued in her sweet, sensible tones. "I received word earlier this week that my godfather Mr Bell, who was traveling in Cádiz, is near death and was asking for me to come to him. I have little family left, and I could not sit idly by without attempting to see him once more.

"I had hoped to speak with you upon boarding to beg your leave and protection for a safe passage. Circumstances, it would seem," her eyes flicked to Thornton, "were not favorable for an uneventful journey.

"Mr Thornton has been a loyal and trusted friend of my family. I was most grateful to find that he intended to sail on the same ship, and I am honoured that he would attempt to care for me during my injury. I assure you, Captain, that if his intentions had been less than honourable, he would not have corrected the doctor's initial assumption that we were, in fact, already married. I was, at the time, rather incapacitated."

The captain glared silently. The doctor blushed at his mistake. Then, seeing a chance to turn the topic from his error, he cleared his throat. "Excuse me, Miss Hale, but did you say your godfather's name was Bell?"

She blinked. "Yes. Thomas Bell. He was my father's closest friend from Oxford, and I believe he had business affairs on the Continent he was trying to settle."

The doctor's jovial grin broke through. "Fancy that! I never thought to hear of the old fellow again. You see, Miss Hale," he glanced to the captain as he explained, "my own father wished me to become a scholar instead of a navy doctor. I spent a year at Oxford and I remember your Mr Bell, as he was one of the upperclassmen at the time. I believe I may even remember your father; his name jogs a memory. One could not forget Bell, though. He had a dry wit, that one! I am very sorry to hear he is doing poorly!"

Margaret dipped her head gratefully. It was a pleasure to encounter someone who might know another so dear to her, and she hoped to have a chance later to speak to the doctor more about her friend.

The captain's attention turned to his daughter. "You knew of this?"

Melanie lifted her chin and squared her shoulders in a perfect mimic of Margaret. "Yes, Papa, she told me. Margaret is a respectable lady, Papa, and I beg you would not treat her so rudely."

The captain thinned his lips thoughtfully. He decided to converse more with his daughter later. As he resolved on this, the door clicked open and his wife stepped in firmly. Her level gaze and arch expression told him all he needed to know. Seeing himself outnumbered in the matter of his opinion of Miss Hale's honour, he shook his head in exasperation.

Having cleared Margaret of the accusation of wantonness, he turned his ire on Thornton. "You, sir, I take issue with your actions. If you did indeed intend to protect Miss Hale, you seem to have failed to shield her from yourself! How is it I found you as I did?"

John's ears burned in shame. The captain's words had struck a nerve. How could he claim to be defending her reputation when he had sullied it himself? "I offer no excuse, Captain. You are correct, my behavior has been reprehensible. I can only beg Miss Hale's forgiveness."

The captain paced, clasping his hands behind his back once more. "Miss Hale is traveling aboard my ship, and as such, her honour is necessarily my concern. I am afraid I must insist upon an immediate marriage." He swiveled to stare at the younger man, almost willing him to defy his orders.

The couple in question met each other's eyes. Margaret's cheeks were bright pink, but she met his gaze with equanimity rather than alarm. Thornton took a deep breath. "We intend to marry, sir. We had not discussed time or place yet...."

"The time is right *now,* Mr Thornton." The captain's tone brooked no argument. "As you are aware, I have the authority to conduct a marriage right here, which will remain binding once you return home to England."

John closed his eyes. This was not how he had wanted to begin his life with Margaret; hushed and secretively, as though they had some shame to hide. "If we may have a moment alone, sir, I would like to speak with...."

"I would think," the captain interrupted, "that you have had *more* than the appropriate amount of time alone, Mr Thornton." Carter glared him into silence.

John surrendered immediately. He knew the captain had every reason to think the worst, but for now, at least, the man seemed willing to take him at his word. He doubted the captain's magnanimity would endure much testing.

"Miss Hale?" Carter turned to Margaret. "You are of age, correct? Will you consent?"

John watched her carefully. He found himself the object of the captain's orders and knew that Carter would exert nearly any coercion- possibly including even handcuffing him- to spare the reputation of a lady. On the other hand, he could see that the captain would not force the lady in question to marry immediately if she objected.

But if she wants to marry.... His entire body thrilled at the thought. She could be his within a matter of minutes! The momentary flight of ecstasy was stilled by the worry that she could regret a bond made precipitously, shrouded in scandal.

She gazed quietly at the captain's stern face, then her eyes shifted to his. All traces of hesitation vanished. She met his hopeful stare with calm assurance as a small, embarrassed smile began to tug at her lips. She turned back to the captain and steadily replied, "I will."

His heart began to race. She had consented! She would be his this very day! Without consciously willing it, he found himself standing near her, looking down into her eyes. "You will?" he asked softly. "You will not regret such haste?"

Smiling, she shook her head firmly. "The result will be the same, will it not? I already knew I wished to marry you."

They twined their fingers together, wordlessly waiting. Captain Carter rustled in his desk for the proper papers. "You have no ring, I expect," he grumbled. "Well, no matter. You can attend to that later." He shuffled a few more leaves about. Presently he approached, his mood lightening somewhat. Scandal averted; the captain allowed himself to enjoy what was one of the rarest but quite possibly the most pleasurable of all a sea captain's duties.

"Dr. Grayson, will you stand as witness please?" That gentleman attempted to nod solemnly, but his face betrayed his delight. The captain turned to his daughter and wife. "I suppose that you will be wanting to remain as well?" They both asserted that they would.

"Well, then. If you will both come here, please." He cleared his throat and spread the marriage documents on his desk, indicating where they should complete the information on the license. With shaking hands, each took their turn with the pen.

After they had inked their names together, Carter gestured to where they should stand while he read the solemn vows. Margaret's eyes glittered as she repeated the sacred words. Their hands clung together tightly.

John could scarcely believe his ears. The woman he had loved in vain for so long was at that very moment swearing to bind herself to him for the rest of their lives. The ceremony was over almost as soon as it had begun.

In later years he would not remember the words the captain required them to repeat, but the way Margaret's face shone as she held his hand. How could so momentous a thing fill such a brief span of time?

Nevertheless, it was done. His heart light and full, he gently kissed his bride. Her eyes, shining up at him, were pouring forth volumes of her adoration. Grayson was clapping him on the back with congratulations, and even Carter seemed pleased.

Margaret was immediately swept into the embraces of Melanie and Mrs Carter. "Aye, lass, 'tis a good man you have there! Many blessings to you both," the dear lady enthused.

Melanie fairly bubbled with delight. "Oh, Margaret, I am so pleased for you! I know how you love each other; you will be so happy!"

Margaret thanked them both graciously, then turned to face her husband. Husband! He nearly burst with the pride of it. Her cheeks were rosy and glowing in radiant bliss as she tucked her small hand in his. "I love you, Margaret Thornton," he whispered, exulting in her new name.

She blinked back tears of sheer joy as she returned his words of affection. "And I love you, John Thornton," she repeated back for his ears alone.

Carter folded and sealed the signed marriage documents, then handed them to Thornton. He tucked them safely in the breast pocket of his waistcoat, next to his heart.

"I think it best," Carter was telling them, "that you continue in your berth in steerage, Mr Thornton. There are a number among our passengers who are not privy to these goings-on, and it will be easier all round if we let them remain that way." He finished with a stern look and an arched brow at John.

His heart sank. Of course, he knew it was for the best, but he had never imagined he would not spend his wedding night with his bride. She was truly his own now, in heart and in fact, and he wanted to spend every second by her side.

Nevertheless, he bit back his disappointment and managed a respectful reply. "Of course, Captain. I will just escort her to her cabin." On this, he would not yield. The captain acquiesced with a skeptical expression.

Margaret shyly took his arm, the significance of the act not lost on either of them. She had placed her life and future into his keeping. He wrapped a protective hand over hers, and with a heartfelt smile, led her back to her cabin.

Twenty

ONCE INSIDE, HE SWEPT her into his embrace without speaking a word and kissed her firmly. She laughed, wrapping her arm around his neck. Having lost her mouth, he pursued her jaw, her cheeks, her neck. She sighed luxuriantly and nestled her head to his heart.

"Are you content, my love?" he nuzzled close to her ear. "I hope you are not regretting the haste...." Eyes questioning, he drew back a little to look at her.

Margaret laughed lightly. "I confess I did not wake this morning thinking it would be our wedding day, but I am not sorry." She stroked his cheek. "You know, I always did want a simple wedding."

"Did you? Tell me," he smiled, and began to kiss her forehead.

"Oh! If I tell you all, you will be very angry!" she teased. He raised an eyebrow, waiting for whatever provocative story she might tell. She tilted her head playfully.

"No, I think not. I do believe you will not like it if I were to tell you how I dreamed aloud one day of simply walking to the church in Helstone in my favorite old dress. You certainly would behave badly when I tell you that Edith's brother-in-law, Henry, took my words a little too much to heart, and presumed that I was... hinting." She stole a look at his face, mirth glinting from her eyes.

His shock was evident. "You are right, *Mrs Thornton.* I may indeed behave badly." The warning tone in his voice was mollified by a spark of mischief in his eyes. He picked her up quickly, carried her to the bunk, and deposited her on it, tumbling laughingly on top of her. Distantly she marveled that even in his passionate playfulness, he had taken great care with her injured shoulder.

Margaret shrieked with laughter as he pressed her downward with his body. "You are mine now, you minx! No London dandy will carry you off now!" His breath was hot against her neck as his lips did devastating things to her. He captured her impertinent mouth, kissing her deeply with a hunger he had never unleashed upon her.

Her laughter silenced and she pulled him closer, reveling in the feel of him. His fingers plundered her hair and caressed her silken features. When she began to gasp in breathlessness, he traced her tender jawbone with his lips, nuzzling and dropping feathery kisses over her.

With evident difficulty, he finally sighed and released her. "If I do not stop now, I will not stop at all," he explained ruefully.

She toyed with the hair falling darkly over his eyes. "John, I am yours now. You do not need to stop."

Fire shot through his veins at her words, the thrill of what she had spoken surging like electricity through him. He closed his eyes, fighting his every urge. "No," he made answer lightly, though through clenched teeth. "I have dreamed so long of you, of what it would be like to hold you. Our first night together will be something I will wish to remember the rest of my life. I don't want it to be on a cramped cot on board a rolling ship." He kissed her again, tenderly. "We land tomorrow. Beastly as I am, I think I can wait that long!"

She laughed again, breaking the tension. "'Beastly' is not a word I would apply to you. Giraud perhaps...." Instantly she regretted mentioning his name.

John's face clouded, and he eased off of her. Offering his hand, he helped her to a sitting position and placed himself beside her. "Will you tell me what he said to you?"

She hesitated, knowing what she had to say would anger him, but saw that he meant to find out what had happened. "He said he wished some kind of a partnership with you... implied that he and I could form some kind of..." her cheeks flushed scarlet, "alliance." She swallowed hard, not looking at him.

"He also said you would need him, and his capital...." her voice trailed off. She finally dared to look up. A chill came over her when she saw his broken and hollow expression. "John? Is something the matter? Is there something you haven't told me?"

He gave a low throaty noise, a small bitter laugh. "Have I ever told you how much I have enjoyed hearing you call me by my name?"

Her face lost some of its worry, but she had already read his conflict. She would not be easily distracted, and he owed her a full disclosure.

"My precious love," he murmured, stroking her cheek again. "There is something I must tell you."

Her eyes studied his, waiting wordlessly. "Margaret, I did not believe it possible for a man to love a woman as I love you. I never had any hope that I would even see you again, much less that you could ever care for me! The temptation to call you my own was too great! But I should not have," the last words were choked with emotion, "I fear I have misled you! I wish to care for you properly, but I may well have nothing left to offer but my own heart, small as it is."

"I do not understand. What more could I want but your heart? It is greater than my own, I believe, in that you have always known it better. I shall want for nothing else!"

His held breath came out as a sob. "If that were only enough to live on! Oh, my darling! But I have other concerns, as you must soon discover." Impatiently he jerked to his feet, paced the small room, and turned back to face her. She also had stood, a hand reaching hesitantly for him. He brushed her fingers lightly with his, a touch of reassurance, then dropped his hand in sorrow.

"The mill is very near failure. Recovery has been slow, orders have been scarce, and the capital which was to help me ride out times such as these is nearly all invested or used. If this partnership in Spain does not prove fruitful, I will be forced to sell out.

"I will have no debts, no shame, but I will have nothing left to offer you. I will have to look out for some other situation, some other position which will allow me to provide for my mother. I cannot ask you to share my disgrace! It is not too late-" his voice broke, "we can still have an annulment if you regret...." He broke off, his breath ragged.

During this speech he had held her gaze steadily, waiting for the wrenching moment when revulsion would cause her to look away. It had been a wild stretch once, so long ago, to imagine she might be content as the wife of a successful mill owner. He had allowed himself to dare to hope that somehow, he had earned a way to be worthy of her regard.

But a gently bred lady- trained from birth to look down upon tradesmen- bonded irrevocably to a failed manufacturer? She could never find happiness in their union. She would come to resent and revile him. Better to have never loved her!

Margaret's eyes never wavered. Rather than turning away, as he fully expected, she took a deep breath, then a firm step closer. She laid a hand upon his arm. He stiffened, not daring to believe she could feel other than betrayal and disgust with him. To have taken such liberties, recited their vows, then to lay out the truth of his situation! Surely, she had every right to be indignant and offended.

"John, I have never desired wealth or position. Surely," she looked down, embarrassed at the memory, "our past dealings would have proven that." She looked back up, held his gaze. "I am not afraid of struggle and I care nothing for what others think. I was wrong! So wrong, about you, about Milton, about so many things," she blinked back sudden tears.

"I did not think you could overlook my wrongs or forgive my offenses against you. I know now that your mother was right about you. You have the most faithful heart of anyone I have ever encountered, and if you will trust me with it, I want nothing more than to be by your side." She took a deep gulp of air, surprised at her own forthrightness, but satisfied with all she had said.

Tears forced themselves into his eyes. He reached for her face in disbelief and found her cheeks wet with emotion as well. His trembling hand smoothed her hair and he kissed her tears away. "Are you sure?" he whispered. "We may have little enough to live on, certainly no luxuries. Are you quite sure you can bear it?"

She laughed through her tears and nodded resolutely. "Let me simply be with you, and I will be content." She pressed her face into his chest. The deep well of loneliness she had known for so long finally began to recede. They stood long, at peace simply remaining in each other's' embrace.

At length he turned her in his arms, pulling her shoulders close to him and nuzzling the side of her neck. Gently he guided her back to the little bunk, then sat near to her, pulling her snugly to his side. She rested her head on his shoulder, and he sighed in deep release. She would stand by him, and somehow that simple knowledge made the hurdles he faced seem insignificant.

Then, remembering something suddenly, she brightened. "I do have some little inheritance from my mother. It is not a great deal, but it is enough to keep your mother in modest comforts, while we save whatever we can."

He did not release her, but his voice was strong and clear. "No. My love, I will not touch a penny of yours. The inheritance, whatever it is, is yours to spend as you wish. It is my responsibility alone to support our family. I cannot in good conscience deplete your funds while acting a sluggard in regard to my income."

Margaret pulled away from him, lifting her chin defiantly. "John Thornton, I will not yield on this point! I insist that you allow me to bring whatever I can to our marriage to help. You could no more be a sluggard than you could cease breathing! I do not wish to be a painted China doll, to be kept and fawned over and never expected to contribute. I wish to be a partner! I do not expect my small income to meet all of our needs, but I must insist we share absolutely everything or our marriage would be a sham!"

A slow smile spread on his lips. *This* was the spirited, stubborn woman he had dreamed of all those lonely nights. "You wish to share everything? Even... a bedroom? You do realize… we will not be able to afford a large place." His eyes sparked with mirth and something else deeper.

Heat crawled up her neck, flushing her face crimson. She was glad to see his departure from low spirits, but she felt his tease deserved a serious answer. She had never considered such an idea- had scarcely considered marriage for herself in a serious light before the last couple of days. Now she did, and she came to her conclusion quickly.

Catching her breath, she forced herself to reply. "Yes," she said slowly. "I know it is not considered the norm- my parents never shared a bedroom but I do not quite wish to emulate all points of their marriage. I have seen many couples in Milton who are forced, of necessity, to share a bed. I cannot say they are not the happier for it." She stopped, not trusting herself to say more.

Scooping her into his arms, he growled into her ear with pleasure, "I accept your terms." His lips descended on her face, her neck, nibbling and teasing. She gasped and closed her eyes in ecstasy. "I want," said he, between kisses, "to go to sleep every night for the rest of my life holding you close and listening to your soft breathing. I want to wake every morning with you nestled near to my heart, your hair strewn all about me. I want to run my hands over your belly when it swells with my child, and to clasp you by my side through all the rest of my days." He ceased speaking when he claimed her mouth, kissing her deeply.

She melted into his embrace. He pulled back and smiled in satisfaction at the passionate daze in her eyes. How he ached to remain cloistered in her cabin with her, tasting the hidden delights which were now his for the asking!

He had never dared to hope she might respond to him with such honest intensity. He had somehow formed the expectation that if she ever accepted him, she would receive his advances with maidenly dignity, never fully surrendering her genteel modesty. This woman in his arms was a new creature to him, one who desired his caresses as fervently as he longed to bestow them. Delicious, enticing, breathtaking Margaret, now his very own!

He pressed his lips into her hair. "Perhaps we should go for a walk," he rumbled. "If we remain here longer, I fear I will break my promise to the captain."

"I would not wish to be responsible for causing you to break a promise! Will you escort me to the dining room, sir?"

He chuckled, clasping her hand to his heart. So many life-changing moments had already occurred this day, and they had yet to break their fast! With one more tender, lingering kiss on her lips, he led her out of the small cabin and into the fresh sea air.

THE NEW COUPLE LOITERED together above decks the entire morning and most of the afternoon. Sometimes Melanie was in their company, sometimes they strolled alone. Margaret worried that the bruise on her jaw would be obvious to others, but John tied her black bonnet snugly under her chin, assuring her that nothing was noticeable.

Margaret introduced him to the young Sheffield family, careful to avert her adoring eyes to protect their privacy. John lifted the little boy he had noticed on the very first day and tickled him, eliciting the most glorious laughter from the child.

After the little family had gone on their way, John caught his new wife's gaze. "A son would be a fine thing, but I think I should fancy a daughter first," he remarked with a knowing twinkle in his eyes.

She tossed her head airily. "Placing orders already, sir? What sort of control do you think a woman has over such matters?"

"She shall have dark little curls, round little cheeks, and little dimples on each finger," he insisted with a grin. "I believe we shall call her Maria, for her dear grandmother, but our second daughter of course, we shall name after my mother, just to be fair."

"You, sir, are incorrigible!" she laughed. "Suppose I do not wish to have children?"

"You wound me, Madam. I know of only one method to purposely prevent that occurrence. While it has certainly proven efficacious to date, I doubt that in light of new circumstances I shall have a great deal of continued success adhering to such a scheme. You *did* promise, after all, that you would keep me warm during the long, cold Northern winter," he lamented, affecting a mournful face.

Margaret's face bloomed red, her eyes like saucers as she processed this suggestive, playful side of the steady, serious man she thought she knew. She recovered quickly, resolving not to allow him the upper hand. "Correct me if I am wrong, my dear husband, but there must be a good deal more to the matter than simply keeping you warm," she retorted saucily.

He laughed deliriously, his pulse thrumming in his ears. "I certainly hope so! I suspect, however, that a young lady raised in the country might have some rather practical knowledge on the subject." He paused to enjoy the slyly arched eyebrows slanted in his direction.

"I shall very much look forward to your tutelage," he murmured in her ear. Once again, he was able to admire the bright staining on her cheeks, but the approach of other passengers put an end to any further teasing.

MARGARET ACCEPTED AN INVITATION from Melanie and Mrs Carter to tea, and John reluctantly turned loose of her hand. Knowing he still needed to protect her reputation as his "sister" while on the ship, he tore his eyes from her retreating form and focused on the sea. It did not keep his mind off her. He spent the entire time she was gone leaning over the stern rail in a dreamy haze.

"So, Margaret dear, how are you this afternoon?" Mrs Carter asked cheerfully. She passed Margaret a tray of sandwiches, which Margaret gratefully accepted. It was good to feel her appetite returning.

"I am very well, Mrs Carter. My shoulder pains me less and less each day," Margaret answered respectfully. The woman pursed her lips with a little sparkle in her eyes, encouraging a less sterile response to her question. "I am also very happy," she continued, dipping her head a little shyly.

Mrs Carter gave a curt nod of satisfaction. "Aye, that is exactly as it should be, my dear. I hope my husband did not frighten you before. He can be a touch overbearing when he is aboard his ship. Sea captains!" she rolled her eyes sweetly.

"You need not apologize, Mrs Carter. He was perfectly in the right. I am glad your husband is such a man. It was my original intention to ask for his protection, and I am happy to know my trust would not have been ill placed."

"Not at all, my dear," the older woman patted her hand comfortably. "He is a good man, is my husband, but it is *your* husband I wanted to talk to you about."

Margaret frowned. "I do not understand. Do you disapprove of my choice?"

"Not in the slightest, Lass! He seems a good man, your Mr Thornton. I daresay, even if I did disapprove, it would do me no good to voice such an opinion. And I thought my Melanie was a headstrong one," she tsked gently, shaking her head with a little chuckle. Margaret and Melanie exchanged a bemused glance.

"No, no, my dear," she continued, "I only worried for you, with matters so rushed as they were. Most young wives get a little advance warning before their wedding!"

Margaret blushed. "I have no complaints, Madam." She dropped her gaze demurely to her hands.

"Mmm," the lady raised her cup, gazing speculatively at Margaret. She wondered whether this young woman had any motherly counsel in her life. The poor girl had lost her own mother some while before, and in any case, she was at the moment quite far removed from any family. With a reluctant sigh, she at last decided that Margaret, in her modesty, might not welcome unasked advice from an acquaintance of only two days' time- no matter how badly she might need it.

Perhaps Mr Thornton had a mother or a sister back in England who would take his young wife under her wing. Though, she thought wryly to herself, such counsel would not come before the new bride's wedding night. Well, well, she decided, the young gentleman seemed thoroughly enamored with his lovely bride, and she with him. They would survive.

"Margaret, Mama and I would like to ask to call upon you once you are settled," Melanie inquired. "Would that suit?"

"Of course!" Margaret agreed eagerly. "Though, I do not know how long that shall be. Our plans in Spain are not fixed. May I write down an address for you?"

"We can call upon you at Marlborough Mills, can we not?" asked Mrs Carter.

Margaret hesitated. "I... do not know for certain. You know that matters in Milton are still rather difficult. We may find it... necessary to remove." She bit her lip. She suddenly began to realize that if the mill failed, she would never feel shame or remorse for herself, but for what others might say or think about John. For his sake, she did not wish to cast the mill's financial difficulties in any sort of unfavorable light, but neither would she disgrace him by hiding the truth. She would face whatever the future held as bravely as he.

Shrewd Mrs Carter watched the play of emotions over the young woman's face. From long experience, her reading of Margaret's dilemma and resolve was not far from the mark. "I will write down my address in Scarborough for you, my dear. I do hope you would come and call at any time that is convenient for you. After this journey, I anticipate I shall be back home for good."

Margaret's gratitude was palpable. "I have some family in London as well," she offered. "Melanie, perhaps we could call upon each other when I am there to visit?" Melanie agreed energetically. Addresses were exchanged, and they relaxed in each other's company for the rest of the visit.

Margaret had come already to truly cherish Melanie. She had never encountered another so forthright and clever. Melanie was like herself in so many ways, yet she sparkled with her own peculiar energy. How glad she was to have found such a friend, one in whom she found she could trust! She looked forward to keeping up their connection.

Mrs Carter, too, seemed a worthy and kind woman, one she felt she could turn to as a mentor and a friend. Her situation in Scarborough was not so very far, nearer even than London to Milton. Smiling privately into her cup, Margaret felt a little shiver of anticipation at returning to that city on John's arm, and to call it her home once more.

Oh, dear, what would his mother think?

Twenty-One

In the fading light of the Milton sun, Hannah Thornton slowly paraded through the shipping yard of the mill. Most of the workers had gone home for the day. Only a few lingered- those whose duties did not end when the lines shut down each evening. Everyone was as familiar with her stern presence as they were the Master's, and each worker dodged her carefully.

John had only been gone a few days, but the oppressive weight of her loneliness was like a sodden drape over her routine. Her son was her light, her reason to thrive. With him gone, her entire household was sullen and bleak.

She almost wished he had stayed, given over immediately and gone to live in some quiet situation so that she would not have to endure his absence. Each time the selfish thought came to mind, she ruthlessly rejected it for the foolishness she knew it to be. Her brave, proud son would never give up while there was a fighting chance to preserve his life's work, nor would she have it so.

Mrs Thornton knew each detail of the docks and the yard. The cracks in the pavement, the battered wagons, the heavy clamor of equipment; all were printed in her mind to perfection. Each worker buzzed about his duty with synchronized harmony, none wishing to attract her notice by discordant variation. Walking the yards, she found, was no break to the monotony of her days.

Without precisely knowing why, she bent her steps toward the little outbuilding in a far corner of the yard. Several months earlier, John had allowed the hands to start up a dining hall for the dinner hour. She had been against the scheme, thinking it would turn into charity of the worst kind- costing John a great deal and allowing the men to take advantage of him. After once voicing her opinion, she had stayed well out of his business. She had good cause to suspect the idea had been inspired by a particular southern lass and did not wish to be too closely connected to its failure.

All these months later, from everything she could tell, the plan had flourished. Marlborough Mills had long been the most highly sought-after employer in town due to John's infallibly fair treatment of his workers, but this was more than that. The dining hall, and by extension the Master who authorized it, had drawn high praise from the very men who had sought to ruin him only a few months earlier. *It was gracious indeed of him to make such concessions!* She could not forgive the insults of the last year as easily as her son had. Still, her utter boredom led her to investigate what had long been a source of curiosity for her.

She had not intended to set a foot inside. She knew that John regarded the small building as nearly sacred to the workers, never intruding unless he were specifically invited. As she drew near, however, her interest was piqued when she noticed that the door stood yet ajar.

Coming close so that she might peer inside, she spied a young woman with her back turned. Her slender frame shook as she busily scrubbed a large soup pot. For just a moment, Mrs Thornton remembered those harsh days of want and worry, when she and her meagre household had survived on just a few shillings per week. She wondered distantly if those days would soon be upon her again, and how she would manage without the vigour of youth to sustain her.

A sharp tug on her skirt made her jump. Startled, Mrs Thornton looked round to see a small boy, perhaps seven years of age, but possessing large age-old grey eyes which seemed out of place in his youthful face. His clothes were ill-fitting and in need of mending, but his face and hands were freshly scrubbed.

He gazed at her in stony silence for a moment, while she looked back in wide-eyed amazement. Solemnly he searched his pocket, drawing out a small sweetie and wordlessly offering it to her. Confused, but not wishing to offend the lad's generosity, she shook her head in wondering silence.

Mrs Thornton's attention was drawn back to the young cook when she heard a sharp clatter and a little exclamation of surprise. "Johnny!" The cook, barely more than a girl, Mrs Thornton could now see, rushed to the boy. Nervously she clutched for his hand to draw him inside.

"Please 'scuse 'im Ma'am, 'e don't mean no offense, he dusna'!" The girl bobbed a respectful curtsey, wiping a stray wisp of hair out of her flushed face.

"He does not offend me," she informed the girl primly.

"I know 'e's n'a s'pposed to be in the yard, but wi' a' the men gone Ma'am, and me not done wi' my duties...."

Mrs Thornton held up a hand to stay the girl's explanations. The girl was perfectly right; a child of his age had no business at the mill. John was a stickler for the rules, and this small youth was by law too young for factory work. John forbade the younger ones on site and had been vehement about enforcing that rule ever since one small child had been run over in the yard. In this case, Mrs Thornton reasoned, there was almost no one about and the child was quite safe.

"Does the child come often?" she asked sharply. Though to be fully reasonable, she saw no immediate danger to the child, it would not do to continue so. Minor infractions tended to blossom if not brought to a halt.

The young cook shook her head. "Only whe' Father and me is both workin' late. 'E goes to the primer school, and 'tis too far for 'im to walk 'ome alone. Me da' won't allow it."

Mrs Thornton lifted her chin. "And may I ask which is your father, Miss...?"

"Higgins," she bobbed another little awkward curtsey. "Mary Higgins, and me da' is Nicholas Higgins."

Mrs Thornton's face froze. That name was well known to her, though she had never met the man in person. All of Milton remembered him as one of the lead instigators in the strike, but Mrs Thornton also remembered him as a personal friend of Margaret Hale's. Why John had taken him on later she could well imagine, though she had been firmly against that idea too. Once again, she had been proven wrong, as John claimed Higgins to be one of his very best.

"I trust, Miss Higgins, that you will finish your duties quickly and keep your brother safe inside the building with you," she charged gravely.

Mary cast her eyes to the floor. It was the first time she had ever had words with The Dragon, as some of the girls called the master's hard-lined mother. Mary had kept her head down and avoided the woman, but now that she saw her in person, she thought that Ice Queen was perhaps a more fitting appellation for this frosty widow.

"Yes, Ma'am. Only, 'e's not my brother Ma'am. 'E was one of the Boucher children. Me da' and me 'as been lookin' after 'im and the others."

Mrs Thornton's eyes widened in wonder. Boucher was another familiar name- a troublemaker for the Union, if she remembered correctly, who had eventually committed suicide. John had been deeply troubled over the affair, though none, not even the Union, could have called it his fault.

Hannah had suspected at the time that the mode of the fellow's death had struck a painful chord within her son. The man had left behind six hungry children and an ailing wife who did not long outlive her husband. And this precocious little urchin, with the unsettling grey eyes and surprising generosity, this was one of those orphans.

"He- he appears to be doing very well under your care, Miss Higgins."

Mary Higgins blushed at the unexpected compliment. "I thank ye kindly, Ma'am." She looked down at the small boy with a flash of genuine affection. "'E's a good lad, 'e is. 'E didn'a speak much for a long time, 'e missed 'is ma so. Da' was so grateful to Mr Thornton for helpin' 'im get into the school. 'E's done so well there."

Mrs Thornton almost managed to conceal her surprise. "Indeed," she deadpanned. She expected that if she were to check her son's personal ledgers, she would find that he had been supporting all of the Boucher children in one way or another, even those too young to attend school.

That boy, she sighed. She could not help but admire John's benevolent compassion, though she sometimes wondered at his direction. Kind and true son that he was, she half feared that his goodness would one day prove his undoing.

Without warning, the child- Johnny- thrust a book toward her and from nowhere offered a beatific smile. "Will you help me read, Mrs Thornton?" His inflection was crisp and precise, obviously the result of careful instruction in the school.

"No, Johnny!" Mary gasped in horror. "'Scuse 'im please, 'e's not used to addressin' a lady." Mary tugged the boy more closely to her, her embarrassment at his question causing her to treat him a little more roughly than she perhaps intended.

After a few seconds Mrs Thornton recovered from her shock. "I am not in the habit of reading with children," she answered slowly.

"I'm so sorry Ma'am, 'e dusna' know better," Mary stammered, her head hanging.

"I have not finished, Miss Higgins," she replied serenely, turning her attention back to the girl. "How long before you will have finished your duties?"

Mary shook her head a little in bewilderment. She fully expected she was about to lose her job. "Abou' 'alf an hour Ma'am. W'ull be on our way soon as can be."

Mrs Thornton nodded gravely, then looked back to the singular child before her. "Then, Master Boucher, I would be honoured to read with you for half an hour." She noted the pleased light in the boy's eyes with satisfaction. Her head still spun a little. She could not quite put her finger on her reasons for granting the boy's request, but at least he had the good sense to be grateful.

Mary felt her knees tremble beneath her. Johnny graced her with an angelic smile before turning loose of her hand and taking Mrs Thornton's. It was clear the older woman was quite at a loss for a moment to have this waif of a child presuming to lead her about, but she gracefully submitted to Johnny's direction. He led her to his usual table, where he was in the habit of doing his studies on those days when he waited for Mary.

Mary still stood rooted to the floor, her mouth slightly agape. The Dragon was reputed to be strict with everyone in her employ, making no exceptions for even the children. Johnny Boucher was a sweet little fellow, the apple of her father's eye, but he was still no more than the orphaned son of a worthless weaver. Mrs Thornton was one of the most well-to-do women in the entire city, yet Mary watched with her own eyes as the older woman seated herself with quiet dignity on the rough-hewn bench, her attention on the sandy-haired child.

With a start, she chided herself. It would not do to stand gawking and useless in Mrs Thornton's presence! Many a girl had been sent packing for such an offense. She scrambled back to her pots.

Mrs Thornton accepted the worn book Johnny handed her. She blinked in some disbelief when she beheld the title. *Robinson Crusoe.* Rubbing her fingers over the embossed lettering, she felt a rush of nostalgia. "Johnny," she asked softly, turning to her young companion, "do you like this book?"

The grey eyes brightened and he nodded. "Yes, Mrs Thornton, it is my favorite," he answered with perfect manners. Then those uncanny eyes twinkled and he leaned conspiratorially close. "I think Friday is funny," he whispered.

Her face flickering with emotion, she let the book fall open in her hands. "Do you know, Johnny, that this was also a favorite of my son's when he was your age? In fact, you and he even share the same name."

"It *is* the best name, Mrs Thornton," he sighed with confident little-boy pleasure. "You are very lucky to have your own Johnny."

Her eyes misted over and she shone a rare smile back at him. "Yes, Johnny, I am."

"HOMESICK, MR THORNTON?"

John turned from the starboard paddles to find the object of his daydreams sliding under his arm. He gave her an affectionate squeeze, but ever mindful of propriety, he hooked her elbow through his to create a little space between them. "It was not my home that I was missing, my wife. Why do you ask?"

She tilted her head toward the large churning wheel, which splattered droplets of sea foam on her gown from such a close range. "You were gazing at that rather impressive piece of machinery. I thought perhaps it reminded you of home." She turned to smile at him, without a trace of the irony or condescension which had laced her speech in former days when they had spoken of such things.

"Hmm. I suppose it does. It is much the same mechanism which drives the looms."

"Really? Tell me," she turned her face toward the belching stacks, then back to the wheel in bright curiosity. With unexpected pleasure, he began to explain the mechanics of the steam engine; how the compression built, how the drive was generated and then how it was transmitted to the powerful paddles. He was delighted with the quickness of her mind for such matters as he had never suspected.

She stood transfixed for a moment, her classic features silhouetted against the sunlit spray. Her upturned chin raised to examine the wheel closely, and little diamonds of seawater sparkled upon her dark lashes. Her full lips parted slightly in interest. Her wide intelligent eyes tracked from one point to another, taking in the various intricacies of the design.

He looked on in rapt adoration. *Mine,* he thought proudly, with a tremor through his being. Coherent thought failed him. He felt a rush of emotions- gratitude, satisfaction, unworthiness, admiration, but most of all he felt as if his heart were now beating outside his chest.

Margaret smiled a little as her mind pieced together a part of the mechanical wonder before her, and she turned to share her discovery with John. She found instead that his eyes were misty and he looked quite incapable of speech. Her eyes full of concern, she touched his hand.

His lips quivered. "I am well, Love," he rasped. Glancing surreptitiously about to be certain they were not observed, he raised her hand to his mouth. "Very well, indeed."

THAT EVENING HE BADE her a tender goodnight at the door of her cabin. She turned in some surprise. "You are not coming in?"

He shook his head. "I had better not. I would not leave," he added huskily, a wry smirk tightening his mouth.

In the privacy of the narrow corridor, she traced her fingers lightly over his bristling cheek. "You leave me to wrestle with my sling on my own then," she pouted, a provocative lilt in her voice.

His eyes kindled, and he trapped her little fingers in his to kiss them. "Only for this one last night," he promised hoarsely. "Then I fear you shall never be rid of me!"

Her face warmed. "I hope not." She risked a gentle kiss on his lips, a secret smile, then she slowly closed the door between them. Just before the latch clicked into place, he caught a final glimpse of her tempting lips, curved invitingly for him. It took the last shreds of his restraint to step away for the night.

Twenty-Two

BY THE TIME THE first streaks of dawn lit fire to the morning sky, the *Esperanza* was drawing into her harbor in the port of Cádiz. Captain Carter once again had good cause to be pleased with the performance of his ship and his crew, as they were hours ahead of his original projections.

John met Margaret at her door and found Melanie already inside his wife's cabin. *My wife!* Had he glanced in a mirror, he felt sure he would have discovered his face wreathed in a grin of foolish pleasure, but he did not care. Melanie was helping Margaret pack the last of her belongings so the trunk could be sent ashore. Glancing slyly at her friend, she made a pitifully transparent excuse for herself and left them alone.

Margaret moved into his arms with a pleased sigh. "Good morning my husband," she murmured. He clasped her close, reveling in her words. After a moment she turned in his arms to study his face. Her rosy lips curved in appreciation as she stroked his newly soft cheeks. "Oh, my! I have never kissed a freshly shaven man before."

"I should hate to deny you such an opportunity. I know how you savour new experiences." With much enjoyment he lowered his face for her inspection and approval.

"Mmmm. That is one experience worth repeating, and very often," she decided after a few rapturous moments.

"I was hoping you would find it so." He buried his face in her sweet hair. "We can go ashore anytime now. I just spoke with Dr. Grayson. He tells me the ship will be in port a few hours yet, restocking supplies before they leave for Italy."

Margaret nodded into his chest. "How are you to know your contact for the cotton? Is he expecting you, or will we need to seek him out?"

"I sent word a couple of days ahead of my own departure. He ought to be expecting me. A Mr Marshall, I believe, will be the man I should be looking for."

Margaret frowned. "An Englishman? How odd."

"Yes, he is the one who contacted my banker. It seems he is the younger partner in the firm. I am fortunate that he appears to speak English, for my Spanish is not very good," he chuckled ruefully. "I expect your father schooled you in about fifteen languages, did he not?"

"Only five," she admitted guiltily, knowing full well how he would have relished a chance at such an education as she had always taken for granted. "Unfortunately, Spanish was not one of them, and in any case I doubt if I should be able to make myself understood. I have not the accent. My Medieval French is rather passable, though, to say nothing of my Latin," she smiled sweetly up into his face.

"That should serve us very well if we run into Cicero or Abelard, but that does not seem likely. What of Frederick? I imagine you did not send him any word ahead and rushed off heedlessly the very morning after receiving his letter."

"You know me too well, my husband!" she poked playfully him in the ribs.

"Well, when a man has been married as long as I have...." He bent to kiss her temple. "I assume you know how to reach him?"

"I know he has an office near the wharf, and I have the name of his neighborhood written down. I do not think I can pronounce it."

"We will find him first, then, unless my Mr Marshall is awaiting me on the pier," he decided. "And since he may be, we ought to go ashore soon. Are you ready, my love?"

"I must say goodbye to Melanie, and Mrs Carter. Go down, John, do not keep your Mr Marshall waiting."

He quirked a dubious eyebrow. "And leave you to go ashore alone? Not likely. I prefer to see you safely ashore myself."

"It is nothing more than a ramp, John. If you prefer, I can have Melanie walk with me."

He shook his head. "I am not losing track of you in a strange country. That wharf is a confusing place."

Sensing she would not change his mind, and deeply appreciating his touching concern for her well-being, she relented. "What if I promise to wait for you to come back?" She stood on her toes, her lips creeping toward his ear temptingly. "You must not annoy your Mr Marshall by being tardy," she whispered.

He groaned, tugging her closer. "You are frightfully devious, my dearest! I had no idea what I was letting myself in for." He allowed her to draw his face to hers for a little more temptation. "What other secrets will I discover about you?"

She trailed fingers lightly over his lips. "You will never know unless we go ashore," she smiled mischievously.

"Unless...." he looped his arm lower about her waist and made to drag her toward her bunk.

"John!" she protested laughingly.

"Oh, very well. Go to Melanie and Mrs Carter. I will return shortly." He tightened his arms around her for one last loving caress before he turned her loose.

FREDERICK STOOD BEFORE THE mirror in his office straightening his tie. One of the young Spaniards in Señor Barbour's employ had just notified him that the *Esperanza* was in harbor ahead of schedule. He took a long breath, squaring his jacket, then dropped his tall hat on his head. In meeting a proper English businessman like Mr Thornton of Marlborough Mills, he needed to look the part, regardless of the Spanish summer heat.

The dock was not as crowded as he had expected. He was late. A little nervously, he began to search the periphery of the throng of people, all either coming or going from the ship. He felt sure he would be able to identify Thornton on sight. His glances at the man over a year ago had both been fleeting, but Frederick remembered a tall, dark haired, powerful looking fellow. He had not given the impression that he was a very amiable chap, but he had at least appeared highly respectable.

Frederick did not see anyone to match the description he had formed in his mind upon the docks. He began to scan the face of each person approaching the ramp to walk off the ship. After very few moments, his patience was rewarded.

The man who caught his attention matched the physical dimensions and colouring of the fellow he remembered. His expression, however, was so vastly different that he almost did not appear to be the same man. Thornton's disagreeable scowl was the primary feature that had truly fixed him in Frederick's memory. This man's countenance reflected a light, easy manner.

Frederick watched him carefully as he approached the bottom of the ramp. There could be no doubt about it, this was most definitely his man, and his expression spoke plainly of his buoyant expectations. He felt some of his tension ebb. Perhaps the man was not such a churl after all. His father had gotten on with Thornton well enough, but in Frederick's opinion that spoke nothing of Thornton's character. Frederick believed that no one could possibly take issue with his gentle old father.

Frederick stepped near to where Thornton was walking, the tall black hat swiveling about as Thornton, no doubt, was also searching for him. Raising his hand and stepping nearer, he pronounced the man's name. Thornton turned sharply, as though his ears had been trained for that very sound.

As he approached, Frederick took his opportunity to study his potential partner. Thornton looked to be roughly his own age, perhaps a year or two older. His frame was tall and well-formed beneath the black half-tailored garb typical to tradesmen. He carried himself with a lithe grace which eloquently bespoke of manly strength and an active lifestyle. He fairly exuded confidence, but Frederick, a keen observer, did not sense arrogance in his demeanor. Rather, he seemed swathed in noble dignity.

A most singular fellow, this Thornton. This was a man who knew exactly what he wanted and how to get it, and Frederick agreed with Mr Bell's assessment that he would not be a good man to cross. He might, however, be just the ally he needed if they could respect one another.

Thornton had drawn near and was regarding him rather quizzically. Frederick stuck out his hand. "Mr Thornton, I presume? I am pleased to meet you. My name is Marshall."

Thornton smiled, the careful smile of one who has discovered an advantage. He clasped Frederick's hand in a firm, respectable grip. "I am very pleased to meet you as well... Mr Hale."

MARGARET HAD WALKED TO the deck with John and left him at the captain's quarters. She watched him as he walked completely out of sight, lingering until even the tip of his hat disappeared. *Margaret Hale... Thornton! You are a lovesick fool.* She felt an enormous smile growing on her face.

With a deep sigh of perfect serenity, she knocked on Mrs Carter's door. A young maid appeared momentarily and informed her that the captain had just now taken his lady and daughter ashore to visit a particular millinery shop of which Mrs Carter had been previously fond. She did not know when her mistress should return, as the duration of the captain's brief liberty depended entirely upon his obligations toward restocking his ship.

Nodding a murmured thanks, she turned to watch the milling crew, scuffling cargo about the ship. Most of the passengers, even those staying aboard for the trip to Italy, had taken their opportunity to go ashore to sample the local hospitality.

Stepping to the rail, Margaret leaned over to see if she could spot John below. It was not difficult. He had gone scarcely a dozen paces from the ramp. She watched him turn abruptly as something caught his attention, then he was walking toward someone. She assumed it was his Mr Marshall, who must have been below waiting after all.

The man was obscured from her view for only a moment. When a few passers-by cleared out of her line of sight, Margaret sucked in her breath. Her chest burst in joy. Frederick!

FREDERICK'S GRIP WAVERED IN Thornton's grasp. His eyes widened in shock and he drew back, suddenly apprehensive. Reason failed him for a heartbeat.

For so long had he lived under the pall of a death sentence should he ever be discovered. To hear his true name uttered by a stranger, one from his own home country, stole his nerve. What did he really know of this enigmatic businessman, who seemed to know far more than he ought?

Sensing himself trapped, Frederick tensed and cast about himself for possible avenues of escape. Thornton did not seem to present a threatening manner, but Frederick could not be certain. Fear for Dolores made him begin to quiver.

Without warning, a smaller dark shape stepped round from behind the other man. A female voice cried out his name, and suddenly his sister was in his arms. Her face was wet with happy tears and she embraced him without reserve. Her untied bonnet fluttered to the ground in his embrace as she kissed his cheeks again and again.

"Margaret? What are you...? How? I did not expect...." He stood in aghast wonder as she released him, moving with curious familiarity to take Thornton's arm.

Thornton had placed a possessive hand over Margaret's, a little frown of disapproval on his face. "You promised me you would wait," he was murmuring.

If Frederick had noticed Margaret's playfully apologetic look or the mildly teasing light in Thornton's eyes, he might have been set at his ease. Instead, his gaze became fixed on the linen sling binding his sister's arm and the purple mar on her beloved face as she turned her head. Thornton's chastising words fell upon his tumbling thoughts and rage welled up within him.

Thornton scarcely had torn his eyes from Margaret when he was staggered by a fierce blow to the mouth. He was just in time to dodge a second blow.

"Fred!" Margaret was crying, trying ineffectively to drag at her brother's arm. "Stop! Oh, stop, please!"

Frederick shook off her hold, snarling out an epithet having something to do with the other man's dubious parentage. "*How dare you hurt my sister!*" He dove for the taller man again, both fists up.

Thornton wiped a trickle of blood from his lip as he ducked. He did not dream of retaliating. Margaret would not wish him to hurt her brother, and it was clear that Frederick believed him responsible for Margaret's injuries. He would scarcely have done less himself.

He could not allow this to continue, though. Margaret was too close and pleading too insistently with Frederick. He was afraid he might inadvertently hurt his wife while trying to stop his enraged brother-in-law.

Moving like lightning, Thornton clamped down Frederick's bicep in a painful grip. He drew close, shoulder to shoulder, and hissed the words into Frederick's ear. "Hale, this is not the time or the place! We have much to discuss. Let us go where we can talk."

Frederick wrestled out of his grasp. "I have nothing to say to you!" he spat. "Margaret! Come away. You will be safe here!" He reached for his sister's arm but she drew herself to her full height and leveled a determined stare at him.

"I am not leaving Mr Thornton, Fred," she spoke softly, but with steel in her voice. She took Thornton's arm again. "Please, let us go as he said!"

Frederick looked from one to the other, his fists still balled. His eyes narrowed again on Thornton and his voice trembled in fury. "*You* are no gentleman, sir! I will not have dealings with such a man!"

He wished to snatch his sister's hand from this fiend, but Margaret had made it impossible. Her strong left hand was anchored firmly around Thornton's arm and her other hand was bound by a sling. What manner of injury she had he could not tell, but he did not dare pull her forcibly away.

"Things are not as you think, sir," Thornton rumbled in a low, grave tone. "You will not sway her to go with you alone, and as we are drawing attention at the moment, I suggest we all walk to your place of business."

Frederick looked about himself and found that Thornton was right. A few casual onlookers had slowed about their business to watch events unfold. He could scarcely afford to appear so conspicuous among so many foreign travelers.

Glowering back at the man before him, he agreed that it was necessary to make a strategic withdrawal. "Margaret, come with me! He can follow if he wants to."

"Our luggage! My friends! Fred, please," she protested, nearly in tears again.

"I will send someone for your luggage!" he snapped impatiently. "Margaret! Come!"

Margaret's expression remained withered and sorrowful. Thornton gave her a reassuring look and murmured soft words which only she could hear. Frederick watched in scandalized fascination as this powerful fellow held mysterious sway over his headstrong sister. She took a deep relenting breath, then, blinking rapidly, released Thornton's arm to take his.

Frederick spun her about and marched on, leaving Thornton trailing behind. He kept his eye surreptitiously on Margaret's downcast face. Her quivering lips and nearly closed eyes revealed her torment. Once or twice, she glanced over her shoulder. He did not have to look to know that Thornton was there, nearly close enough to touch.

He seethed with rage at the audacity of the man. What familiarity he presumed! How would he try to explain Margaret's injuries? She seemed reluctant to leave the man as well, which worried him even more. Had he some power over her?

A new concern edged into his thoughts. His father had told him once that Thornton was a magistrate. An officer of English law.... Cold fear crept up his spine.

Could Thornton have discovered his identity somehow, and was that what had truly brought him here? Could he be using Margaret to reach him? Had he threatened her? The coincidences were too strong.

No matter the cost to himself, he could not let his sister fall to harm. He had failed to watch over her all these years, he had lured her here, and now he owed her her safety.

Gritting his teeth and issuing a silent plea for Dolores' forgiveness, Frederick girded up his courage. He would deal with this Thornton like the scoundrel he was.

Twenty-Three

At last, the uncomfortable party reached Frederick's office. It was a small affair, as Barbour did most of his work from his study at home. This rented space served merely as a station near the docks to receive those merchants and hired men not welcomed at the house.

It was really not much more than a furnished room dominated by an ornate old seaman's desk littered with shipping invoices. There were just enough chairs for them all, but Frederick did not intend to invite Thornton to make himself comfortable. He eased Margaret into a chair, then whirled to face the imposing man before him.

"What do you want, Thornton?" he snapped. "If you have come to drag me back to England, then let us go right now, but leave my sister out of this!" He braced himself, adopting a balanced fighter's stance. He ignored Margaret's cry of protest. Protect her he would, but he would not surrender easily.

Thornton sighed heavily, shaking his head. He removed his hat and ran his fingers through his hair. "I am afraid, Hale, that you mistake me completely. I have no intentions to bring harm to you, and certainly never to her. Quite to the contrary, in fact."

Frederick straightened, standing stiffly but no longer in a striking pose. "How do you explain my sister's injuries? What are you doing traveling with her? No gentleman would presume so!"

Thornton dropped his hand and cast an imploring look to Margaret. Frederick turned curiously to her. Quietly she rose and came to his side. She slipped her little hand in his and looked beseechingly into his eyes. "Please, Fred, let me explain. John has been protecting me- I could not have done without...."

Frederick raised an eyebrow. "'*John*'?" he interrupted incredulously. "You were barely on speaking terms with Thornton when I was last in England, and now it's '*John*'?"

She squared her shoulders, looking him stubbornly in the eye. "*John* and I... we were married yesterday Fred... by the captain of the *Esperanza,*" she finished softly.

His mouth fell open. He spun from one to the other, verifying the truth of her words in Thornton's firm expression. He looked back to Margaret. "How!" he sputtered.

Suddenly her implication shone clearly. He pivoted again to face Thornton. "*You compromised my sister!*" Balling his fists, he struggled for composure. "We are leaving for England at once to have this annulled! Margaret, you must come back here to live with us. I will not have you forced to live your life with this cad!"

Thornton had remained silent, his head wagging in self-castigation. Margaret held herself aloof, her head thrown back with an indignant spirit. Her voice remained steady and determined. "No, Fred. I wish to remain with John."

He stared disbelievingly, his breath harsh and panting. He searched to discover the meaning behind her words. Had she determined to endure marriage to the man because it was better than disgrace, or was she trying to tell him that she was inconceivably fond of this great fellow?

Margaret herself answered the question when she abandoned him in the middle of the room and moved to stand close by Thornton's side. He watched Thornton take a long sigh of relief and affectionately tuck Margaret's hand into his.

Frederick pursed his lips thoughtfully. "You had better both be seated. It seems we do have much to talk over." He observed them both narrowly as Thornton carefully helped Margaret to a chair. He then drew his own near, and as soon as he had seated himself their hands met once more.

Margaret leaned forward with insistent concern. "Fred, how is Mr Bell? We have not yet spoken of it. Is he...?"

Frederick found his interrogation disarmed. "He is still alive, Dearest. He is very unwell; I fear you have only just come in time."

Margaret sat back in profound relief. "I *am* in time though. I am glad. Oh, Fred, may we go to him? I have had such fears, that I would be too late!"

"Shortly, Margaret, I promise. We will be on our way soon. Before we go, however, I must know all that has happened here." He spoke sharply and shot Thornton an expectant glare. "Let us begin with my sister's injuries. How is it, sir, that she came to be so knocked about while under your *protection*?"

The couple met each other's eyes and then took turns unfolding the events of the past few days. Margaret began with an embarrassed explanation of her intent to travel alone, against his admonitions and without her aunt's approval. Frederick was annoyed, of course, but hardly surprised.

Thornton picked up the narrative at the point of her unfortunate accident, warmly praising her spirit and fortitude. With some remorse and shame, he admitted to claiming that Margaret was his sister so he could watch over her in her injured state.

In a very few moments Frederick became convinced that he had judged Thornton wrongly. While not strictly honest in every particular, Thornton had protected his sister as a gentleman and a friend of the family should. He began to relax.

Once satisfied that the man was truly innocent of dishonourable intentions, he began to be amused at the way they related their tale. They spoke together seamlessly, even finishing each other's sentences. The warm glances they shared spoke of a real and vibrant affection, of the kind which, Frederick suspected, had its foundations far beyond the events of which they spoke.

When they reached the incident involving the other passenger's assault on Margaret, Frederick began to tremble once more with rage. He was gratified to hear of Thornton's harsh dispatch of the blackguard, but his alarmed gaze swept over Margaret. Sensing his concern, she turned loose of Thornton's hand and reached for his. "Fred, do not fear. I am well, truly I am!"

He released a quavering breath, conviction dawning. Margaret was not fearless because she had not been harmed, for she had, and brutally so. She was brave yet because of the man who had stood faithfully by her side, comforting, and protecting, just as he had stood by their broken and feeble parents during their last days. Frederick felt keenly the oppressive weight of the debt he owed this Northern manufacturer.

There was an uncomfortable pause. Both parties had sensed his swirling emotions, and he felt abashed that they had been obliged to wait for him. "I... forgive me, please. Do go on."

Thornton looked long and carefully to Margaret. Some kind of unspoken understanding passed between them, and he looked down, fingering the brim of the hat in his lap. "Hale, I fear that my behavior just after the attack on Margaret was not such that I ought to be proud."

Frederick's gaze wandered to Margaret, noting the vivid colour which suddenly flashed onto her cheeks. He had a fair idea of what might have taken place next. He was, after all, a man devoted to a woman himself. He knew exactly how he would have tried to comfort his Dolores had someone attempted to harm her. Thornton hedged some in his description- no doubt to protect Margaret's modesty- but Frederick had a very clear picture of the subsequent events and the pressure for an immediate marriage.

He held up a hand. “You need say no more. I can see, Thornton, that you have done nothing more than I myself would have.”

Thornton gave a great sigh of relief. “Thank you, Hale.”

Frederick stood and offered his hand. “I expect, Thornton, that I have made a regular ass of myself. Will you forgive me?”

Thornton stood as well, taking his hand firmly. “As a matter of fact, Hale, I suddenly have the highest regard for you.” He flashed an easy smile at Margaret. “Anyone who wishes to defend my wife has my deepest gratitude. I only hope,” he added with a wry grin, “that you will never again feel it necessary to defend her from me!”

Frederick returned the good will cautiously, then glanced down to their locked hands. For the first time he noticed the angry scrapes on the other’s knuckles.

Thornton answered his raising eyes with a steely gaze. “I would give my life for her,” he vowed in a low voice.

“Then we understand each other. Welcome to the family, Brother.” Frederick released Thornton’s hand. “And now, my dear sister, there is someone waiting very anxiously to see you.”

Margaret followed her beloved brother as he led them through the quaint, wending streets of his adopted home city. The Barbour family were old stock; sailors tracing their lineage from both conquistadores and pirates. Their seat was in an older part of the city, one reserved for the more respectable and well-heeled members of the community.

She looked about in fascination, noticing that John was doing the same. The narrow twisting streets, all sparkling and glimmering with pristine stucco houses, were an absolute novelty to them. John reached out once to brush his fingers experimentally along the peculiar material.

Very soon they were at Frederick’s home. Grinning like a boy, he ushered them into the cozy sitting room where a young woman, nearly bursting with child, was sewing. An older woman sat with her. Both had shimmering, elegantly coiffed, raven-black hair, sparkling dark eyes, plump exotic lips and flawless Mediterranean complexion. Margaret thought the young woman one of the most exquisitely beautiful creatures she had ever seen.

Frederick held his hand out for the young woman, helping her ponderously to her feet. He spoke softly in Spanish to her and her bright eyes widened in supreme pleasure. Pride glowed on his face as he drew her near to them. "Margaret, Mr Thornton, may I present my wife, Dolores."

Margaret extended her hand for the customary civilities, but Dolores would have none of it. She had wished for so long to be able to meet her husband's elegant sister, and the surprise of seeing her in her own home so unexpectedly overwhelmed her. She flung herself into her sister-in-law's embrace, shocking Margaret not a little. She kissed her cheeks in greeting, bubbling with pure joy, but for a moment Margaret could not understand her words.

Margaret did not know precisely how to respond to such overpowering warmth- it was not the way of a properly bred English lady to embrace a near stranger in such a casual manner. She knew from what Frederick had told her before that it was perfectly customary in his new home for family and friends to greet each other with utter familiarity, but Margaret was not yet comfortable behaving with such abandon.

When Dolores finally drew back, she caught her breath, her little hand fluttering excitedly over her breast. "M-Miss M-Margaret Hale," she stammered nervously, her eyes shifting questioningly to her husband to be certain she was employing the proper address. "We are... happy! So happy you are come here! We make you welcome!" She spoke a little haltingly, blushing furiously, but her radiant smile remained undiminished.

Frederick was still grinning indulgently, but he dipped his head lower to his wife's ear. "*Mi amor*, Margaret is recently married. This is her husband, Mr Thornton. By happy coincidence, he is the Englishman I told you I was waiting to meet."

Dolores' flashing eyes widened still more if that were indeed possible. With joyous enthusiasm, she welcomed John as a brother, kissing him on the cheeks too. He could have fainted of mortification on the spot. Until two days ago, the only woman to ever touch him with any degree of familiarity had been his mother with her stiff affections. Margaret's caresses were an entirely different matter altogether. He had no idea how to process the ebullient greetings of his new sister-in-law.

Margaret stifled a laugh as she watched his extreme discomposure. She could not be certain, but she thought she detected a thin line of sweat forming upon his brow. Stepping back from Frederick's wife as politely as he could, he instinctively sought Margaret's hand. He clutched it as if she were a lifeline to all that was proper and decent.

Margaret smiled privately to herself, and, looking up, caught a similar expression upon her brother's face. Frederick was used to the open, hospitable ways of his adopted country, but it was clear that John had a deal of adapting to do. Margaret did not wish to embarrass John any further, though she was not certain that Frederick would not relish such a chance.

"Fred," she asked with sudden inspiration, "what do you mean that John is the man you wished to meet?"

He cocked his head. "You did not tell her, Thornton? Why, certainly you must have known of it, Margaret. He came to speak to me about the cotton. Thornton, if Margaret did not make that connection for you, how did you know who I was?"

John cleared his throat uncomfortably. "There is a rather strong family resemblance. You look- you both look- a deal like your father." His gaze wandered to Margaret's, holding hers for a moment in an eloquent silence. "Also," he added softly, "I doubt you will remember, but we saw each other from a distance once."

"Ah, yes, the train station. I told Margaret at the time that you looked to be a very unpleasant chap. Sorry about that, old man. In her defense, she disagreed with me. Still, I am surprised to hear that you would remember me from such a fleeting glance. She must have told you of me long ago then?" He frowned, not entirely pleased at the prospect that Margaret might have revealed his visit to England to others, breaking her long-ago promise to conceal his presence.

"No," Thornton interpreted his thoughts perfectly and sought to clear Margaret of any blame. "She did not tell me of you until very recently. I still did not know you and Mr Marshall were one and the same until you introduced yourself on the dock."

"I see. Yes, Margaret, you had never known that. You and our family have always written to me under the name of Dickenson, but Marshall is the name I have long used for business correspondence. It always reminded me of what awaited at home, should I ever lose my resolve and try to return to England. Although," he reached for Dolores' hand and gave it a gentle kiss, "I no longer need such a reminder. My heart now belongs in Cádiz."

Frederick returned his gaze to his sister's face, then quickly looked back down to his wife's little hand. His baby sister and her new husband were no longer paying him any heed, lost as they were in each other's eyes. He confirmed his prior suspicion that he had unraveled a part of the mystery of their sudden marriage. There was nothing sudden about the affection they shared.

Thomas Bell's eyes fluttered open from his morning drowse when the latch of his door began to click. Through his bleared vision, he observed his godson, approaching with a gentle smile as always. Then, from behind him... "Margaret," he breathed in relief.

His old friend's daughter knelt at his side, wrapping her cool fingers over his fevered hand. "Mr Bell, I have come. Oh, you are so warm!" Her sweet features were inscribed with concern and sorrow.

"There, there, my dear girl," he patted her hand with his other. "You are come, it is very good of you. I was hoping," he paused to catch his breath, "for this gift. To see you at the last... very good of you, my girl."

"Mr Bell," her voice trembled, "please do not speak so! You will be well! You are looking so much better than... than I feared!" A tear began to waver upon her cheek as her tones failed to a whisper.

A hand dropped over her shoulder, squeezing and consoling. She closed her eyes and rocked her head toward it, grateful for the comfort it offered. Bell's gaze followed the hand up to identify its owner. "Thornton!"

"Mr Bell," the younger man smiled kindly, his eyes shining with compassion and friendship.

Bell's shrewd gaze returned to Thornton's hand, still resting on Margaret's shoulder, then back to his face. "By thunder," he wheezed, "it is about time. Well done, my boy." He let his head fall upon his pillow, his fingers slackening contentedly in Margaret's grasp. "Very well done."

Frederick and John left Margaret with her dear Mr Bell and retreated to the study to begin discussing their business interests. Frederick poured them both a drink, early as it was yet in the day. John, reasoning that the routines of the day flowed differently in this nearly tropical clime, made no objection to sharing a morning drink with his new brother.

"My father-in-law is away at present," Frederick explained apologetically, taking his seat. "Normally he would take part in our discussion, but we are hoping for his return by this afternoon, or tomorrow at the latest. He had some affairs to tend at the court in Madrid."

John was surprised. "He must be very well connected indeed!"

Frederick shrugged, swirling his drink. "He is, but not so highly as you might be led to believe. He is only an auxiliary to the present affairs. I believe that the Queen has been quarreling with Pierce over Cuba yet again. Barbour has interests in Cuba and likes to keep close tabs on whatever mischief Isabella might be up to." He shook his head in exasperation. "I love my new home, but sometimes I could wish for a good, sensible woman on the throne! It seems England got her first."

John raised his glass. "God save the Queen," he toasted.

"Both of them," Frederick agreed. "Now, then, down to it." He drew some papers from his desk, shuffling them a moment until he had found the proper pages. "Here it is. This is the proposal that your Mr Dalton should have shown you. Does everything look the same?"

John took the papers and began to scan them carefully. After a few minutes, he nodded in agreement. "It does. I am curious, though; why not simply sell the raw cotton yourself? There are plenty of buyers, more now than ever. Why become involved in the finished product?"

"I can see why you would ask, but it's really simple enough. Barbour already has an established clientele with his shipping interests. His trade routes are well-tested and profitable, and he does not wish to take on the marketing of a raw material to an entirely different clientele right now. His buyers are typically higher-end merchants in the larger cities who cater to the wealthiest customers. Obviously, none of them have an interest in raw cotton, but there is a growing interest in cotton textiles.

"With all the unrest in the Americas, cotton prices are only going to go up for a time. That instability affects both raw materials and finished products, so Barbour stands to profit either way. However, he is hoping to consistently supply a product which others cannot. His clients are looking for finer weaves, higher grade materials, and as yet there are few mills which can handle large orders of such quality. That, my friend, is where you come in."

"Hmm." John stroked his chin thoughtfully. "That is an interesting idea. I wonder, though, that if his trade routes are already profitable why he would purchase the interest in the plantation at all. What is his long-range plan?"

"Oh, actually he did not purchase it. Bell did, a few months ago via correspondence. He wrote me at the time asking me to market the cotton, as I am so much closer- and I suspect he had other motives as well. We agreed to it, but only on the condition that it not disrupt our regular flow of commerce."

John started in surprise. "Mr Bell? I suppose that would explain what he would be doing here!"

"Yes. He came here to settle the final details of that transaction, and through the same agent he was conducting some other business as well- I still don't know all the details. He refused to tell me much, only that he was hoping to see Margaret and that I would learn more soon enough."

John narrowed his eyes. "He really expected her to come, did he not? I could almost be angry with him for knowing her so well, putting her in such danger."

Frederick snorted. "Don't underestimate that old geezer. I half wondered when we saw him a bit ago if he did not somehow anticipate you would be on her ship!" He shook his head, chuckling. "That would be impossible, I know, but he certainly did not seem one bit surprised to see you together!"

John pursed his lips and sighed nostalgically. "He always used to like to rile things up. Hale, I had the very greatest respect for your father. We enjoyed many splendid discussions round the fire. I have never known a finer man. Our conversations took on an unusual spirit, however, when Bell was present. I used to marvel at it- he used to irritate me a great deal. He's a clever fellow, always calculating and pulling his old tricks. I wonder...."

Frederick leaned closer. "I don't. I know exactly what Bell is like, and now that I have seen you with Margaret, I can imagine what he saw. She's a tough one, is my sister, and I never thought I would see her change her opinions so drastically, but she obviously did. He was challenging *her*, not you."

"Oh, he challenged me as well," he mused, his eyes fixed on some distant point. "Hale," he changed the subject abruptly, "before we get back to business, there is something more pressing I must attend to. Would you mind suspending our discussion an hour or two?"

Frederick shrugged agreeably, and John began to rise. Suddenly he paused. "I would be most grateful for your assistance if you can render it. I do not know the local shops, nor do I speak Spanish."

Frederick grinned, a mischievous light making his eyes sparkle very like his sister's. "I'm right behind you."

Twenty-Four

HENRY LENNOX HAD BEEN in his office already two hours this morning, but he had really accomplished nothing. He stared blankly at the pile of documents before him- wills, mostly, all awaiting his perusal before they could receive the legal stamp of approval. It was simple enough, for one as experienced as he had become, but his mind would not apply itself to the task.

He worried for Margaret. He had flipped through his calendar and checked with the shipping yards and knew that her ship was scheduled to arrive in Cádiz today. Possibly it was already in port. *If* her passage had been a smooth one, and *if* she had been able to travel in safety and protection, she ought to be securely ensconced in her brother's home by nightfall, at the very latest.

He frowned. *If* she knew how to contact her brother in the country. A deep sigh racked him. There were far too many unknowns, and there was simply nothing he could do about it.

He rubbed his eyes and resolved to return to his task. He had made one editorial mark on the first paper when a sharp rap came at his office door. Somewhat grateful for the interruption, he sprang up and answered it.

"Captain Harper!" He stood aside to allow the grizzled sea captain entry. "It is good of you to call. I did not know you had returned to port yet."

"Aye, lad, jest last evening. Me wife said ye'd left me a note, and well do I remember yer fine spirits." The old salt's eyes twinkled in good humour.

Henry showed the man to a seat and procured the requested drink. "I am very glad you came to see me. I have some questions, and I was hoping you might help me to find the answers."

"Aye, I got yer letter." Harper drew Henry's note out of his breast pocket, and a second sheaf of paper scrawled in his own curious hand. "Ye were trying to find out about the *Esperanza,* were ye not, lad?"

"Yes, do you know the captain at all?"

"Aye, a good man, Carter. We served together aboard the *Russell* as fancy young lieutenants, would ye believe. Done well for 'isself, since leavin' the navy, 'e 'as. Fine ship, good routes."

Henry leaned intently forward. "Is he an honourable man, do you think? Would he see to the protection of a lady, would you suppose?"

Harper's gaze sharpened craftily. "Aye," he answered slowly. "'E's a married man, and 'e 'as a pair of daughters 'isself. I s'pect 'e would. 'E's as gen'l'manly as e'er I saw."

Henry blew out a huff of profound relief. His expression was not lost on the old sea dog. Harper pressed the second paper he had drawn from his pocket down on the desk, sliding it across to him. "That there," he pointed, "be a copy of the final passenger manifest. These be the folk what act'lly boarded, per the vessel, not just them as paid the ticket a' the office."

Henry glanced up in grateful surprise. Here at least would be confirmation that Margaret had made it safely aboard. He himself had tried quietly to obtain such a list from the booking office, but the agents had been rather tight-lipped. He could, perhaps, have pursued a legal avenue to gain possession of the manifest, but he had feared raising too much interest in the subject.

His eyes scanned the list once, twice, and did not find her name. His breath quickened in alarm. Forcing himself to remain calm, he reasoned that she may perhaps have traveled under a different name. Margaret was no fool and would not willingly lead anyone to her brother. He began to search specifically for the names of women traveling alone. He found only one. "Melanie Carter," he murmured softly.

"Oh, aye, the cap'n's daughter. A spry thing, that one," Harper chuckled. "Know'd her as a wee lass, I did. Been two or three year since I saw 'er. S'pect she'd be mighty 'andsome by now."

Henry wilted in despair. So, the young woman was not Margaret. Where was she?

"One other thing, though I canna' say if it be of interest to ye. I know a fish house on the wharf. Old Madge's place," the captain smiled fondly. "I stop in for my pot o' stew sometimes. She told me some lady 'ad been 'urt on the docks. One o' the porters, she says, 'e fell on 'er and 'urt 'er arm, then she was brought up to Madge's. The leech from the *Esperanza* was called to tend to 'er."

Henry straightened. "Injured? Was she taken to a hospital, then?" Nervous fear made him tremble. Could Margaret have been lying, injured and unknown, in some hospital all these days? How serious was the injury?

"Just a mite 'o shoulder in'ury. She din'na know where the lady went. The gentleman wha' brought 'er in, 'e paid for Madge's trouble, but she said the lady walked to'rd the ship with the men, last she saw."

Henry sagged again. If the woman had been Margaret, there would not have been any gentleman with her. It sounded as though this woman had boarded the ship anyway, and therefore could not have been Margaret. Where might she be?

Harper tossed back the last of his drink and began to rise. "Lennox," he stuck out his weathered hand, "yer ale is as fine as I remember."

Doing his best to present a grateful reply to his guest, Henry took the captain's hand and murmured his thanks. Harper still read his mournful expression through his bold front.

"I be on leave the next fortnight. Ye know where to find me." The captain's tanned skin crinkled around sun-bleached eyes as he offered a compassionate smile.

Henry nodded his acknowledgement. "May I keep this manifest?"

"Aye, lad. I've no use for it. G'day to ye."

"Good day, Captain."

After seeing the captain out, Henry dropped heavily back into his desk chair. He carefully searched the manifest again and again, hoping desperately for some clue. Families, couples, single men.... His eyes stopped abruptly and hovered over the last entry. *John Thornton, Milton; and sister Miss Thornton; 1 First Class Cabin, 1 steerage berth.*

Henry tapped his fingers in deep contemplation. He had never been to Milton, but he seemed to remember something mentioned about a Mr Thornton. Mr Bell had mentioned his name, he thought. Ah yes, that was it. A friend of old Mr Hale's, and also Mr Bell's tenant. One of Milton's most well-known manufacturers.

Henry narrowed his eyes as he tried to remember every detail. Had not that Watson fellow married Thornton's sister? The news of Watson's successful rail speculation had created ripples that none in London could have missed, particularly not an attorney who specialized in estates and financial transactions.

Henry jumped to his feet and began to pace. Odd, wasn't it, that Thornton's sister should be traveling with him? Why would she not have remained home with her husband?

A quick glance again at the manifest confirmed that Watson was not listed among the passengers. Perhaps there was a second sister.

Still, what would Thornton be doing traveling to Cádiz? Surely, he too would not have run off to see Mr Bell, even though he was his landlord. There would be no call for such a trip- as he recalled from Bell's comments, the two men were not very close. Henry chewed his lip, utterly confounded. Nothing made any sense.

The one thing Henry did know was that he needed to dig more deeply. Though Margaret's recent behavior had baffled and scandalized his previous notions of her, he had to be sure that she was safe somehow. If she had not made it aboard the ship, where the devil could she be?

He racked his brain for options. He could speak with Maxwell, but certainly not Edith, not yet. He could not share his concerns with his sister-in-law until he had more information, and he was afraid Maxwell would not be able to conceal his troubles from his wife.

Bell had agents in town, surely, but he wasn't sure how that would help. He felt his answer yet lay along the wharfs somewhere. Could she have accidentally boarded the wrong ship? He would be surprised if she had made such a mistake. Those docks could be a confusing place, but Margaret was a clever woman.

Perhaps, he mused, she had recognized Thornton boarding the very ship she intended to take and had decided not to board herself. Perhaps she chose instead to sail indirectly via France, to conceal her travels from anyone who might remember her or make a connection to Frederick Hale.

Scowling in frustration, he sloppily folded the paper, stuffing it into his jacket pocket. He could not focus on his work while his mind roiled with such doubts and worries. He had to do *something*. Snatching his hat, he turned out of his office door and marched down the street toward the harbor.

John pinched the exquisite gold band between his fingers and held it up for inspection. A single diamond adorned the center, encircled by small, bright amethysts. The gems caught the light most strikingly. Fine white gold filigree formed an intricate bed for the jewels. The uniquely crafted ring was at once vibrant and delicate, much like the woman he intended to give it to.

The jeweler, a short, balding fellow, jabbered bewilderingly to Frederick as he pitched the sale. John could not begin to follow the lilt and drawl of the man's speech, but Frederick simply nodded and translated, naming the jeweler's price.

John bobbed his head quickly in agreement. "Yes, that will do."

"Oh, Thornton! You disappoint me. You truly do not understand how to haggle in these markets. You must offer a lower price!"

He tore his eyes off the lovely piece of jewelry and his thoughts from the even lovelier woman who would wear it. "I must?"

"Of course! That is how these fellows rake the tourists over the coals. They wait for poor, smitten men to walk in here and pay any figure to please their ladies. I had thought *you* more sensible than that."

"Oh. Well, then, offer him something lower for me."

"Hmmf." Frederick groused. "We ought to leave right now. You'll never get a better deal from him after he's seen your face. Besotted, that's what you are."

John grinned with pleasure. "Yes, and what of it? This is Margaret's ring, and I do not intend to leave without it."

Frederick sighed and returned to the proprietor of the jewelry shop. Already the man's face was gloating in silent glee at his conquest. Frederick did manage to talk him down a precious little, but not anywhere close to what he would have considered a fair price. Thornton paid the money without complaint and waited for the ring to be boxed up.

As they turned out of the store, Frederick grumbled in mock disdain. "And here I always heard you were something of a skinflint. 'Keen businessman,' Mr Bell said, 'never wastes a penny,' 'puts everything to good use!' Remind me never to allow you to negotiate on my behalf!"

John drew a long breath in pure satisfaction, patting his bulging pocket. "Not when it comes to Margaret. She is my very heart."

Frederick chuckled in sympathy. "I know what you mean."

They passed a few more shops, then a window display of some chiffon confection caught John's eye. He halted abruptly, almost tripping Frederick who was half a pace behind him. "Margaret ought to have something other than black," he thought aloud.

Frederick grunted. "She does. Our Aunt Shaw would have seen to that. Like as not, she has an entire closet full back in London. The question is rather if she would *wear* anything else."

John gazed up at the little dress shop's swinging signboard, as though he could read it. "Margaret has had a hard go of it, Hale," he murmured gently. "More so, I think, than you can know."

Frederick closed his eyes and sighed. "I am sure she has. You would probably not have known it, but it was Margaret who was the strong one when Mother passed on. Father and I- we were lost. Margaret comforted me a great deal, when it was I who had come to lend strength to her."

John turned back to Frederick, his face unreadable. "I knew it," he replied, in a voice almost too low to hear. "She has borne much, and all too often alone. Perhaps now I can persuade her to put the grief behind her for good."

Frederick shrugged in defeat. "You are right of course. I, too, would be glad to see her put the mourning aside- at least... for a short while. I doubt she will though, Father has only been gone a few months." He peered over John's shoulder with distaste at the shop beyond. "Still, I would be grateful to you for any gladness you could bring her. I give you fair warning though; you are marching into the lion's den."

John firmed his mouth in desperate resolve. "It is mine to care for her now, and a bride ought to have something cheerful and fine. This is, as it turns out, our wedding trip, is it not?"

Frederick grimaced as though the thought of entering the bastion of femininity brought him actual physical pain. "It is that. You are either braver than I, or more foolhardy. Lead on!"

The door jingled as they walked into the little dress shop. They were, of course, the only men present, but a pair of ladies with their backs turned appeared to be dressed as English women. John felt reassured that the Spanish shop might have on hand such attire as Margaret would feel comfortable wearing.

Just then, one of the women turned and he recognized Melanie Carter. "Mr Thornton!" she greeted him with enthusiasm. "I am so happy we could run into you!" She directed her bright eyes to Frederick with open curiosity.

Mrs Carter had now turned as well and greeted him with genuine friendliness. "Mr Thornton," she curtseyed. "How is your dear Margaret this morning? I am afraid we missed her as she left the ship. My husband had only a short window of time in which to see us to town, and we had to take it, you see. He will be back for us shortly; we are set to depart soon."

He returned her courtesy. "Margaret is very well, thank you Mrs Carter. She is with her godfather now; she was most eager to see him."

"Ah, I am glad, the poor lass! She was so worried she would not be in time. Has the gentleman any chance of recovery?"

John looked toward his brother-in-law. Frederick could answer the question more faithfully and accurately than he. Frederick shook his head discretely.

"Oh, I am sorry to hear that," the woman clucked sorrowfully. She glanced expectantly back to Thornton.

He jumped. "Forgive me, please! This is Mr Marshall, an associate of Mr Bell's, and my own as well. May I present Mrs Carter and her daughter Melanie? We made their acquaintance on the journey."

"Delighted, ladies," Frederick bowed with a flourish.

Melanie beamed charmingly and offered a curtsey. "Mr Thornton, are you here looking for something for Margaret?" she queried with a knowing smile.

"Well, as a matter of fact... yes, I am. Perhaps you might advise me, since you are here. Would you be willing?"

Melanie hopped girlishly and clapped her hands in delight. "Certainly! I even know her size. Leave everything to me, Mr Thornton!"

It was with very little trepidation that he gave Melanie a roll of bills and then escaped safely outside the shop with Frederick. He trusted Melanie's judgement, as she was a well-dressed and respectable-looking young woman herself, and her mother would offer wise counsel. Besides, what did he know of a lady's attire? Nothing! Nothing... yet! He struggled to contain the ridiculous smile which threatened to turn his face lopsided.

After they had been waiting some while, they spotted Carter making his way toward them on the walkway. Frederick narrowed his eyes, looking more closely. "Excuse me, Thornton, but I believe I should make myself scarce for a few moments." Just in time to avoid the captain's notice, Frederick dipped his hat lower over his face and disappeared around a corner.

"Why, Mr Thornton!" boomed the captain jovially as he approached. "A fine thing to run into you just now. How are you and your lady finding Spain?" He pumped John's hand cheerfully, all of the prior day's events apparently forgotten.

"Quite well, Captain," he replied. "She is with her godfather at present, and your good wife and daughter agreed to help me do a little shopping for her."

"Capital! A good-hearted girl, my Melanie," he grinned proudly. "She thinks very highly of your wife. I do hope you will forgive me for all but calling you a scoundrel yesterday."

John shook his head. "I deserved it. You were perfectly within your rights. I do not complain about the end result- I have wished to marry her for longer than you can know," he finished with a wistful little smile.

"Hmm. Well, you are a good man, Thornton, and true to your word. I'm glad the lass will be taken care of. Ho! There you are, my girl!" the captain greeted his daughter as the door of the shop jingled open.

"Hello, Papa!" Melanie chirped. Her arms were laden with parcels and bags and she turned to John to pass off her burden. "There are two new gowns, Mr Thornton, as well as traveling suit and a few... well, a few other necessities. Oh, and here! This is a hat that I had purchased this morning, but I truly have so many, and as Mamma says, not even room in my cabin for more! Margaret really only brought that drab thing, she could do with something more jolly."

"I do not know how to thank you," he replied with heartfelt earnestness. "All of you," he extended his gratitude to the entire family. "If ever you should find your way to Milton, I wish for you to please call upon us! Margaret would like it very much, as would I."

"Aye, we shall do that," Mrs Carter agreed. "I would be most glad to see the lass again. You'll give her our love, will you not?"

"Of course. Thank you Mrs Carter, Miss Carter. Captain," he offered his hand once more, "It has been a pleasure. I hope our paths may cross again someday."

Twenty-Five

MARGARET LOOKED UP FROM her reading when Mr Bell's breath began to rattle in his throat. Concerned, she leaned nearer, but determined he had only drifted to sleep. Gently she laid aside *The Taming of the Shrew*, careful not to make a sound that might disturb him. He was no longer in the mood to chuckle over Petruchio's machinations.

She stretched in her hard wooden seat and glanced at the clock on the mantelpiece. She had been reading for over two hours! With great caution, she began to shift her weight out of the creaky chair and to her feet. Tiptoeing slowly to the door, she at last let out a long breath when it clicked silently behind her.

Margaret looked up and down the hallway outside Mr Bell's room. She heard voices from the sitting room where she had first met Dolores and decided to follow the sound. She felt somewhat awkward interrupting, particularly without Frederick present. She need not have felt any concern, she discovered. Dolores practically glowed with happiness when she entered the room.

"How is Señor Bell?" she asked in her soft lisping tones.

Margaret frowned dubiously. "He is resting for now. Has he shown any improvement at all since he has been here?"

Dolores bit her plump little lips. "No, he... how do you say... *peor*... worse, yes? He puffs up," she gestured to her fingers and her face, attempting to demonstrate the swelling in Mr Bell's extremities.

Margaret sighed sadly. "Yes, I know. I spoke briefly with the ship's doctor yesterday afternoon, and he suspected from what Frederick said in his letter that might be the case. There seems very little that can be done."

"Si," Dolores frowned. "The doctor, he use... how do you say... *dedalara*... Dig... Diji...."

"Digitalis?" Margaret finished. Dolores nodded in confirmation. "Yes, that is what Dr. Grayson said ought to be used. And he is not responding well, you said?" She shook her head sorrowfully. "Poor Mr Bell!"

Dolores patted her shoulder kindly. "He is very happy you came, no?"

Margaret returned a trembling smile. "Yes, I do believe he is. So am I! I am so glad to meet you finally!"

Dolores took Margaret's hand firmly. "You are not yet *refrescada.* I show you your room?"

Margaret agreed, realizing how badly she needed such refreshment. It had been long hours since she had had a moment to herself, and she was stifling in the growing heat of the day.

She willingly followed as Dolores slowly led her up a narrow staircase and to an upstairs room. The room was fresh and airy, with a light but elegant décor. A pair of shuttered doors were fastened open, leading to a shaded portico of stucco and red tile. The walls of the little patio were festooned with fragrant Mediterranean flora of every kind she could imagine. Margaret gasped in rapt appreciation. "It is beautiful!"

Dolores blushed with pride. "This was my room before I marry."

Margaret turned and took her sister-in-law's hand. "Thank you, Dolores! You have made me feel so welcome in your home."

"You and Señor Thornton will be comfortable here, si?"

Margaret's heart fluttered in her throat. In a rush of thrill mingled with panic, she caught her breath. From now on she would belong to him, sharing even the most private of moments in their mutual bedchamber. Another glance about the room confirmed that both her trunk and his suitcase had been delivered and placed near a little dressing alcove. Her pulse began to thud erratically. She loved John and was proud to be his wife, but the reality of her new circumstances hit her like a brick. She felt so ill prepared!

"Margarita?" Dolores' voice was hesitant as she interrupted her thoughts.

She jerked her attention back to Dolores and noted the concern written on the young woman's face.

Dolores studied her wordlessly for a moment, her intelligent dark eyes casting a sense of calm to her nervous sister. "You are... very recent married, si?"

Margaret nodded. "Only yesterday," she answered breathlessly.

Dolores smothered a bright grin in sudden insight. "You are not... How do you say... fear? Of your husband?"

"No!" Margaret jumped a little, then swallowed. "No," she amended her response apologetically. "I could never be afraid of John."

"Good," the little woman bobbed her head in satisfaction. "He will treat you very kind. He is good man?"

"The very best." Margaret released a pent-up breath, beginning to relax again.

Dolores took her hand again with a reassuring smile. She leaned near to Margaret's ear with a conspiratorial whisper. "You must trust. Everything is... very nice."

Margaret's face began to flame, but she was secretly grateful for the other woman's reassurances. "Thank you," she stammered.

Dolores gave her hand a last comforting squeeze. "Do you need help with...." She gestured toward her own shoulder, pantomiming Margaret's sling.

"Oh, I... no, I think not for now, thank you. I will only be a few moments. Will you be returning downstairs?"

She nodded cheerfully. "Mamá and I sew clothes for the baby. Is it you would wish to help?"

"I would very much," Margaret smiled. "Thank you, Dolores, I will be down shortly."

HANNAH THORNTON PUSHED HER needle again and again through the dark cloth, tying off a final knot. *There*. That was the very last of her mending. She looked about herself at the tidy little stacks of various items. She had scrounged them from all parts of the house. Towels, stockings, linens of all sizes, every scrap of fabric she could find that could in any way be imagined worn.

In a stately fashion, she gathered each little bundle and put it away herself, personally ascertaining that all was in order. She felt a little swell of satisfaction. Her home was well in hand, with nothing at all possibly wanting her attention. *Nothing*. She sighed.

Her eyes found the clock, slowly ticking the hours away. John ought to be in Cádiz by now, she realized hopefully. It had been about long enough to accomplish the passage. Fleetingly she wished for the reassurance of a telegram, but such a message sent from so far through so many international relays would be outrageously dear and might likely not even arrive. John had offered to try to send word anyway, but she would not hear of it.

Without realizing it, she had begun to pace her dining room. She glanced again at the clock. The whistle would be sounding for the dinner break in half an hour. Her thoughts suddenly turned to the young wisp of a girl who would be scurrying madly about her soup kitchen in the yard, making the last of the meal preparations.

Hannah had wandered by again on the previous evening, and once again that curious child Johnny Boucher had arrested her attention. He had smilingly charmed her into reading with him once more. Last night it had been a rather new book, and a questionable one in Mrs Thornton's eyes. The schoolmaster was a young man and had been unable to satisfy the voracious appetite of the precocious reader. He had sent Johnny home with a copy of *Moby Dick* from his meagre personal collection.

She had eyed the book dubiously, but when she saw the story come to life in his sterling eyes, she withheld whatever judgement she might once have brandished. He reminded her so much of John at that age! To be sure, they looked nothing alike, but this young boy shared her son's zest for knowledge and his indomitable will to better himself.

Hannah had spent a bitter evening after that. How many times had she scoffed at her adult son's longing to return to the classics of his school days? He had been cruelly robbed of the opportunity freely given to so many other boys, many of whom never even appreciated such a gift.

She never thought he regretted his loss overmuch until she saw him leap at the chance to reclaim that education. He had been master of his life, wanting nothing of material consequence. He certainly did not need the training to succeed in some craft. Yet he pled for her understanding, her blessing even.

In his eyes, the pursuit of higher learning had not been time wasted from his business concerns, but a means of sculpting himself into a better man. She had begun to understand why her son would be supporting and encouraging the Boucher children in school. They, too, deserved a shot at raising themselves to be better than their father.

With little thought, Hannah draped her lace shawl over her shoulders and tied her bonnet in place. She proceeded with her usual dignified survey of the yard, once again finding herself at the little kitchen.

A stifled blubbering sound emanated from the closed doorway. Curiously, she pushed the latched door aside. Mary Higgins was crouched on the floor, trying to soothe the sobbing Johnny. She stood back a pace, wondering what could have upset the child so, and what he was doing here at this time of day.

Mary whirled about at the creak of the door hinge, beholding the Mistress' stern expression. "Oh, Missus!" Mary stood, brushing her skirts and apron into order, and dropping a quick curtsey. Johnny turned sullenly to face her as well, head hanging. A fat tear glistened yet from its trail down his dusty cheek.

Mrs Thornton pursed her lips expectantly. She may have been willing to overlook a well-mannered child's presence after hours, when there was no risk of accident, but this! This was clearly outside the bounds of her permissibility. She crossed her hands before her, waiting for an explanation.

"'E's only jest come i', Missus...." Mary chewed her lips nervously. This, she was quite certain, meant the end of her employment at Marlborough Mills. "'E 'ad a day o' it, 'e 'ad," she offered lamely.

Hannah's cool gaze shifted to the sandy-haired lad, who was quickly wiping his eyes and trying to meet her look. "Tell me what happened," she demanded, though not altogether unkindly.

Mary's mouth gaped. Flummoxed, she tried to form a coherent string of words, but the Dragon still made her quake in her boots. Johnny it was who found his voice.

"He called me a- a name," the child replied, in a clear but still wavering voice. "I'm not allowed to repeat it." He stuck his little jaw out defensively, the fierce pride of flinty boyhood ashamed to be caught in grief.

Hannah arched a brow. "The master?" She felt no sympathy for a child disciplined by the schoolmaster. She had not detected rebelliousness in this particular youth, but no child could be without fault. A little harsh correction would do the boy good in the long run.

But Johnny was shaking his head. "No... Joseph Sowers. He said... About my da'...." The boy's chin dipped again in shame. He hung his head silently, then hurriedly wiped his face while it was hidden from her.

It was then that Hannah finally noticed the blotch of ink sprawling over the shoulder of the lad's nondescript chemise and the fresh muddy stains on his knees and elbows. She narrowed her eyes thoughtfully. "May I suppose you then got into a fight?" she queried sternly.

He shook his head again, his stormy eyes leaping indignantly back to hers. "No, Ma'am."

She dropped her focus to the ink blot on his shoulder, then wordlessly back to his face. The little boy shifted his feet nervously, reminding her just how very young he actually was.

"There were three of them, Ma'am," he answered softly. "Master sent me home for the day, but he said he would not punish me."

She sighed pensively. Once again, she was haunted by the image of her own brave son, splattered with mud and stoically shrugging off the insults of the neighborhood boys. The shame of the father was like a stench clinging to the son, drawing bullies like flies. John had been older than this waif, but the savage pride, the almost feral vigilance kindled within her motherly bosom that day was never forgotten.

So lost was she for a second that she fairly jumped when the dinner whistle blasted across the yard. She stared thoughtfully again at the child. The boy had bewitched her, beyond any doubt. Ought she allow it to continue?

Mary blanched in near panic. She looked down to the child at her feet, then spun helplessly toward her stew kettle. Her little hands flew as she dragged a towering stack of plates, bit by bit, from her pantry to the serving board. Whirling about again, she found The Dragon still standing in the doorway; her black gown blotting out the yard beyond, where the men would be gathering any moment.

"If... if yo' 'scuse me Missus, I mun send 'im 'ome. I know 'e canna' be 'ere." She took a step toward the boy to give strict instructions for the walk home, one he was normally forbidden to take on his own.

"That," Mrs Thornton interrupted, "will not be necessary." She faced the child again, and in a gentle tone she had not used in many long years, addressed him. "You may come to my house for the remainder of the afternoon, Master Boucher. Miss Higgins may see you home after she has finished her duties."

Johnny Boucher's tears faded, forgotten in an instant. With an enormous grin, displaying a devilish little gap where his front teeth ought to have been, he reached a hand for his new ally. Somewhat awkwardly, Hannah received the little hand and managed an expression which, if not precisely a smile, might accidentally have been taken for one. She offered a stately nod to the flabbergasted young cook, and together the widow and the orphan left the little soup kitchen.

Twenty-Six

Margaret dropped her valise on a dressing table and began a one-handed search through its contents. In a moment, she found what she had sought: a small bundle wrapped in a rosy-hued silken cloth. She clutched it tightly and brought it to her lips, inhaling her mother's dear scent.

Slowly she treaded to a low-backed seat, placed before a dainty vanity. She stared a moment at the precious bundle, afraid at first to open it. Stroking the silken cloth, she remembered that last summer she had come home to Helstone from London; the last year of "normal life" before the bottom of her world had fallen out.

Her father had come for her, meaning to escort her home as he always did. She had been anxious for them to take their leave as soon as possible, but he had lingered reluctantly, delaying their departure an entire day. They strolled through some of Margaret's favorite haunts; the park she frequented, the lanes leading to quieter paths outside of town, but it was on their return that her father had surprised her. He asked her to take him to the shop where Edith had her gowns made.

Mr Hale had entered the establishment with bewilderment, not even quite sure where to start. At length, he had moved softly to the saleswoman and spoken low words to her. Margaret had stood back, watching her father with some fascination. He gestured to a beautiful gown of soft green, but the woman shook her head. She tried to interest him in a brown shawl instead, but he demurred. Another dress had caught his eye, and the saleswoman again was unable to satisfy him. She directed his attention then to a case draped with fine silken handkerchiefs, trimmed with exquisite lace.

Mr Hale had stood forlornly for a moment, blankly stroking the nearest specimen. As Margaret watched, he slowly drew out his pocketbook and made his purchase. The woman wrapped it and he returned silently to Margaret, his eyes down.

He said not a word until they were almost back to her aunt's house. He had turned to face her then. "Your mother will like it, do you not think?" His voice had trembled with hope, tottering on the edge of despair.

Margaret had smiled encouragingly, clutching her father's arm. "Yes, Father, I am sure she will," she had whispered.

Her fingers smoothed the creases in the cloth, stroking the fine lace edges and tucking the corners. The tears began anew, quivering at the points of her eyes and choking her breath. *Oh, how I miss you both!*

She gritted her teeth and fought for the faintest measure of control. It had been some while since she had allowed herself a good long cry. She longed to drown her tears in John's arms, sensing the first sweetness through all the bitter. He would hold her and soothe her sorrows, helping to dull the pain she had tried for so long to blunt on her own. That tender knowledge brought a hope back to her breast. Still clutching the little bundle to her mouth, she prayed, a simple prayer from a thankful heart.

She took a long refreshing breath, lowering the precious knot she held to the vanity before her. For the first time in many months, she dared to unwrap it. She lifted each little corner slowly, training her ears on some splendid, winged creature just outside her room who sang a song of both joy and lament.

At last, she unrolled the final laced bit and two bright metal bands shone forth from their soft casing. She blinked. She had quite forgotten that she had, at the last, wrapped her father's wedding band up with her mother's. With dainty fingers, she lifted each piece fondly.

Her mother's ring must have cost her father dearly, else been some heirloom passed down from his own mother. Perhaps Frederick knew the story. It was a lovely thing, set with a single sapphire- not large, but very beautiful- and twined elegantly in gold. She held it up to the light, admiring the cerulean facets and the soft glow of the setting.

Her father had made mention, some weeks after her mother's passing, that Frederick ought to have taken the ring, but he had sadly not thought of it in time. Margaret had immediately settled with herself that, should she ever have a chance to make it so, the ring would belong to Dolores.

She replaced the sparkling band in the handkerchief and drew out the other. This one was simple and unadorned, yet thick and strong still after so many years of loving wear. Margaret smiled. Once, perhaps, she might have given this ring to Frederick as well, but now there was another man with a claim upon it.

Nicholas Higgins heaved a great sigh of relief when the dinner whistle pierced the carding room racket. He stayed to be sure that the lines were properly shut down and all of the children had safely clambered out from beneath the teeth of the massive carding machines before he moved to the door and the fresh air himself. Following the very last girl out, he tugged his cap and mopped his drenched forehead.

He scanned the clipboard he had been carrying for days now. His pencil was worn to a nub but he eked out a few last marks from the flattened point. Williams had been steadily teaching him to monitor every detail of the mill, from receiving to shipping and every fiber and scrap in between. He was learning to juggle not only the limitations of the machines and the demands of the workers, but also the necessities of the orders, the accounting of the supplies, and the perfect synchrony which kept all parts churning as a smoothly run whole.

He blew out a huff in near exasperation. From weaver to clerk- he could not quite decide how he liked the change. This was either Thornton's idea of a promotion, or some twisted sort of revenge.

He laughed a little at that lark, fancying Thornton lounging in some exotic port and smugly picturing his former union nemesis slowly unraveling back at home. *Ha!* A pretty notion, that. The idea of Thornton taking his ease was even more far-fetched than a Union boss taking on the mantle of management.

Still smiling at his little private joke, he made his steady way up the wrought iron staircase to the overseer's office. Williams was there, mumbling over a stack of fresh invoices. He looked up sharply at Higgins' entrance, then gave a casual nod of greeting. He removed his thin glasses and pinched between tired eyes.

"Sir," Higgins placed the clipboard within reach for Williams' inspection.

Williams waved dismissively. "I don't need to see it today. You've been precise to your numbers all week. If you don't mind, I've this lot, then the payroll to muddle through."

Higgins drew back his board, warmed by the off-handed compliment. "Aye, sir," he nodded.

Williams reached to the far side of his desk, grunting with the effort of flattening his ample middle and avoiding the precarious stack of invoices. "Here," he tossed a battered notebook to Higgins. "These are the rest of the week's orders. You'll need to see to it that all of those get filled. Mind, the Bath order is set to the finer weave, and the one for Liverpool must be done on the widest loom."

Higgins ran his hands over the beaten surface and opened the book somewhat reverently. Williams had just handed him a great deal more responsibility. The full force of his supervisor's confidence shook him.

Thornton may have had his own reasons for trusting him, but the same could not be said of Williams. The overseer was not the hardened Master that Thornton was, that was true, but he had made no secret in the beginning of his suspicions regarding Higgins' allegiances. Higgins had to earn every shred of Williams' grudging respect, and now here was proof that at last he had done so. Blinking and nodding wordlessly, he gave a little salute and left the overseer's office, tucking the bulging book beneath his arm.

He made it to the dinner hall as most of the crush were leaving. A few of the less useful hands had begun already to give him a wider berth, but the better ones, many of whom he had shouldered burdens with for long years, still greeted him with friendly respect. Sighing, he eased himself onto the bench between two of his fellows.

Mary came quickly with a plate for him, but as soon as she had set it down, she was clutching his sleeve. "Da!" she hissed. "'Tis Johnny!"

Nicholas set down the fork he had just raised. "Wha's that, Lass?" He turned to his daughter in confusion. Her eyes darted to the other men then she looked back to him with a subtle shake of her head.

With a groan, he lurched back to his tired feet and followed Mary to a quiet little corner by her stove. "Now wha's this a' 'bout, Lass?"

"Johnny- 'e go' picked on a' school and the Master sen' 'im 'ome."

"'E's walked alone?" Higgins set his mouth in frustration. There was little else to be done if the lad had been sent home, but he did not like it. The boy knew his way, certainly, but Higgins worried about the heavy traffic of a market day, and he would have to go all the way across town. Like as not, the boy would have his nose buried in a book rather than watching for traffic as he walked.

"No! The Dragon... er, Missus Thornton, she took 'im!"

"Yer no' makin' sense, Lass! Took 'im where? No' 'ome! She wouldna' do that. Do ye mean she *sent* 'im 'ome?"

"No, she took 'im to the big 'ouse! Wi' 'er!" Mary fairly danced with the strain of her excitement. There were rumours of Mrs Thornton's charitable acts, but by and large the woman was not renowned for her kindness.

Still, there could be no mistaking the widow's response to young Johnny Boucher. She seemed genuinely taken with the boy, and he not at all intimidated by her. Haltingly, as she still was serving the occasional dinner plate, Mary described the last couple of evenings with Johnny reading his studies aloud with Mrs Thornton. Higgins listened in baffled silence.

"Doesn'a make sense," he murmured, more to himself than to Mary. What should he do? He was due to return to his duties in fifteen minutes, there was little time. Still, the lad was his responsibility. "Mary, bundle me up a roll, girl. I mun' go for 'im."

With the fat book of orders under one arm and a meagre bite of dinner in his other hand, Higgins set off across the long yard as quickly as he could. The forbidding gray house sat at the far end, between the long warehouse entrance and the heavy wooden gates.

Hesitantly he knocked and was admitted by a skeptical maid. She appeared to know his business already- surely the presence of a grubby child in the Mistress' house would have raised some eyebrows among her staff. Doffing his sweat-stained cap, he crumpled it in his free hand as the woman- Jane, if he remembered correctly- ushered him into the ornate dining room. "Mr Higgins, Ma'am," she announced crisply, and left him to his own devices in the Mistress' presence.

Mrs Thornton raised her head curiously as he stepped falteringly into the room. Johnny, sitting beside her at the massive table, paused his reading and smiled timidly at his adoptive father. Mrs Thornton arched her eyebrow. "Mr Higgins. How nice to finally meet you," she intoned dryly.

He bobbed his head respectfully. "Aye, Madam," he stammered. "'Tis a pleasure." He swallowed, biting his lower lip, then gestured to the child. "I'll thank ye kindly, Madam, fer lookin' after me lad."

She rose serenely. "Do you not have some duties to be about, Mr Higgins?" Her eyes fell upon the familiar order book. So, John and his overseer had tapped this fellow for extra responsibilities during John's absence? She wondered briefly at the wisdom of such a decision, and at her own ignorance of it. Her son did not tell her everything these days.

Higgins was nodding, his eyes on the rich carpet. He felt suddenly ashamed of his soiled shoes. "Aye, Madam, tho' I would take the lad so ye'll na' be troubled."

"He does not trouble me. You may return for him this evening. I trust that there will be no further disturbances of the kind?" She tilted her head haughtily, casting a stern glance at the child, but Johnny was not cowed. Instead, he smiled sheepishly and nodded his head in agreement.

Higgins stood dumbfounded. His widened eyes shifted between the boy and the matron, standing in expectant dignity before him. Finally, he managed a numb, "Aye, Madam." He touched his knuckles to his forehead in salute and made his hazy way to the door. "A wonder!" he breathed. He shook his head, muttering to himself. "Th'ould Dragon 'as a' soft a 'eart as a dame!"

He showed himself out of the door of the house, still awestruck. He came to himself when the whistle blasted once more, calling the hands back to their posts. Higgins picked up his step, not wishing to betray Williams' newfound trust in him. Still, he marveled at what he had just seen. "What wi' the young Master think on tha'!" he chuckled wonderingly.

MARGARET STEPPED SOFTLY DOWN the stone staircase, her fingers trailing the cool walls. Everything here had such a different look, a new feel that she had never encountered. It felt hard, cool, permanent. There was a fresh elegance, so unlike the ornate richness of a fine English home.

At the bottom of the stairs, she decided impulsively to check on Mr Bell before following Dolores' invitation to sew. Nudging the door aside, she began to step into the room and found, to her surprised pleasure, that John was already there. Mr Bell smiled weakly at her approach.

John rose and helped her into the seat nearest Mr Bell, which had just been his, and took another himself. "I thought you would be with Frederick," she touched his hand thankfully.

"We returned a short while ago and he had another matter to attend." John smiled gently at his bride, faintly sensing a return of the old fragility to her manner. He worried a little- Margaret had been so crushed by grief, and it seemed that she was facing it yet again.

"Mr Thornton here," Bell interrupted, "was just telling me the wildest tale, Margaret. I am sure you will find it diverting as well, my dear. Married by a sea captain! Ho, ho, my girl, the stories a man makes up when the lady is not present to defend herself!" Bell gasped to catch his breath but his amused grin never wavered.

Margaret chuckled and wrapped her arm through John's, lacing his fingers with her own. "You may credit his words as the truth, Mr Bell." Her face shone adoringly up to her husband and John's usually firm features melted as he basked in her glow.

Bell gazed admiringly at the contented couple before him. "How pleased Richard would be!" he murmured. "Are you seeing this, my old friend?" he cast his eyes to the ceiling in jest. A sudden cough seized him and he choked pitifully. The young couple leapt to their feet, one on each side of him, trying to offer what comfort they could. He waved them off and, wheezing, dropped back to his pillow.

"Margaret," he gasped, "I intended to look out for you myself." He paused as she offered him a sip of water.

"You have," she answered him gently. "You have been more than good to me!"

"You do not understand. I... Oh, there you are, my lad." Bell's attention turned to Frederick, who had just entered carrying a dinner tray.

Frederick placed the tray near the bedside himself. "Your favorite soup, Mr Bell," he offered. He tilted his head to Margaret by way of explanation, "This recipe is special to Dolores' family, and Mr Bell finds it agrees with his palate."

Bell groused a little, putting on a show for the benefit of his visitors. "They eat far too much fish here. Dreadful stuff and covered in horrid spices to hide the ghastly flavor. Morbid on the stomach! Give me a plain poultry any day." He winked at Frederick, who was merely shaking his head and laughing. "Here is your tea, sir," he rotated a cup within the old man's reach.

Mr Bell grunted and began to lift his spoon. Another coughing fit shook him, leaving him visibly weakened when it had passed. Margaret drew near with a napkin to offer whatever help she could. John, who was still on his opposite side, braced an arm behind Bell's pillow to help prop him up, and Margaret began gently to spoon the soup for him.

"There, that's enough," he muttered hoarsely after only a few bites. "Go on now, you must eat yourselves. Let an old man alone to rest." He emphasized his remarks by drooping back on his pillow and closing his eyes.

Margaret looked helplessly to Frederick, who shrugged sympathetically, but rose to go. Once outside, he shut the door softly. “He will sleep for hours now. Come, Dolores has the meal waiting.”

Twenty-Seven

JOHN AND MARGARET HAD rarely seen such a feast as they were presented for the midday meal. Various courses of fish, shrimp, soups, meat cutlets, and casseroles were rolled out, one after another. Mr Bell had been right about the liberal use of the spices. Margaret's mouth flamed, causing her to gulp the water, until Frederick hinted subtly that she might use the back of her tongue to savour the feast.

With each successive course, both the English guests declared themselves well satisfied, but Dolores' mother was insistent. Margaret could not help a small laugh as the little woman railed at them in Spanish for their poor appetites. They could not understand most of her words, but her militant hospitality would brook no arguments.

Finally, the dessert course was placed before them. They both sighed in relief; not only was the dessert a highly familiar and soothing ice cream dish, but it also signaled the end of the bountiful repast. Dolores' mother nodded in satisfaction that her guests seemed well pleased with the final course. She left them shortly after the meal was ended, allowing the conversation to flow exclusively in English.

Frederick leaned back from the table, smiling tenderly at his wife. Margaret watched them with growing satisfaction, pleased that her beloved brother had found someone to whom he could give his heart. "Oh, Dolores," she suddenly remembered her gift, secreted in a little pocket of her gown. Withdrawing it, she rose and brought it to the young woman's side. "My father wanted you to have this."

Dolores smiled and nodded gratefully, taking the small silken package with reverent care. "Oh!" she exclaimed as she unwrapped it. She plucked the sapphire ring from its nest, her face reflecting awe and gratitude. Her eyes flashed with uncertainty to Margaret's, then to her husband's.

Frederick leaned near and took the ring from her fingers with a tremulous smile. "Mother's ring," he murmured in awe. "But Margaret, it ought to go to you!"

She shook her head resolutely, unknowingly triggering a sly grin from her own husband. "No, Father and I decided long ago- it should be yours. Do you know anything about where Father got it?"

"Grandmother Hale's, I believe, but I was never certain. She passed on before I was born, you know. Mother never spoke of her."

"Yes, I thought that," Margaret replied, a little sadly. It was a shame that an entire heritage was forgotten with the passing of a single generation. Her eyes rose to John's, taking heart from his warm gaze. They would begin to forge their own heritage, she decided.

Frederick took his wife's hand and placed the ring on her fourth finger, nestling it close to the plain gold band she already wore. Kissing it, he looked back to his sister. "Thank you, Margaret. This means a great deal to me- to us."

Margaret nodded, her eyes unconsciously falling back to the silken cloth with a wistfulness she did not intend to make obvious. She began to retreat to her seat when her sister-in-law's soft hand froze her. "This is yours, Margarita," she offered, gently placing the handkerchief back in her possession. Margaret blinked in silent gratitude and smiled her genuine thanks.

Frederick murmured something in a low voice to his wife, receiving a quiet nod in reply. He rose, helping his wife also to her feet, then casting a significant glance across the table to his new brother-in-law. "We'll retire for a while. Thornton, shall we resume our discussion at half past three?"

John, rising himself, acknowledged the plan with a sage nod of his head. He claimed Margaret's hand. "Half past three. I thank you, Madam, for your hospitality," he bowed toward Dolores. With an invisible caress to her fingers, he steered Margaret out of the dining room and led her toward the stairs.

"I trust you can be my guide from here," he murmured once they were alone, approaching the stone staircase.

She fixed him with an impish gaze to quelch the flutterings through her being. "Where are we going?"

He grinned, stroking her palm with his thumb. "*Siesta*," was his cryptic reply.

Her brow furrowed. "Where is that?"

He laughed. "Had you never heard of it? It is too hot to do much work during the middle of the day, so the Spaniards eat that unholy large meal then take a long rest. They tend to be about their business somewhat later into the evening as a result. It is quite the norm here."

"A... a nap? In the middle of the day? How very odd!" she exclaimed, allowing him to place his hand low on her back and guide her up the steps. She paused before the door Dolores had shown her before, waiting for him to open it for her. He did so with a flourish, dipping his head chivalrously as she passed by him with a curious frown. When she stepped into the room, she was met with a small tower of boxes which had not been there before. "What... what are these?" she turned to him in confusion.

He closed the door and drew near, taking her hand. "These are for you," he answered softly. "I wanted you to have some wedding clothes, something other than mourning. I hope you will wear them. We will get more once we return home, but this is a start for now."

She shook her head vehemently in protest. "But, John, I don't need... It is so much! No, we cannot possibly...."

He stilled her objections with a gentle kiss. "Do not fret, my love. I- *we-* are not precisely destitute, and this day has already brought me much hope for the future." She drew away, beginning to object once more, but he trapped her face in his hands. "Margaret, please, just trust me. I want you to accept these."

Blinking, she relented. "Thank you, John," she whispered.

His face lit in happiness. "Do not thank me just yet. I am not exactly certain what it is I have bought! I ran into Miss Carter and her mother in the city, they offered to make the selections for you."

Margaret laughed lightly, thanking him again for his thoughtfulness. He wrapped her in his arms and encouraged her in a low voice to open the larger boxes. She relented, expecting she would enjoy his face as she opened her boxes far more than the gifts themselves. Giddy as a schoolboy, he snagged her free hand and brought her to the little stack. Three larger boxes were piled to one side, while two smaller parcels rested atop a hatbox nearby.

Smiling abashedly, she carefully lifted the top lid of the nearest box. Crusted inside was a lovely emerald silk, boasting an elegantly daring neckline. A dense lace décolletage swept over the shoulders, narrowing to a point at the waist to preserve the modesty of the gown, and intricate beaded embellishments adorned the bodice. She gasped in awe, stroking the cloth admiringly. It was far more delicate and less serviceable than she had been used to wear, but clearly intended as a day dress for an elegant lady.

John pulled the gown from the box for her full inspection, draping it artfully over a nearby chair. The waist was sculpted fashionably low, cinched with delicious tucks and a single flounce. The skirt bore a lesser number of the same details copied from the bodice, all tastefully arrayed to enhance the flowing design. Margaret's fingertips hovered near her lips. She had oft preferred dark colours for everyday wear, but the richness of this gown left her speechless. She did not know how she could dare to wear it! A look at her husband's adoring gaze lent her the courage she wanted. Clearly, he was already envisioning her robed in his gift. She drew a deep breath and graced him with a thankful smile.

The next box revealed a plum-coloured traveling suit, crisply trimmed to dignified lines, yet softly feminine to flatter her figure. John drew this out for her as well, and then he showed her the hat which Melanie had purchased. He was pleased to discover it was in a close straw weave, quite simply styled and very like the one he remembered her wearing in Milton. It was trimmed daintily with a silver pin and a narrow pink ribbon. The back of the hat flared up in the latest fashion, and Margaret found it suited her tastes very well.

Margaret almost became reluctant to lift the lid of the last large box. These gowns were too much! John persisted though- he wished to see them for himself, and to imagine his bride wearing each of his gifts to her. With a smiling sigh, she tugged the string and opened it. A rosy chiffon gauze peeped from within. This last gown he draped reverently over the bed, taking as much delight in the garment's examination as she.

The bodice was swathed in a shirred wrap style, with individual pleats arching from the shoulders and crossing at the bosom. The dusty pink colour deepened as the filmy layers cascaded downward, forming delicate petals about the skirt. Clearly the heritage of the Spanish shop where the gown had been purchased impacted the gauzy and free-flowing design, but it would still be suitable for a summer dinner party back at home. Margaret fingered the sheer fabric, thinking how light and feminine it would feel to wear. It suited her simpler tastes, yet there was a romantic grace to its flowing form.

John drew close behind her, dropping his arms about her waist and nuzzling the back of her neck. "Are you pleased, my love?"

She swallowed and nodded mutely. She had never owned a gown to match it; the closest rival was the white one she had worn both to Edith's wedding and to the Thorntons' dinner party.

"Good," he spoke warmly into her ear. "Will you wear it for me tonight? I would very much like to see my enchanting southern rose so fittingly attired."

She chuckled a little then turned in his arms. "I would be honoured, kind sir," she teased lightly, bestowing a soft kiss upon his chin. "Thank you, John. I shall truly *feel* like a rose in this gown!"

"Ah, that reminds me," he paused, dropping to one knee before her. "There is something else I should long ago have given you." He drew out his pocketbook and opened it, revealing a handful of pressed, dried blooms. Carefully he removed the fragile buds, and, blue eyes gazing up, offered them into her hand. "Do you recognize these?"

She stared at them wonderingly for a moment, then recognition sparked in her eyes. "They are from Helstone, are they not? I know these deep indentations round the leaves. You were there?"

"Yes, on my return from Havre, you may remember- it was while your father went away to Oxford. I wanted to see where my Margaret grew up, even then at the worst of times, when I had no hope of calling her my own."

Her lips quivered uncontrollably. How touched she was that he had thought lovingly of her, even then! She tugged at his hand, pleading wordlessly with him to rise so she could lose herself in his embrace, but he remained where he was.

"Not yet, my darling, I have not done." He bent his head to search another pocket and presented to her a small box. "Margaret, my dearest love, will you wear this all the days of our lives?"

She bit her lip, the tears beginning to flow freely. Without even opening the box, she was nodding emphatically. He smiled hugely at her acceptance, but insisted, "You must look at it, you know!"

She laughed through her tears and raised the lid of the little box. The glorious diamond caused another gasp of dismayed surprise. "Oh, but John!" she protested.

"Shhh," he rose, placing a quelling finger over her lips. "You already promised you would wear it, and you cannot back out now." Still grinning like a boy, he plucked the tiny sparkling thing from the box. He slid his other hand along hers, and held the ring poised at the tip of her fourth finger.

Bowing his head, he repeated the sacred words which had been omitted from their own abbreviated vows. "With this ring I thee wed, with my body I thee worship, and with all my worldly goods I thee endow: In the name of the Father, and of the Son, and of the Holy Ghost."

He tenderly guided the ring onto her finger, then bent to seal his oath with a kiss. "Amen," he whispered, holding her eyes with an intense, fervent joy.

He dropped his hands to her waist, meaning to draw her to his chest, but she bounced away from him. "Oh! Stay but a moment!" She whirled out of his grasp, moving quickly to the little vanity. Snatching up something, she sashayed back to his laughing embrace.

"This one is for you," she smiled shyly. She held aloft a soft golden band. He marveled but a second. Where had she obtained a man's wedding ring on such short notice? "It belonged to Father," she murmured in answer to his unspoken question. "I think he would be pleased now, knowing it will be yours."

He clasped his hand over hers, holding the ring. "It would be my honour," he answered hoarsely. He could think of nothing he liked better than to receive his dear friend's heirloom and to wear it in good faith, proclaiming to all his love for that man's precious daughter.

She slipped the ring on his offered finger, following his lead and pledging her troth once more. At her last syllables, he twined his arms around her, lifting her for an exuberant embrace. "My Margaret!" he cried joyfully, but she silenced any further outbursts with a firm kiss. He made no objection.

He settled her back on her feet, his hands reaching to cup her face. Fingers tracing over her soft skin, he kissed her again, this time gently brushing the tip of his tongue over her lips. She drew her breath sharply in surprise but remained still. At his encouragement, she hesitantly responded in kind. They stood several delicious minutes, exploring new tastes, new sensations. Fearing he might overwhelm her, at last he drew back with a light kiss to the tip of her nose.

"Margaret," he whispered, "may I see your hair down?"

Her eyebrows rose in mild surprise. "In the middle of the day? Would that not appear strange?"

A heated gleam came to his eye. "Do you remember what I told you about siesta? There will be no one about below for some while."

Her breath stilled. "Do you mean... for how long?"

That sly smirk returned. "I am not to meet again with your brother for three hours yet. Mr Bell will be resting as well; if you remember, Frederick made a point of telling us as much."

Margaret's eyes flew open in a scandalized gasp. "Oh, but... but Frederick! He cannot think...."

John touched her lips with his fingers, smilingly halting her protests. "Frederick is a married man, my love," he whispered. "So," he curved his face around hers to drop tantalizing little kisses along her ear, "what say you, my Margaret? Will you allow me to see your hair down, or shall we sit on the balcony there and read some Plato?"

She laughed, a nervous little trill quite unlike herself. "Plato sounds... indescribably boring at the moment!"

"I quite agree," he grinned.

Twenty-Eight

JOHN TUGGED HER CLOSE, brushing his palms up the backs of her arms to reverently encircle the slender column of her neck. Gently he skewered her hair with his fingers, seeking the pins binding it into prim coils. Lacking experience, he did not at first know where to look for them, but Margaret found she quite enjoyed his searching efforts.

She tipped her chin a little higher and kissed him lightly as he drew the last few pins from the tumbling ringlets. Her hair fell at last in a dark cascade, curling over her shoulders and down her back. He drew back to receive the full effect; his love's face framed by her softly furled tresses, gazing up at him with tender affection, was a sight he longed to burn into his memory.

He turned her as she stood before him, pivoting her to face away from him so he could stroke the ebony silk, tumbling almost to her waist. He sighed and buried his face in it, so deeply that she could feel his breath tickling through her thick hair to her scalp, then lower to her neck.

His hands began to rove tenderly over her hips, thumbs caressing up and down her back. He might have stayed thus for hours, but he was rapidly becoming intoxicated by the nearness of her. He was already quivering in exquisite anticipation. "Shall I unbind your arm?" he queried softly.

Her eyes fluttered open and she tilted her head back to look at his face. She bit her lip and nodded silently. He stroked her thick hair aside, carefully arraying it over her opposite shoulder. This time there was no tantalizing delay. He loosened the sling binding her, letting it fall freely to the floor, and brought his own hand up to support her arm from behind. He immediately descended upon her neck and ear with his mouth, teasing and savouring her sweet skin. His free hand curled round her waist, then began to explore upward, splaying searching fingers over her abdomen.

Margaret dropped her head back, resting upon his shoulder. Her breath began to come in long sighs, her eyes fell closed, and she gave herself over to his passionate ministrations.

After a few moments, he daringly tickled his fingers up to the curve of her breast. Margaret gasped once more in surprise, her breathing quickening uncontrollably. Tracing lightly over her form, his fingers wandered until they hovered over the buttons of her bodice. Without warning, he stopped, turning her again to face him.

"John?" she gazed up at him in confusion. "Is something wrong?"

"No!" he bit his lip, shaking his head. "Margaret, you... you move me beyond measure! I was not prepared... I could never have known how you would arouse such powerful feelings within me."

She smiled in relief. "Nor I!"

He clasped her hands, quieting his bounding pulse. "Margaret, I am so afraid I might hurt you, or frighten you. I could never forgive myself."

She was shaking her head in denial. "John," she murmured, touching his face, "I do not fear, and you have never been anything other than perfectly gentle with me. You need not worry for my shoulder; it is feeling much better."

He swallowed. "It is not your shoulder which concerns me. My love, have you any knowledge of what takes place in the marriage bed?"

Her cheeks burned crimson, and she lost her nerve. She dropped her eyes. "A- a little," she faltered. She gulped. "Not much."

He tipped her chin up with his fingers. "I probably have not much more understanding than you. That is part of what troubles me."

Her eyes widened. She had never thought of it, but somehow, she had expected....

He read her thoughts. "I know, it is common for men of means to... to sport with women, but I always thought it disgraceful. From the age of fourteen I was helpmeet to my mother and father to my sister. With the care of two women falling to me, I could never look at another with so little regard for her person. I told you once before, and it is true- I never loved anyone until you, Margaret. My only 'knowledge' comes of the bawdy conversations I have overheard from others, most of which 'advice' I do not care to heed."

Margaret chewed her lip, looking down still. Suddenly she looked up, full into his face. "I am glad!" she whispered.

His eyes lightened. "So am I!" he replied fervently. He stroked her cheek lovingly. "I shall never have memories of any but you, and that is exactly as it should be- as I should wish it. My only worry is that I desire so much to please you, Margaret, and I do not know how."

A smile of encouragement blossomed upon her lips. "John, you do please me."

He looked intently down at her, willing her to understand his fears. "I am afraid," he replied softly, "that it may indeed hurt you at first. I do not know how to avoid that."

She pressed her lips firmly together, then wrapped her arm around him, laying her head upon his chest. "I understand."

Slowly he released a long breath, relaxing some in her embrace and pulling her yet closer. "You must promise me something," he murmured gently in her ear. "You must promise to talk to me, tell me what pleases you and what does not. I wish to know you; every inch of you, every sigh, every sense. There can be no room for shame or embarrassment between us. Promise me, Margaret!" He lifted her chin to gaze directly into her violet eyes.

With hesitation at first, then growing certainty, she nodded in reply. A new urge grew within her- perhaps a primal temerity previously foreign to her- to give him all the assurance she could. She could not suffer her husband, who had known so little affection in his life, to ever again be in doubt of her feelings for him.

His smile returned as he bent to kiss her again. Margaret surprised him with the fervency of her response, drawing him close and tantalizing him, meeting him with soft lips and tongue. His pulse throbbed fiercely. She feathered her fingers through his hair, following down to the curve of his neck until it disappeared beneath his collar.

She traced her fingers around the line of his clothing until she encountered his narrow tie. Drawing back and holding his gaze with a coquettish gleam in her eyes, she slowly tugged until the knot failed and the ends hung loosely down his chest. His lips curled in growing desire as she slyly worked her finger under the first button of his collar, then a second. He moaned softly when her warm lips searched down his throat, to the hollow just above his chest where his pulse beat the strongest.

A third button now disappeared as her questing continued lower. "Oh!" she inhaled suddenly when she encountered the coarse hair spreading over his chest. His body shook with restrained laughter as she, with flirtatious boldness, explored the new curiosity she had discovered.

After a moment he pushed her back, his eyes dancing with mirth. "Normally I start with the coat," he chuckled. She watched with interest as he quickly divested himself of both jacket and waistcoat, tossing them carelessly on the floor so he could return his hands to a more absorbing pursuit. He laced his fingers low upon her waist, rapturously stroking the curves of her form and waiting for whatever beguiling endeavor she might commence.

Margaret narrowed her eyes, discovering now how fully she held him in her power. Her flushed lips curved sensually as she returned them to his neck. She hooked the fingers of her sore arm in the lowest button of his shirt for support and began to investigate his naked chest with her other.

More buttons gave way to her inquisitive caresses. His head relaxed backward as a long shuddering sigh escaped him. How delicious her soft fingers felt! And how delighted he was with her adventurous explorations! He emitted a low throaty groan as her lips and fingertips brushed over the most sensitive parts of his torso. She was full of surprises, his enchanting lover!

Fearing his self-control would unravel too quickly, he stilled her hand. "My turn," he rasped. He turned her away from him again, repeating his tender assault on her neck, and stroking his hands possessively over her curves. When her head lolled back against his chest, his fingers traced lightly over the tiny buttons of her bodice. "May I?" he rumbled low in her ear. She nodded breathlessly.

He wanted no further encouragement. Deftly he eased free each little rounded button in its turn, keeping his fingers strictly to their task. The bodice of her gown draped loosely in a moment. With a quivering breath, he gently swept it back, taking care to not jostle her sore shoulder. Closing his eyes, he gathered the skirts of her gown at her hips. "Lift your arms, Love," he requested softly.

Her breath catching, she complied to the best of her ability, and he raised the voluminous folds over her head. The fine black silk gown unceremoniously joined his coat on the floor. Gentle fingers urged her to face him once more, and as she looked up to his face, he opened his eyes. "Oh-h-h," he sighed. His gaze caressed her form, lingering upon the softly rounded swell of her bosom as it rose above her corset. "Margaret, my lover, my wife!" he murmured, pressing his lips to the treasure revealed to him. "You are more beautiful than I could have imagined."

Her breast began to heave as his mouth traced fire over her untouched skin. His hands roved gently over her curves, teasing and fondling the secret delights belonging only to him. She arched into his hand, closing her eyes and sighing. Her heart pattered erratically, a thrill of nervous anticipation quivering through her stomach.

His fingers tracked the bony ridges of her corset, boldly slipping under the top edge to brush the soft flesh hidden beneath. She felt a growing tremor through her abdomen, piercing right through the center of her being as he explored her body. His other hand searched out the laces on the back of her corset, finding the ties and slowly loosening them to allow his fingers easier access. Margaret's body began to sway as she leaned toward him, trusting, whispering his name.

With a few deft flicks, he learned the secret of the hooks on the front of her corset. It tumbled unheeded to the floor. Her skin was so soft and warm! Thoroughly addicted, he stroked again and again over her bared flesh. This was the real, vibrant Margaret pulsing eagerly beneath his fingertips, a dream so long and agonizingly desired that her willing invitation was doubly sweet. With innocent seductiveness, she rose to his ardent touch.

His own desire had grown painfully unbearable. He had to know all of her! His fingers began awkwardly to tear through the lacing on her crinoline, drawing a surprised little laugh from her as he jerkily freed her of its encumbrance. He slid his arms around her and lifted her close for a kiss, sweeping her feet clear of the collapsed bundle of linen and wire. He rested her back on her toes, but only for a heartbeat. Claiming a better hold on her body, he cradled her in his arms and bore her to the bed.

Margaret's eyes slowly flitted open. A little surprised, she looked about drowsily; she had not realized she had fallen asleep. Her head was pillowed on her husband's shoulder, her cheek resting just above the beginnings of the dark hair curling over his chest. His body rose and fell in deep, rhythmic breaths. He was still asleep. Dearest, weary John! At last, he could rest a little. Nestling her head into the soft flesh of his shoulder, she inhaled his scent and closed her eyes in contentment.

The slight movement of her head roused him fractionally. His fingers curled reflexively over her bare skin, possessively brushing a part of her body none but he had ever touched. "Mmm," he nuzzled into the cascade of her hair. They remained tangled in one another's embrace, neither willing to leave the blissful peace which had settled upon them.

Margaret's right arm was uppermost, her hand resting just beneath her chin. Drowsily she began to toy with the hair covering his torso, twirling it gently about her fingertips. The crisp ringlets whorled curiously as she brushed her fingers through them, stroking the contours of his upper body. Encouraged by his euphoric sigh, she allowed her fingers to wander over the whole of his chest.

He lay passively, a little smile creeping upon his face, but he did not open his eyes. Margaret accepted that as a challenge, and her lips parted mischievously. Slipping her hand under the sheet, she continued her ministrations over his ribs to his navel, twisting and tickling.

He was most decidedly becoming more alert with her ongoing explorations. His hand tightened over her lower extremities. "Margaret," he rumbled warningly, "if you continue so, we shall not be leaving this bed any time soon."

"You would keep me here against my will?" she arched one brow saucily.

"The argument could be made, my love, that you do not appear to be very unwilling." He lifted his head from the pillows to kiss her forehead. She narrowed her eyes, leveling a bewitching smile at him, and blatantly allowed her hand to drift still lower.

"Right, then," he breathed. In one swift motion he rolled her lower body up and over his own, reaching to guide her descent with his other hand.

Margaret gasped in shock. "John!" she laughed, a little scandalized at finding herself brazenly straddling his abdomen.

"Hush," he joked gruffly. "I'm very busy." Pulling her down to his mouth, he began to nuzzle and then kiss her soft feminine shape. He intended, very soon, to make good on his promise to acquaint himself with every inch of her.

Quite some while later, sated and exhausted, they collapsed in each other's arms. Lying on their sides and facing one another, they shared gentle kisses and soft endearments. They learned to indulge in the profound pleasure of lovers' talk; tender words punctuated by meaningful silences.

He stroked her hair, letting the silken threads slip over his fingers as he brushed through them. "I hope I have not hurt you, my Margaret," he spoke in low concern.

A languorous smile came over her face as she reassured him. "Only a bit, and just at the very first. Everything after was... I had no idea it could be so wonderful," she murmured. She trailed her fingers over the new stubble already sprouting on his cheek.

He let out a breath in relief. "If it were not, I would consider myself to have failed miserably!" He tipped her chin near, brushing tantalizing little kisses over her lower lip.

His pulse drummed headily as he drank in her responsiveness, so soon after finding satisfaction in his arms. Already she was arching her neck closer to his sensitive mouth. "Do you not know, my love?" he whispered, mesmerized. "Can you understand how you bewitch me? You were made to be loved, and loved well."

He let his lips wander gently over her face, caressing her soft cheeks, brushing her closed eyes, softly enticing her with his breath blowing soft little kisses over the corners of her mouth. He drew back, basking in the view. Margaret gazed silkily up at him from her repose; no longer a mysterious and sacrosanct lady to him but a woman- *his* woman- bathed in all her seductive glory and unveiling her beauty to him alone.

He had never dared to hope his fondest dreams might one day be realized. Nestled rapturously in his arms at long last was the one woman he had ever loved; his perfect match, his very heart, and she had entrusted herself completely to him. All the fears and doubts he had ever held about her had washed away in the last hours. She had melded to him utterly, loving generously and fully as he loved her. Finally, no barriers remained between them.

His fingers traced admiringly up and down the sweep of her feminine contours, wondering at the delicacy of her form and marveling at the hidden strength he had found beneath. His sweet bride settled her head in the crook of his arm, her breath softly tickling the tender places of his ribs.

With the greatest reluctance, he glanced over the luscious curve of her hip toward the open window to the outdoors. The sun was sinking rather lower in the sky than he had realized. Cold alarm filled him. It would not do to be late for his appointment with Frederick.

He had always prided himself on his punctuality, feeling that tardiness robbed others of their valuable time. It always goaded him very greatly when others revealed that weakness. He did not wish to commence his dealings with his new brother-in-law and business partner in such a way.

His alarm, however, grew more out of a sense of embarrassment than anything else. As he had so suggestively informed his bride earlier, her brother was no innocent and would most assuredly know exactly why he was late. Mumbling his excuses, he began to rise from the bed.

"John?" she murmured groggily. She sat up, her hair tumbling enticingly down her shoulders and the sheet falling delightfully away.

He groaned. His days, he began to realize, were now to be characterized by a new kind of torment; the exquisite agony of counting the minutes until he could come back to her. "I must see your brother," he gently reminded her.

The same sort of apprehension he had felt suddenly appeared on her face. "Oh! How long have we been?" She gathered the sheet modestly to her breast and began to cast her gaze about, searching the walls in vain for a time piece.

"Not long enough." He lowered his face to hers for one last kiss. Straightening, he pivoted his body and stretched his long legs to the floor. He stood, heedless of his fully undressed state as he strode to the heap of clothing they had tossed aside so long ago. Bending down, he sorted through them until he found his own articles, searching out his silver pocket watch. He cursed himself inwardly when his eyes registered the position of the watch hands. He would only just be in time, if he hurried.

Distracted now, he bent once more to hurriedly gather the remainder of his garments. At last, he drew back up to his full height to apologize to Margaret for his haste. He found her hiding a wicked grin behind the sheet, her face bright red and her eyes brazenly roving over his body. "What...?" He looked down. "Oh." He flushed in embarrassment. "I'm sorry." He moved the bundle of clothing in his arms to shield his nether regions.

"Oh, no, that will never do! No secrets, remember?" She leapt from the bed herself, dragging the sheet, he noticed, and tugged the offending clothing from her line of view. "Much better," she jerked her head in bold satisfaction.

"You are a minx!" he growled. "I thought I married a lady!" He snatched the sheet from her. It was only fair, he decided, and he felt no compunction against openly admiring the figure she presented.

Rather than shrink in modesty, Margaret daringly lifted her shoulders. "Come now, John," she teased, tilting her smile enticingly up toward his jawline. "Would a lady sail alone with a gentleman who is not her husband?"

"Touché." He grinned roguishly, lifting her off her feet.

Twenty-Nine

FREDERICK DID NOT HURRY to his study. He sauntered in, ten minutes late himself, and chuckled when he found the room completely empty. Pouring a cool drink, he draped himself over a comfortable chair with a copy of Shakespeare and settled in to wait as long as necessary.

He rather enjoyed the notion of the entrepreneurial machine of Mr Bell's description being softened by his own sister. Softened! By all he could see, Thornton would leap to the moon at Margaret's bidding. A wry grin split his face as he swirled his drink. And this, the tough negotiator he had been warned of! It would be a mellow man indeed who walked into his study this afternoon.

He had made it through several sonnets when the door at last creaked open, admitting a humbled Thornton to the study. Frederick tossed his book aside with deliberate casualness. "Ah, there you are, Thornton." He stretched and yawned with dramatic flair before he stood, enjoying his brother-in-law's reddening face.

"Hale, I must apologize for my tardiness," he faltered.

Frederick waved his hand as he straightened, looking Thornton directly in the eye. "Think nothing of it. You have just had a long, hard journey. You must both be tired. Did Margaret rest well?"

John narrowed his eyes. In all the time he had known old Mr Hale, and even the frail Mrs Hale, he had never identified in them the rather puckish sense of humour their children seemed to share. Then again, until very lately he had only glimpsed a rare smile from Margaret. He'd had no inkling of the lively wit to which he would fall victim. "She is well enough," he replied, with as much dignity as he could muster.

Frederick nodded, smirking a little. For all of Thornton's affectations of remorse over his tardiness, the man seemed smugly pleased with himself. "Right, then, let's get down to business."

PHILIPPE GIRAUD STEPPED FINALLY into the hot sun of the Spanish afternoon. Carter's men had turned him over to the local authority immediately upon the ship's arrival in port. Scarcely had that ship left the harbor, however, when he had regained his freedom.

He jingled the remaining coins in his pocket. The Spanish authorities were as corrupt as any he had found. It had cost him dearly to purchase his freedom, however, and he pondered how best to replenish his traveling funds. A round of cards seemed a promising solution- he had always had good luck.

Turning up and down the street, he settled his gaze upon one man, dressed like himself as a gentleman traveler. He set out to follow him, assuming that where one man found bed and board, another might as well.

Margaret peeped hesitantly into Mr Bell's room, feeling guilty at her long absence. The old gentleman's eyes drifted open. He lifted his lips in a peaceful smile, then his eyes fell closed again. "Read to me a little more, will you my dear? I have not at present the energy."

"Of course." Margaret feared the hollow, lisping quality his voice had taken on just since that very morning. After once seeing her mother fade listlessly away, she could never forget that dreaded progression.

She found her page in *The Taming of the Shrew* and began. After only two lines, Bell interrupted her. "Oh, no, not that. Have you anything else? I think I should like to hear something about love- real love."

She closed the book softly and turned it over in her hands. Glancing furtively about the room, she saw no shelves or trunks which might contain more reading material. "Do you have a preference? Perhaps I might borrow something from Frederick," she suggested. Bell's eyes flickered open and he grunted mutely in agreement.

She excused herself from his room and made her way to the place where she thought she might find Dolores. Upon her entry, her young sister-in-law looked up from her needlework with bright cheer. "Ah, Margarita, is it you rested well?"

Margaret flushed a little and nodded. "I am quite refreshed. I want to thank you for sending Maria to me a while ago, she was a great help in dressing."

Dolores' eyes sparkled. "Ah, bueno. Good! Your gown is so beautiful!" She hefted herself to her feet to draw nearer. She gazed at the rose gown admiringly. "Frederick, he tells me about your Señor Thornton, he gives you such nice gifts!"

Margaret blushed again. "It seems a good deal too fancy for every evening, but John specifically asked me to wear it tonight."

"No, no! Is... how do you say... perfect. My father, he comes home just a while ago, and we have a feast this night! He rests now, but he will be with Frederick soon." Dolores' white teeth flashed as she smiled delightedly, tilting her head this way and that to better appreciate the lovely gown. "My father, he will love to see you."

Margaret thanked her for the generous compliments. "I wonder if you could tell me where Frederick keeps his books?" she asked. "Mr Bell would like another selection if I can find one."

"Oh, si!" Dolores took her familiarly by the hand, leading her down an airy corridor to a heavy, ornate wooden door. She entered boldly, without knocking, and Margaret found herself standing directly in Frederick's study. Her brother and husband stood hunched over a desk, each with a pen and a stack of papers at hand, deeply engrossed in their discussion.

Both men straightened at their intrusion. Margaret paled a little and would have backed out of the door but for the immediate smiles their appearance generated. John was at her side in a moment, asking her if all was well.

"Y- yes," she stammered. "Mr Bell asked me to find a different book to read to him, and I thought...." She turned her embarrassed gaze to Dolores, then to Frederick. "I am so sorry to intrude." John clasped her hand and kissed it in reassurance; whatever her sensibilities might be, he could not picture himself ever being displeased at an intrusion by his enchanting wife into the duller matters of business.

"Nonsense, Margaret, it is no bother." Frederick strode to a little side table near a plush chair, chose a small stack of well-loved volumes, and returned to her with them. He extended them within her reach with an appraising smile. "You look beautiful, Dearest," he complimented, his eyes twinkling. "It is good to see you in something other than black once again."

Margaret thanked him and looked to John with a bashful smile. Clearly, he agreed with Frederick, but his admiration for her appearance spoke more eloquently through his eyes. Just before Dolores could steal her away again, he brushed a tender kiss to her forehead, not caring one bit that her brother was watching. "I will come to you in a while," he promised.

"Oh," she remembered, drawing a letter from the folds of her gown. She had composed it for her aunt but did not know the safest way to send it from Frederick's home. She handed it to John, who nodded in understanding as he took it.

The ladies disappeared back through the door, and Frederick turned back to the desk and his guest. "I say, Thornton, my sister looks to have blossomed just since her arrival this morning."

John sighed serenely. "The gown suits her well, does it not?"

"That it does, but it was her countenance I was remarking upon. She has more colour, do you not agree? Ah, it was the rest, surely that was all she needed, the poor girl. Perhaps you ought to consider taking our siesta tradition home with you."

John stood still in shock for a moment. Frederick had nonchalantly returned to the crop forecasts, his face tipped low to his papers so his expression could not be read. Still, John had the distinct impression that Frederick was having the time of his life laughing at his expense.

His lips twitched. John Thornton was a man who could give as well as he got. "Perhaps," he replied slowly, causing Frederick to look back up. "Then again, there is something to be said for retiring with the sun, and not having to break one's rest for many hours together." He flashed his brother a sportive grin, causing both of their composed façades to crack into mirthful chuckles.

HANNAH THORNTON HAD DISCOVERED during her long afternoon with Johnny Boucher that the lad's precisely schooled dialect tended to crumble during ordinary conversation. He spoke clearly enough in short sentences, and his precocious reading, of course, followed the usage of the literature. He would falter, however, when asked to engage in discourse of any duration. His infractions ranged from minor pronunciation errors to grievous grammatical felonies.

She had decided instantly that the boy wanted a good deal more practice than could be obtained within the strictures of the school room. Living and laboring in a home such as the Higgins' would most decidedly preclude the possibility of such refined pursuits, but Hannah had recognized a spark within this child. He had it within him to make something of himself. He could never gain the respect of his societal betters while bearing the handicap of such vulgar speech, and she was the very one to school him.

She had begun with simple table manners. Johnny had a barbaric way with a teacup, and absolutely no concept for the correct posture and manner at table. She instructed patiently, taking comfort in the knowledge that the skills learnt at her table might serve the boy for the rest of his life.

"Not that way," she would slant a stern expression his direction, and he would instantly resume the correct finger posture while holding spoon or cup or knife. At a glance from her, he recalled the proper placement and use of his napkin.

He would manage for a few minutes, then slip again. In the wake of each correction, he survived longer before the next mistake. By the time tea was over, he had only spilled twice, and lost just one spoon to the abyss under the table. In spite of his deep humiliation, Hannah gave a grim nod of satisfaction. He had a good will and he appeared to be eminently teachable.

"Have you much practice with figures?" she probed as the tea things were removed. There was little more useful skill a child could learn if he were to enter the world of business.

He nodded with a lopsided grin. She raised an eyebrow and he straightened. "I mean, yes, Ma'am, I am learning some." He squared his tiny shoulders proudly and those silver eyes fairly sparked. Were she a softer hearted woman, which she most decidedly was *not*, she would in that moment have reflected that he was quite an adorable child.

She rose with dignity and returned with her household ledgers. "Let us see how you manage," she replied coolly. She drew her chair near his to observe his work, and the pair spent a solid hour poring over the flow of expenditures and income of her housekeeping.

At first the boy had great trouble fathoming a figure larger than a pence or a shilling. His eyes grew large, and once he blurted, "Ye must be the richest lady in England!"

She fixed him with a firm stare, her pen poised in the air. "Young man, that is not a proper comment."

"Oh," he bobbed his sandy head apologetically. "I meant 'You,' Ma'am," he amended.

She could not help rolling her eyes. "It is not proper to make comment on another person's wealth, or lack thereof."

The boy's face fell as he digested this new rule. "Ma'am?" She raised her chin in silent acknowledgement. "Father was poor. Is that 'lack the-rub'?"

She drew a long-suffering sigh. "Yes, child, I suppose it is."

His face brightened. "Then I ain't… I mean I shan't talk about that. I can talk about Mr Nicholas, though, because he's not the one or the other."

She peered over the rim of her reading glasses. "No, child, I do not think that would be fitting either. One does not discuss financial matters in polite company."

His little brow furrowed. "But it's not… fun-anshal. He looks after me. You know, he takes care of us. Father couldn'a… I mean, he could not. I don't know why. I think he wanted to." He looked back to her mortified face questioningly. "Don't you think?"

Frozen, she made herself form some reply. "I expect, child, that any mother or father would do all they could to care for their children." Slowly she rose from the table, her mind stumbling through a seventeen-year-old fog. "That is enough ciphering for today," she mumbled roughly. "Let us see what can be done for the stain on your clothing."

In the end, she gave up on the ink-stained chemise. Searching through her charity sewing basket, she found a half-completed garment of nearly his size. It only wanted some finishing. While she sat with her needle, she instructed him to run through his catechism. Having finished that, he offered to recite his figures, then the first conjugation Latin verbs.

"Latin?" she frowned. She still thought that particular exercise an exhaustive waste of time. This young arrow ought to be nocked and aimed carefully into a trade which could raise him from the drudgery whence he came. She set the shirt aside for the moment and returned with a book from John's library. The book contained various diagrams and mechanical explanations detailing the steam engine. "Study this, then you shall describe for me what you have learned."

The child leaned over the book, chin propped rudely on his knuckles, and tried to study while she finished. Once or twice his toes would tap restlessly, but then he would glance up nervously, stilling his little body. She watched in shrewd silence the child's valiant efforts against unsanctioned movement.

As she tugged free the last stitch of the hem, she glanced at the mantle clock. Three hours yet remained before Higgins could realistically be expected to have finished for the day. She sighed, glancing out the window. It was too fine of a day to keep the lad indoors. It had not been so long since her own son was a boy that she had completely forgotten the boundless energy which bubbled constantly near the surface in a child's small body.

"Try this on," she instructed, holding the shirt out. He eagerly jumped from his seat, leaving John's book carelessly flopped over the arm of his chair. She sent him to the washroom to change, setting the book more carefully upon the side table after he had left.

He came out quickly, wearing the new shirt and an enormous, crooked smile. "Thank you, Mrs Thornton," the winsome scamp grinned, giving a very proper little bow.

She pursed her twitching lips. "Come, child, we shall take some air. Straighten your collar and check your shoelaces."

So it was that a quarter hour later saw prim Mrs Thornton, the widowed matron of Marlborough Mills, escorting a miniature John Boucher of Francis Street through the busy market square. Not a few heads were turned at the spectacle of the severe Mistress giving her hand to a freckled seven-year-old worker's child.

Hannah was not unaware of the curious eyes upon her as they walked. Though she habitually held her head high and refused to be unnerved by any untoward attention, she quietly directed her path out of the town. "Tell me," she queried the lad at her heels, "what did you learn in your book?"

Johnny was silent, his eyes on the pavement.

"Well?" she demanded.

He looked back up. "I forgot," he whispered guiltily.

Hannah sighed. "Did you examine the diagrams? What do you remember?"

His little brow wrinkled. "I dinna'... I think... there was a wheel?"

"I see," she answered stiffly. "Perhaps we will look over the book together at a later time."

Johnny's curious gaze swept the neighborhood they were passing through. "Where are we going, Ma'am?"

Hannah walked on without reply. To be truthful, she did not precisely know where they were going, but she did not wish to linger in Crampton. The quiet paths leading up the hill out of the city were all she could think of. Johnny's tongue was loosed as they came out of the populated areas. He began to chatter happily, his little fingers flexing comfortably in her hand.

Hannah was at first disconcerted by his nonstop prattle. The boy pointed out every scattering bird, every interesting rock, each little whirl of breeze rustling by. By the time they had reached the long hill leading up to overlook the town, she had begun to be inured to his babble. His happiness was evident, and perhaps it was that quality which riveted her eyes more and more steadily on his little form.

It had been a long time since she had looked on the world through a child's eyes... since John's childhood, in truth. With some sadness, she admitted to herself that Fanny had not had the same mother as John. Her cares had been greater in those days, her heart not as light as it once had been. It was with a wondering curiosity that she began to heed the child's words, as he described his world to her.

He told her of his oldest sister, only a year older than himself. "She don't say... I mean she doesn't talk very much. She mostly helps Mary with the yung'uns... I mean my other brothers and my baby sister. Nellie never gets in trouble, but she says I do too much. She don't... I mean she doesn't understand what it's like to be a boy!" he declared with childish flair, gesturing expressively with his thin little arms. He raised worshipful eyes to his adored patroness. "*You* understand boys, don't you Mrs Thornton?"

Hannah discovered a little quirk breaking free of the frosty set to her lips. She peered down to the child's admiring gaze, a small sparkle growing in her eye. "What makes you say that, child?"

"Ye... I mean you are Mr Thornton's ma, ain't... I mean, aren't you? Mr Nicholas says he's not so bad for a Master. Ye musta been a good ma... mother." The child bit his lip with an impish little grin as he amended himself.

She could not help but chuckle at his innocent deductions, but she did not answer. It was not necessary. The boy did not need a co-conversant, as he managed well enough on his own. At length he pointed to a little knoll, not many yards from the path on which they walked. "That's where me da'... my dad and my mum are buried," he informed her nonchalantly.

She glanced down with surprise. His cavalier attitude did not sit well with her. "You ought not to speak irreverently of the deceased," she scolded him.

His crystal eyes flashed back to hers. "I dinna' mean to be... what is that word again?"

"Reverent," she repeated firmly. "It means respectful. We do not speak of those who have passed on with careless disregard."

He nodded slowly, a thoughtful look tickling his expression. "I remember now. That's what Miss Marget used to tell me, when she brought me here. She said I ought to be... what was that word? Rev'rent. You must be a lot like Miss Marget, because she said the same things you do."

She narrowed her eyes. "Miss... Marget?"

"That's what Mr Nicholas calls her. She used to come talk to me after me da' died. She was nice. Then her own da' died and she had to move. I miss her," his little fingers tightened around hers, "but I like you too, Mrs Thornton."

Hanna's jaw clenched. It did not greatly please her to hear that young woman's name mentioned again. She ought not to have been surprised; she knew that Margaret Hale had befriended the Higgins family, but it had not occurred to her that young Johnny might yet cherish fond memories of her.

"Miss Marget... is that her proper name, Mrs Thornton? I don't suppose you knew her. She would read with me, before Mr Thornton got me into the school. She was the one that give me Robinson Crusoe," he confided, his gaze blithely roaming about the edges of the graveyard along which they walked.

After many paces, Hannah finally spoke. "Miss Hale," she supplied, her voice low. "Yes, I knew her."

Johnny's head snapped back up to her. His attention had just been diverted to a small melancholy display by one of the headstones, and the subject of a moment ago was already forgotten by him. "Aye... y-yes," he stammered. "That was it. She was really nice. I s'pose she's got married by now and forgot all about us."

Hannah did not answer.

Thirty

"YOU SEEM HAPPY, MY dear."

Margaret lowered *Ivanhoe* when Mr Bell's raspy voice interrupted the joust match between the Disinherited Knight and Bois-Guilbert. It took her a moment to drag her thoughts back to the present. She looked up to see his faded eyes smiling at her from his swollen face. "Why do you say so, Mr Bell?"

He gasped a little, trying not to cough. "You seem... brighter than when I saw you last. More like when I first knew you. No," his face clouded a little. "More brilliant, even, than that."

She favored him with a tender smile, taking his hand. "I am happy, Mr Bell."

He tightened his fingers around hers. "You deserve it, my dear. I have wondered many times, most especially when we went to Helstone, what it was between you and Thornton. I know you asked me not to speak of Frederick to him, but do you know, I intended to defy your wishes as soon as I returned home," he winked. "I am very glad to see that, at least, is settled."

Margaret laughed. "Yes, Mr Bell, all is in the past. We understand each other very well now."

"Ah, that is well. He will take good care of you, will Thornton. Very devoted to you, I daresay. I worried so, when you would be left alone...." His voice trailed off as he gasped a little, regulating his erratic breath. "You will be good for him too, my dear. Long has Thornton needed a little joy in his life, and the softness of a woman to lighten his manner. 'It is not good that man should be alone,' the Good Book says."

She smiled more broadly now, a flattered blush staining her cheeks. "He was not alone, Mr Bell. He has always had his mother, and I believe her to be a fine, strong woman."

"Oh! I see how it is now. Butter her up, will you? Ah but you are right to speak so, my girl. You did not know her husband, or her family. I grew up there, you know, and I remember her as a maid. Dignified she was always, but a fair sight pleasanter in those days. Her father disapproved of George Thornton, but she would have her way. Pity. Oh! What does it matter now. It will do the old dame good to have you about. You may liven that dour old house a great deal."

Margaret lowered her gaze doubtfully. "I hope we shall get on. She has never thought very highly of me."

"She has no taste then," retorted the cantankerous old gentleman loyally. Seeing Margaret's genuine concern, he softened. "There, there, child," he wheezed. "The way into old Mrs Thornton's good graces has ever been through her son, and I daresay you have a stout advocate on your side. She will come round, do not you fear."

Margaret smiled hopefully. "You seem very confident of that."

"Indeed, my girl. Indeed." He rested his head on the pillows, a wistful gaze lingering on her face.

A perfunctory knock at the door brought a short, rounded man in, clutching a black satchel. He straightened in surprise upon perceiving a lady in the room and bowed deeply. Margaret rose with dignity and the little man came forward, introducing himself in Spanish.

"Ah, there you are, Doctor. Here is my goddaughter, Mrs Thornton. She has been good enough to sit with me, have you not, Margaret?"

Margaret turned mutely to her godfather, her eyes widening. It was the first time she had been introduced by her new name. How should she not be confused with the other woman who bore the same?

"Delighted to meet you at last, Mrs Thornton. Mr Bell has told me much of you." He bowed again. "My name is Gallego."

Margaret greeted him properly, impressed with his precise English. Frederick had evidently not exaggerated the doctor's credentials. Margaret exchanged pleasantries with Gallego, then excused herself so the doctor could examine his patient.

In the sitting room she once again found Dolores, and happily joined her young sister in her sewing. Dolores proudly showed Margaret the bounty of clothing her child would inherit at birth. Margaret complimented her sincerely, but privately she could not imagine what more could possibly be wanting from the infant's layette. What remained to be sewn? Dolores must have perceived her dubious expression, for she made shy references to the seeming likelihood of a twin pregnancy, noting that it would be far from the first such occurrence in the Barbour family.

Absorbed in such pursuits, Margaret spent a very pleasant half hour getting to know her young sister better. Dolores' mother, who sat with them, largely remained quiet, but Margaret suspected it was not the natural state of affairs for that lady. She seemed an exuberant, talkative personality like her daughter, but even Señora Barbour was not quite bold enough to try to carry on small talk in a language with which she was utterly unfamiliar. Not comfortable ignoring her completely, Margaret cast frequent inviting smiles in the older woman's direction.

Margaret's eyes also wandered quite often to the open breezeway which passed by the sitting room. The doctor was taking such a long while! She wondered what could be keeping him.

Some time later a hearty laugh echoed in the corridor behind her. She turned her head to behold a new face. Stocky and possessing a shock of thick black hair, a Spanish gentleman in a blousy white lawn and a gold-hued brocaded vest entered the room. Closely behind him followed Frederick and John.

The gentleman turned kindly eyes upon her, clasping his hands together in unbridled delight. "Ah, *mi yerno*, this must be your sister, yes?"

Frederick came to stand at the gentleman's shoulder. "Si, Señor," he smiled. "Margaret, may I present my father-in-law, Salvador Barbour."

Barbour bowed with a courtly flourish, offering his hand to the young lady. Margaret smiled and curtseyed, taking Barbour's hand and allowing him to bestow a gallant kiss upon her fingers. "Ah, Frederick, you do not exaggerate. Señor Thornton, you are a very lucky man!"

Margaret flushed at the bold compliment as John drew near to take her arm. He looked down to her and was treated to her brilliant smile as her face shone up to him. "Yes, Señor, I am," he agreed heartily.

Margaret, embarrassed as she was, forced herself to make polite answer. "I am honoured to make your acquaintance, sir, and I thank you for your hospitality."

"The honour is mine, muchacha! Your brother, he is a son to me. It is I who am most pleased that you have come!" Barbour clapped a familiar hand on Frederick's shoulder and another on John's. "Your husband is a clever man! Drives a hard bargain, my son tells me, but he is an Englishman I can work with. We celebrate tonight! Sofia, Dolores!" he called to his wife and grown daughter.

The pair of smiling ladies had drawn near. Barbour greeted both with expansive affection and declared an end to their feminine labors for the day. "It is time for the meal!" he asserted, steering his wife toward the dining parlour.

John was grinning broadly as they fell into step behind the rest of the party. "It is going well, then?" Margaret inquired softly.

"Very. They are a formidable pair- your brother has a keen head and Barbour is craftier than he lets on, but we have nearly come to full agreement in all the particulars."

"Then the mill is safe!" she cried in relief.

"It looks that way." He frowned. "It will still be a pinch for a while, as we will yet be rather short of capital. I may have to lay off some of the hands for a time until we see some returns."

Margaret looked with regret down to her exquisite gown and the sparkling ring embellishing her finger. "We should not keep these," she whispered guiltily.

He tightened his grip upon her arm. "Do not speak so, Margaret. It is but a small expense in the larger scheme, and we may yet find a way to avoid such a measure."

She bit her lip in continued worry. "Margaret," he interrupted her thoughts. "I beg you would trust me. I will look after my own." She glanced up at his face in time to see a reassuring wink.

"Smile, Beloved. Barbour wishes us to celebrate with him this evening. I expect we should be prepared for something of a feast," he finished, with a warning expression softened by mirth.

At long last, the day's final responsibilities were done. Nicholas Higgins had tallied the day's counts over and again to be certain of his numbers. Slowly he climbed the wrought-iron staircase, his eyes still scrolling down the pages he flipped over. The sheer volume of cotton bolt produced by the mill in a single day was no less staggering on paper than it was in real life.

Now, however, he knew the price of those hours of sweat. The order book had lain open before his eyes the entire afternoon. On the backs of his tally sheets, he had sketched a few quick figures. It was these numbers, not the final tally of the day, which still held his attention.

It was true, the great steam-powered wheels turned a handsome figure on paper, but Higgins knew exactly how much manpower must be costing Thornton's mill. He had a faint grasp of the price of cotton and made a wild stab at what he thought might be some of the mill's other overhead costs. He felt he could make a fairly educated guess at Marlborough Mills' net profit at the end of each week.

He mopped his sweating forehead once again with his weathered cap as he looked at the figure at the bottom of the page. The number was far more modest than he might once have thought. Cotton prices had risen, he knew, and as yet the demand for finished goods had not caught up with the spiraling cost of the raw material. It would, given time- it always did. He heaved a great sigh. He hoped his employer would have the luxury of waiting things out.

At his knock on the overseer's office door, a tired voice bade him to enter. He found Williams still behind his tower of papers, but nearly done for the day himself. Higgins felt his stomach drop when he surveyed the chaos that was Williams' domain. It seemed nothing had changed from several hours ago. How frustrating it must be to never see a notable improvement after one has been laboring all day!

Yet Williams seemed well pleased, declaring he had gotten to much more than he might have been able, had Higgins not taken over his duties about the mill. Higgins shook his head, still marveling at the great number of things he had always taken for granted.

"If yo'll please, sir, I mu'n see to me lad. Is anythin' wantin'?"

Williams gave him a nonchalant wave of his hand, scarcely looking back up from his desk. He had only a handful of payroll notes left to calculate and had every intention of spending this one evening with his wife.

Higgins shifted his cap in his hands, gave a polite nod, and departed. A few minutes more and he was once again at the great oaken door to the Thornton residence. Jane answered to his knock and showed him to her mistress' parlour.

Mrs Thornton raised her stern features at his entrance. "Mr Higgins," she greeted him, but her customary brittleness was absent from her tone.

"Madam," he bowed shortly. "I'll thank ye kindly again fer lookin' after me lad."

He wished to say much more. How he wondered that a lady of her station and reputation would take an interest in a worker's orphan! He would have liked to speak of how some of the young mothers in the mill- after hearing rumours of her care of the lad- were whispering of Mrs Thornton's goodness to them at one time or another. As though it were some shameful secret! With the Dragon, however, rumours of good deeds had always been carefully guarded.

Mrs Thornton came toward him with stately grace. She rang a small bell, and Jane reappeared. "Jane, will you fetch Mr Higgins' child? I sent him to the washroom only a moment ago." The maid bobbed a curtsey and went to do her mistress' bidding.

Mrs Thornton turned a cool gaze upon him. "Mr Higgins, it has come to my attention that your child wants a deal of training in proper etiquette. You must see to it he receives it."

"I... Aye, Madam." Flustered, he looked down once again to the ornate carpet at Mrs Thornton's feet. Etiquette? He was a simple man with simple manners, and his children were no more than he. How was he to go about schooling the lad in fine behaviors, and more importantly, why should he?

"Is there a problem, Mr Higgins?" His gaze rose again to her face; the skeptical arched brow, the demanding tilt to her head which he now knew well from his familiarity with the woman's son.

"'Tis only, Madam.... that I be'nt the best to instruct 'im in such things. I know nothin' of it meself." He thinned his lips in some embarrassment, but this time refused to look to the floor. He would not be ashamed in her presence!

"I see," she responded quietly, her eyes shifting to the side. "There you are, child. Your father has come to take you home."

Higgins turned to behold a freshly scrubbed boy with a glowing countenance entering the room behind him. He serenely tilted his head this way and that, encouraging his foster father to notice his very handsome grooming. "Mrs Thornton cut my hair, Mr Nicholas!" he boasted, not quite able to contain himself. He puffed out his little chest, raising his arms. "And just see! She had a new shirt *just* my size, so I needn't wear the ink-stained one to school!"

Higgins stood flabbergasted. His amazed eyes searched the good lady's face but found no flicker of emotion playing across her granite features. He might have expected exasperated scolding, or some kind of denial, but she appeared to observe the boy's exuberant praises with perfect equanimity.

She turned to him with well composed dignity. "Mr Higgins, as you claim no education in etiquette yourself, I insist that the child must come regularly for instruction. Would tomorrow after school be convenient to the boy's schedule?"

Higgins' mouth dropped open. Brow furrowed in astonishment, he absolutely stared for several seconds. At length, he only managed a mute nod.

"Mr Higgins, you must *try* to adopt better manners, for the child's sake." She tilted her head a little toward him, eyebrows arched challengingly. Surely if he knew her a little better, he would have been able to interpret that gleam in her eye- for quite certainly she had no sense of humour, but he knew no other meaning to which he might attribute her expression.

"I... Aye, Madam," he stammered again. Johnny tensed in delight beside him, his wiry body quivering with glee. It seemed the pair had bewitched one another! He had never seen the boy more taken with anyone- not even the adored "Miss Marget" had captured the child's fancy in quite the same way this staid and frosty widow had.

"That will do well," she nodded gravely. Her gaze slid to the child. "Master Boucher, I shall be expecting you tomorrow at Four O'clock for tea."

Beside Higgins, young Johnny suddenly straightened and responded to Mrs Thornton's formal invitation with a precise little bow. "Thank you, Mrs Thornton, I shall be delighted," he answered with careful inflection.

Mrs Thornton's eyes twinkled strangely again, and she inclined her head solemnly to her callers. "I bid you good evening then, Gentlemen."

Thirty-One

"GOOD EVENING, MY DEAREST Margaret." John could not keep the smile out of his tones as he slid his arms around his wife's silk-clad waist in the privacy of their chamber. She had retired earlier to dress for bed, while he had lingered over drinks with Frederick and Señor Barbour. He had certainly enjoyed the pair's company but had been silently counting the minutes until he could decently excuse himself.

He was fairly positive that Frederick had intentionally brought up that question about Arkwright just as he had been about to bid them goodnight. The younger Mr Hale was far more sly and devious than the senior had been. At long last though, he had extricated himself. Here, finally, he was rewarded at the end of the day by Margaret's loving embrace. He nuzzled her hair as she came willingly into his arms.

"Good evening, John." Margaret giggled a little as she snuggled against his chest. How formal her words sounded on the surface, when the reality was far warmer and more intimate. No longer was she nervous- rather, she relished the chance to draw close to him once more. She inhaled his scent deeply again, as if afraid she might forget it.

"I do not remember you wearing this before," he mused, tracing his fingers over the satiny curves of her garment. "What else have you been hiding from me?"

"When exactly should I have worn it?" she inquired primly. "At tea on board the ship, or perhaps to meet Frederick's family? In truth though, I only received it earlier today. It was in one of the smaller boxes that you gave me."

"Really?" he admired her robe again with increasing interest. "I have exquisite taste, do I not?"

She laughed, wrapping her arms about his body. "I suppose I am bound to agree! Though, I do not think you can take full credit for the selection of these garments."

"There are more?" He lifted the silken binding of the robe at her shoulder and tried to peer at the filmy material hidden beneath.

She arched playfully away from him. "John Thornton! You are no gentleman at all!"

"I never said I was," he answered reasonably. "I believe we have already settled that you are no lady, so we are even." His fingers returned stubbornly to the edges of her robe, while his other hand tugged her closer. She had begun to laughingly object, but he silenced her in the best way he knew. As she melted into him, he began to kiss her in all the ways he had discovered she liked. His lips tripped over her warm flesh, and he proudly delighted in the euphoric sighs his caresses elicited.

While she was thus distracted, he smoothly released the tie on her robe then slipped his hands between the slick folds of cloth. A slight flick of his fingers and the satiny garment slipped off her shoulders.

She made a little muffled noise and lifted her mouth from his. "John..." her lashes fluttered hesitantly downward, "I think it would be best if... if we do not...."

He narrowed his eyes. "So, I *did* hurt you before." He pulled her to his chest and kissed her hair. "You promised you would tell me," he chided gently.

"It was only a little!" she pleaded. "I only think I would rather rest... just for tonight."

"Of course, Love" he replied easily. "I trust you will not deny me the pleasure of holding you, at least? You will not mind if I admire my good fortune a little more, will you?" She shook her head, smiling.

With a grin, John turned to shed his outer clothing, draping them over a chair. Then, bundling his precious wife in his arms, he nestled her between the sheets and snuggled her close to him. Margaret pressed her face into his chest as they wrapped their arms about each other. He sighed rapturously, tucking the loving friend of his heart under his chin as they settled into the pillows.

"John?" she asked sleepily after some minutes.

"Hmm," he murmured.

"Did you ask Frederick about writing home? I promised to send word once I arrived."

"I did. He actually advised against writing, though he said if you insisted, he would send your letter. He said he currently sends mail through an old comrade; someone he trusts who has settled in Antwerp. It might take many days before it arrived, in which time we will likely have returned ourselves."

Margaret bit her lip. She knew her Aunt Shaw and Edith would be worried out of their minds, but Frederick was probably right. It was not worth compromising his safety for the sake of a letter that would not arrive any sooner. In that case, it meant that Frederick also thought that Mr Bell.... She gasped a sorrowful breath.

John tightened his arms around her and kissed her forehead in empathy. She traced her fingers over his chest, bravely fighting back her grief over an inevitability she could not prevent. She stubbornly refused to cry on this, their first real night together.

She forcibly turned her thoughts in a happier direction. She was married to John! That withering and long-neglected hope had not died. Her life had begun in an entirely new path. Her brow furrowed as she thought again of her dear aunt and cousin. They no doubt waited anxiously for word of Margaret's safety and would be denied the warning of her letter.

"I expect when we do return, my poor aunt will have quite a shock!" she thought aloud. John gave a short chortle in reply. Then, in a shy voice, "How will your mother take our news, do you think?"

"Sitting down, I hope," he retorted dryly. It was Margaret's turn to stifle a chuckle, but it died in a sigh of worry. John interpreted her concerns perfectly. "Fear not, my love. She has only ever desired my happiness. It may take some adjustment for her, but she will hold you as a daughter."

Margaret drew a pensive breath. As a daughter? The proud, jealous mother she remembered might not welcome such an intrusion upon her son's affections. She could only hope and pray that the senior Mrs Thornton would see her not as a threat, but as the loyal helpmeet she intended to be.

Sensing her continued doubt, John whispered into her ear. "She has a soft spot for children, you know."

Margaret's eyes widened, digesting the idea. Children! The thought of prim Mrs Thornton doting upon a young one was almost scandalously fantastic. Yet, was it possible? For surely none should know her better than her own son. "Do you really think...?"

Laughing lightly, John rolled her gently beneath him and kissed the tip of her nose. "That she will come round? Or that we will be blessed with children?" He did not give her much chance at response for long delicious moments. She laced her fingers through his hair, tenderly pulling him to her heart.

When she finally did catch her breath, she tipped his chin to look carefully into his eyes. "I hope for both," she whispered.

"It is a hard duty, but I will do what I can to help- on *both* counts," he smirked, resting his chin comfortably on her breast. "However, for the latter I believe a deal of practice must be wanted."

Margaret gazed steadily, lovingly into his face. Slowly she moved beneath him, invitingly curling her body round his. He shook his head in gentle denial. "No, Love, I would not hurt you."

"I am suddenly feeling quite well recovered." She drew his face back to hers, an impish curve playing at her lips. "And as you say, much practice is wanted." His laugh was soon drowned out in the search of more delightful pursuits.

GIRAUD TAPPED HIS MUG again on the table, signaling a raven-haired serving girl to refill it. He eyed the girl's slim waist and ample bosom appraisingly. He had never before been to Spain, but he expected the hospitality here was as welcoming as in other places. For now, however, he needed to finish replenishing his traveling funds.

His gaze shifted back to his companions around the card table. He had made substantial headway, thankfully, toward that end. The other players had mostly proven wealthy enough to gamble high and foolish enough to lose generously. The man nearest him was an English lieutenant by the name of Jackson who had sneered disdainfully at first at the Frenchman. Now the fellow regarded him through eyes narrowed in grudging respect.

Giraud allowed himself the pleasure of staring at the lieutenant for a moment. The man drank and played like a sailor, with the abandon typical of one of Her Majesty's finest when on leave. Like as not, he had friends who were similarly inclined. He would do well not to thoroughly alienate this Englishman. A strategic loss or two, a few more drinks and some nostalgic tales, and he might even call the man a comrade.

MORNING BROUGHT A SWEET breeze, perfumed with tropical flowers, wafting into the bedroom. Margaret stretched languorously, looking about herself at the empty bed. John was already up and gone. Dimly she recalled his kiss and his warmth leaving her, a long while ago. She rose, grimacing as she identified stiffness and aches previously unfamiliar to her.

She tiptoed across the stone floor to the dressing table and poured herself a little cool water from the laver. She splashed her face and hands, dragging herself to full alertness. With a start, she realized that her shoulder was scarcely troubling her. Slowly and experimentally, she stretched forth her right hand. She could not hold it out for very long, and turning her wrist elicited a sharp stab of pain, but she felt greatly improved. A day or two ago she could scarcely lift it at all.

She found the little bell to call Maria to help her dress. A short while later, she descended the stairs in her new emerald gown. Maria showed her where Dolores and her mother were breakfasting, and she settled herself with a delicious cup of brewed chocolate. The flavor was a little unfamiliar to her, but she found it much to her liking- smooth and rich like coffee, and yet with a light clarity more akin to tea.

She spent the early morning with the two ladies, sewing and reading until word came to her that Mr Bell had wakened and had been refreshed. Excusing herself, she thanked the dark-eyed boy who had brought her the report. She rose and hurried to her godfather's side.

His face was grayer than the day before, his eyes puffier. She thinned her lips and resolved not to allow her dismay to show. She did not wish to dishearten him. "May I read for you some?" she asked gently. Bell nodded weakly, his eyes half closed. Margaret picked up *Ivanhoe* and began to search for her place when he stopped her.

"Did the doctor say anything to you my dear?" he wheezed.

"No, he did not. I did not see him again last evening," she admitted. She had looked in on Bell before going upstairs for the evening but had found him peacefully asleep.

"You know what he would have said, don't you?" the faint voice rasped.

Margaret lowered her eyes. "No, I do not," she denied stubbornly.

"Please do not play the fool, my dear. It does not become you," he whispered, his breath hissing through a sudden spasm of pain in his chest. She started in concern, her eyes whirling about the room for some means to offer him comfort. All she had to give was her hand, tightly clasping his.

The door creaked softly on its hinges. Her relieved expression welcomed John and Frederick, each stepping discretely into the room. John sat near her, while Frederick took his post on the opposite side of Mr Bell's bed. She looked to her husband with a faint question in her eyes.

"The little niño, Frederick called him, he said Bell was asking for us," he whispered lowly into her ear. Nodding almost imperceptibly, her face full of pity, she returned her gaze to her godfather.

Bell tightened his fingers around hers, reaching for Frederick's hand as well. "I never thought to have this last gift," he sighed painfully. "No children of my own. You are my children now, the both of you." Margaret met her brother's eyes, noting the pinched agony mirrored there. Bell's grip tightened reflexively again as another paroxysm seized his lungs.

"Shhh," she crooned gently, pulling her other hand from John, and caressing the old gentleman's cheek. "Do not speak now, you must rest."

"Please do not interrupt me, my dear. I have not long now, and you must know." Her brow furrowed and she dropped her eyes to his fevered hand. "I am leaving all my properties in England to you. My Spanish plantation goes to Frederick; it is already in his name. The bulk of everything else is yours."

Margaret gaped, her heart drumming in fear and wonder. "You cannot leave me so much! No, you must not! Surely, there is some other, some relative!"

"Hush, my dear," he whispered hoarsely. "There is not, and even if there were, this is what pleases me. No, it is already settled." He looked for the first time that morning to Thornton, whose face had gone pale. "I worried, my dear, that even everything I could give you would not be enough." He nodded gratefully to the younger man. "Now I see you already have all you needed."

Margaret was sobbing, the tears she had choked back earlier now rushing again to the fore. "Oh, Mr Bell! Please do not speak so. You can- you must not give up all hope!"

He shook his head gently. "You mistake me, my dear. I have a great deal more hope now than I have had in a very, very long time." He extended the hand she had gripped to Thornton and grasped the other man's firmly. "It is yours now, everything; though it all pales in comparison to the jewel you already possess." Bell tensed, grimacing against a coughing fit.

John swallowed hard. All that he had striven for, all those years of his tears and sweat, and now at a word everything was handed to him freely. Yet, with utter force of conviction, he fully agreed with the dying man before him. His true treasure was sitting next to him, twining her fingers over his and Mr Bell's. Blinking rapidly, he looked back to the old gentleman's face. Words failed him. All he could do was to nod in simple gratitude. Bell's eyes twinkled in understanding.

Frederick had sat in silence, an errant tear sliding down his sea-roughened cheek. He quivered in joy for Margaret and her manufacturer. His little sister would be well cared for in every way that was possible; every way that he could have wished to provide himself.

He squeezed Bell's hand thankfully, yet still he ached for the life that was passing before his eyes. The last of a generation of learned men, thoughtful watchmen of a bygone era; a lonely yet a beautiful soul sat poised at the gates of eternity. A tremor of grief turned into a loud gasp of heartbreak and his tears began to flow freely. He bowed his head and covered his face with his free hand as his shoulders shook with sobs.

Margaret and John leaned close together, he offering her comfort and strength. Her head low, she too began to give way to her grief, grateful for her husband's arm about her.

"There, now, both of you," the old man rasped weakly. "You will leave me no alternative but to march out of the room if you carry on so." John alone was capable of appreciating Bell's wry quip. The faded face on the pillow offered him a small wink as Richard Hale's children tried to compose themselves.

"Freddie," Bell murmured, with evident difficulty, "are you not angry with me for playing favorites?" The old fellow's eyes kindled with a lingering spark of mischief.

Frederick wiped his eyes, trying to laugh through his roiling emotions. "You know better than that, Godfather."

"You were always a good lad, Freddie," he whispered, his head rolling down the pillow in fatigue. "You have a good place here. My properties in France," he coughed, "I had long thought to pass them to you, but when I learned you were here for good...." He paused, clenching his eyes.

"You sold them to buy the plantation," Frederick finished. "And Barbour told me you sold him your South American properties." He smiled in gratitude. "You have been more than good, Godfather. I do not deserve your generosity, but I thank you, from the very bottom of my heart."

Bell smiled faintly, his eyes closing and his breath escaping as an inarticulate response. Exhausted, he said no more, and the parties about his bed bowed their heads in reverent sentry.

Thirty-Two

"NO!" THE TODDLER CRIED, stamping his foot and repeating the one word he seemed to always remember.

Edith Lennox was at her wit's end. Sholto, her lively twenty-month-old son, stared down from his perch atop his mother's wing-back sewing chair. His little shod feet balanced precariously on the top edge of the furnishing, and he steadied himself by stretching for the gilded bird cage which stood behind it. Defiance glinting from his hazel eyes, he fairly dared her to make him move from his little castle.

"Sholto! You must come down this instant!" Fear for her child's safety forced Edith to make a crude grasp for his chubby little arms.

"No!" he repeated with emphasis. As he was in the habit of doing when she reached for him, he turned and attempted to wriggle away. He might have succeeded too, if the bird cage by which he balanced had been more suited to his purposes. It was, however, designed for fine parlors rather than a child's jungle gym. It began to sway dangerously backward, and only a desperate lurch on his mother's part saved both child and bird from disaster.

Edith clasped her writhing son to her breast, a mother's relief temporarily overriding her annoyance with the child. He, however, was impeded by no such swell of emotion. Pushing against her arms, Sholto arched away from her and wormed his way to freedom. She grasped his sweaty little fingers as he slipped to the floor, but he tugged away. Edith was bested and they both knew it.

With a squeal of rebellion and delight, he pillaged his way out of the room and attacked the stairs, nearly tripping poor old Dixon as she lumbered down. The aging maid peered questioningly through to the parlour, where Edith slumped in shame and defeat. She tugged her handkerchief from the folds of her gown as tears of humiliation and torment pricked her eyes. She dabbed her lashes daintily so as not to disturb her perfect cosmetics, but her frustration was genuine. How was she to manage such a hellion of a child?

Dixon limped near, her expression full of sympathy, yet... was that amusement lighting the woman's eyes? Edith cared not to ask. She was more greatly agitated that it had to be Dixon who witnessed the scene. Her own maids were crisply polished and professional, utterly discrete. Dixon, however, seemed to air opinions of her own, and Margaret had not taken care to squelch them. *Margaret....*

With a renewal of her distress, Edith buried her face in her handkerchief and sobbed uncontrollably. "There, now, Mistress, there's no need for that." Dixon's voice, an odd mixture of comfort and practicality, broke through Edith's self-pity.

"Oh, Dixon!" she wailed, shaking her perfect curls as she strove for speech. "I just do not know what is to be done with him! Margaret always knows just what to do and here she is gone off, and I do not know if she will ever come back to us! What shall I do?"

It was fortunate, perhaps, that Edith was still lost to her feelings and missed the weary roll of Dixon's eyes. "The lad is a Beresford, and no mistake," she mumbled under her breath. In a more audible tone, she added, "Do not you fret about the child, Mistress. He only wants a bit of management."

Edith stopped her tears and glared speechlessly at Dixon's audacity. To make the claim that her precious baby needed a firmer hand would have immediately sent any of the other household staff in search of new employment. Dixon, however, she could not touch. She began to open her mouth in impotent consternation when a clamour, again from the direction of the stairs, dispelled all thought.

Margaret had painstakingly taught Sholto how to manage the stairs on his own by turning round and stepping down backward. Edith had at first objected- surely it was his nurse's duty to carry him up and down stairs at all times! Margaret had sweetly insisted, however, that it was important for a lively child's safety that he should know what to do in any case. So, just as she and Frederick had been taught on the steps of the modest parsonage, soon she had Sholto confidently navigating the massive spiral staircase for himself.

He was now putting that knowledge to good use, gleefully slipping his nurse's collar as she clambered down in harried pursuit. He only giggled in delight and moved faster, nearly sliding rather than crawling down backward. Gaining the bottom, he turned and toddled back to the protection of his mother, depending upon her to not let Nurse carry him to his bed like the naughty boy he was.

Clinging to her skirts, he beamed a cherubic, drooling smile up at her. Exasperated, Edith picked him up. Beside her, Dixon was silently pressing her lips together. Edith did not miss this look of disapproval, and some part of her wished to prove herself better than Dixon apparently thought. *Think!* she admonished herself. *What would Margaret do?*

Straightening, Edith took a deep breath and set the rebellious toddler back on the floor. The embarrassed nurse finally caught up, and shamefully dropped her gaze before the Mistress.

"Sholto," Edith's voice quavered uncertainly. "You must mind Nurse. Go now, and you may return when Nurse says your manners have improved." *Margaret would have managed the wayward child herself,* Edith thought glumly, but surely her cousin would approve of this small display of maternal authority, at least.

Three astonished expressions greeted her. The young nurse, a competent woman from a large family, looked to her mistress in grateful relief. Dixon's lips twitched in endorsement. Sholto's face, however, crumpled in aggrieved betrayal. Mother never remanded him to Nurse's custody when she was about to take him away! He wailed his disappointment as he was carried off, flopping and writhing in his caretaker's firm embrace.

Taking a bracing draught of air, Edith spread her trembling hands over her skirts. Dixon, her eyes sparkling oddly, made her typical abbreviated curtsey and began to turn away. A fresh scone and a hot cup of coffee were calling to her.

"Dixon, wait!" Edith stopped her. The maid turned back, her eyebrows arching expectantly. "Margaret..." She choked back a sob and started again. "How long did Margaret say she would be away? She *is* coming back, is she not?" Edith's tones broke. Dearest Margaret! Why would she have gone away so?

Dixon's mouth fluttered and she began to blink rapidly. Margaret was as dear to her old heart as she ever could be to Edith, but Dixon had more faith in Margaret's fortitude. Her girl would come back, she had every confidence, and no doubt the happier for it. Nothing would have set the girl's mind at ease if she had not gone off, but it was impossible to make Edith understand her more single-minded cousin.

"Depend on it, Mistress, she'll be back. Master Frederick will be taking good care of 'er until then. Just ye wait and see, Miss Margaret will come back in good time." She set her jaw and gave a definitive nod for emphasis.

Edith shook her head, the tears beginning to flow again. "But it is so dangerous, so shocking! What could have made her do it, Dixon? She could meet with any manner of people on such a journey, and Frederick could not be there to help! How could she do this to us?" Edith buried her face again in her handkerchief, weeping helplessly.

Dixon was ordinarily wont to simply roll her eyes at what she perceived as Mrs Lennox's frivolity, but the young mistress' last comment raised her hackles. "*Do* what to us? Miss Margaret 'as done nothing but care for others and doin' just what they'd 'ave 'er do! Sakes and nonsense, don't the girl deserve some 'appiness? She's been down in the mouth for months. If y'ask me, she left 'alf 'er 'eart in Milton. Aye, mourning or no, she's not the same as she was there, no ma'am. First time I saw any spark in 'er at all was when she made up her mind to go. Count on it Mistress, she'll come back and you won't know her! She'll be that much stronger, she will."

Edith stared in horror and amazement at the pert old maid. Dixon, her ire fading, fully grasped the impropriety of all she had said. She flushed scarlet and dropped her gaze. "If you'll forgive me, Ma'am...." She shuffled off awkwardly, head bowed.

Edith toppled gracelessly into her chair, still incapable of speech or thought. Dixon's words, more than her complete lack of deference, shook her to her core. An agonized sob racked her and she broke down completely.

"Dearest?" Her husband's voice drifted into the room a moment later. "Edith, there you are! Darling, what is the matter?" Maxwell Lennox strode into the room, his confident manner belying the concern in his voice. He was not a man of deep feelings and tended to dismiss his wife's hysterics as common to all fair creatures of her sex. "Edith, whatever is troubling you?" he asked again, more gently when her tears did not cease.

"Oh, Max!" she cried, and flung herself into his shocked embrace. Through blubbering gasps he was able to make out Margaret's name once or twice, but no more.

He patted her back, still mystified, and looked over his shoulder to his brother, who had just been calling. Henry hung reluctantly in the entryway, not liking to take his part in a scene between husband and wife.

"Now, Edith," Maxwell pushed her shoulders back a little, forcing Edith to compose herself. "Whatever is this all about?"

"M-m-m..." she sniffled. "M-Margaret! She is m-miserable here and will never want to come b-back!"

Maxwell frowned, glancing again at his brother. "Where are you getting this notion, my sweet? You know Margaret adores you, and she absolutely dotes on dear little Sholto. How can you say she is so unhappy here?"

"D-Dixon s-says so!" she wailed, drenching the shoulder of her husband's morning coat with her tears. She took a great gulp of air and her words came out in an unbroken rush.

"She says M-margaret was unhappy and th-that is why she w-went off, and if she does not w-want to come b-back I do not know what I sh-shall do!"

"My dear," he could not keep the patronizing roll out of his tones, "you ought to know better than to listen to Dixon. She's a sour old maid, and that's that. Here," he offered his own perfectly pressed handkerchief and grimaced a little as Edith spoilt it in a most unladylike fashion. "Come, now, you must go lie down until you are thinking clearly."

Edith meekly submitted to her husband's guiding hand. Not until she had neared the entryway of the room did she notice Henry, lurking in the shadows of the hall just outside. Poor Henry! How distraught he must be at Margaret's disappearance! She began to snuffle again, losing whatever composure she had gained.

Maxwell groaned. "Sarah!" he called. A young maid appeared promptly, as though she had been hovering nearby and only waited to hear her name. He sighed in relief. A good girl, that, and deserving of a raise. "Take Mrs Lennox to her room and see she is comfortable," he directed. Sarah curtseyed and took over the care of her weeping mistress.

Once she had safely scaled the staircase, Maxwell spared a significant glance for his brother. Henry met his brother's arched brow with a silent, level gaze. Maxwell pressed his lips together and wordlessly led the way to his study. He closed the door and bolted it, then rounded on his brother. "Well, now! What do you make of all that? Save that my wife is somewhat the worse for wear?" He sat heavily in his chair, rubbing his temples and reaching for a whiskey glass.

Henry seated himself, his eyes on the floor. He rubbed his upper lip thoughtfully with the back of his finger. "I think she may be right," he answered softly.

"What?" Maxwell almost gagged in surprise on the strong spirits he was sipping. He cleared his throat and set his glass down. "What makes you say so?" he demanded.

Henry shook his head wearily. He had lost a deal of sleep of late. "Margaret has not been herself since she returned from the North. I thought at first it was due to grief over her father, but now I am not so sure- at least, there must be more to it. I think she must have been desperately unhappy before she heard Mr Bell's news, else she would have been more willing to speak to Mrs Shaw and Edith about her concerns. Do not you?"

"I've no idea. I never understood her myself. Such a quiet one, but in truth she is a little intimidating. So... well, so stoic and aloof she can be. I feel as if she does not quite approve of me sometimes. Do not you dare *ever* repeat that!" he glared, pointing an accusing finger at Henry.

Henry sighed, ignoring his brother's frustrated drinking. "Margaret is not intimidating," he mused. "She is simply... direct. And determined. Yes, I suppose that is it. She knows what she wants and will not be swayed from it."

Maxwell dropped his glass to the bureau with a bang. "And you were not it, were you Brother?"

Henry's face admitted all. His shoulders drooped and he stared wordlessly at the carpet.

"I thought as much." Maxwell refilled his glass, pouring a second this time for Henry which went untouched. "I tell you, the girl is proud and a fool."

Henry's brown eyes flashed to his brother's. "Margaret is no fool," he whispered through clenched jaw. "Nor is she prideful. We were friends. I thought once, perhaps, that we could be more, but that is in the past. All I can pray for now is her safe return, that she be restored to those she loves. I shall hope that she will be content to remain in London, but I have little confidence of that."

"You think so too, then? Tell me, what is this obvious change in her demeanor which everyone save myself claims to have witnessed? She is withdrawn, but then she always was to a certain extent, and she is in mourning besides."

"Have you not heard her speak, then? I cannot believe I missed it. Little interests her but matters of business these days. She was far too refined to speak of such things before. I have some banking contacts in common with her Mr Bell, and when I speak of financial matters in the North her eyes finally light up. She is greedy for any news and does all but come right out and ask how matters stand with the unions and the bosses up there. I think she must have a good many friends she cares about still there, but she says nothing of them."

Maxwell grunted. His interest in the matter was fading, as he only really concerned himself with affairs as they directly impacted his household. He swirled his drink, then pivoted in his chair to plop his feet directly on his desk. He smirked a little at Henry's pained expression. He always did love goading his younger brother when he could.

"Why was it you were calling this morning? I must assume after all this that it had something to do with Margaret."

Henry sat up straight, suddenly remembering the concerns he intended now to share. "Maxwell... I cannot be sure she actually sailed for Spain."

"What do you mean? Of course, she did! Why, where else might she have gone? Eloped with someone?" Maxwell snorted disbelievingly. "Hardly likely."

"No, certainly I do not believe she had any ruinous intentions. Odd though her behavior seems, *that* would be impossible, I believe. What I mean is that I obtained a copy of the ship's complete passenger list. Her name is not on it."

"Are you certain it was accurate? Perhaps she used an assumed name."

"I thought of that. The only unaccompanied woman listed was identified to me as the captain's own daughter." Henry related the rest of his conversation with Harper, mentioning the injured woman he had heard of. He even produced Harper's list for his brother's inspection.

"So, what do you think?" Maxwell asked, for the first time displaying a pinch of worry between his brows. "You mentioned that Thornton fellow, you think she may have taken a different ship to avoid notice?"

"If she did, she covered her tracks well, but I have never known Margaret to be duplicitous in any way." Henry began to nervously pluck his eyebrow, a distracting habit from school days which he had effectively killed off in his adult years. Stress, it seemed, had rekindled the old vice.

"I checked, and there were only two other ships she could have taken that morning. Both were small ships bound for France. Her name does not appear on their lists either-both claim that no unaccompanied women traveled."

"I see...." Maxwell chewed his lip, then impatiently tossed back the glass he had poured for Henry. "Well, I do not know what exactly we can do, Brother. If she had wanted to be followed, I say she could have made it easier."

"There is one lead still to follow up. I am visiting the fish warehouse on the docks, the one Harper told me about. Perhaps this 'Old Madge' he speaks of will remember the injured woman who was brought in and can describe her. I was hoping you might come with me."

"Why me? And why you? You are starting to sound like a private investigator. Besides, from what you told me, that could not possibly have been her."

"It's all I've got." Henry sighed deeply, said no more for a moment. He began to think he had been wrong in coming to Maxwell. No good could come from it, other than the relief of his own private anxiety by sharing the worry.

Maxwell was not unconcerned about Margaret, but he was a pragmatist. He would not fret himself over something he could not control, but he might well accidentally let some word slip to his wife. Edith certainly needed no further fuel for her agitation, and Henry had really no proof of anything- not yet.

He realized his fingers had begun to pluck his eyebrow again and he forced himself to still them. He held his hand up in a gesture of defeat. "Never mind. You are right, of course. Forgive me for disturbing your morning."

"Not at all." Maxwell dropped his feet to the floor and stood. He pressed his lips together in sympathy at last. "I am sorry, Henry. I wish there were more we could do. Surely, if she is safe, she will send word. Margaret was always a faithful correspondent."

"I know," he breathed, standing slowly. "It may be many days yet, though. She said as much in that letter she left you. If she should prove *not* to be safe, that is a deal of time to lose."

Maxwell frowned and nodded silently. Clapping his hand on his brother's shoulder, he showed him to the front door. Henry departed in a morose gloom.

Maxwell watched him from a front window as he shuffled down the street, head down. He shook his own head. He knew his brother like no other, and to him it looked like the man was giving up. A shame, he thought, that Henry had fallen for such a proud young woman and that she had failed to see what was good for her. Henry was an upright fellow, and he would make any woman a kind and faithful husband. Maxwell could not predict what might yet happen with Margaret, but he hoped that someday his brother might be rewarded with happiness.

Thirty-Three

HANNAH THORNTON STROLLED WITH quiet dignity through the great looms in her son's mill. It may, she reflected, be one of her last opportunities to do so. The power and the wondrous technology represented in this room alone had always impressed her. Though the noise was deafening and wearying, she never tired in her fascinated study of the weaving process.

With clock-like precision, a row of workers- women, mostly- marched the arm of the great machine forward for the next loop of the weave. As the arm was withdrawn again, two children, about twelve years of age, scrambled beneath to reclaim wasted cotton. They scurried back out as the arm was pushed forward again. The entire team moved with a mesmerizing rhythm, perfect in synchrony.

A couple of the women allowed their gazes to drift toward her as they worked. All by now had heard rumours of the master's mother and the Boucher child. She had not seemed quite human to many of them, until now. Some still regarded her with dubious appraisal.

Hannah was no fool. She knew precisely the reason for the questioning glances. Well, what matter if they thought her behavior unusual? Had not she, a widow presently bereft of her son and only joy, the right to show kindness once again to a child? Had not the boy, robbed of a mother's care, felt both the pleasure and the advantage of her attentions? Satisfying herself that her actions were above reproach, she held her head a little loftier.

With a grave nod and a slightly challenging lift of her eyebrows, she met the gaze of the most overtly curious young woman on the line. The woman's eyes widened and she snapped them back to her work, her cheeks stained pink. Hannah allowed her expression to warm ever so slightly in triumph. Another young woman, not quite so easily cowed, gaped in silent wonder as the line marched backward.

This amused her greatly. She liked a bold face, and she offered a slight upward curve of her lower lip. The young woman's brow knit, then without warning a lovely smile blossomed to the full. Hannah could not stop- did not realize, perhaps- an answering twitch to the corners of her mouth. Her dark eyes flashed kindly. Inclining her head once more, she took her leave of the plucky young worker. Little did she know, she left in her wake more generous feelings than perhaps ever before.

She wandered on, searching faces for once rather than machinery and able arms. It was the same throughout the mill. Some did their best to ignore her, keeping their eyes studiously to their task. Others gazed intrepidly, daring to meet her eyes, and finding an unaccounted warmth there. Often it was instantly returned, and the effect was multiplied the longer it went on.

Her heart soared curiously. She had never been well-liked in most circles. Years of brushing aside others' grudging tolerance of her shy stoicism had built a roughened and calloused character. Where once it had needed a thoughtful and patient companion to truly draw her out enough to appreciate her charm, now most would claim no such allure ever existed.

The mill workers, however, lacked the pride of circumstance possessed by many of her acquaintances. They looked only for a kind word or a smile to sweeten the bitterness of their long day. The tender places of her heart thawed, ever so reluctantly, at the workers' immediate responses to her small overtures.

She had been expecting to encounter Nicholas Higgins at any time. There would be no way of predicting his whereabouts- rather than remaining at a station he would be flitting about the entire mill if he were faithfully performing his duties. She admitted to herself a great curiosity and wondered if she would have an opportunity to see John's favorite at work. After about half an hour, her expectations were fulfilled.

One of the spinners was broken down again. She paused at a discrete distance to observe the men, led by Higgins, as they wrestled with the recalcitrant piece of machinery. Higgins clambered up to a peak to reach the lines above, more nimbly than she might have expected for a man of his age and stature. He bore a large wrench, using it to expertly tap and tinker with the release valve. At his word, a man waiting below jerked the lever to engage the machine and it roared to life. Higgins descended to grateful claps on his shoulder and general esteem among his peers.

"A'right, Lads, that be it. C'mon, now, back to work!" The men grumbled good-naturedly but turned their hands immediately to their tasks as Higgins walked away. His path lay directly before Hannah, and he pulled up short.

"G'day, Ma'am," he touched his sweat-stained cap respectfully.

"Good day to you, Mr Higgins," she greeted him cordially, then spoke no more.

He glanced from side to side under her silent gaze. Higgins was not a man to be shaken by a firm word from the Master, but his mother was another matter. He did not understand her at all and suspected that few ever did. "Be there somethin' wantin'?" he ventured at length.

"Not at all, Mr Higgins," she replied serenely, yet she did not move. She draped one hand over the other and rested them across her black skirts.

Higgins stared wordlessly, feeling too self-conscious to meet her eyes. She seemed perversely to enjoy intimidating him. Distantly, he noted for the first time that the Mistress' hands were gnarled and cragged, like those which had known hard work in their day. He cleared his throat, trying to break the uncomfortable silence. "I, uh... I'll be about me duties then, Madam," he tipped his hat.

Mrs Thornton inclined her head graciously and stepped aside to let him pass. "I will see you this evening, then," she reminded him.

"Aye, Ma'am," he nodded awkwardly. He began to move away, then paused. He summoned his courage, looking her full in the face with the same impertinent twinkle in his eye which amused the Master. "I'll thank ye again, Ma'am, for takin' an interest in me lad. 'E's been a fair sight 'appier these days."

The black-clad widow's expression suddenly cleared of her customary frost. Something like genuine pleasure played about her eyes and mouth. If he were not mistaken, a faint hint of rosy warmth teased her cheeks. Though some years older than himself, he thought fleetingly that she might once have been a fair lass.

She hesitated for the barest breath, her dark lashes fluttering uncertainly. "The pleasure has been mine, Mr Higgins." Her voice was low, barely audible over the clamour of the looms and the boom of the steam engine, but her meaning could not be missed. Higgins responded with an audacious wink, dipped his head, and ambled away.

MARGARET DID NOT LEAVE her beloved Mr Bell's side all day. She held watchful vigilance over every agonized breath, every flutter of his eyes as his earthly body began to slip away. John and Frederick had left her only briefly, and in shifts so that she was never fully alone in her sentinel. Frederick returned to them now, trading her a tray of refreshment for *Ivanhoe* and taking his turn at reading. Dolores came with him and eased her small ponderous frame into a chair next to her husband.

Margaret gratefully dipped a piece of bread in the soup which Frederick had brought. Soon she found that she had no appetite, though her stomach cried out for nourishment. Frustrated, she forced herself to gag down a few mouthfuls, but quickly set the tray aside.

Her entire body hurt from sitting so long in one posture. She rolled her good shoulder, rocking her head from side to side. Much to her relief, strong warm fingers volunteered to knead her tired muscles. The release of tension was immediate and she let out a long ragged breath.

She smiled gratefully at John, realizing that he was likely as weary as she, and not knowing how she could offer him the same comfort. She trapped his fingers in her good hand as he withdrew and kissed them boldly. The light which came into his eyes assured her that it was thanks enough for him.

Across the sickbed, Dolores caught their private exchange. Her luscious lips puckered in delight. *Margarita,* as she called her adored new sister, appeared fortunate in her marriage. It brought her cheer not only for Margaret's sake, but also for Frederick's. Surely, he would worry a great deal less about his distant sister now.

Dolores, too, stretched uncomfortably and rubbed a hand over her bulging midsection. Frederick's hand strayed to hers in sympathy as he read. He had already made her promise to leave the room if she began to weary, though he doubted she would keep her word. He understood- his spritely Dolores would only naturally demand her rightful place beside him during this final vigil over one so dear.

Some time after the dinner hour, well into the evening, Bell's breathing rhythm changed. Those in attendance sharpened their gazes upon him. His chest fluttered quick and shallow. Fluid rattled in his lungs and he could not get the air he needed. At length, his eyes opened again. He stared unseeingly at the wall when Margaret's sweet voice caught his attention.

Slowly the bleary gaze found her. His swollen cheeks tensed into his best approximation of a smile. His lips, now cracking, mouthed her name but there was no sound behind it. Margaret had taken his hand, and she squeezed his fingers gently. Raptly he gazed into her beloved face, taking heart in her faithful smile. His breath rattled in his throat as his breathing continued to dip.

Feeling faint, he let eyes roll closed again, but as if he realized something he had forgotten, he opened them immediately. His aching gaze sought his godson, the only child he had watched grow to manhood. He felt as proud of this strapping son and graceful woman as if they had been his very own. Frederick took his hand and grinned roguishly, reminding him of better days. Bell took one last long breath and closed his eyes in peace. He never opened them again.

His body lingered on, fighting valiantly for every morsel of fresh air, but it was no use. A mere hour later, his earthly soul passed on to his reward. Margaret and Frederick were by now numb with grief. The tears rolled silently down their cheeks, but they did not break down as they had before. Their spouses, staying near with misty eyes of their own, shared in their mourning and comforted as they could.

Margaret leaned heavily on John's shoulder, thanking the good Lord for bringing them back together at such a time so she might not have to grieve alone. He cradled her against him, not speaking but simply holding her. Her grief was his, and he ached for her return to sorrow and mourning.

At length he persuaded her to try to get some sleep, as it was by now very late. Frederick relented as well, more out of sympathy for his wife's condition than in admission that he ought to abandon his post. Dolores gave soft directions in Spanish to someone of the household for the disposition of Mr Bell's room and dragged her reluctant husband to bed.

John and Margaret followed slowly, she depending upon him perhaps more than she knew. When they met with the stairs, he no longer wished for her to struggle on. Without giving her an opportunity to object, he wrapped her into his arms to carry her. She was not heavy, though her voluminous gown made it difficult to hold her securely. Still, he had never carried her so far up long stairs and was quite winded when they gained the top.

He set her down at their door and she turned to him with her first smile all day. She reached to kiss his cheek. "Thank you," she whispered simply. He pulled her close for long breaths, feeling the tension ebbing from her as she nestled into his arms.

He helped her dress for bed, then encouraged her to turn away from him so that he might wrap his body comfortingly around her as she rested. She sighed deeply, leaning wearily against his chest, and pillowing her head on his arm. In minutes she fell into an exhausted sleep.

JOHN WAS HABITUALLY AN early riser, but the next day he lingered. It was only his second morning waking up to the sublime pleasure of Margaret cradled in his arms. There would be no urgency to rise quickly and meet with Frederick this morning, so he contented himself with watching her soft breathing.

Her hair he had loosed the night before, and it tumbled gloriously over the pillow. She was so beautiful, swathed in the warm glow of morning! He could still scarcely believe she was his.

He propped his head upon his hand, not touching her to disturb her slumber. How long he remained thus, simply savouring her angelic presence, he could not say. As he watched, her breathing would change from time to time, her eyes moving beneath her dark lashes.

She was dreaming, but as the dream wore on, he could tell it was not a pleasant one. Her lovely features pinched, her closed eyes blinking more rapidly. He considered waking her for no other reason than to have the privilege of reassuring her, but with a gasp she woke herself.

She sat bolt upright, a quiver of moisture in the corners of her eyes. It was clear she did not quite register her surroundings at first. He stroked a soothing hand over her back. "What is it, Love?" he murmured.

Her eyes flew to his in a rush of relief. "Oh, John! The most terrifying dream!"

"Tell me," he encouraged, drawing her to his chest.

"I- I don't recall all the details. I just know I lost you. Something took you away and I could not find you again." She drew a tremulous breath, blinking the emotions away. "I suppose it sounds silly, now."

He chuckled silently. "Not silly. I am glad to know you would be sorry to lose me." He continued to stroke her hair, pressing his lips to her temple. "You know I would never leave you, my darling," he spoke as a solemn vow.

She shook with a deep sigh, then draped her head over his shoulder. "I know. It just seemed so real, and I was so devastated."

He kissed her lightly, relishing the sweetness of being the one she turned to for comfort. "I am sure it comes from losing so many others you love, do you not think? You have been somewhat battered this past year, I am afraid."

She allowed him to pull her back down to a lying position, grateful to find her fears vanished in the truth of morning. At the mention of her past griefs, her eyes misted again. "John," she whispered. "I... I miss them all so much."

"I know, Love," he tightened his arms about her. "I miss them too. Your father was perhaps the best friend I ever had. And Mr Bell... I have no words yet."

Margaret sniffled, willing herself not to burst into helpless tears. "He was always so good to me. And still! I feel so unworthy of... of everything."

"He did not think you so. You must trust in that. He thought the world of you, my love."

She was quiet for a moment, biting at her fingertips as she blinked away her sorrow. The new day was upon her, and with it, a new sense of obligation. "We must put his gift to good use, John," she pleaded. "I would like to find some way to honour his memory."

"I have been thinking of that. What of establishing a library in Milton, in his honour? Perhaps we could do more as well, but it will take some time and thought. I am sure he would like it if we found ways for the Mill to truly improve people's lives. What do you think?"

"I like it very much! What of a school at the Mill, or some place for the youngest children to be near their families? I know it is hard for some of them."

"I was thinking grander, even, than that. You remember what I told Giraud, about the new Mill towns? Perhaps that is a dream we can aspire to someday as well. But let it rest for a time. I do not like speaking of such things just now."

Margaret nodded into his chest. She felt secretly that Bell would be delighted with John's ideas, but she understood his discomfort; she, too wished to remain deferential to their recently departed friend's memory. It would not be difficult, for her godfather was all she could think of. At least she could turn her thoughts of him in a cheerful direction. "I think he was happy," she sighed meaningfully, settling her head more snugly in the crook of John's arm.

"I believe so. He surprised me, how pleased he was for us. I rather expected him to be sorry you had not married better," John chuckled, reaching to nuzzle her cheek with his morning stubble.

"Not I," she returned stoutly, but slowly a mischievous curve came to her mouth. He was relieved to see it so soon again after the day before. She quirked a saucy brow. "He knew I was a hopeless case. He was likely grateful some poor soul would have me! Who it was did not particularly matter." She grinned impishly, expectantly.

Oh, how he loved it when she teased him! It delighted him all the more to have evidence of her willingness to allow him to help dim her sorrow. He could not let her down. "I 'do not particularly matter'!" he cried in mock offense. "Oh, you shall pay for that remark!"

Laughing freely, he seized her hand, confining her near his side. He rolled toward her and began to rake his rough chin over her neck. Margaret shrieked in laughter as he tickled the sensitive places near her ear and the curve of her shoulder. She tried reflexively to worm away, but he tortured her mercilessly.

"Tell me," he ordered playfully between nibbles, "tell me you cannot live without me."

Margaret tensed, forcing herself to endure his delicious torment long enough to make a cheeky reply. "Why, Mr Thornton, that would be a lie! I did very well without you for many years."

"Is that how it is going to be? Very well, two can play at that game!" He pushed her flat, pinning her down with his body, and began to tickle his fingers over her ribs. Margaret gasped and squirmed beneath him. He found the little hollow just beneath her good arm and teased her, prodding gently as she squealed in laughter.

"Oh, stop, please!" she giggled, but she was still well within herself. He arched an eyebrow and decided she could stand just a little more.

"Say it," he demanded as his lips found her earlobe. His hand gave her a temporary reprieve as it trailed down her side, under the cup of her knee, and pulled her foot within reach. He felt her tense and quiver in anticipation. "'John, my husband, my only lover, you fulfill all my desires and I cannot live without you,'" he dictated, narrowing his eyes in a provoking dare.

Seeing her defiantly arched brow, he leaned closer in a playful threat. "Say it," he decreed, his voice dropping low. His fingers quivered menacingly.

She pulled her head away from his tormenting lips to look him boldly in the eye. Her chin twitching merrily, she stared him down and made as if to comply with his request. "Mr Thornton, I find it most convenient to have the honour of your company," she informed him primly.

He grinned, accepting the challenge. "Not good enough, you minx!" Snagging the sensitive bottom of the foot he had trapped, he lightly traced his fingertips over her delicate arch. She shrieked and tried to twist away, but he was stronger.

He leaned over her, coming eye level with her bosom. His eyebrows rose as inspiration struck, and he impulsively added a new torment. He nipped and nuzzled her tender flesh through the filmy silk of her nightgown and listened with satisfaction when her panicked gasps took on a throatier quality.

"Do you surrender?" he queried, his voice threaded now with heat. "Let me hear it, or I shall torture you even more cruelly!"

"Oh, my!" she cried in exaggerated distress. "Not that!" Distracted as he was, she succeeded in a surprise jerk of her foot, hooking her leg around his and preventing further harassment. She wove the fingers of her left hand through his hair, and, in an unexpected shift of demeanor, she pulled his head up to look her in the face.

His eyes wide now with interest, he allowed her to drag his ear to her mouth. "I say," she purred into his cheek, "that you are bound to catch more flies with honey, *Mr Thornton*."

He turned again to admire the sensual light flickering in her eyes, caught helplessly in her snare. "Duly noted," he panted.

Thirty-Four

THERE WOULD BE NO funeral for Thomas Bell of Oxford, England. He had already informed Frederick that this detail was specified in his will, but it chafed the sensibilities of his godchildren. He had desired to be quietly interred in Spain, "Without a lot of pomp and fanfare," as he had at one time groused. "After all, what use will I have for such nonsense?"

Frederick had reminded him that such ceremonies were often a balm for those left to grieve, but Bell had waved him off. "I would much rather, Freddy, that you remember me when you read a good sonnet than by dressing in some monkey suit and pulling a long face for an hour."

After breaking their fast, Frederick and John had gone early to report the old gentleman's passing to his local Spanish agent. The man himself returned with them to the house, and the three men were closeted in Frederick's study for over an hour.

John had expected that Margaret would need to be present for the initial sorting out of the will, as she was the named party, not himself. She declined however, asking him if he would mind taking on the grim duty in her stead. It would be a long procedure, she had no doubt, and she had little head for business matters at present. John would handle the tedious details efficiently and expertly.

She felt her own time would be better served helping prepare her old friend's body. Her old shock at such ideas had long been worn away, to be replaced by the hope of making herself useful. When Dolores learned her intent, she declared her own desire to help in whatever way she could. "I think there is little we can do," Margaret counseled her gently, "but I would like to honour him in my small way."

Dolores nodded her hearty agreement and the pair set to work. Together they shaved Mr Bell's face and bathed his hands, anointing his beloved old features with a special olive oil produced by Dolores. Margaret was still hindered by her sling, and Dolores by her ample middle, but they worked so seamlessly together that they scarcely felt their disadvantages. Dolores supported Mr Bell's head and Margaret carefully combed his hair, roughened and shaggy as it was from his decline. She slicked it into the style she remembered him wearing, then Dolores gently rested his head back on the white pillow.

The two women stood back, evaluating their work. Margaret had retained her composure admirably during the distraction of their labors, but now the finality of it all caused her eyes to fog once more. Dolores offered her a comforting hand. "He is not hurting now, si?" she consoled her sister.

Margaret turned and nodded wordlessly, and the two young women sought comfort in each other's embrace. Dolores bore her tears bravely, speaking soothing words and holding her dignified English sister as tightly as her growing belly would allow.

"Margaret." The door opened silently behind them. Frederick stood there, holding his arms out to his little sister. She went to him, confident in his sympathy. He bore his sorrows plainly for all to see, and his sadness was no less deep or painful than hers. He clasped her close for long minutes.

At length he released her. "John is waiting for you," he told her. "We've got all the details figured out, but the agent needs your signature now." She nodded, accepting her brother's arm wound tightly about her. Dolores came as well, taking her husband's other arm, but she left them as they passed by the parlor.

When they entered the study, John took her by the hand. He squeezed it, searching her face deeply. "Are you well?" he asked softly.

She nodded, putting on a brave face. "I am better. Thank you for helping to cheer me up this morning," she offered him a shy, intimate smile.

He returned it immediately, his entire face blossoming in that endearing way she had always liked. "Believe me, the pleasure was all mine," he whispered feelingly.

"Mrs Thornton," a nasally voice interrupted.

Margaret turned, a little embarrassed at her rudeness. Before her was a spidery little man, somewhere in the autumn of life. He wore a thin outdated monocle, and his hair formed a disheveled ruff around his balding pate. He came forward to present himself with a bow.

"Margaret, this is Mr Spaulding, Mr Bell's agent in the country," John introduced.

"You are English!" she blurted in surprise, then coloured in shock. She was certainly not beginning this acquaintance well. She shrank a little in mortification but noticed her husband's eyes sparkling in amusement. Some years later, after several similar blunders, he would confess that her outspoken bluntness had always enchanted him.

The little man barely seemed to notice her bad manners. He was, Margaret learned very quickly, little more than a ledger book. He thought in numbers and forecasts, and troubled not with general niceties. He was the perfect international agent for wealthy English investors who demanded accuracy and were not present to care about social graces.

The contrition in her face faded as the little machine of a man directed her attention to a summary sheet. "This," he informed her, "is a compilation of Mr Bell's Last Will and Testament. I understand, Mrs Thornton, that you have married since this document was prepared. Have you proof that you are, in fact, the same lady known formerly as Margaret Hale of Twenty-Six Harley Street, London?"

"I have," John answered for her. He drew their folded marriage document from the inner pocket of his jacket and handed it to her. Margaret glanced at him with a queer little smile. It seemed a sweet, sentimental gesture of his to keep this evidence of their union close to his heart. She would have thought by now he would have locked it safely away with the business papers in his suitcase.

She passed the marriage license to Mr Spaulding for his perusal. "Very good." He nodded quickly, then the document was returned to John's breast pocket. "Now, then, if you please..." he handed her a sheaf of papers.

She stared at them blankly for a moment, turning the pages unseeingly. Her brow furrowed. It was a lot to take in. Thirty pages on legal paper at least, and if she were not mistaken, another large pile of addendums lay on Frederick's desk.

John leaned closer, explaining softly in her ear. "Mr Bell had several wills and codicils, and the most recent one always trumps all others. However, where there is no contradiction in terms, only different information, the older wills must be taken into account as well. The will itself details his estate and wishes, and there are a number of other documents explaining those items in further detail."

She nodded fractionally. "And why was it here? I would have thought the documents would all still be in England," she whispered.

"Apparently Mr Bell had enough worry for his health that he brought copies of everything with him," he murmured back. "There is a note enclosed by the attorney in London who drew everything up, verifying that this is a faithful copy of everything filed in his office. It was all sealed and dated on the day he left England and recorded in the Spanish agent's office the day he arrived.

"These copies are for simplification only; we will have to repeat this process back in London, but it will be less cumbersome for we will have already begun the transfer proceedings. Mr Spaulding will be in touch with the attorney himself."

"If you will excuse me, Madam," Spaulding cleared his throat. Margaret jumped, chastising herself for her inattentiveness. "Thank you, Madam. Now, as you will see...." The agent began a dry list of the finalized details.

Margaret's stomach began to flutter and her breath trembled as he went on. Mr Bell had been more wealthy than she had ever realized. By the time he had finished reading, the penniless young woman of former days had fallen heiress to a sizeable fortune.

She was now the holder of four entire neighborhoods in Milton, the Empress Hotel, several small lots in the market square, a moderately sized paper mill, a lumber yard with a mill, and one very large and consequential cotton mill. She thought she detected a pleased little twitch to John's lip as that last item was read.

In addition, there was what remained of Mr Bell's family estate, which had not been sold off in the onrush of industry. One hundred acres of rocky soil; not much good for farming, but still comfortably situated near a growing city and sure to skyrocket in value. There was a substantial bank account as well, but other than noting that it was in good standing, the agent could not disclose the sum of it, for those numbers had not been made available to him.

Margaret, her eyes glazed, let the papers fall into her lap. The businesslike little man, eager to keep his ducks in a row, reclaimed them from her to order them neatly again on the desk. "Mrs Thornton, your signature is required," he reminded her.

"Oh," she breathed. "Y-yes, of course." With a glance at John, who gave her a tight gentle smile, she moved to take the pen. A dip of ink, a little scribble- fumbling a little over her new name- and it was done.

"Thank you, Madam," Spaulding reacted quickly. His obligations here finished, he was eager to get back to his office. He snapped the documents into a worn leather portfolio, nearly snatching them from Margaret's hand as she finished her signature. He bowed to the lady, then shook the gentlemen's hands. "I will send an express message to Mr Bell's attorney in London, a Mr Gentry of Gentry, Harlow, and Jacobs. He will be expecting you, Mrs Thornton. Good-day Mr Thornton, Mr Marshall."

Frederick showed the man out, leaving John and Margaret alone in the study. She was still breathless, overcome. She turned her eyes to him, full of wonder. "Did you hear...?" she gasped.

He pulled her into his arms, gazing steadily down at her. "I heard him call you 'Mrs Thornton'," he replied, grinning. "I rather liked that."

Margaret was still aghast, not to be deterred from her amazement. "But... but so much! I never thought.... What are we to do with it all?" she exclaimed. "I would not know where to begin!"

"You are an intelligent woman," he murmured, nuzzling her ear. "I am sure you can think of something."

She drew back to look him full in the face, a small smile growing. "The mill is safe," she whispered exultantly. "And the workers are safe! Oh, John, do you know what this means?"

"It means I quite prudently married myself an heiress. Very clever of me, don't you think?" he winked.

Margaret's face was still awash in wonder, unable to take it all in. She laughed, her breath coming in erratic little puffs. Wrapping her arm around his neck, she stood on her tiptoes to kiss him firmly, gleefully on the chin.

Not satisfied with her hasty retreat, he followed her lips as she dropped back to her heels. Cupping her face with gentle fingers, he tipped her chin up again to meet him. Never had he kissed her so patiently, with such loving restraint.

She melted into his chest as he tenderly explored every point, every minute detail of her mouth. Their breathing synchronized as he caressed her lips, her tongue, even her teeth. His thumbs stroked the sides of her face lightly, affectionately as he loved her. Margaret splayed her fingers through his hair, willingly opening to his ministrations and inviting him more deeply.

"*Ahem...*"

Mortified at being discovered, Margaret spun away from John, her cheeks already flaming. Frederick leaned casually against the doorframe of the study, one leg crossed nonchalantly over the other as though he had been there some while. He surveyed his fingertips indifferently, brushing at an imaginary smudge of ink.

"Whenever you're ready, Thornton. I can come back in an hour or so...."

Margaret felt her face burning. She did not dare meet her brother's eyes at first. Such shocking behavior she had become guilty of lately! She shifted her downcast gaze to the side, watching John's fingers brush hers. His voice came cheerfully over her shoulder. "No, Hale, I am quite ready. If you will excuse me just a moment?"

"Take your time." Frederick did not move, his twinkling eyes fastened on his sister's flushed countenance.

Margaret slowly looked up to her husband. "What does he mean?" she asked.

"We've some baled cotton samples to examine," he answered, his face still shining in pleasure from their shared embrace. "Some fiber types are better for weaving than others, and I can get a better feel for our finished product if I can actually get my hands on it. We thought it would be best to do this today...."

She nodded in understanding. Though she would have liked to stay longer in her brother's home, it was a selfish desire. They had agreed it would be best for John to wrap up his own business with Frederick quickly, as both were eager to return to those waiting anxiously back at home. The men had lost an entire business day already. "How long will you be?"

"I am not sure. He says the warehouse is near the docks, so we will not have to go far, but I will need to spend a good deal of time there. One field alone can produce quite a bit of variety, which can complicate matters. We need to look for consistency through the entire storehouse."

He glanced pointedly at Frederick, still smirking in the doorway. He deliberately took his time saying a tender goodbye to his wife, savouring the joy and contentment which were now his in her embrace. With a last soft kiss on her lips, he released her and left.

GIRAUD STRETCHED IN THE hard bed of the boardinghouse in which he had taken up residence. It was cheap, that was about all that was to be said for it. Well, that and the company wasn't bad. He allowed himself a satisfied smile. The little hoyden who had warmed his bed last night was long gone, but he knew where to find her again.

He reached to the wobbly stool which served as a nightstand, first lighting a cigar, then checking the shoddy timepiece on the wall. The morning was no longer young. He stroked his mustache thoughtfully.

He had nearly regained a respectable amount of pocket money. He was just vain enough to desire the services of a good barber and a bath house before seeking out the man he had come to find. The amenities of the boardinghouse were primitive, at best.

He would need a new suit of clothes to make his call, as well. His own had been tattered and stained in the crude hold of the *Esperanza*, and he would never see his trunk again. English sailors! Thieves and scoundrels, all of them!

Sitting back against the bare wall, he puffed his slender cigar and permitted his thoughts to turn back to the ship. That English tart... *oh, la!* He toyed the tip of his cigar with his lips and crafted detailed visions of that lovely strumpet. She was no lady, he was quite sure- far too saucy and spirited, too clever and stubborn. Yet she *appeared* to be everything elegant and refined, seemingly modest and sheltered. An enigma, she was, but what a figure!

His eyes narrowed and his lips curled in lascivious pleasure as he imagined what other liberties he might have taken. Those lips! How he had wanted to break that scornful gaze she cast upon him, to force her haughty guard down. No, she was no worthless socialite, petty and spineless. Beneath that dignified exterior simmered a vibrant woman of intense passion, he was sure of it. His fingers curled as he imagined her once more in his grasp. He saw himself revealing her secrets, teaching her in the carnal ways of pleasure.

His lip curled in frustration at last. No doubt that Thornton fellow had already discovered the lady's deepest intimacies and unlocked her delicious ardor. He would have to be blind not to see the way she looked at the Milton man. He had been close, so close to tasting that same prize! Willing or no at first, she would not have resisted him for long. Then Thornton, again. Always that man!

His face clouded, his pleasant visions shattered. Thornton's name had long inspired both admiration and envy. The man's rise from obscurity to notoriety in trade circles was something of a fascination for him. Sure, he was on hard times now, but given half a chance the Milton business machine would remain a fierce competitor in the market.

He chewed the butt of his nearly spent cigar. Thornton never had confessed to him the purpose of his journey to Spain, though he had tried with all his might to discover it. He was a close one, that was certain, and no buffoon. It did not take much insight, however, to determine that the man was likely on the same mission he himself was. Why else would a cotton miller, one in financial straits from what he could tell, pay a sudden visit to Cádiz just now?

He frowned sullenly. Thornton had likely already snared the contract he had come about for himself. The business contact here in Spain had been lukewarm in his response- rather discouraging in fact- when he had written back. Still, the idea was so revolutionary that he had felt compelled to investigate himself. If he could get a substantial leap ahead of the competition through novel trade practices, he pictured his new cotton mill succeeding marvelously.

He crushed the ashes off his cigar, sighing. No doubt the seasoned Englishman had already wooed away his contract, but there was yet reason for hope. Raw cotton was becoming a hot commodity, but many others had gotten their start the old-fashioned way, and he could too.

And who knew? Perhaps the Milton manufacturer's present liabilities were too much for the Spanish plantation to stomach. Anything was fair in business.

Thirty-Five

John plucked a small wad of fibers off another bale and rubbed them between delicate fingers. He closed his eyes as he concentrated on the weight, the loft, the density. Pleased, he then lifted them to the lamp which Frederick held for him and examined them under his magnifying glass.

Frederick pursed his lips patiently. His brother-in-law knew his business- that much was obvious. Thornton had spoken almost nothing in the last hour, consumed as he was with every detail of every lot they examined. Still, Frederick Hale had not come so far without learning to masterfully read expressions.

Thornton had an excellent poker face, but Frederick had learned to peer through the chinks in this particular man. Seeing him through Margaret's eyes had made all the difference. Thornton was imposing; though young, he was a consummate man of business and probably the most expert authority on his trade to be found anywhere in Europe, but he was as human as the next man.

Frederick was confident in his product, and by the little flicker in Thornton's eyes, he could tell the other man was impressed. The plantation Mr Bell had purchased had been well chosen. It had been carefully tended for generations and was large enough that some fields were always rotating in either beans or wheat. As a result, the soil was excellent and the production remained high. In addition, this particular cotton variety had long been jealously guarded, supposedly some local secret. It was, indeed, a generous offering.

It was a marvel that it had ever been let for sale at such a time, with the market only climbing, but Frederick knew that old Bell had had his tricks. He was a persuasive fellow, and no doubt had a fair number of resources to leverage to get what he wanted. Frederick doubted that, even if possessed of the full amount of Bell's former reserves, he would have ever been able to make so handsome a purchase. Old Spanish families tended to never sell their ancestral land, but Bell had been in the right place at the right time.

Frederick smiled privately as he followed his brother-in-law to yet another lot of cotton bales. Thornton was, indeed, exactly the man he had needed to meet to make his vision a reality. He had come to truly believe that his introduction to this fellow had been no accident. It was Bell who had first dropped the hint of exploring new direct marketing ideas, though he vehemently denied it later. *The old devil,* he thought fondly as he held the lamp up for Thornton again.

Thornton repeated the same procedure with every set of bales he examined, methodically treating every sample to the same scrutiny. Each of the pieces he had inspected he had dropped into a small bag he carried. Finally, as they finished the last lot, he turned back to Frederick with a carefully neutral expression.

"Well?" he inquired, his eyebrow quirking.

Thornton said nothing, but a slow tug on one cheek produced a satisfied expression. His eyes narrowing, he gave a small jerk of his head and led the way to a low accounting table in the corner of the warehouse.

Frederick carefully positioned the lantern on the table as Thornton withdrew his samples, spreading them out. "Notice anything?" he asked.

Frederick looked them over thoughtfully, wondering what specifically stood out to the experienced manufacturer's eyes. "There is almost no waste material, the colour is uniformly white, the bales are all strikingly clean..." he glanced up to Thornton, noting that the other appeared to be waiting for more. He stopped, wondering what it was.

Thornton produced a small ruler from his pocket, prompting Frederick to wonder what else the man carried around with him. His marriage license in one pocket, a magnifying glass in another....

Thornton aligned the little ruler with the fibers and pointed to his findings. "The fibers are very long for a European variety. In fact, I would hazard a guess that this strain originally came out of South America. How long did you say they had been growing here?"

"Three or four generations, at least. They were an old family; Barbour knew of them. The land is situated in an isolated region of the province, so I don't think any local cross strains can have developed. The family had begun to make a name for themselves in cotton, I am surprised they ever sold out."

"Hmm." John thoughtfully plucked a few individual fibers from several samples and arrayed them parallel to each other. "See here, they are all consistently about an inch and an eighth. Most fibers from the Continent and from Asia are scarcely an inch, and some even less. That is why the Americas have gained such dominance in the export. It seems a small difference, but it wreaks havoc with machinery. We have to reset everything and keep the entire building even more humid to tame the fibers so they can be woven, which makes it harder on the workers as well."

Frederick nodded, pulling out a few fibers for his own examination. "I was told this variety was quite strong in comparison to others. You have more experience in that, what do you think?"

Thornton's eyebrows jerked, betraying his enthusiasm at last. "Indeed. Very high quality. And you are sure of your annual yield?"

"I persuaded the old plantation foreman to stay on, and I have all of his numbers for the last twenty years at least. He seems a scrupulous man, and now that I know his management practices will be carried forward, I can answer with confidence. We are subject to weather and natural disaster as everyone else is, but I can predict with as much accuracy as anyone can. We've never had a weevil infestation either, which is a mercy."

Thornton nodded emphatically. "Keep your plantation isolated, whatever you do. You can't help wind, but workers going from field to field can do a lot of damage. You'd almost be ahead to find them year-round work with you in some capacity or other, rather than allow contamination from outside sources."

Frederick grinned. "You've been around Margaret too long. She's starting to rub off on you."

At this the façade of the cautious manufacturer crumbled completely. Thornton's expression broke into open pleasure. "I would not consider that a bad thing!" He was silent a few seconds, his eyes shining brightly. Softly, a little timidly, perhaps, he confessed the long-hidden secret of his heart. "She is everything to me, Hale. I count myself the luckiest man alive."

"No, I think that honour goes to me, but I'll not argue with you. You clearly have excellent taste, and no man could watch over her more devotedly. That much is clear, as is the fact that you have won her over completely." He shook his head, marveling. "I'll never know how you did it, but I'm glad, for both of you."

Thornton laughed. "Did she never tell you? How madly jealous I was after seeing her with you at the train station, and how she refused to explain herself? That Leonards fellow died later, did you know, which prompted an investigation into events that night until you were ruled out as a suspect. She protected you like a lioness with her cub." He heaved a quavering breath, reflecting on that dark time.

"Huh!" Frederick exclaimed. "Well, now, that *does* explain a few things! Poor Margaret, she had so much to bear! Wait..." Frederick fixed the other in a prying stare. "You were jealous... I see now, you must have spoken to her before I ever came back. You did!" he nearly jumped as Thornton began to shake his head, an embarrassed smile in evidence. "Now I understand things better. How badly did she abuse you?"

"Oh! Please do not remind me. We have both repented of that day!"

"That badly, then? My word. Yet she would not let me put you down when you came to call on Father and Mother. I was in a foul mood, I admit, but she jumped all over me when I called you 'some tradesman.' She must have grudgingly liked you even then- or maybe she just felt guilty."

"Any guilt to be had was mine, particularly after that investigation. I was rather harsh on her, I am afraid. We did not speak to each other voluntarily for months. Left to our own devices, we likely never would have again."

"Until she became your landlady," Frederick pointed out.

"Yes! I suppose that might have changed things. Who can say? But it does not matter now. What matters is that she and your own lovely bride are waiting for us back at your house with open arms." He allowed himself a lopsided grin. "What *matters* is that she is coming back with me to Milton, and I will never lose her again."

"Indeed! Have you given any thought to when you wish to leave?"

Thornton nodded. "I would like to ship out as soon as possible. We must see to Mr Bell's affairs, of course, but I am quite satisfied with everything we have discussed. If we are to make a go of this, there is no time like the present to begin."

"I had expected something like that. I have a steamer that can be ready in two days with the initial shipment through Liverpool. You can catch a ride back home at the same time."

"That should do. Margaret and I will have to take a train immediately for London, but it serves better than shipping the cotton through there." He paused, eyeing his brother-in-law, whose face had started to wilt in regret. "I know Margaret will wish to return as often as we can," he supplied softly.

Frederick's gaze snapped up in surprise that he could be so easily read. He pressed his mouth tightly and shook his head slowly in agreement. "I thank you, Thornton. I would like that, too. I have missed her so, these many years! I wish I could have been there more for her. You'll bring her back soon, won't you? That is..." his lips twitched in sudden mirth, "if she is fit to travel."

Thornton arched a brow, deliberately misunderstanding the joke. "I imagine she will rise to the occasion. Perhaps if I need help keeping her quiet and well-behaved, we will bring along Dixon. I have no doubt she can manage things."

"Now you're threatening me!" Frederick laughed. "She'll give me a tongue lashing like you've never heard for settling in a papist country! Ah, but it would be worth enduring to see her again. I've told Dolores so many tales! But come, rather than merely speaking of fair ladies, let us go enjoy their company."

"That," his partner agreed, "is the best idea I've heard all day."

THE DOCTOR HAD SENT men for Mr Bell's body just after Frederick and John had left. Though it was Señor Barbour's house, Margaret it was who managed the affair. She was Mr Bell's legal heir, and with her host's assistance at translating, she directed the arrangement and disposition of whatever was left uncertain in Bell's will.

The man in charge of the body's direction glanced sideways at her more than once, unaccustomed as he was to working with a lady- and a foreign one at that. Barbour, however, staunchly redirected any queries made of him back to Margaret.

He only intervened once; there was some difficulty expected with the Church, as neither Mr Bell nor his heir were Catholic. Barbour would not hear of his houseguest being interred indecently, and after a few strongly worded phrases in Spanish- no doubt enforced by Barbour's standing in the Church- the man visibly backed off. At length, everything was settled to Margaret's satisfaction.

After the melancholy party had retreated from the house with their burden, Margaret put her hand briefly to her forehead. She felt faint and tired. The wild emotions of the past several days- *was that all it was?*- wore on her terribly. Now, this sad last duty was come to an end for her. She would visit the grave, of course, but there was nothing else she could do for her old friend. She released a long pent-up breath, trembling as it left her.

Barbour proved to be as gentlemanly as her first impression had led her to believe. His English was nearly flawless, and his concern for his young guest genuine. Her weariness was clear to him, and he tactfully guided her back to the parlour where Dolores and her mother sewed.

He spoke cheerful words to them in Spanish, then turned to translate for the benefit of his guest. "How do you like some music, Señora? Come, you sit with us and enjoy until the meal. Eh, bueno, Dolores!" he exclaimed as his daughter rose to take another seat in a different part of the room.

"Señora, please be comfortable," he gallantly showed Margaret to a plush leather seat. Smiling wonderingly, she took it and turned her full attention to her host and his daughter. Barbour seated himself on an armless stool next to Dolores, picking up a curious stringed instrument. It looked to her vaguely like a fat, elongated violin, or perhaps a small cello, but he held it cradled in his arms. Margaret tilted her head in interest. She had heard of the *guitarro,* but had never seen one.

Barbour's fingers began to dance over the strings, making the instrument sing out in dulcet tones. Dolores brought her elegant arms up and began an intricate clapping, keeping tempo and adding punctuation to the music. It was unlike anything Margaret had ever heard. Dolores and her father shared joyful smiles as they performed the spirited music, and Margaret felt the emotions of the players trickling warmly through her own being.

The song ended, to her regret, but Barbour was not finished. A magnanimous performer and something of a showman, he had found a willing and enchanted audience. He struck up another song, this one sounding more romantic than frolicsome. Dolores did not clap this time, but she and her mother took turns lifting their voices to the melody. Both had lovely voices, and though she could not understand the words, Margaret felt the song disarming all her tensions. Soon she was breathing deeply and lightly, a smile of true enjoyment playing at her lips.

"Señora!" Barbour claimed her attention from the song as it finished. "Do you sing?"

"Oh! No, not I, though I am fond of music."

"Come!" he insisted as she tried to beg off. "We play something you know!" His fingers tickled the strings again and within a few bars of the introduction, Margaret found her eyes narrowing thoughtfully. "Come, Señora!" Barbour laughed. "You must help, I do not know the words!"

Margaret was smiling widely now, her brow knit in wonder. Could it possibly be? Dolores's thick dark lashes winked across the room at her and Margaret knew. She began to laugh as well. Frederick had taught his new family an old sea shanty he used to sing to her in girlhood, before joining the Navy. The tune she remembered, but the verses were mostly lost to time. Her toes tapped helplessly and she thought carefully of the words before joining in. Her voice, shaky and faltering at first, gradually grew in strength until it swelled from her heart.

"But the standing toast
That pleased the most,
Was 'The wind that blows,
The Ship that goes,
And the lass that loves a sailor!
Some drank 'The Prince,'
And some 'Our Land,'
This glorious land of freedom!
Some that our tars
May never stand
For heroes brave to lead them!
That she who's in distress may find,
Such friends as ne'er will fail her.
But the standing toast
That pleased the most,
Was 'The wind that blows,
The Ship that goes,
And the lass that loves a sailor!'

Sometime during this performance, John and Frederick had come softly into the room behind her. Both were thoroughly charmed and moved discretely so as not to interrupt the shy singer. Frederick was immediately taken back to long-ago days, perched in his favorite apple tree with his little sister following doggedly at his heels and trying to emulate everything that he did.

John was simply filled with breathless admiration. He had never before heard Margaret sing, and whether it was the skill of the singer or his love for the same, his heart declared he had never heard a voice to rival hers.

"Bravo, Señora!" Barbour, seeing his son's return, set his *guitarro* to the side and rose with expansive praise. "Eh, Federico, why is it you did not say before how beautiful sings your sister?" He came near to clap his son-in-law on the shoulder.

Margaret, only now realizing that she had had an audience, flushed a little in embarrassed pleasure. She was not accustomed to performing in any way, and Barbour's accolades discomfited her somewhat. Bashfully she rose her eyes to meet the two men she loved best. John's were sparkling fluently back at her, his heart too full for simple words of praise.

Frederick had greeted his father-in-law then turned back to her. "There are many things about Margaret I did not tell you, Señor!" he chuckled. "If I had, there is no telling what you might put her up to!" Then, leaning close to kiss his sister on the cheek, "That was lovely, Dearest. I am glad you still remember!"

Margaret's eyes were brimming with tenderness for her beloved brother as he held her gaze for a moment. So many years they had lost! Yet, she thought with great comfort, in their own small way they had found each other again. Though they would soon be again forced to be family only by way of the pen, their letters would now take on a new depth.

She knew his family now, and how they lived. She would be able to picture his children running about these halls, and to smell the aroma of spices and flowers as she savoured his letters. Dolores was her living, breathing sister in reality, not a faceless mystery.

And John! How she marveled at the thick camaraderie which had kindled between her new husband and her brother. Even now as she watched, Frederick was freely ribbing John over some trifle with their business affairs, and John was energetically rising to the bait. He, too, would profit from their connection. She knew John had few men of whom he truly thought well, and even fewer with whom he could be so at ease.

As she gazed at him in contentment, John turned to catch her eye. Scooping his arm around her, he pulled her close to nuzzle her ear, openly displaying affections she felt he never would have without the influence of her brother's family. The last of Margaret's tensions for the day dissolved. Swirling grief might surround her, but here in this moment, all was right with the world.

Thirty-Six

After the midday meal, another magnificent spread, the family separated to their various places of rest. While it could not be accurately reported that the newlyweds did a great deal of resting, still they emerged some while later thoroughly refreshed. Though her gown was once again black, Margaret's good cheer had returned, much to the relieved delight of her steady companion.

They found Frederick in his study, poring industriously over a stack of export documents needing his attention. His puckered brow smoothed at their entry. "There you are. Dolores was very fatigued, so she is resting yet. I'm afraid, Margaret, you'll have to bear with rather dull company for an hour or two," he bowed self-deprecatingly.

"Is she well?" Margaret asked, suddenly concerned.

"Oh, yes, certainly. She tires more easily these days," he shot a surreptitious wink at John, who received it with an arched brow. "Thornton, I'm sorry to say I have a deal of paperwork to get through myself, if we are to have your shipment ready the day after tomorrow. Would you and Margaret care to stroll the garden?"

"If we are to be at our leisure for a time," John glanced speculatively at his young wife, "I think I should prefer to see more of the city. It is magnificent. What do you think, my love?"

"Oh! Yes, I think that a fine idea." Margaret had, in fact, not even considered being a tourist until that moment. Here she was in one of the most beautiful ports in the world, and she had yet to examine any sights beyond the confines of her brother's home.

"Of course," Frederick bobbed his head with enthusiasm. "I wish I had time to show you around myself, but I am sure you will manage. I'll have Bernardo fit out the curricle for you to take you about."

"Surely, that is not necessary," Margaret objected. "Can we not rather walk?" She looked to her husband for his opinion.

"Well..." Frederick deliberated. "I know you would prefer it, Little Sister, but it is easy to become lost. There are parts of the city I would not wish you to venture into."

"Perhaps if you gave us directions," John suggested, wishing to satisfy his wife's craving for her favored long strolls and also heed her brother's advice. "I am afraid we have not the time at present to take in all of the city's sights, so what would you recommend first?"

Frederick pursed his lips. "The *Catedral Nueva* is a usual stop for foreign travelers. Father could have spent days on end there, but I think I know you better than that, Margaret. I think you would like *La Caleta*. It's a beach, and so different from our shores in England that you cannot begin to imagine! There is the advantage of the sea air as well, which you will no doubt find preferable to the confines of the city in the late afternoon. It's not terribly far; within walking distance for you, to be sure. You should not have to pass any dangerous neighborhoods from here."

The tourists bowed to his more experienced opinion, and a map was quickly sketched out. John studied it, trying to memorize as much as he could so that he might not have to pull it out much while walking, thus branding himself as one who did not know his way around.

The way was stunning. If John had wished to not appear the foreigner, he failed utterly in his astonished marvel at every new vista. Margaret was no less wonderstruck. Architecture was nothing new to them; London had its share of ancient structures and sweeping monuments. It was the sheer brilliance of everything which took their fancy. Rarely did the sun shine so intensely in London as on that tropical port. The light glittered and sparkled on every surface, purifying the entire city in their eyes.

The walk to the beach was accomplished quickly. Indeed, they could hear the surf thundering at the house, and as they came closer the tang of salt air grew more intense. As they rounded the last block, however, and the sea came into view, Margaret gasped audibly. John looked quickly to her, his eyes alight as well, and squeezed her hand.

Neither had spared much attention for the sea when they had first arrived in Spain. Now with eyes wide, they took in the sprawling white sand where the foaming surf billowed over a brilliant emerald froth. Margaret had been accustomed to think of the ocean as a dark, brooding thing, unfathomable and frigid. Sea air to her had always been a bracing draught- fresh, to be sure, but not without a trace of cold aloofness. This shoreline was bright, inviting, even invigorating.

Their spirits buoyed with each passing moment, and with no sense of time they wandered the entire stretch of the exposed shoreline. The sandy beach was dotted here and there with other revelers and their umbrellas- mostly families, Margaret noted. Here and there she spotted a sandcastle as raven-haired youngsters labored with spade and bucket to craft their own fantasies. Frequently, upon beholding a particularly captivating sight, their eyes would meet to share their silent amusement.

They spoke little. Their comfort with each other had grown so completely that they were both at peace simply marveling at all they saw without struggling to find words to match their feelings. It was not necessary. The radiant bliss emanating from Margaret's being was mirrored in John's quiet enchantment. His fingers trailing lightly over her hand communicated his joy, his matchless contentment, and all his hopes for their future.

Frederick had been right about the crisp salt breeze. Had it not been so, undoubtedly, they could not have long borne the heat of the late summer afternoon. Margaret in particular, swathed as she was in dark layers made for another climate and handicapped by a lady's fashion, would have soon become exhausted. The fresh air, however, only added to her energy after so many days of idleness. She felt she could have walked for miles.

At length John diverted her with a boyish grin to a little shanty not far from the walkway, where a vendor peddled ice cream and other refreshments. Stumbling over the communication barrier, they managed to purchase some cool treats, and retired to a nearby bench to enjoy them. They gazed out over the rolling expanse, meditating on the turquoise waves and listening to the sea birds as they savoured their ice cream in companionable quiet.

"I suppose," he said ruefully after a little while, "that we will not have another afternoon like this for a very long time." He smiled down at her. "The sea shores at home are nothing at all the like of this."

"Not at all!" she agreed. "Yet I do enjoy visiting the coast. It is different, to be sure, but I love it all the same."

"We will have to take a trip once we return, then. I had no idea you had such a fondness for it."

Margaret was silent for a moment. "Edith and my aunt took me with them when last they went. It was... it was good for me, I think. I spent many a lonely hour staring out at those waves."

"Hmm," he wrapped his arm around her shoulders. "Tell me what you were thinking about."

She turned to meet the sterling blue of his eyes as they reflected the water. "You," she answered simply.

A slow, humbled smile warmed his face for an entirely different reason than a moment ago. "I was a fool to ever let you leave Milton," he murmured huskily. His speaking eyes studied her lovingly for a moment. "Would you have stayed? That last day, when you came to say goodbye- if I had found the courage to speak, as I so wished- would it have done any good?"

She looked long and hard into his cherished face, trying to put herself back into that heart-wrenching day. "I do not know," she decided at last. "Now I cannot imagine that I could have walked away, had I thought you could still care for me. I was not myself then, though."

"Then," he smiled whimsically, "I ought to have come sooner. The night before you left, before your father's funeral. Your aunt had just arrived and I came to ask after you."

She straightened. "You did? I never knew."

He nodded. "I wanted to see you, but I could not. Mr Bell walked home with me- he came to stay with us. As we left I saw you in the window, with your hand over your face and I could almost feel your pain. I very nearly ran back into the house. If Bell had not been there, I doubt not that I would have done.

"What I thought I could do, I do not know, but throwing you over my shoulder and dragging you back home with me would have been at the top of the list!" He gave a low chuckle, enjoying the playful sparkle which came into her eyes at his impulsive notion. "Would you have even seen me, had I asked?"

"That I would have," she answered thoughtfully. "I wanted to see you, even if I was still afraid of what you thought of me." Her lips thinned pensively. "There are few who can truly understand times like those," she whispered, causing him to tighten his arm around her.

"Yes," she declared again, more positively this time. "I would have wanted to see you, though I do not know if at the time I would have found the courage to ask my aunt for privacy. I doubt she would have given way easily, and little of any value could have been said in her presence."

"Before that, then," he turned his attention back to the waves, beginning to have fun with his little fantasy. "Fanny's wedding? I ought to have overridden the guest list, seen to it that you and your father were invited to the breakfast after the ceremony. Then, as no doubt would have occurred, I could have found you out when you retreated to a safe corner from the hen party. You would have had no choice but to speak to me then."

"You forget your duties as a host!" Margaret laughed. "Oh, no, that would not do. Too many others would have commanded your attention. You would have either appeared to be staring mysteriously at me from the other side of the room, which I no doubt would have misinterpreted, or hiding in the corner with me and shunning your other guests."

"You are quite right. I suppose, then, I should have sought you out on your walks. Followed- nay, stalked you, like some poor neglected dog until you relented and gave me the time of day." He affected a mournful little pout for emphasis.

"You do not account for my stubborn and silly nature, then!" she tilted her head to observe him slyly. "Humble yourself needlessly though you might have, you seem to believe I could have been prevailed upon to be reasonable!"

"You do yourself too little justice, my love! I have found you *most* amenable, particularly when I do this." Here he tipped her chin up to kiss her deeply, sweetly.

Margaret lost herself for a few seconds, then recalled to reality. "*John!*" she hissed, reddening. "We are in public!"

"And we know no one here." He grinned. "Had I known how efficacious it would prove, I might have tried this long ago." He drew her close for a much longer kiss. Margaret responded stiffly, reluctantly at first. Her every impulse rebelled against such a blatant display.

John, however, had not wasted this past week with her. He had been a quick study, and rapidly learned how to assail her defenses. He put his knowledge to good use now, enticing and tempting her. Before she had quite realized it, she was well on her way to permitting liberties on that open park bench which she would have once thought indecent in perfect privacy.

Gasping quickly, she at last pulled from his intoxicating embrace. He did not move, but languorously opened his eyes in a perfectly satisfied euphoria, a crooked smile in evidence. Margaret looked quickly about, noting that no one appeared to be staring, but feeling conspicuous all the same. How had she come to the place where she so easily surrendered whenever he touched her?

"John Thornton!" she snapped, although not altogether as exasperated as she tried to sound. "You are no gentleman!"

"No," he winked, still leaning toward her. "I'm not."

GIRAUD HAD FOUND THE establishments in the older part of town to be a veritable fount for him. He had ventured toward the better-heeled parts of the city in search of a new wardrobe but discovered many reasons to linger there afterward.

The current argument in favor of higher-class establishments lay on the table before him. He kept his expression carefully neutral as he swept an appreciable stack of coins toward his growing pile of winnings.

The clientele in this particular place of business included the requisite English naval officers, of course, but also a goodly number of foreign travelers and Spanish gentlemen with money to lose and nothing better to do. Some were shrewd players, but he had learned to watch for those and to avoid them.

The other thing he had learned from long experience was not to stay on a winning streak for too long. One built a reputation that way, and that tended to dampen future winnings. Bowing ingratiatingly to his fellow players, who were none too sorry to see him go, he pocketed his prize money and left.

Outside, he drew a deep breath, wrinkling his nose slightly in distaste. Pungent, sea air was, and even more so in humid climates. He would be glad to get back home, and- yes, by the feel of his purse, he could now afford the passage. At least in this part of town he was some distance from the wharfs, where the odor of stinking fish was the strongest.

His pocket watch had been another casualty of those cursed English sailors. He glanced speculatively at the sun, trying to ascertain the time of evening. It was growing late, probably a little too late to make it back to the docks to inquire about a ship home. Not quite sure of his direction, he began to wander the narrow streets.

The street came to an abrupt end, dumping him unceremoniously before a long sandy beach. Glancing up and down, he chose a direction at random and strolled aimlessly forward. Occasionally he would pass one of the officers with whom he had played, as they, for the most part, came to the shoreline to admire beautiful Spanish girls after losing at cards. The English officers generally pretended not to recognize the French businessman, an arrangement which satisfied everyone.

After a quarter hour of purposeless boredom, some familiar shape caught his eye. His gaze sharpened, honing in on the fleeting glance. A pair of tourists on a bench, watching the sea... or... not precisely watching the sea.

His body surged with adrenaline as he recognized John Thornton and that mysterious woman of his. His fingers flexed and his pulse quickened. Whoever that Margaret wench was, it was plainly obvious to all now that she was *not* his sister.

He fairly quivered with a strange mixture of emotions. Jealousy, bitterness, desire, and utterly unbridled curiosity all combined to make his stomach lurch queerly. Recalling his senses, he slipped unobtrusively out of the couple's possible line of sight, determined to at least gawk at them unobserved.

Their intimate moment ended with the lady not very convincingly acting put out with the gentleman for his liberties. Thornton apparently obtained her forgiveness, as she bestowed one last favour upon him before he rose to help her to her feet.

Unsure of his purpose, Giraud began to follow them. His caution apparently had begun to slip, as he realized he had caught up with them far more closely than was wise. He was almost near enough to command their attention with a normal speaking tone, should he have wished it. No, this would not do. He did not know yet what he would do with this information.

Just as he checked his stride to allow the couple to outpace him again, he recognized one of his English lieutenants approaching. That would be Jackson, a gracious loser, and a frequent companion during his stay. The lieutenant could not fail to notice him. With a sinking feeling, Giraud felt sure of detection.

Instead of staring at him, however, the lieutenant's head snapped around after the couple passed him. He had been walking alone, and now he stood gaping after the retreating figures. He remained stock still, his fingers twitching uselessly at his side and entirely heedless of Giraud's approach.

Curiosity arrested Giraud. "Bonsoir, Monsieur," he greeted the other man cordially.

The lieutenant turned, his eyes hardening. He spared Giraud a curt nod, but offered no other greeting. Silently, he began to retrace his steps, hesitantly following after the object of his interest.

Not willing to be so dismissed, Giraud kept pace. "Pardon," he interrupted the other, "but is it you follow after zat lady?"

The lieutenant stopped cold, finally turning his attention to the Frenchman. "Why do you ask?" he demanded.

"Well," he smiled ingratiatingly. "I 'ave 'ad some passing acquaintance wit' ze lady myself. Is it zat you know 'er?"

The Lieutenant's eyes narrowed. He was silent a moment, staring after her. "I cannot be sure. I think she came from the same village as I. *She* looks the same, but..." his voice trailed off. He craned his neck, his uncertain gaze not yet willing to lose sight of his quarry.

"If I may, Monsieur," Giraud ventured cautiously, "what is ze name of ze lady you remember?"

The Lieutenant grit his teeth, galled by the other's probing questions. Still, his own interest had been sparked and he answered, almost to himself. "Margaret Hale. She was the rector's daughter."

Margaret Hale. So that *was her real name.* Out loud, he agreed. "Oui, Margaret, zat is 'ow I know 'er. Ze lady was on my ship."

The Lieutenant finally began to take him seriously. "Tell me," his voice dropped urgently, "*what she is doing here*!"

"Zat I could not say, Monsieur," he shrugged. "Ze lady is mysterieuse, you see."

The fellow scowled, then turned away from him to resume his trail after the couple. He had quickened his steps noticeably, but the pair had already gained considerable distance on them. Giraud caught up with the officer.

"Monsieur," he demanded again. "Ze lady is of interest to me as well. Per'aps we could 'elp each other, nôn? What is it you wish to know of 'er?" Hopefully if he could provide whatever clue the lieutenant sought, the Englishman might do him the same service.

The lieutenant swore under his breath, as he was having a hard time keeping sight of the black figures in a sea of other men dressed in the same colour. Eventually he relented, more out of frustration than anything else. "Her brother is wanted for mutiny."

Giraud choked back a gasp. In dazed wonder he fixed his eyes on the shapely figure retreating from him. The lady's mysteries deepened the more he knew of her! His eyes narrowed.

"If I may, Monsieur..." he advanced slowly.

"Yes?" the Lieutenant snapped.

"You do not know 'er brozer? Or at least you do not know where 'e is to be found?"

The lieutenant stopped, muttering an exasperated oath. The couple had taken a side street or slipped from his view in the split second he had turned his gaze. Irritation with the persistent Frenchman made him clench his fists. "No! I would scarcely remember him, he was older than I. Now, have you anything of use to tell me, or do you annoy me for no better purpose than your own amusement?"

"Why, *bien sur*," Giraud beamed smoothly. "For you see, zat man wit' 'er *is* 'er brozer.

Thirty-Seven

Hannah's eyes sparkled in satisfaction as her young pupil set down his tea cup. This, the third afternoon at her table, had seen a remarkable improvement in the lad's manners. He straightened his shoulders and lifted his chin, meeting her expression of approval with pride shining in his little face.

"Excellent," she pronounced with evident pleasure. A forbidden impish grin broke out on his face at her words, but she did not have the heart to chide him. The lad tried so hard to please her!

"Mr Higgins, Ma'am," Nancy's crisp tones distracted her. She turned her head in some surprise. It was nearly a full hour earlier than she had expected him. To be sure, the whistle had blown some while ago to dismiss everyone else, but Higgins' new duties had been normally detaining him much after. She rose from the table to greet the man, in her unaccustomed sunny mood perhaps offering more civility than was strictly warranted.

"Ma'am," he dipped his head. He shifted his familiar old hat around in his hands as his eyes tried unobtrusively to take in the new surroundings of the dining room.

Johnny also rose with scripted precision, coming forward to offer his foster father a crisp little bow. "Good evening, Mr Nicholas," he greeted. His twinkling eyes shifted to Mrs Thornton's, seeking her endorsement.

They had had some debate over what he ought to properly be calling Mr Higgins. She had lobbied for either "Father" or "Mr Higgins," but the lad rejected the first as too reminiscent of his real parent, and the second as too formal for the man who cared for him. In the end, he stuck resolutely to his accustomed address.

Hannah drew a miniscule sigh of resignation, crossing her hands before her as she typically did. Higgins gave a shy little smile, his stubbly cheeks quirking curiously. "I'll thank ye again Ma'am," he nodded. "I'll bid ye g'dev'nin, then." He extended his hand with unmistakable affection to the boy, and the child came obediently.

Johnny then paused, his grey eyes turning hopefully back to her. "Mrs Thornton, am I to come next week?" he asked politely.

A pinched expression crossed her features. That was why Higgins was early- the work week was over and done, and the late hours of the last few days had purchased him something of a reprieve on Saturday night. Her Sabbath would be spent in her typical sacred pursuits, with neither her son nor her new protégé for company. As for what the next week would bring... John's return, she hoped, but what that would entail was still unknown to her.

"Yes," she answered at length, her eyes fixed somewhere above the lad's head. "At least, for a few days."

Higgins was too astute to miss the sudden uncertainty in her voice. His hawk-like gaze fastened upon her, shrewd brown eyes wrinkling mysteriously. He offered another silent, half comradely little smile, nodded discreetly, and turned the lad to go.

Hannah's eyes fell now upon her empty table. *Not precisely empty*. It was still laden with food, the dessert course having just been brought, but was now devoid of company. "One moment, please," the words left her lips without her specific will to speak them.

Higgins paused. Two pairs of curious eyes met her.

Her throat constricted, but she had committed herself now. "We were not quite finished. Mr Higgins, would you care to join us for a few moments more?"

She felt sure the blood drained from Higgins' face, just as it had suddenly done from hers. Johnny looked imploringly to his foster father, silently begging him to accept.

Higgins' mouth gaped in bewilderment, rather like a fish as he sought words which would not come. Hannah closed her eyes briefly in shock at herself. *What on earth would have come over me to make me ask that man to stay*?

Higgins choked a moment more. He felt afraid to give offense, but even more afraid of Mrs Thornton- or at least the legend of her. The woman before him baffled him utterly. There was a warmth there he had never detected, and what was more, a longing for companionship none would ever have noticed when her son was near. "I... I, uh, think we best get on home. Th' other yung'uns, ye see... But thank ye, most kindly M'lady."

And that is what he called her from that day forth. Though he had been utterly terrified by her uncharacteristic overture, a flicker of respectful kinship grew out of their mutual affection for an orphaned child. Mrs Thornton at once won his fealty, and for the rest of his days he would stout-heartedly defend her honour against any slight.

BREAKFAST IN FREDERICK'S HOUSE was, as every meal, a sumptuous affair. On the Sunday of the week, however, Margaret noted that Frederick's family observed the same traditions as they had at home- the meal was of a simpler style and everything had been prepared the day before.

It was still a lavish offering. Margaret delighted in the variety of fresh fruits available, many of which were previously unfamiliar to her. She bit her lip as she strove discretely to extract the juicy pulp of a grapefruit, while John beside her was doing full justice to the mangoes. There was, she noted, no shortage of cold meats on his plate either.

"Thornton," Frederick was saying between courses, "we must leave in an hour for Mass. We always walk on Sundays, so everyone has the day off," he explained. "I...." Here he glanced in some discomfort at his in-laws. "I expect you will not be attending with us?"

John cleared his throat and glanced to his wife, whose suddenly paled face registered all he needed to know. "I think not, Hale. We appreciate your welcome, but... no, I think we should prefer to remain."

Frederick acknowledged the plan with some relief. He had been less concerned for Thornton's comfort than for Margaret's. She was still a stout Anglican, despite their father's dissention. While she had never once mentioned any concerns for his eternal soul, Frederick knew she would feel out of place and downright irreverent stepping foot into a Catholic Mass.

After the meal, Frederick motioned them aside to his study and closed the door. He went to a locked compartment of his desk and withdrew both and Anglican Bible and a Book of Common Prayer. "If you want to read this morning..." he mumbled uncomfortably. "I have been fully adopted here, but I keep these in Father's memory, you know. He gave them to me when I put to sea."

Margaret brushed her hand reverently over the battered leather covers. She opened the Bible to the dedication page and blinked rapidly as she found her father's familiar old scrawl. "Did he ever say anything, Margaret?" Frederick's voice, now trembling slightly, interrupted her thoughts.

She sniffed a little and shook her head. "No. He never told me why, only that he had doubts. He never said what they were."

"He told me," John offered. The others pinned him with focused expressions, their need for this one answer burning intensely.

He blinked in some mild surprise. "He never explained? I am sorry, I did not know. He told me he could no longer put faith in the rites and ceremonies. He did not see how they really helped anyone come to true faith. He also saw things in the management of the Church which disturbed him, made him question priorities."

Margaret, whose face was troubled and white, dropped her eyes to the floor as she digested these ideas. She wished her father had had the courage to come to her, but at least he had found a solid platform for discussion in his favorite pupil.

John rested his hand on her shoulder, drawing her gaze back up. "He never lost faith, Margaret. You must know that," he spoke gently. She drew a long breath of relief. She would have sworn to that fact herself, but John's reassurance soothed her a great deal.

Frederick, too, was affected. He was biting his upper lip and holding his face to the side. "Thank you, Thornton. I am glad you told us."

"Thank you, Hale, for the use of these." He smiled at Margaret. "We will return here after you leave to hold our own little service."

As they were leaving the study together, a teenaged boy accosted Frederick in the hallway with a note. Frederick thanked the messenger, then opened the paper. John and Margaret tried to discreetly look away, granting him privacy for his affairs, but his annoyed grunt and twisted mouth drew their attention back.

"Blast!" he sighed in frustration. "My loading supervisor fell from a scaffold this morning and cannot walk. Now, not a blessed soul in that warehouse has any clue how to read the bill of lading. I'll have to go down there myself."

"Today!" Margaret cried. "But Fred, it is Sunday!"

Her husband and brother exchanged glances. "The port doesn't stop for holy days, Margaret," Frederick informed her gently. "It's a bad business, but there it is. If the cotton is not aboard by early afternoon, you won't be heading home tomorrow. My captain knows his business, but he has enough to do without overseeing the warehouse operations this morning. If I don't go, goodness knows what sort of load you'll get. Beans and China-ware, more likely." He shook his head, growling. "That may be a slight exaggeration, but some of those lads down there I've had trouble with before," he elaborated.

At about this time, Frederick's family had begun to file into the entryway of the home, all in their finery and prepared to walk to Mass. Frederick turned to Barbour and began to explain the situation in hasty Spanish. Both cast regretful glances to their wives, but it seemed both were arguing to take on the unpleasant duty themselves.

"Wait a moment," John spoke up. All eyes turned toward him. "I will go. I know I do not speak the language, but I can point and yell to make myself understood with the best of them. We have nowhere special to go," he tilted his head toward Margaret as he spoke. "Besides, it will give me the advantage of choosing my own lots for this first shipment, so we have a good sampling."

Frederick squinted thoughtfully. "I can't let you take that on yourself. Professional courtesy, and all of that. I'll go, but if you insist you may come along." The two argued a few moments more, both determined, but John eventually prevailed.

Frederick at last shook his head in resignation. "Have your own way, then. If nothing else, Thornton, it proves one thing."

"What is that?" he asked.

"That you've enough mettle to stand up to my sister!" he winked. He reached for his hat and extended his arm to Dolores. "We will be back in time for the noon meal. If you have not returned by then, I will come join you."

"Understood," John gave a quick jerk of his head, stepping out of the way of the family as they departed.

He turned back to his beautiful wife, expecting a remonstration from her. Instead of reproof, he found her brow creased ever so slightly. "I am sorry, my love. I felt it right to do this myself. We will hold our own little prayer service when I return."

"It is not that," she sighed. "I just... are you certain you will be all right? You were with Frederick before, and I remember not liking the look of that neighborhood."

"My darling," he took her in his arms, his voice gently chiding, "I have seen and dealt with a good many things in my life which would appall you. I would not take you with me, but believe me when I say I have been through some of the roughest areas in all of England. I do know how to handle myself."

She clamped her teeth against further objections. This was going to take some getting used to, she knew. John was independent and savvy, and little as she liked it, she knew he spoke from the truth of his experiences. She imagined if she were ever to ask him, she would be horrified at some of the things he had endured during those years of hardship.

John kissed her hair, relishing the scent and feel of her in his arms. "Will you be very lonely while I am away? I hate to leave you so, in an unfamiliar house with no one about."

Margaret searched and found her reserves of strength, fortified as they had been these past few days in his arms. She lifted her chin against her recent grief, refusing to knuckle under her sorrows. "I will be fine, John. Just come back quickly."

"Oh, I intend to." He thumbed her chin, lifting it for a sweet caress. His kiss was lingering and gentle, laced with passion but tempered by loving tenderness. After some minutes, he traced a line up her jaw with soft lips. "And when I return," he whispered in her ear, "I thought we could do some liturgical studies together. It has been some while since I contemplated the Song of Solomon. I think it could be a very *long* sermon."

"John!" she scolded, but he was laughingly unrepentant. He kissed her pert little mouth again until all the salt had gone out of her embrace. Married life, he decided, was most definitely going to agree with him! With sudden inspiration, he was almost wild to be away with her on board ship. Three and a half days, keeping her all to himself- and this time, he was going to lock himself in her cabin every night!

He continued kissing her, caressing nearly every surface of exposed skin. He was filled with regret to let her go even for a moment, but burning with energy to sweep her back home with him. The sooner the ship was loaded, the sooner he could reclaim her warm affections. "I will be back soon," he promised lowly.

She traced her fingers over his cheeks, smiling bravely into his eyes. "See that you do. I love you and I cannot live without you, John."

A sparkling grin split his face, the memory of their joke the day before lending speed to his desire to get his duties over and done with. "I love you, my Margaret." He kissed her once more, then he was gone. Margaret crossed her left arm over her sling, hugging her arms tensely to her chest.

TWO HOURS LATER, JOHN was mopping his streaked forehead with the sleeve of his shirt. The warehouse was stifling and he, like the Spaniards, had eschewed his formal black coat and went about in his simple white shirt. It had been a rocky morning, peopled by a torpid and indolent handful of workers staffing the warehouse, none of whom understood a word he said. As he had reassured his brother-in-law, he had managed to make his instructions clear enough, but his voice was now raspy in his parched throat.

It was fortunate that most of the load had already been marked by the usual supervisor, or he might have been there for many hours yet. John glanced back to the bill of lading and verified that they had, indeed, acquired the full complement of the ship's destined cargo. A quarter mile away in her anchorage lay the *Sparrow,* the ship they would sail upon. John draped his dusty coat over his arm and snagged one of the last drayage carts as it rumbled by, hitching a ride.

As quickly as possible, he consigned the cotton to the ship's cargo master and washed his hands of the job. There was something much more pleasant to look forward to. His mood lightening, he struck out in a jaunty walk, whistling a little as he went. The wharf was crowded, but he threaded his way through with scarcely a glance for those in his way.

Just after he turned up the first street, a rough pair of hands ripped him around by the shoulders. He tensed automatically, swinging a fist about in reflex and dropping his coat. His carelessly aimed fist skittered harmlessly alongside a burly seaman's jaw. He did not fare so well himself, as the blow was returned with better aim.

Dazed, he swayed slightly. "Who are you?" he demanded angrily. "What do you want?"

The burly man did not answer, but a steely faced younger man in a glittering blue uniform stepped close to look him in the eye. "That's him," he pronounced. "Take him."

John looked between them in panting confusion. He had thought this was a mugging, but he could not fathom why a man in uniform would wish to identify him. The heavier man grabbed his collar to drag him somewhere, but he ducked, writhed away, and landed a successful punch to the man's temple. The first man tumbled to his knees. Whirling, he twisted away, but another pair of hands was behind him. The last thing he remembered was a close-up of the third man's knuckles.

Thirty-Eight

Margaret's nails dug mercilessly into the soft leather of her chair. "*Tell me!*" she insisted again. Frederick paced before her, pale and shaken. He had insisted she sit down before he related what he knew, but he doubted it would matter. She would not stay seated for long once he had spoken.

He raked his fingers through his sweat-streaked hair. "He wasn't at the warehouse. Everyone there was gone. They said he had been at the ship to sign over the documents, and then nobody knows what happened. That was over four hours ago. I don't know any more."

Margaret bolted upright, her little white fists clenching in agony. Her face was streaked with tears of fright, her cheeks stained bright with distress against her bloodless features. "Where was that?" She stalked to the hall, ripping a random bonnet off its hook before he could stop her. She clamped it on her head, jerking the ribbon with her good hand. Her fingers fumbled, and in a cry of rage and anguish, she snatched and tore at the sling hindering her progress.

Frederick caught her up and locked her into a restrictive embrace. His strong sister crumbled, sobbing onto his shoulder. "Shhh, Dearest. We will find him," he soothed. "I'm sure there is some explanation. You know John, he probably went to buy you a pair of diamond earrings or something."

Margaret shook her head in vehement denial. "No, he would not have, Fred! We both know that." She covered her face with her soaked fingers and gave way to her fears. "Something has happened, Fred! I have to go find him!"

"*You*," he pushed against her shoulders firmly, staring her down, "are in no condition to go *anywhere*." He stubbornly held her gaze until she backed down first. He could take no chances that she might run out after he left. Thornton was a strong, imposing man, well able to take care of himself, but Margaret was an entirely different matter.

"I have about twenty of my own people scouring the streets for him, and Barbour has gone to the police. I am going to my office to oversee things from there. We *will* find him, Margaret, but you have to trust me. You have to stay here! I cannot risk having you lost, too."

She bit her lip sullenly, refusing to meet his eyes. "Margaret…" he warned. "Don't even consider it! You can do us no good out there." He seized at one last hope of detaining her. "John will expect to find you here when he comes back."

Her tear-smudged eyes rose silently to his. She hated this feeling of impotence. She longed to be out pounding the streets, doing something- anything!- to distract herself from her gnawing sense of worry.

"Promise me!" Frederick demanded, cupping her wet cheeks.

She drew a tremulous breath and nodded fractionally. He did not release her quite yet. "I- I promise, Fred," she muttered hoarsely, reluctantly.

"Good. Now, Dolores is going to stay with you. Try not to wear my wife out just now, will you? *Stay.*" He glared affectionately at her one last time. Finally convinced she had tendered the best promise he was going to get, he spun out the door and hurried down the street.

John groaned and put his hands to his head. His face throbbed and his equilibrium spun wildly. *What happened?*

"Good afternoon, Lieutenant Hale," a crisp British voice sliced through his foggy thoughts.

He blinked a few times, wincing at the pain over his eye socket. "Wh… what did you say?" He tried pushing himself up and found he was laying on a planked floor with a single rough woolen blanket for comfort. He rolled slightly and found his ankle shackled by a heavy chain.

The same officer he had seen in the street sat before him on a half barrel. "Oh, it's no good pretending, Lieutenant Hale. My name is Lieutenant Jackson. You are on board the HMS *Marlborough*, of Her Majesty's Mediterranean fleet, under the command of Captain Edward Wharton and bound for England."

He shook his head slightly, mindful of the dizziness which would result from much movement. "I do not understand. There has been some mistake. My name is John Thornton of Milton."

The young officer laughed, a low menacing chuckle. "Yes, so this document says," he held aloft a fluttering paper between pinched fingers. John squinted and recognized his precious marriage license.

"A clever ruse," the officer continued. "Traveling with your sister under another name, pretending an elopement to conceal your identity so you might leave the country undetected. You might have invented a more convincing alias, though."

John's brow was furrowed in utter confusion. He was only now beginning to sense the full measure of the jeopardy in which he found himself. Righteous anger would do him no good here; he had to appeal to what reason the officer possessed. "You make no sense. That is a legitimate marriage license. I wed Margaret Hale, originally of Helstone in Hampshire, last Wednesday."

"Indeed." The officer snorted derisively. "Did anyone tell you it is not the norm to carry such an important document in your pocket? Nor is it usual to flee the country and be 'married' at sea! And what is it you do, Mr... excuse me, what was it you claimed your name was?"

He clenched his teeth. "John Thornton. I am Master at Marlborough Mills, a cotton manufacturing plant."

The officer laughed aloud this time, slapping his knee in affected mirth. "Well, they don't make them that imaginative anymore, do they? Your head is addled, man. *Marlborough* was the name of this ship. And as for your 'marriage'..." his tones dropped dangerously, "I, too am from Helstone, and the Margaret Hale I knew of would *never* marry a tradesman. First rule of disguise, man; Know Thyself."

He rose to his feet, glancing scornfully down at his prisoner. "You may remember, Hale, that for the usual slops we conduct court-martials aboard ship, but you are lucky. Captain Wharton wishes to make a special example of you in London, since there we are bound anyway. I suppose if one is going to mutiny, it pays to do so with such notoriety. You, my friend, are destined for Whitehall. I expect you have at least four days before you dangle."

The haughty officer took his little lamp and left him alone in the dark, slamming the hold door. John dropped his aching head breathlessly back to the planked floor. His thoughts whirled desperately. How was he to prove his identity under such circumstances? The only document he had carried with him had been his marriage license, and the lieutenant had shot his own opinionated holes through that evidence.

Sinking fear turned slowly to panic. *Margaret!* She would be out of her mind with fear for him, and justly so. She could have no way of knowing what had become of him, and even if she could somehow find him, there was nothing she could do to help. What if... what if the worst happened? What if... a choking sob broke shamelessly loose in his breast.

If he could not prove his identity in time, he would hang in Frederick Hale's place. He could not, would not betray Margaret's brother, even if someone would have believed him. But Margaret! To have gained her, only to lose her so soon! His chest began to heave with the unfairness of it all. He had held her, loved her, and she him. He had looked forward to years at her side, and now at the whims of fancy, she was snatched from him again.

His fears for himself spiraled as his able mind worked out all the possible outcomes. Few were promising. It was quite natural that his own instinct for self-preservation should come alive first, but rapidly on the heels of it was another fear, a greater one. What would become of Margaret?

The Navy had their marriage license. She had no proof of anything now. True, her own family in London could identify her as Margaret Hale for the purposes of Mr Bell's will, but she had signed her name as Margaret Thornton. What explanations would then be required?

And what if... it was possible, quite possible, that she might already be carrying his child- a child he might never see. To return home after such a hasty departure in such a condition with no husband and no marriage document....

Sickening, he curled into a ball, his body and soul in agony. His mind black with fear, he buried his face into the unyielding planks and wept for Margaret.

***

Frederick prowled the floor of his cramped office, hands clasping and unclasping behind his back. He had promised overtime pay to all the dock and warehouse workers he could find, and had set them upon the streets of the city. He had no doubt that some were "looking" for Thornton in the local brothels, but that could not be helped. Occasionally someone would report back to him, but always he would say he had found nothing.

He scowled in frustration, chewing his inner cheeks as he mentally churned over the problem. There was absolutely no possibility in his mind that Thornton had gone off deliberately. He was too madly in love with Margaret, for one thing. In addition, Frederick felt he had a good measure of the man, and a more responsible, dedicated fellow he had never met.

That left accident or foul play. Thornton had been to the docks and the warehouse before, and he was a clever enough man. He could not have become so badly lost in those few blocks that he would not turn up hours later. A mugging? Frederick had personally checked the hospital and Barbour the police station, and they had found nothing. The man had simply vanished.

Stalking back to his desk, his hand slammed down on the port schedule again. He had checked over and over, and had yet to find a ship which had been scheduled to sail today which Thornton might have been on. Frigates, cargo vessels, and that sparkling new British Navy gunship he had admired from afar. Some arrivals, but no passenger vessels departing, as it was Sunday.

Like Margaret, he was wild to be doing something which felt useful. He was about to abandon his post to begin tossing the streets himself when someone beat on his door. Hope springing to his chest, he leaped to answer it.

The man he found there immediately disappointed his hopes. He was a slender, elegant man, dressed stylishly in clothes that looked freshly tailored and pressed despite the sweltering day. The man extended his hand, but it looked to Frederick more as though he were bestowing kingly favor than offering a greeting. "Good day, sir," he spoke in heavily accented English, "Monsieur Marshall, I presume?"

Frederick fought a little flinch of his cheek muscles. He had a fair idea of who this fellow was and what he wanted. He thought he had told the man he wasn't interested. "I am. And you are?"

"Philippe Giraud, I believe we 'ave exchanged proposals of business." The man strode into the office, looking speculatively about. "Your ideas are very interesting, Monsieur."

Frederick felt his voice growing cold. "I have entered another contract already, sir. I am afraid I cannot offer you anything. Now, if you will excuse me, I have another matter of some urgency requiring my attention."

Giraud turned about, tilting a patronizing smile at him. In the light of the window, Frederick could not be sure but he thought he detected fading bruises on the man's right cheek. Though he appeared a spotless dandy, he had evidently been playing rough somewhere.

"Oh, oui, Monsieur, I expect anozer was 'ere before. Ze Monsieur T'ornton, from England, nôn? Ah yes, I know of ze man. Very clever, oui. Mais, 'e is in some financial trouble, did you know?"

Frederick narrowed his eyes. "Actually he is quite stable. Where are you getting your information, I wonder?"

"Oh! Well, zat is not what word in ze industry says. Pardon if I am mistaken. It must be true, for Monsieur T'ornton would not lie to a business partner, nôn?"

The hairs on the back of Frederick's neck were beginning to prickle. Something was amiss. "No, I do not believe so. Tell me, Monsieur Giraud, have you ever met Thornton?"

"I? Well, I also would not lie." Giraud smiled ingratiatingly. "Oui, I met 'im in passing. It 'appened we sailed ze same ship, you see, but I was delayed in seeking you out by some personal matters."

"I see." Very well, in fact. Had Margaret ever told him who her attacker was? Frederick doubted not that he had found the scoundrel. As if it had been planned, one of Frederick's dock workers knocked on the office door at that exact second. "Excuse me please, Monsieur."

Frederick did not welcome his employee in; rather he put his head just outside to speak privately. The man had no good news, but it did not matter now. Frederick knew what he needed to do next. After giving a few instructions, he dismissed his worker and turned back to his guest.

"Well, Monsieur Giraud, it seems my erstwhile partner has left the country unexpectedly. Perhaps Thornton is not as honourable as I previously thought. Do you think you and I could discuss matters?"

"Ah, I am glad to 'ear you speak so! Where shall we begin?" the Frenchman enthused.

"Why, the warehouse, of course," Frederick grinned. "It is not far, a short walk really." Frederick led the way out, holding the door for the Frenchman. Together they walked the three blocks to the warehouse. Giraud had questions which Frederick hoped he answered with convincing civility. He ushered the other man in the side door of the enormous building.

"Oh, là!" the other cried, doffing his silly looking hat. "You do not disappoint, Monsieur Marshall. Zis is enough to supply my mill for t'ree mont's!"

"The plantation is rather large," Frederick commented neutrally. "We just loaded a shipment this morning, and I have more inbound from Sevilla by next week." Frederick's eyes skimmed the perimeter of the building.

"Zat shipment- it is bound for T'ornton's mill, oui?" the Frenchman inquired.

"Perhaps," he replied nonchalantly. "I can change the export documentation, send it to a different destination, but it will take at least another day to re-file the paperwork. If Thornton is so quick to abandon the prospect, I may be forced to do so." He lightly clasped his hands behind his back, wagging his fingers.

Giraud chuckled low. "Ah, yes, zat T'ornton- he seemed occupied with *ozer* matters on ze ship," he quirked an eyebrow suggestively. "I do not t'ink his mind was entirely on ze business."

Easy, Frederick cautioned himself. It would be counterproductive to lose his cool now. "Oh? Do you mean the man is a gambler?" Movement caught the corner of his eye. *Almost*.

"*Nôn*! Not a gambler, but perhaps a... 'ow do you say... philanderer? Oh là, Monsieur! Ze man chooses excellent companionship!"

"A true scoundrel, then. I say, Monsieur Giraud, I have another very important question for you."

"Oui?" he asked, still laughing a little.

In a flash, Frederick had a handful of Giraud's stylish new shirt, his fist cocked back menacingly. He slammed his weight forward, forcing Giraud to bow over backward. Giraud gaped, his mouth and eyes flown wide. "*Where is he?*" Frederick bellowed.

Six strong warehouse workers, their sleeves rolled up, surrounded them. Giraud's eyes darted helplessly around the little circle. "Start talking!" ordered Frederick. "And don't leave anything out."

Thirty-Nine

"SO, THAT'S EVERYTHING HE told me." Frederick pulled his weeping sister close to his side as Dolores held her hand. "We turned him over to the police after that. They've got him locked up. It seems he bribed his way out before, but not this time."

Margaret shook in fury and outrage. Why would anyone do such a thing? Her pure honest mind could not conceive of it. She was terrified for her husband. What could happen to him?

"Fred," she choked, "what will they do to him?"

Frederick exchanged glances with Dolores and Barbour, who sagged morosely in a nearby chair. "It depends, Dearest. I am certain now they took him on the *Marlborough*, which left today. I made inquiries and learned that the captain did not conduct any court martials in port, which is good news. Since the ship was scheduled for London anyway, Wharton will turn him over to the authorities at Whitehall. That will buy us some time."

She sniffled, struggling to contain herself and make her voice obey her will. "Time for what, Fred? Will he be able to prove who he is?"

Frederick set his teeth grimly. "He will when I turn myself in."

Cold horror washed over her. "No, Fred!" Dolores next to her bowed her head, tears dripping from her cheeks. "You cannot do it!"

"Nor can I let an innocent man hang in my place. I have run long enough, Margaret. It is time I faced the consequences. I moved the schedule up, the *Sparrow* weighs anchor in two hours. We'll both be on it."

"No!" she cried. "Fred, you are innocent too! Surely there is some other way! John has any number of contacts in England who can identify him. He has business documents and... and... oh, Fred, he has our license! His name is everywhere, surely!"

"He has a marriage license issued in haste which lists 'Hale' as your maiden name, Margaret. That's a liability, if I know the Navy. They'll use it as evidence that he's really me traveling under an assumed name. Giraud told them the man was your brother, and that is what they will believe. They won't let him contact anyone directly who can come identify him- not unless he gets a halfway honest lawyer, and that is not something worth placing your hopes on. Time is of the essence with the Navy. No, Margaret, I have to come with you. It's the only way."

"Not quite," Barbour's voice broke in for the first time. All eyes turned to him- Frederick's lifeless, Margaret's desperate, and Dolores' hopeful. "I am legally business partner too, eh? I bring business contracts with his name and we bring Spaulding to testify. And Señora, I buy time. You find others, bring witnesses, si?"

"Yes! Oh, Fred, please listen to him. Think of Dolores!"

"I am, Margaret." He squeezed his wife's hand, looking with deepest apology into her beloved eyes. "I would not dishonour my wife and my family by allowing John to die in my stead. I could not live with myself."

"But he is right, Fred! So many people know John if we can only get them there. Why, all of Milton could identify him, and likely several in London. He is even a magistrate, his signature is everywhere! The court could not refuse such evidence. What further good can it do to sacrifice yourself?"

"It is a sure thing, Margaret. The court wants a neck to stretch, and they don't particularly care whose. You would have to have a good number of very determined witnesses to sway them. Who can you possibly get on such short notice who will storm the court with you?"

Margaret bowed her head briefly, then suddenly lifted it again, light glowing in her eyes. "You have not met my mother-in-law."

John jumped to his feet when the door opened to his little cell. It was not the lieutenant or any other officer as he had hoped. Just the same orderly as always, bringing hard biscuit and water. "There's been a mistake!" he cried. "I need to speak with the captain!" The young orderly- little more than a boy- stalwartly refused to acknowledge him. He had evidently been well trained to ignore the prisoners.

John slumped hopelessly back on the floor. He dropped his head to rest in his hands, between his knees. It had been two days of utter solitude, locked away with his fears and worries. So far, everyone he came into brief contact with ignored his protests. How was he to make his case? Would there be any hope of legal counsel once he reached London? Prospects were dim.

He thought, still, of Margaret. Frederick would take care of her, of that he was sure, but he knew his fiery wife well. She would be searching everywhere, and there would be nothing for her to turn up. What had tipped off the Navy he still did not know, but he worried that if they did discover he was the wrong man, they might go back to Càdiz to resume the search. If that happened, neither she nor her brother would be safe.

His poor mother! How sorry she had been to see him go that morning, just over a week ago. Would she ever receive word of what had become of him? Margaret would write her, he was sure. Even then she could not tell his whereabouts, only the strange circumstances which had thrown them back together.

He had little hope that their fractured relationship could be mended in the light of his disappearance. They, who would need each other the most, would scarcely know how to speak to one another. His mother in particular would be bitter about Margaret's role in his sudden absence. He wondered if she could look past whatever blame she might assign to Margaret so that they become a comfort to each other.

Not knowing what else to do, he heaved a weary sigh and sent up the same fervent prayer he had prayed already for two days.

"SEÑORA, PLEASE, YOU MUST save your strength," Barbour urged once again. He had been a steady and supportive escort through the entire voyage, but Margaret could not stem her restlessness.

She turned a wan smile on him. "I cannot go below just now, Mr Barbour. I cannot remain still. I would simply pace the cabin."

"Si, this I know, but it grows cold. Señor Thornton, he would not wish you to take ill, no?"

Margaret sighed through clenched teeth. She had grown to recognize this tactic. Barbour would employ John's name only when he was at the end of his persuasive abilities.

On the whole, he was a loyal and gentle traveling companion who cared wonderfully for her welfare, but he was not the man she wanted.

She closed her eyes and shook her head at her own willfulness. Barbour was doing the best he could. He had provided amply for her comfort, both physically and emotionally. He had brought a ladies' maid from his own home to assist her. He had even rousted Spaulding from his bed the night they departed and demanded the little agent accompany them. The man was initially very displeased, but somehow Barbour had soothed his ruffled feathers.

"Your, eh, your shoulder? It does not pain you any longer?" Barbour gestured hesitantly to Margaret's sling. She had, in a fit of pique, nearly thrown the sling overboard the day before when she could not fasten it herself and had no John to help her. A few moments of her arm hanging unsupported had cured her of that whim, and it had taken the rest of the evening for the sharp ache to subside.

"I am better, thank you," she replied softly. Offering a little smile of contrition, she bowed to her companion's concerns. "I think you are right, I should go indoors. Perhaps I will go for some tea."

"Ay, muy bien," he agreed. He gallantly offered his beefy arm and Margaret accepted it. It was impossible not to compare his height, his walk, his voice, his very feel to the man who was not there- the man who had become a part of her. *Stop this!* she ordered herself. *You will only drive yourself mad!*

She grit her teeth, swallowing again the sickening lurch of worry and powerlessness which threatened to overcome her. "Mr Barbour, do you think the *Marlborough* can have docked yet?" Her stomach fluttering tensely, she prayed not. The longer that vessel took for the passage, the better her chances of reaching John.

"Possible, Señora, possible," he mused. "In fact I am certain. She is fast, is the ship of the line! I..." he stopped when he beheld Margaret's white face. "But the *Sparrow* now, she is fast too!" he reassured her. "She is English built! Federico, he say they are the best, no? We reach Liverpool in the morning, you will see!"

Margaret's heart sank. It was a solid four hours, possibly more from Liverpool to London. Frederick had not been able to change the export documents in time, and they were obliged to sail to their original port. In addition, she intended to make a detour to present herself at Marlborough Mills to find anyone she could to accompany her.

She quailed a little at the prospect of facing down the senior Mrs Thornton. What would she think? She had no doubt of her immediate compliance. Mrs Thornton would do anything for her son, but at what cost? She imagined herself receiving the brunt of the widow's scalding ire. She set her jaw. For John, she would do it, and bravely.

HENRY LENNOX, WORN OUT from his long day, at last dropped the final pages into his filing box. He had worked late today to make up for lost time this past week. He had resigned himself to waiting and watching, and there was nothing he could do to hasten word of Margaret.

He had told his brother that he would pay a visit to the docks again, but his better sense took over. Maxwell was right. What was the point? It was not as though that same injured woman would still be sitting there, and the likelihood that she was Margaret was slimmer still.

He fastened his briefcase and was sliding into his coat when his door opened without a knock. Startled, he craned his neck to see who would be so audacious. "Harper! What brings you here at this hour?"

"I've jest heered something what might interest ye, Lad." The grizzled captain glanced over his shoulder, as if worried he might have been followed, then pressed the door closed. He hobbled his way to the chair opposite Henry's desk, not even bothering to ask for a drink.

Henry quivered with anxiety. What could have brought the old captain here at this hour? It must be something important. "Well?" he leaned forward urgently, hands splayed over his desk.

"That feller from old Reid's crew, the one what mutinied."

"Frederick Hale?"

"Aye, ye were his att'rney, weren't ye?"

"Y-yes," stammered Henry. "But I have no idea of his whereabouts. Why, what's happened?"

"They've got 'im. Heered it this evening. *Marlborough* put in and they 'ave a pris'ner, fresh from Spain. Word travels fast, mate." Harper leaned back wearily. "Court martial set for t'morrow, they say."

The blood drained from Henry's face. What could have brought Hale into custody? And if they had found him, what did that mean for Margaret's safety? Numbly, he thanked the captain by handing him an entire bottle of his best brandy.

After Harper left, Henry scrambled together every document he had ever filed on Frederick Hale's case. He stuffed the bulging stack into his briefcase. This could not wait. He had to get to Whitehall.

Almost everything was abandoned this late in the evening. All the offices were closed, but Henry had been to the naval offices before. There was always someone to let him in with sufficient inducement.

He got past the first set of guards, though somewhat more impoverished than before. After several frustrating delays haggling with uncooperative minor functionaries, eventually he got through to the hall where prisoners awaited trial.

A bored attendant- too old for his drab midshipman's uniform- leaned over the desk. "State your business," he yawned.

Henry snorted a little. "I am here to see a prisoner who was just brought in, a Lieutenant Hale. I am his legal counsel."

"No visits after hours. Come back in the morning." The attendant yawned again.

"See here, Midshipman! I will have you on report to the Admiralty for your slovenly conduct! I will take this to Henry Eden himself, whose wife is related to my client. Now, I demand you allow me entrance!"

The lowly officer, jolted to attention by this mention of a member of the Admiralty, leapt from his seat. Shaken, he blustered, "One moment, sir, I will see what I can do."

Henry released a tight breath and nervously smoothed the front of his jacket. In truth, he had never met Eden and had no means of introduction, but he had overheard Mrs Shaw once brag that Eden had married a third cousin of hers. It would have to do.

A few moments more, and Henry was shown formally to the prison block. He had hoped he would never need to see this place again. He looked about glumly as he was ushered into a little white room set aside for interrogations. Things did not look good for Frederick Hale this time.

He took a seat at a little table and began to rifle through his documents. The door from the other side rattled, hinges whining, and a guard pushed someone into the room. "Ten minutes," he rumbled. "You want more, come back tomorrow."

Henry stared at the man shackled before him. This was *not* Frederick Hale. He was tall- taller than Hale, and slightly darker complected. His unshaven face was bruised and his clothing tattered from rough handling, but he stood with quiet strength in the center of the room. He, too, was silently evaluating.

"There must be some mistake," Henry found his voice first.

"There is, indeed." The man's voice was deep and sure. He came forward extending his manacled hand, relief evident in his face. "John Thornton, at your service."

Thornton! But he was supposed to be in Spain! Henry's mouth fell open. As pieces of an exploded puzzle, several things began to click back together for him at once. Henry sat down roughly, unable to support himself in his great shock. Thornton arched an eyebrow skeptically, then assumed the other seat himself.

"And you are?" Thornton prodded.

Henry shook his head slightly, clearing his thoughts. "Henry Lennox, Attorney at Law."

Thornton's doubtful expression washed away, replaced by sudden recognition. He caught his breath.

"You have heard my name before," Henry observed. "Then perhaps you can tell me-*where is Margaret Hale*?"

An expression somewhat close to a smile, if it were not so full of pain, graced the man's features. "Lennox, there is a great deal to tell you, and very little time. Now, listen very carefully...."

Henry listened in confounded wonder as Thornton related the details of his relationship with Margaret. His heart twisted in final resignation when he heard of their abrupt marriage, but the more he listened, the more he believed the truth of it all. Some things were finally making sense. Thornton kept his tale brief, but Henry at last understood both Margaret's motives and the dire situation Thornton found himself in.

He leaned back in his chair, staring at the face of the man Margaret loved, and racked his brain for ideas. He was not so mean or low as to wish him harm out of jealous spite. It stabbed him painfully, to be sure, but in truth he had already known her heart could not belong to him.

With full conviction he also knew that he, as a friend, would do whatever he could to help her husband. He drew out a new leaf of paper and a pen from his briefcase, staring at them blankly.

"You will need names of witnesses, I imagine," Thornton prompted. "I have to establish my identity somehow."

Henry passed him the paper and watched as he scrawled out some names. "Send a telegram to my mother," he fairly pleaded. "If... if it is too late for her to see me, will you tell her all I have told you about Margaret? She does not know."

Henry nodded solemnly. "I will."

"And Lennox-" he leveled a determined stare, "I will not have Frederick Hale compromised. Under *no* circumstances. Do we understand each other?"

Henry swallowed. Thornton had guts. Did he just understand the man properly? "Do you mean you will face the gallows rather than turn him in? Don't be a fool, man!"

"I mean exactly that. If Margaret..." his voice broke. "If Margaret is to lose one of us, it will not be because I acted the coward." His eyes dropped to his hands, and Henry was sure he saw the man blinking away tears. "I could never do that to her," Thornton murmured quietly.

Henry covered his mouth with his hand. If he could have ever wondered whether Thornton cared truly for Margaret, that worry was now dead. The man before him was willing to sacrifice everything for her.

The door opened again, a gruff-faced guard frowning and crossing his arms. Thornton rose reluctantly to go. "One more thing," he paused, turning back.

"Anything you need. What is it?"

Thornton stepped close, his tones low and broken. "Margaret. If things go badly for me, will you take care of her?"

Henry stared mutely, his eyes glazing.

"Swear it, Lennox!" Thornton demanded, his voice suddenly heated. "I know you care for her too, or you would not be here! She will need you. Promise you will look after her! And tell her- tell her I love her."

Henry's eyes pricked with emotion. He nodded, his heart breaking. "I swear it. But we will get you out of here, Thornton. You can tell her yourself."

Thornton nodded wearily, at last satisfied. He had done all he could for his cherished Margaret. He walked back and submitted once more to the guards with a final lingering look to his legal counsel.

Henry sat in a daze for another moment. He tried to picture himself in Thornton's shoes. Could he have had the same courage? What selfless devotion it must take to face what Thornton faced, unwilling to speak a word which might cause his wife more pain. Even staring blankly into the unknown, the man was still willing to consign the care of the woman he loved to another, in the hope that she might be kept safe.

Sighing deeply, he closed his eyes and scrubbed his tired face with sweaty palms. If Thornton could sacrifice his own desires for her good, then he could do no less. He resolved to pit his every wit and every resource against Her Majesty's Navy.

Forty

Hannah Thornton was always an early riser. Today was no different, as she carefully dressed herself to descend the stairs. The week was nearly spent, and as yet she had no word from John. Everything depended upon how long he'd had to remain in Spain, but she hoped he would be back on firm English soil by the time the week was out.

Young Johnny Boucher had continued his visits to her. It had seemed only natural on his first visit of the new week to send home with him the remainder of the large, toothsome chocolate cake they had shared. After all, his parched frame could tolerate cake better than her aging figure. And if her cook was surprised on the next day at the larger portion of dessert dishes the Mistress had planned for the afternoon tea, she had the good sense to hold her tongue. It was important, Hannah reasoned, that the child ought to encounter a variety of dishes during his etiquette training.

Beside the lad's daily lessons, she had taken to walking the mill every morning of late. The good cheer her visits had begun to engender brightened her own dreary days as well. She found it a pleasant break to her monotony until her protégé should arrive each afternoon.

The day before in the carding room, one young girl- a new hire- had been crying over her workstation. Mrs Thornton had assumed she was ill and had intended to send her home. The girl denied it. "'Tis the noise," she had wept. "Me 'ead, it 'urts sometimes."

Hannah had stood silently a moment, eying the young worker thoughtfully. She seemed earnest enough and showed a strong desire to remain. Wordlessly she had gathered a few scraps of fluff, showing her how to fashion plugs for her ears. The girl had been able to finish the day out, much to Hannah's satisfaction.

Today as she passed, the young woman put on a brave smile. Hannah could still read the discomfort in her face, but she was at least functioning. Perhaps... perhaps if things settled out well for the mill, they might find her another workstation. The entire mill was noisy, but some areas were worse than others. She liked a girl who worked with a will.

She slowly paraded about the mill, cautiously returning shy smiles when they were offered. She made her way to her favorite vantage point, taking the wrought iron steps up to the scaffolding. Nicholas Higgins found her thus, as she leaned elegantly over the observation deck to survey the room. "G'day, M'lady," he lifted his cap jauntily.

She acknowledged him with a slow gracious nod. "How are the week's orders progressing?" she inquired.

"W'ull be done 'bout three hours 'head of schedule, M'lady." Higgins' voice was cheery but his face betrayed a hint of worry.

"Is something wrong, Mr Higgins?"

"Aye- w'ull 'bout run up on cotton, M'lady," he answered reluctantly. "'Nother week... Some o' the hands, well, they're a'feared."

She pressed her lips together grimly. "My son has the situation under control, Mr Higgins. Have no doubt," she asserted, with a confidence she did not feel.

He caught her eye with a steady, reassuring gaze. "I know, M'lady. I trust the Master."

She drew an uneven sigh, blinking. "Thank you, Mr Higgins." His word went a long way to that effect because she knew the hands would follow him. They stood a moment, looking over the looms together.

"Well, I best be gettin' on," Higgins sighed at length. He moved to descend the scaffolding, but his way was blocked by a liveried messenger.

"Mrs Thornton, I presume?" the man asked, craning his neck upward.

"I am," she answered grandly. Higgins stood out of the way so the messenger could ascend to them.

"Telegram for Mrs Thornton," he announced, passing the paper into her hand. "Sign here, please." He extended a clipboard for her signature, then backed down the stairs.

Hannah passed trembling fingers over the seal. Higgins tipped his cap silently and moved to follow the messenger down the stair railing to grant her privacy.

"Wait," she stopped him. "This... this will be from John." He stopped and held her eye. Both shared a silent hope as she hastily broke the seal of the telegram. Her eyes flew over the printed script. She began to breathe erratically and he watched her eyes scan from top to bottom again in disbelief.

"Bad news, M'lady?" he started in concern. Her hand fell slack, and the telegram would have slipped to the floor below but for his quick action. Mrs Thornton, strong woman that she was, tottered and swayed.

"Hold it!" he cried, and utterly heedless of the lady's dignity, he swooped his shoulder under her arm to support her lest she fall to her death below.

"John!" she was sobbing, her eyes unseeing. "Not John!"

Horrified at what the nature of the telegram might be, Higgins could not stop himself. He looked at the scrap of paper in his hand and read.

Marlborough Mills, Milton
17 July 1856
Thornton, Mrs Hannah
John Thornton held prisoner in Whitehall on charge of mutiny. Mistaken identity. Court martial proceedings begin immediately. Request witnesses.
Lennox, Henry Atty.

Mrs Thornton was shaking, her face a staring white. Blindly she sought the railing of the scaffolding. "I have to go to him!" she cried. "Let me go!" she wrested free of Higgins' supporting arm.

"Nay, M'lady, ye canna'!" he argued. Gripping her arm again, afraid she might still fall, he pulled her roughly around. He knew he should be fired and perhaps imprisoned on the spot for treating the Mistress in such a way, but he needed to snap her back to reality. "Ye'r in no condition!" he insisted sharply.

"Mister Higgins!" she rounded on him, her full ire blazing. "Out of my way *this instant!* I intend to be on the next train to London!"

He screwed his mouth stubbornly. "Not alone, y'er not."

HENRY HAD SUCCEEDED IN one more visit to Thornton in the morning. The first thing Thornton had asked, oddly, was whether the *Esperanza* had returned to port. Henry nearly slapped his brow in frustration with himself. He had written off his interest in that ship once he had settled it with himself that Margaret would no longer be aboard it. "Get Carter," Thornton had insisted.

Henry had nodded quickly. "Any other contacts in London? I do not know how many witnesses from Milton we can get here. I sent telegrams to Mrs Thornton and Mr Dalton at your bank, as well as a Mr Hamper and a Mr Slickson."

"The last two won't come, count on it," he grumbled sourly. Thornton had squinted thoughtfully a moment, then, "Mr Gentry at Gentry, Harlow, and Jacobs. He was Mr Bell's attorney, and he may have a copy of the signed will by now. I doubt that would be much evidence."

"Probably not. You never met the man? The navy prosecutor already has your marriage license and a convenient explanation for it, so I doubt an additional document- also a recent one- would add much weight to it. I might try to bring my brother and his wife down- he's a retired Captain in the Regulars and has some credibility."

"They have never met me either. How does that help?"

"They've met Frederick Hale."

Thornton shook his head. "I do not want to draw attention back to him. We need people who can testify that I am John Thornton, not people who will merely say I'm not Frederick Hale."

Henry had relented, knowing Thornton was right. It was too weak of a defense from a trial standpoint anyway, but it was almost all he had to work with until his witnesses could arrive. That would not be for several hours at best. His best hope until then was to plant the seeds of doubt in the minds of the Board of Admirals.

The court official present at the time informed him that court martial proceedings would begin at 10 this morning, sharp. He had submitted to the court a brief declaring that his client stood falsely accused under a case of mistaken identity. Now he paced the floor outside the admiral's chambers as the board reviewed his paperwork.

After what seemed an eternity, a minor official stepped out of the room. Henry approached respectfully. The withered old man unrolled an official-looking document and read aloud to those assembled in the room. The preamble was long and Henry missed most of it. What he waited to hear finally came forth.

"...In light of present claim to mistaken identity, the Defence shall be granted until 1400 hours on this day, 17 July, in the year of our Lord 1856, to disprove the Defendant's identification as one Lieutenant Frederick Hale of Her Majesty's Naval Forces. If sufficient evidence is not presented by such time, court martial proceedings shall begin promptly."

Henry glanced at his pocket watch. It was 9:25 now. Hours, hopefully enough time for at least a speckling of the requested Milton witnesses to arrive. Thornton clearly expected his mother and likely his banker, at least, would come. Henry hoped he was right about that latter. The banker's testimony would carry more weight than a distraught mother's would. A man with business dealings would have official documents with signatures, and that might prove vital.

He wished he knew how to contact Margaret. She would want to be here. From what Thornton said, she could have had no way of knowing what had happened to him, but both knew her to be a clever and determined woman. She and her brother would have figured something out, surely. Henry began to hope against hope that she had at least possessed the instinct to sail for home, but he knew she would not have unless she had exhausted every other avenue of search. She could still be days out, and her husband did not have that much time.

Glancing again at his watch to make certain he had read it aright, Henry took up his briefcase. The *Esperanza* seemed the most hopeful thing to look for at the moment.

It took him nearly an hour to get down to the port. The ticket office seemed the best place to inquire first, but there was a long line before he could ask anyone his question. "Due back today" was the only answer he could get out of anyone.

Scowling, he stared at his watch again as though it could speak back to him. Not having any better ideas at the moment, he resolved to wait on the pier for any sign of the returning ship. Two hours, he gave himself. After that, he had to figure something else out.

MARGARET HAD HER VALISE in her hand and was gripping the starboard rail well before the *Sparrow* actually docked. Barbour had pleaded with her to wait in a safer, more comfortable place. "Señora, you cannot make her sail any faster! Sit now, while you can!" he had urged, but to no avail. Margaret could not have sat if the ship were under heavy seas and tossing her about.

The lines could not be thrown fast enough, the tug not efficient enough, to satisfy her yearning. She was aching to be on firm ground and on her way. At last, deciding that her hands were beginning to cramp with anxiety and the force of her grip, she commanded herself to be still.

Maria, the girl who had come to help her from Frederick's home, timidly approached. Likely enough she had come only at Barbour's behest, but Margaret forced a welcoming smile. Maria spoke not a word of English, so their communication had been largely in gestures, but she was a comforting presence, nonetheless. She would not be going on to London with them; Barbour had made provisions for her to return immediately upon the *Sparrow* once it had taken on its return cargo.

At long last, the ship settled into her anchorage. A cargo vessel rather than a passenger ship, the *Sparrow* was obliged to moor in an industrial area of the port. *That much further from the rail station!* Margaret screamed with internal frustration.

Her feet hit the docks first, followed by Barbour and Spaulding. The former was chastening the latter to keep up with the little woman who marched briskly ahead of them in a swish of black skirts. Spaulding was having some difficulty managing both his briefcase and his bag, but he determinedly pushed his glasses up his peaked nose and struggled on. He had already learned not to cross this particular young lady.

Margaret, used to walking as she was, decided to hail a cab to transport them and their baggage to the station. Speed was all she cared about. Soon she was jumping out of the carriage, scarcely even waiting for Barbour to offer his hand for her support. At the ticket office, however, she met with disappointment. She scanned the train schedules again and again in denial.

She had intended to take the train through Milton first to gather whomever she might know. If she did that, however, she would not arrive in London until very late in the evening. It would take an hour or two in Milton, and with a sinking feeling she knew she would miss every train save the last one out. She simply could not risk the delay. She would have to go directly to John, without stopping. She prayed his mother would forgive her-and that forgiveness was more likely to come if she were successful at reaching him!

Hastily they purchased tickets to take them the southerly route, through Birmingham. It was a little shorter route anyway, she comforted herself. They had at least arrived in time for that train, and still had at forty-five minutes before it was scheduled to leave. Barbour and Spaulding sank gratefully into freshly painted waiting benches, both panting just a little.

Margaret prowled the floor, her eyes wandering the waiting room. Then, from the far end of the room, inspiration struck. She strode quickly over to the bespectacled man in his little cage. "Excuse me, sir, how much to send a telegram to Milton?"

Forty-One

HANNAH PERCHED GINGERLY ON the hard seat of the rail car, her white knuckles gripping the hand railing. Across from her, the only other occupant of their small compartment, sat Higgins. He uncomfortably avoided looking at her, twitching his fingers nervously.

Neither of them had ever been to London. Hannah had ridden a train once- John had insisted on taking her to the coast a few years ago for her birthday, but as a general rule she had not cared to leave her home. The rolling and clattering had not troubled her, but the sense of dread and the unanswered questions hovered over her like a shroud.

How on earth had John been confused with some sailor, and accused of mutiny, of all things? He was the last man in the world who could commit such an act! She only hoped that whoever this attorney was who had written her was a competent and dedicated professional. She was going to demand some answers.

She was still bitter about her lack of success in rallying more witnesses for John's cause. Fanny and Watson were away on holiday and could not be reached. She had called at the bank and at the local office of the Ministry of Justice. Dalton had been called away on "urgent business," his assistant claimed, and the Ministry assured her that they would send one or two of the other magistrates "as soon as they could be found."

Some of John's peers, fellow mill owners, refused to be troubled. This cut the deepest to her. John was the best of them, a leader among his fellows, and they denied any aid. The telegram seemed suspicious to them, they claimed. More likely, she thought angrily, knowing of John's business troubles they had evidently decided to distance themselves somewhat. His failure could only help them.

Finally deciding that she was out of time to make her train, she had gathered what evidences she could of John's identity and descended upon the rail station. In all that time, Higgins had scarcely left her side. Ironic, thought she, that the man who stormed and ranted about John to the Union a year ago was now the only one she could find to stand by him.

She closed her eyes wearily. She had not been sleeping well at all during John's absence, and the heightened distress of the morning had worn her down. She felt suddenly old, weak, and tired. She was not used to her life spinning out of control; the last several years for her had been a well-ordered routine for the most part, with everything- almost everything- going according to her plan.

Higgins was propping his chin on his fingers, brushing over his scruff of beard growth, and averting his eyes to the window. Once or twice he took a breath and opened his mouth as if to speak, then lacking courage, closed it again.

"Something on your mind, Mr Higgins?" she asked guardedly, more to break the tightly strung silence than anything else.

"I... Aye, M'lady," he answered slowly, a little twinkle in his eye. He took a moment to gather his thought. "I's thinkin'... I wonder if we cou' find Miss Marget... be'n as we're goin' to London, I's thinkin'."

She frowned sulkily. That young woman was the last person she would expect to come to John's assistance. Then again... the man across from her would have formerly made that list as well. She clenched her jaw in silence. She would not go begging anything of Margaret Hale.

But for John? Her feelings rebelled within her. She would do anything for her son, even fall on her knees to make her plea, but the cynical places in her heart doubted it would do any good.

"I do not know how to reach her," she decided at last. Higgins' hopeful gaze drooped, crestfallen. She softened somewhat at his disappointment. "I suppose we can try to reach her if more witnesses are needed. Perhaps that attorney who sent the telegram could help us."

At last! Henry stretched to his fullest height, straining on the tips of his shoes to read the name emblazoned across the hull of the approaching vessel. He had lingered far longer than his determined two hours, but when scouts had sent up word that the *Esperanza* had been sighted approaching port, he had decided to stay.

Thornton clearly believed Carter's word would be weighty testimony, so he was determined to get the man. Time was running short, though. This was going to be close. He hoped his Milton witnesses would be arriving soon, and he worried that they would not find him there to greet and brief them. Another glance at his pocket watch assured him that it was possible. He hoped he could get aboard quickly to speak with Carter.

HANNAH STEPPED OUT OF the rollicking rail car to a teeming, crushing, unfamiliar sight. Higgins, beside her, was similarly overwhelmed. Milton, for all its industry, was nothing to the hurry and bustle of London. She glanced about in a moment of disorientation.

Higgins set his mouth, squared his shoulders, and determined to perform his self-sworn duty to the Mistress. "C'mon, M'lady," he attempted a confident grin. He hefted her bag for her and began to push through the crowds to where he hoped he might find a waiting cab.

Hannah followed hesitantly, surprised at her sudden gratitude for Higgins' presence. He was surely a rough sort, but John had been right about the man. There was a quality about him, and she was glad to have his staunch loyalty at such a time. She did not know how she could have faced London alone.

It took nearly a quarter of an hour to hail a ready cab. They were always taken just before they could reach them. Finally Higgins learned to aggressively lunge for an open door and to effectively bar others from boarding before she could catch up. "Whitehall!" he shouted in relief as the door slammed. The carriage lurched and they were underway.

Once again Higgins proved his worth. "Whitehall" was a rather generic description of their destination. Neither of them really had any idea what it meant, or any scope in their minds of how vast and intricate the array of government buildings might be. Leaning out the carriage window, in his broad Northern dialect, Higgins barked out questions and directions to the driver. Finally satisfied that he had communicated their needs, he settled back on the rear-facing carriage seat.

Hannah's face was bloodless and parched. Her dark eyes danced along the busy street outside the carriage window as they passed the massive structures of the city, each more imposing than the last. Higgins bit his lip, then boldly reached to shutter the windows.

She blinked, taking a long breath. A little colour trickled slowly back to her cheeks. "Thank you, Mr Higgins," she murmured. He nodded curtly, and the rest of their journey was accomplished in relative peace.

"Captain Carter, at your service," the broad-shouldered man offered his hand. Henry at last drew a deep gulp of fresh air. Getting aboard a vessel which had only just docked, and that without any paperwork, had been a small miracle. Cornering the captain in person, amid the scramble of humanity disembarking and issuing orders, had been nothing short of the hand of God himself, Henry decided.

He met the captain's beefy hand. "Henry Lennox, Attorney at Law," he greeted.

The captain arched a white eyebrow. "Am I in some legal trouble, Mr Lennox?" he queried with a smile.

"No! Nothing of the kind, Captain, I assure you. I am here, however, on a rather pressing matter regarding a recent passenger of yours. Do you perhaps recall a Mr John Thornton of Milton who took passage to Spain last week?"

The captain's smile became at once guarded yet also amused. "Remember him? Aye, he caused me a fair bit of trouble, he did!"

Henry glanced about, suddenly aware of the sensitive nature of what he had to convey. "Captain, is there somewhere more private we might confer?"

The captain held his gaze for a moment, as if evaluating Henry's character to determine whether he were some agent of sedition come aboard his vessel. At last he relented. "Aye, lad, come to my cabin."

Henry followed the captain into what was surely a spacious living arrangement for a sea captain, but still seemed cramped to him. Two ladies with their backs to him seemed to be sorting their belongings. As the men entered, the ladies turned. One appeared to be the captain's wife. The other... Henry had to shake himself, making a mental effort to stop staring and to keep his mouth from falling open.

"Mr Lennox," the captain interrupted his gawking, "my wife and daughter." He turned to his little family. "Mr Lennox has some business to do with our Mr Thornton."

At once the young woman crossed the tiny room, her pert features brightening with interest. "Oh! Does he know Margaret too?" she cried, clasping her hands.

"Now, Melanie, the man says he needs to speak with me in private," the captain chided his daughter.

Henry snapped back to reality. "Miss Melanie Carter," he bowed, the meaningless name from Harper's list suddenly coming alive for him. "I am most pleased to make your acquaintance. As a matter of fact, I am old friends with Miss... er, with Mrs Thornton and her family." His eyes never strayed from her face as she received his words with the highest pleasure.

The captain pursed his lips. "I see word travels fast. Please be seated, Mr Lennox." With a look the captain dismissed his wife and daughter, and Henry was disappointed to see that auburn head turn away in obedience. Once they had gone, Henry quickly rambled through the situation with Thornton, careful to omit his own association with the real Frederick Hale.

Carter sat in silent contemplation. He stared at Henry deeply, never breaking eye contact, for a full uncomfortable minute. "And you say the Navy has the marriage license?"

"Yes, Captain. As Mrs Thornton's maiden name was Hale, and there was some rumour that she was his sister, you can see, I suppose, how the mix-up may have occurred."

"Hmm," Carter mused. "I have a fair idea of who might have spread that report. I can testify first-hand though... she is *not* his sister."

Henry reddened, his embarrassed gaze dropping to his hands. "Yes, Captain, I know."

"Well," the captain rose. "Let us away, Lad. I liked that Thornton chap, hate to see him strung up. Now, where did you say Mrs Thornton is now?"

"We do not know, Captain. We are trying to get word to her in Spain, but it will be difficult. Also, if I know her as I think I do, she will not be there any longer."

Carter stopped, staring again with that long penetrating look. "Odd, don't you think, that that Hale fellow has never yet been found? I wonder where a man like that might hide, with a price on his head and all?"

Henry leveled as cool a gaze as he could back at the captain. "He may be dead by now for all we know," he conjectured innocently.

The captain chortled silently. "Indeed." He narrowed his eyes, but Henry refused to back down. "Lad," he asserted quietly, resting an enormous paw on Henry's shoulder, "I never had any use for Reid, and let's leave it at that."

IT HAD BEEN DIFFICULT, but with Higgins' dogged assistance, Hannah finally entered the gilded chambers of the Admiralty. She gazed about, still somewhat intimidated at the opulent surroundings. Higgins stopped, allowing her to go on alone. She turned in mild curiosity.

"The'll be wantin' a better class to speak wi', not an ol' weaver," he winked. "G'on. I'll jest be here," he cocked his head to a nearby waiting bench to her left.

She drew a fortifying breath and marched on, drawing on her old dignity to sustain her. Lifting her chin, she strode up to the young officer behind a reception desk. "I received word that my son, Mr John Thornton, is being held here," she declared, with as august an air as she could muster.

The officer looked up with only his eyes, keeping his face trained on the papers before him. "State your name, please."

"Hannah Thornton, of Milton." The officer recorded it, then proceeded to ignore her.

She snorted indelicately. "I do not believe you may have heard me before." She repeated her introduction, her voice laced with irritation.

"No Thornton in the registry," the man informed her, looking bored.

She withdrew the telegram and held it blatantly before his eyes. "Tell me what to make of this, then!" she huffed, a rush of her Irish temper flaring.

The officer, thoroughly unruffled, glanced back to his book and began to turn some pages. "Mr Lennox is representing a Mr Frederick Hale, accused of mutiny. Trial begins in one hour."

"Wh-what name did you say?" Hannah started in confusion. "Was that 'Hale'?"

"Former Lieutenant Frederick Hale of Her Majesty's Ship, the *Avenger*," the officer dictated crisply, leaning threateningly over his desk. "No visitors allowed."

The room had begun to spin. Summoning the last of her dwindling courage, she opened her mouth. "My son is no naval officer!" she stormed. "He is Master of a cotton mill, Magistrate in the city of Milton, and his name is known in industrial circles across the Continent!"

The officer stood from his chair. "Your *son* Madam, if so he is, is a traitor and a murderer! Corporal!"

Hannah whirled and prepared to unleash her fury on the advancing security guard, but a sharp tug at her elbow silenced her. "C'mon, M'lady," Higgins whispered urgently. "Jest sit a moment." He tossed a sheepish little wave to the guard as he dragged her to a bench. The guard glowered menacingly but returned to his post.

Hannah, white and trembling, carefully lowered herself to a seat. Higgins sat opposite her, his expression grim. "What does it mean?" she asked him tremulously, as though he might be able to answer her. "Why 'Hale'...? Is that...?"

"Aye," Higgins caught her in a steely gaze. "'Tis."

She straightened. "What can you mean?" she demanded, her voice cracking.

"'Er brother," he whispered.

"Brother!" she breathed in wonder. "She never had a brother!"

"Kept it a secret, they did," he replied, his voice low enough for only her ears. "Ye can see why. 'E was up 'ere when th' mother died. Me Mary, she knew o' it."

Hannah leaned back, her features ashen as she gaped blankly at the wall. A memory tickled her conscience, recalling how roundly she had abused the young woman for walking out alone with a young man. She'd accused her of the most blatant impropriety, and now it seemed probable to her that Margaret had only been walking her brother to the train station. Had she not been so horrified for her own son's circumstances, she would have been riddled with guilt for her shameful treatment of a girl in mourning.

"How," she wondered in a whisper, "did John get mixed up with all of this?"

"Tha' M'lady, I dunna. I s'pect, though, that we're 'bout t'find out. Look." He gestured with his eyes to the entrance of the chambers as the doors were swung open.

Hannah followed his gaze. A squarely built man in foreign dress with thick black hair was holding the door for a young woman. She was slim and tall, dressed in full mourning. Her arm was bound by a curious sling, but that did not seem to hamper her determined steps. Her face was still obscured by her bonnet, but Hannah would have known that queenly bearing anywhere.

The young woman strode defiantly the length of the room, her head held high and looking neither to the right nor left. The officer at the desk apprehensively surveyed her approach, one eye trained on her while he pretended to carry on with his registry book.

The foreign gentleman and a scrawny mouse of a man carrying a satchel trailed behind her.

She drew near the desk, and her crisp, bell-like tones echoed clearly in the entire room. "My name is Margaret Thornton, and I have come for my husband!"

That was the last thing Hannah heard before the floor tilted and she collapsed.

Forty-Two

HANNAH BLINKED. COOL GENTLE fingers over her temples began to rouse her to alertness. She opened her eyes and stared. "Easy now, M'lady," she could hear Higgins' voice somewhere to her right.

She shook her head, still in disbelief. "M-Miss Hale?"

Margaret smiled, perhaps the most genuine expression of pleasure she had ever witnessed on the young woman's face. "Mrs Thornton. Can you sit up?"

"I...." she strained, discovering that her head was draped over Margaret's bound shoulder. Higgins extended his hand, a sparkle of pure joy in his eyes as he helped her straighten and re-seat herself.

Hannah took several deep breaths to compose herself. Her awestruck gaze swept over the young woman she had never thought to see again. She wondered at the binding over her arm and the striking smile so foreign to her experience. Her eyes at last fell in mute astonishment on the sparkling diamond adorning Margaret's hand.

Margaret could not miss the direction of her gaze. Hannah absolutely stared, thunderstruck. Her eyes and voice gentle, Margaret reached that hand to touch hers. "There is a deal to tell you, Mrs Thornton," she spoke softly, humbly. "The short of it is that John and I were married last week on board the *Esperanza*."

"*How*?" she found herself asking. In her stupefied condition, it was the only word which would come to mind.

Margaret's lips thinned, blinking. "It would take a very long time to tell how, Mrs Thornton. What matters now is that we prove that John is who he says he is so he can be released. There will be time enough for explanations later."

Hannah stared in wonder, searching, and finding that old iron will she had grudgingly come to respect in the younger woman. She nodded slowly.

Margaret took her hand again in gratitude. "Thank you," she whispered. "I am glad you are here." She looked across to Higgins, finally including him in her warm greeting. "And Nicholas! I am so glad to see you!"

"Aye, Lass, 'tis right pleased I am t'see ye," he grinned, looking as though he could scarcely contain his joy.

Margaret's sparkling eyes returned to her mother-in-law and she sobered. Hannah was still staring, but her expression had kindled to something gentler than her previous shock. "So, Miss... I cannot call you Miss Hale anymore!" Her face rounded in surprise at this revelation.

Margaret laughed lightly, in spite of their awkward position and her tense fears. "My name will do nicely, Mrs Thornton."

She firmed her mouth and began again, all business. "Margaret. What is to be done for John?"

"My... I mean John's partner, Señor Barbour of Spain, is presenting some legal documents to the court right now. They bear John's signature and he is testifying to John's expertise in cotton. That should establish his identity. He took the documents you provided in with him as well, that can only help."

"Partner!" Hannah cried, relief wavering in her tones. "Then his negotiations were successful!"

"Very," Margaret reassured her. "The mill is safe, Mrs Thornton. There is more, however. With Señor Barbour is Mr Bell's land agent, who also has legal documents to present to the court."

"Bell? Do you mean he has a copy of John's lease agreement for the mill? I already brought that," she huffed in annoyance.

"Y-yes, he has that..." Margaret hesitated slightly, darting a glance at Higgins. "We must not only prove who John is, but also that he had a legitimate business contact in Spain. Without legitimate documents the Navy will be calling his travels into question, since they are operating under the belief that he is a fugitive.

"In addition to the lease contract, Mr. Spaulding also has Mr Bell's will. He is recently deceased- he was traveling in Spain when he fell ill. I am his heir."

Hannah's mouth dropped open, aghast. Quickly she closed it. "You... you're *what*!"

Margaret looked down to her hands. "The documents Mr Spaulding is presenting to the court bear my legal married name and testify to the fact that Mr Bell left all of his properties to me."

Higgins was doing a terrible job of hiding his glee. His adored Miss Marget had come back, and in a few sentences, she had both restored the prosperity of the mill and ensured the Master's happiness. A lucky man was Thornton- or, would be, once he was released.

"I only worry," Margaret was continuing, "that the documents we present may not be sufficient evidence. Mrs Thornton, do you know if any other witnesses are expected?"

Hannah snorted gently, a trace of a smile warming her eyes at last. "I think you had better stop calling me 'Mrs Thornton', Margaret. It is going to become very confusing." Margaret stifled a small grin. "As for other witnesses...." She drew the telegram out again and handed it to her daughter-in-law.

Margaret's shock was immediate. "Henry!" she cried. "This is... well, this is wonderful, but how?"

"I was hoping you could tell me," she replied, a little stiffly. Another man with a claim on her favor? This was not to be borne!

Margaret recovered a little. "Henry is my cousin's brother-in-law, and a friend," she soothed, anxious that her loyalties might not be in doubt. "He tried to help... he tried to help my brother. I expect that is how he heard John was here."

Hannah arched an eyebrow and nodded gravely, wishing to put that subject aside for the moment. "And where do you suppose this Mr Lennox is, Miss... Margaret? Does he know of your relationship to my son?" she demanded, a little sharply.

Margaret struggled a moment in silence. "I cannot know that. If he spoke with John, then surely he does. I do not know. Have you not seen him?" Hannah's grave expression was her only answer. Margaret sank into nervous silence. She did not think Henry would abandon John, no matter what the circumstances of their relationship were.

A moment later, Barbour and Spaulding were ejected from the side chambers where they had been presenting their evidence. Margaret looked hopefully to them. Spaulding's face was expressionless as always, but Barbour caught her eye and shrugged.

"They are not convinced?" she quavered.

"Oy, almost Señora, almost. They see a problem but are not quite sure. If we had another, perhaps? I think they are not so willing to give up their prisoner." He glanced at his watch. "They give only fifteen more minutes and then they decide."

Margaret's chest began to heave in fear. Barbour's testimony and Spaulding's documents had been her best hope. Desperately her thoughts plunged about, dragging up any idea she might conceive. Her hands clenched nervously, but then a reassuring strength gripped them. She looked up to Hannah's steely gaze.

"We will go talk to them ourselves, girl," the widow declared stoutly. "We will make them listen, you and I!"

Margaret gathered her courage and nodded. As they were rising, the door to the reception hall swung open again. She looked, her heart buoyed by hope. "Henry! Captain Carter!" she sang in joy.

Both men turned at her voice. "Margaret! Thank God you're safe!" Henry cried. He came forward eagerly to clasp her hand. He looked steadily into her face, sensing her trepidation and her fears. "Don't worry, Margaret," he reassured her before she could speak. "We will get your husband out."

She fairly basked in relief. He knew, and he was helping. She closed her eyes, biting her lips together. "Thank you!" she choked back a little sob.

Henry nodded, a trace of sadness behind his smile, but he gave her hand one last firm grip before he let it go. "Captain, if you will follow me," he turned.

Before he would move on, Carter stooped low to murmur reassuringly, "Aye, lass, 'twill be all right. I'd be obliged to you though, if you could keep my Mellie out of trouble." He chuckled and moved on after Henry.

Margaret blinked and turned around. Following in Carter's wake was his daughter, and after her his wife. Tears of joy tumbled down her cheeks as she embraced her friend. "Thank you for coming, Melanie!" she wept.

The next quarter of an hour was spent in tense anticipation. Margaret clasped her mother-in-law's hand, and Melanie clasped Margaret's. She had the pleasure of introducing Mrs Carter to the senior Mrs Thornton, but there was no conversation.

Higgins paced, swinging his arms back and forth about his torso to battle his own tension. Barbour sat near the ladies and tapped his knee with his fingers. Only Spaulding seemed calm, and Margaret expected that was because the man likely possessed no emotions to bandy about.

At length, the door opened to the chambers again. "The board requests the testimony of Mrs Thornton," a page called out.

Both Hannah and Margaret started to rise. Hannah stopped, meeting Margaret's gaze. "That will be you they are asking for," she conceded, a flash of pained resignation in her eyes. Margaret squeezed her hand and went to the door.

JOHN SAT UP ON the hard bunk when the door to his cell rattled open. A guard beckoned him to rise. With a sinking feeling, he obeyed.

There was no timepiece available to him- they had confiscated everything he had carried. Internally, though, he knew that the allotted time for his trial had come. He grimaced. Still no Henry Lennox had appeared. Perhaps he had misjudged the man, after all. Surely, he would not have minded claiming Margaret as his own.

He extended his hands to the guard so the chains might be removed. For that, at least, he was grateful. No prisoner was to appear in court manacled until he had been proven guilty. Not that he expected it would take the board of Admiralty long to reach a decision. None of them truly cared who they hung, he thought bleakly. It was a mark for fair old England, a chance to make an example of a traitor.

Rubbing his bruised wrists, he walked down a narrow corridor between the guards provided for his escort. The hallways were largely dark and poorly lit, but stumbling was the least of his worries.

He feared for his wife. He'd thought that Lennox fellow would be honourable, but if he were not, and if he were the one to assume protection over Margaret... He recoiled. She would be broken with grief and he angrily cursed Lennox if he should fail to care for her properly.

Then his own sense of justice brought him up short. No, he doubted he had misjudged Lennox. If so, why had the man come back to see him again this morning? Margaret may not have loved the man, but she *had* called him a friend.

Lennox could not be the reprobate of his anguished imagination. There was just nothing to be found on such a short notice, so many hours from Milton. Lennox had simply come up empty-handed and the trial would proceed without him.

The guards stopped him before an oaken door and motioned for him to go ahead of them. Sighing emptily, he stepped forward. The room was bright, and he blinked for a few seconds.

Four admirals in epaulets flanked him on the right as he entered. They stared at him without expression. Quickly his eyes took in the other occupants of the room. He had just identified Lennox when he heard his name uttered in a beloved voice. He spun to his left.

"Margaret!" he cried exultantly.

She was fairly running, barreling into his chest with a sob of relief and elation. She was in his arms now, her left elbow hooked behind his neck as she wet his face with joyous tears. "Oh my love!" she sighed between rapid kisses. "I thought I had lost you!"

He enveloped her completely in his arms, dropping his face to her neck. He could live off the sweet fragrance of her! He wept inarticulately, his hands stroking over her back as though she might vanish at any moment. He sought her lips and drew her in for a sweet, passionate embrace.

"*Ahem*..." one of the nameless admirals cleared his throat.

They broke apart, turning their heads to face the board, but both refused to loosen their hold on the other.

"Well, Captain Carter," one of the admirals muttered, "you were, it seems, quite correct. This man is clearly *not* the former Miss Hale's brother."

Margaret looked at each of the faces in the room curiously. She had assumed they had summoned her in here to answer questions. Henry was looking away, his face bright red. Carter was nearly laughing, as were one or two of the admirals.

The first admiral waved in exasperation. "Get them out of here," he groaned.

John picked her up by the waist and spun her about in giddy relief. "Oh, my Margaret!" he murmured softly in her ear.

"One moment, please," one of the admirals stopped them.

John set her feet back on the floor, both glancing back to the board.

"I would remind Mrs Thornton that aiding and abetting any traitor to the crown is punishable by death." He paused significantly. "If she has any idea of the whereabouts of her *real* brother, I recommend she make her information known."

Henry opened his mouth to speak, but John was first. "You would threaten a woman injured and in mourning, sir?" he snarled roughly. "It ought to be obvious to you that she has lost her entire family, sir! On top of all this you nearly made her a widow this day before you would believe the truth! How *dare* you level threats at my wife?"

The admiral who had spoken clamped his mouth shut. His eyes flickering dangerously, he leaned threateningly forward from his fists on the table. John's outburst had done little to proclaim her innocence.

It was Carter who salvaged the situation. "Nearly all that crew died," he averred. "Fever took them in Argentina, we all know that. Any other rats who fled that God-forsaken hole in the world were caught by the *Reliant* a year later. In any case," he harrumphed, sticking his chin out, "I never heard of a man on the run fool enough to ever contact a relative again. Nothing good can come of harassing this poor woman, if you will excuse me, Admiral."

The admiral straightened back reluctantly. Carter had a point and he knew it. Hounding a young woman in mourning would certainly come as a black eye for the Admiralty in the eyes of the public. He said no more, but clearly, he gave up the point.

Forty-Thre

John's reunion with his mother was more exuberant than he would have ever imagined her capable of. She shed happy tears and kissed him on the cheek. "I am sorry for all of this," he apologized.

She shook her head. "It is done now, and my son has come back to me. Though I beg you not to get into such fool scrapes again, I think you cost me ten years!"

He laughed, pulling her close for an embrace such as they had not shared in a very long time. When she withdrew, she smiled, patted his face lovingly, and looked to Margaret. He glanced back at her questioningly and was met with a brave sparkle in her eyes. His face split into a wide grin and he swept his wife into his arms. Brazenly he kissed her right in front of everyone.

"John!" she rebuked, though not very convincingly. Her cheeks coloured, but she dared a glance at the faces assembled around her. Melanie was clasping her hands in delight. Henry had gone to speak with Melanie, so his back was partially turned, but he shook his head in bashful satisfaction. Captain and Mrs Carter were already maneuvering to the door, pretending not to notice the newlyweds' reunion.

Higgins, his eyes dancing, boldly stepped forward. Though John's arm was still about her waist, Nicholas bent forward and took her left hand. "Welcome back, Lass," he winked, and kissed the back of her hand. Margaret squeezed his back, her perfect happiness radiating from her.

The door to the chambers swung open at that moment, admitting a tall, reedy looking man carrying a fat briefcase. He seemed flustered and harried, his face tight. John's eyes widened in recognition. "Dalton!" he exclaimed.

Dalton's cragged features relaxed. "Thornton! Oh, do forgive my tardiness, I missed the first train as I was gathering documents for- oh, I see you are no longer impounded. Is all well?"

John's grin was perfectly incandescent. "Never better, Mr Dalton. May I have the pleasure of introducing you to my wife Margaret? I believe you met her father at my house before- Mr Hale."

Dalton started, examining the young woman wrapped in Thornton's possessive arm more closely. "Margaret Hale? Why, I received a document only yesterday regarding...." He stopped himself, ashamed at his sudden indelicacy. "Well, Thornton! It seems we have some business to discuss once we return to Milton! I shall await your leisure." He glanced about the motley party assembled before him. "I will bid you good-day, then!" He lifted his hat to the ladies and made for the door.

John impulsively pulled his mother under his other arm, enjoying the girlish flush over her face as he did so. "Shall we?"

Mrs Shaw had finally returned to the drawing room three days ago. Still no word had been had from her niece; but neither were there whispers abounding among her friends, if Edith were to be believed. Margaret was simply "indisposed" until further notice. She had warred with her better judgement against donning black. That would raise too many questions until she knew more!

Edith had joined her in the drawing room with her rowdy little son. Mrs Shaw pressed white fingers to her temples, not accustomed to the noise of a child. Still, it seemed to her that little Sholto's manners had improved of late. She would make a note to praise that nursemaid. She must have done an admirable job of comforting dear little Sholto when his beloved Aunt Margaret had disappeared.

Mrs. Shaw tried to pluck up her needle work, but Sholto chose that moment to toddle over her lap, attempting to shower her in his sticky affections. "Oh! Child, what is the meaning of this?" She grasped his fat little palm, warding it away from her clothing. "Why Edith, he has chocolate all over his hands!"

Edith rose, blushing like any criminal. "I know, Mama. I promised him if he was very good, he could share a treat with me instead of having to return immediately to his room with Nurse."

Mrs. Shaw tsked, shaking her head disparagingly. "I thought only Margaret guilty of such nonsense. You, Edith, ought to know better! A child must be taught more decorum."

Edith suppressed a sad little sigh but favored her son with a tender look. "He is finished now, at any rate. Come, Sholto, it is time for your nap. You must go with Nurse to help clean you up!"

Sholto waddled obediently to his mother's side, stretching up his short chubby arms. Edith smiled and scooped up her little boy. Unafraid of his sticky cheeks, she planted a kiss on his face as she passed him off. What a difference from the week before! He reached willingly for his nurse, submitting cheerfully to her instructions. Edith drew a satisfied little sigh. If only Margaret could see her now!

Dixon had become a surprising help to her in the last days. Of all the people in the house, Dixon alone could stand up to the Mistress and tell her what she was doing wrong. Edith had not liked it, but Dixon's comments had borne fruit she could not deny. Poor Dixon! She wished the woman's gout was no longer flaring up. Dixon was resting upstairs now after a particularly bad morning. Edith hoped she would be feeling better by evening.

She turned to resume her seat when the maid interrupted her. "Pardon me, Ma'am, but Mr Lennox has arrived, and he has guests. Shall I show them in?"

Edith's brow furrowed. "Guests? Of course, show them in, and please call Captain Lennox." She licked her finger to clean Sholto's sticky smudge off her cheek- hoping her mother would not notice- then hurried to arrange herself decently on her chair. It was her duty to present a proper image to whomever she was about to meet.

Henry strode in, glancing somewhat trepidatiously behind himself as he entered. Edith stood to acknowledge him, but the personage behind him caught her attention instead. Her breath left her. "Margaret!" she cried. "Oh, Margaret, you are safe!" Stumbling, Edith flung herself heedlessly into her cousin's embrace. She held her long, eyes squeezed shut and leaking happy tears.

"Oh, Edith!" Margaret was crying. "I have so much to tell you!"

Edith drew back to examine her cousin's face, her teary smile radiant. Her gaze was quickly diverted from Margaret to a man she had never seen, standing close behind her with a strangely intimate grin on his scruffy face.

Margaret perceived the change in her demeanor and pulled back slightly, closer to the strange man. "Edith," she drew a sharp breath, biting her lip, "I want to introduce you to my husband, John Thornton."

MARGARET DID NOT NEED the maid to show her up to her old room. Edith had graciously invited them to stay a few days; in part to recover from her shock at the last two weeks' events, and in part out of practicality. The new couple had business to conduct in London and personal affairs to settle before Margaret would be swept back to Milton. Edith wished to keep her beloved cousin near for as long as she could.

Margaret giggled a little as they reached the door. "What are you laughing about?" tickled a low voice at her ear.

Biting back a very inappropriate snicker, she turned to him as he shut the door behind them. "Edith's face when I told her we would not require separate rooms!"

His face cracked in mirth. "That was nothing to your aunt's! I thought her butler would have to carry her out with a case of the vapors!"

Margaret burst into giggles, hiding her face in his shoulder. He snaked an arm obligingly around her waist. "I imagine your mother was horrified! Oh, dear, what a wanton she must think me!"

"She was laughing- or trying not to, at least. I think she enjoyed watching your aunt's reaction as much as I did."

"I have a deal to learn about her, then! She did not look amused to me."

"It is rather simple, really. When her cheeks twitch like that, she is highly diverted. If you ever hear her laugh out loud, do me a favor and call for the doctor!"

"Noted!" She kissed him soundly for emphasis. His eyebrows lifted in profound interest as she pressed her lips to his. She withdrew softly, her expression no longer humourous. "I have missed you, John!"

"Then come here," he whispered hoarsely. She did as he requested. His touch inflamed her instantly, their time apart serving only to intensify her craving for his arms. In seconds, they were tearing at each other's clothing, aching to satisfy the ragged need building between them.

He wanted to slowly unveil her as he had always done, to feast his eyes upon her soft flesh and stake his claim over every part of her once more. The thought flashed through his mind for the barest fraction of a second before he dismissed it. He wanted her *now*, and her little mewling gasps as he kissed her neck and exposed décolletage only drove him more wild. Madly, he began prying free the little buttons at the top of her gown. Just a little more, that was all he needed to see. His pulse thrummed as she arched her back, drawing as close to his desperate mouth as she could.

Margaret clasped his head to her bosom as he kissed lower, her breath heaving irregularly. Aching for more, she pressed her body to his. His hands settled on her hips, roving, and caressing as he began inching up her skirts, gathering them into his palms. Margaret shuddered and sighed, then dropped her hand to his stomach to explore him. How she had missed this! With a fierce tug, she wrenched a corner of his shirt free from the waistband of his trousers, then energetically ripped the remaining tail so the garment hung rakishly askew.

John drew back, eyeing his savage princess with a pleased growl. She met the fire in his eyes with a light of her own. "Oh, my Margaret!" he breathed, capturing those luscious lips, and invading them without preamble. His abdomen tightened as he felt her fingers threading through the hairs on his chest as she so loved to do. His entire being was quivering for her. He began backing her toward the bed, his fingers still bunching her skirts.

He did not hear the door to Margaret's dressing room open behind him, but he did quite plainly feel the umbrella which viciously clubbed over his head. "*How dare ye, ye scoundrel*!" a heated voice wailed behind him.

He yelped, turning loose of his tempting wife to ward off another clumsy blow. Dixon, her round shining face flushed crimson, gripped her weapon with both hands and looked as though she intended to decapitate him with her next strike. "Out with ye, blackguard!" she thundered, her arms winding up for another swing. "How dare y'enter a lady's room! I will not let ye hurt my lass, I'll have ye up before the magistrates!"

Margaret had moved from behind him, and with a determined snatch she wrested the umbrella from Dixon's grasp.

John's spirits were rumpled in more ways than one. He stared, dumbfounded, clutching his wounded head. "I *am* a magistrate, Miss Dixon! What is the meaning of your intrusion?" His voice carried a threatening edge, and he would have loomed his towering form over the short woman to cow her but for Margaret.

Margaret had tossed the umbrella aside and secured Dixon's menacing right arm, her gaze and grip firm. Only then was it obvious that Dixon troubled herself to recognize the intruder to her young lass' room. It did not seem to surprise her overmuch that

Margaret had returned without warning or ceremony, but she would give no quarter to this offensive cad!

"Mr Thornton!" she huffed. "What ye be doin' violatin' a decent lady in her own house! Go on back to Milton, ye... ye... beast!" Her mouth twisted in fury, she glared him down.

John clenched his fists, biting his lip and looking away, visibly struggling with his temper. Margaret began to intervene, but he held up his hand. "Miss Dixon," he answered, in a surprisingly even tone. "I will indeed be returning to Milton soon, but I intend to take my *wife* with me! As I presume you will wish to accompany her, may I encourage you to begin making whatever arrangements you feel necessary? I assure you, any expenses will be covered, please spend whatever you wish so that all is handled properly. Margaret will explain everything to you in good time, but for right now, I must confess I am tired, hungry, and very much in need of some privacy. Would you be so good as to excuse us?"

Dixon's shock was no less than anyone else's had been. She stood rooted to the floor, her beefy forearm drooping in utter astonishment. She turned wide eyes to her girl, not even knowing which questions to ask to ascertain the truth of his words.

Margaret smiled and patted her shoulder comfortingly. "All is well, Dixon," she promised. "Frederick sends his love, but I will tell you more later. For now, I must ask we do as he says."

Dixon stared mutely, pointedly, at the unbuttoned lace on Margaret's décolletage and her rumpled skirts, still tangled indecently over her crinoline. Margaret's face and neck pinked, but she planted a firm kiss on her old friend's cheek and began to propel her to the door. "Nay, Lass, I know my way out!" she groused.

Dixon opened the door into the hallway just in time to run face-to-face with a grave Mrs Thornton. "Sakes!" she mumbled loudly. "The house is full of 'em! What is it come to?" She limped off, shaking her head.

Through the doorway, Margaret caught Hannah's eye and noticed, for the first time, that the older woman's cheeks were quivering. Hannah's eyebrow quirked and her eyes twinkled strangely as her gaze traveled over Margaret's no-longer immaculate attire. Margaret gulped. With a shaking nod and the most graceful curtsey she could muster under the circumstances, she firmly closed- and *bolted*- the door.

John rolled his eyes and collapsed on his back on the bed. "*That* was embarrassing!" he moaned to the ceiling.

Margaret hugged her arms about herself, her lips twitching helplessly. A wicked chortle escaped, and she spun around to collapse into peals of laughter beside her husband.

"Oh, I see how it is!" he exclaimed, still trying to sound offended. "Laugh at me, will you!"

She shrieked without restraint, her stomach clenching and tears rolling down her cheeks. "Oh, John!" she gasped. "Your face!" She rolled to her side, still struggling for air and unable to stop her giggles. "I do not think I have ever seen you so red!"

"I am glad I can amuse you so," he smirked, not wholly able to maintain his affronted dignity in the face of Margaret's glee. Dear heavens, how he loved her!

"Oh, it is not so bad, John!" she teased, combing her fingers through the beginnings of a thick beard on his chin. "Only think what she might have been treated to if she had come in five minutes later!"

"Margaret!" he sputtered, thoroughly horrified. "Perish the thought!" She dissolved into squeals of laughter once more, delighted that she, for once, had been the one to discomfit him. He rolled roughly on top of her, still gentle with her shoulder, but he intended to silence her uproarious amusement at his expense- once and for all. "You will not laugh so loudly in a moment, Madam," he rasped.

His mouth and hands plundered everything he could reach- her hair, her face, her delicious curves, her trembling throat, and that glorious swell of feminine softness pressed to his chest. His eager fingers raked up under her skirts, urgently seeking to breach their sanctity.

Margaret gasped luxuriantly, plying her fingers through his hair. "I thought you said you were tired and hungry," she whispered into his ear.

"I am," he rumbled. "Here is my feast, and here is my rest."

Epilogue

Margaret Thornton nestled sideways on the loveseat, her feet tucked indecorously on the cushion as she leaned back against her husband's shoulder. His arm draped comfortably around her, his thumb absently brushing her wrists as he attempted with his other hand to wrestle his newspaper. Her book had fallen unheeded to her lap as she reclined her head tiredly against him.

From across the room a gentle gurgle roused her attention, and she turned her head. Hannah, her eyes shining, cradled a small blue bundle in her arms. "He is waking, Margaret," she murmured softly, a little regret in her voice.

Margaret blinked and sighed, arching her back to restore herself to alertness. John brushed a tender kiss into her hair as she rose from his grasp to cross the room. With a grateful smile to her mother-in-law, Margaret eased her son free of his blankets. Richard Thomas Thornton, born exactly ten months to the day after his parents' marriage, had already become quite expert at making his wishes known. Any delay to his meals was regularly met with the greatest consternation.

Hannah had more than once observed that the child was every bit as determined and inflexible as his father, a comment which Margaret always deflected with a kiss to both of her handsome gentlemen. "Not at all!" she would croon, "we just know what we want, do we not?"

John had simply laughed whenever he heard his mother's dry quip, indicating that he would take it under advisement to strive for a sweet-tempered girl next time. "After all," he would joke, "Margaret *did* promise me a daughter!"

Margaret always had some saucy reply for that remark. Hannah would simply shake her head when her son and his wife would dissolve into such foolishness. Some bits of their relationship she would never understand- nor would she have wished to.

The greedy grandmother's eyes followed Margaret as she excused herself to tend their son. Her admiration for the regal young woman was no longer grudging. Margaret's sweetness had flooded her home, imbuing her precious John with the light that had nearly been quenched eighteen years earlier. And that boy! Never had a finer or handsomer child been born, of that she was certain.

"Mother," John's voice interrupted her thoughts. "Will you be coming with us to London for Mr. Lennox and Miss Carter's wedding?"

Hannah blew out a reluctant breath. She still hated London. "How long will you be gone?"

"I thought we would stay a few days after. Margaret would like to stay longer, and she claims she is well enough. She wishes to remain a fortnight, at least. Perhaps...." He folded his paper to set it down.

"Can you really be away from the new construction project so long?" Hannah did not even have to ask if he had considered leaving Margaret in the care of her family while he returned to Milton without her. The couple were scarcely out of each other's sight- and if one or the other were not to be found, it was safest not to go looking for them.

He nodded carefully. "Higgins has taken over the project almost entirely. Whatever he might need me for in those few days can be accomplished by wire at this point."

She remained silent about whether she would travel. She would have to think about that. She had no desire to linger in London, but she did not want to be the cause of Margaret having to leave her family sooner than necessary. John would not hear of either of them traveling alone.

Perhaps the bride's mother might be persuaded to visit her here for some days after the wedding- surely the captain would soon be back at sea. Mrs Carter was a solid, practical woman, and Hannah did not find her in the least offensive.

Her eyes glittered proudly as she watched John gazing dreamily into the evening fire. Her noble son's achievements had been nothing short of meteoric this past year, thanks to the financial backing of Margaret's inheritance and the unique positioning of his partnership with Spain. In all of that, he had not rested but pressed forward, resolving to craft the finest little industrial empire in all of England.

He won wide acclaim for his vision from all quarters of the industry. Employees clamored for a place at Marlborough Mills, as it was well known that John was expanding and the new mill community would be the finest of its kind. He had made innovative and generous provisions for the many young families who hoped to make it their home. It was a prime opportunity for a new life, for many of them. Already the new dyeing plant was opened, and new machinery was arriving weekly.

Truly, he had done very, very well- not only on a professional level, but he had proven himself as a husband and a father as well. Perhaps Hannah's opinion of his worth was somewhat inflated, but she had full assurance that his wife, at least, would agree with her assessment.

Margaret returned shortly, bouncing, and cooing to her son. John rose eagerly and claimed him from her arms before his mother could. He was fortunate to be in time, for Dixon entered the room at that moment to take charge of her young mistress. Between the three of them, he had to snatch moments with his child whenever he could!

He sat again, watching with some amusement as Dixon fussed over Margaret's appetite and eyed his fatherly attentions distrustfully. Margaret was adept at submitting meekly, then rolling her eyes at him only after Dixon's back was turned. It was no mystery to him who really ran the house.

He stifled a laugh and returned his attention to the babe in his arms. Stroking the soft cheeks wonderingly, he lost himself in the miracle of it all. His son! A frisson of joy raced through him. In his arms he held his greatest gift, their living heritage and proof of the love he shared with his wife. In him, all their best had united to become one- to create a new life. He was awed and humbled to consider it.

Margaret's breath tickled his neck as she draped herself over his shoulder. She wound her arms snugly about him, pressing her cheek to his body. How was it possible she had grown to love him even more? The father of her son had woven so deeply into her heart that his very life throbbed with hers. "He has your eyes, you know," she whispered.

"And your ears," he countered, tilting their son's chubby face to see them better. "But I do not think we can lay claim to any more features until he is older."

Margaret chuckled and turned his face to hers for a kiss. Hannah watched with unabashed delight. She had grown accustomed to their easy, intimate style of relating to one another, though it was radically opposite of every notion she'd ever held. If John was pleased to shower affection on his wife, she was no less so for him.

Dixon limped back into the room, a stack of letters in her hand and a sandy-haired boy in tow. She passed the letters to Margaret and managed to conceal her disapproving frown at the lad from Francis Street.

"Mrs Thornton," Johnny bowed precisely as she had taught him. He turned, his mischievous little face as innocent as he could make it. "Mr Thornton and Mrs Thornton," he bowed again.

Margaret's body shook slightly in a repressed laugh at the formal greetings. It still seemed strange to her to share that same name. She and her mother-in-law had solved the problem by using their given names at home, but little Johnny Boucher did his best to please his adored mentor by painstakingly exhibiting the manners she had so carefully inscribed into him.

The odd pair adjourned to the far side of the room to take their evening tea, as Margaret perused her letters. One in the middle captured her interest. She held it up to John, her eyes twinkling. "A letter from Frederick?" he guessed.

She opened it quickly without answering. She roved the pages, relishing the news of her brother's home. "Oh! Dolores is expecting again!"

"Really? So soon?" he reached for the pages to read the letter himself, but she held it playfully away from him. "I thought the twins' birth was rather hard on her."

"So Frederick says, and naturally he is worried, but I expect that Dolores will manage splendidly." She scanned the rest of the letter; the top half a tense report of family concerns from Frederick and the bottom half a calm, reassuring missive from Dolores. They both spoke lovingly of their baby girls, now eight months old, and shared the news from their extended relations- most of whom John and Margaret had never met. Another page was addressed from Frederick to John, detailing business matters.

She raised the pages to her face, inhaling the sweet scent of Frederick's home, before surrendering the letters to John. He traded little Richard for the letters, and out of habit they resumed their prior postures on the loveseat. She loved nestling against John, and Richard was already snuggling under her chin in drowsiness. She sighed rapturously. *Home* echoed in her heart.

After some minutes, John folded the letters and placed them on the side table, atop his newspaper. Margaret was much more interesting to look at, as she basked in radiant motherhood beside him. His fingers traced the sides of her face and she leaned into his hand. A slow smile spread over his lips. He was, indeed, the luckiest of men!

No. Not luck. He had never believed in it. Nor had any of it truly been his own doing. Providence, that had to be it. There was no other possible explanation for the heaven in which he dwelt every day. The last year had held its share of challenges to be sure, but his faith had been restored and he had the constant assurance Margaret's unwavering love. Nothing short of the divine hand could have wrought it all.

He watched hungrily as his son's eyes drifted firmly closed, not to open again without sufficient inducement. Margaret was relaxing too, but she was still quite alert, smiling down at her babe. He brushed his palm surreptitiously over her soft curves. She arched her neck in sudden interest, lifting an eyebrow speculatively at him as she turned her head. His grin deepened.

Without a word, he rose and took their sleeping son from her arms and gently laid him in the bassinette by Margaret's favorite sewing chair. Across the room, his mother shot him a knowing glance, but studiously turned her gaze back to her young pupil and their tea table.

He returned to the loveseat, pausing a moment to admire the sight. His precious Margaret, queen of his home and heart, tilted her head invitingly. Those rosy lips curved deliciously, only for him. "My love, can I interest you in a siesta?"

Her mouth twitched and she took his offered hand, softly caressing his palm with her thumb. "I thought you would never ask, Mr Thornton."

KEEP READING MORE OF Margaret Hale and John Thornton's romance in *Northern Rain* ! What happens when you discover something in common with someone you never understood before?

From Alix

THANK YOU FOR INDULGING with me and spending a little time with John and Margaret.

I hope you've had a delightful escape to Milton. I'd love it if you would share this family with your friends so they can experience a love to last for the ages. As with all my books, I have enabled lending to make it easier to share. If you leave a review for *No Such Thing as Luck* on Amazon, Goodreads, Book Bub or your own blog, I would love to read it! Email me the link at **Author@AlixJames.com**

Would you like to read more of John and Margaret's romance? I have a sweet, friends-to-lovers romance for you to try next! Dive into *Northern Rain* and see what happens when a chance encounter leads to deeper understanding. Can these two find the love they were destined for?

And if you're hungry for more, including a free ebook of satisfying short tales, stay up to date on upcoming releases and sales by **joining my newsletter**!

Keep reading for a sneak preview of *Northern Rain* !

Northern Rain

George Thornton
Beloved Husband and Father
May 6, 1798—October 17, 1837

A LONE FIGURE STOOD before the graven stone, head bowed and hat doffed. A few had passed by, but if any remarked on the novelty of the sight, they did so from a distance and at a whisper. It was an annual pilgrimage; one the man before the headstone made with religious precision at half past three of the appointed day, every single October, and always alone.

John Thornton, one of the most powerful men in the prominent industrial city, was not a man to be ruled by emotion. His life—for the past seventeen years and four minutes to be exact—had been one of mechanical drive and unswerving purpose. The work of his life had been allotted him at an exceedingly young age, and he had accepted it as a man.

Ensuring his family's welfare had been his first duty. Restoring its honour had been his second. Everything after that had been another step in the logical progression of his life, as the ambitious young man had risen up the ranks in business. The man who stood today before the cold slab of granite was a man who held his head high among his peers, and at whose command hundreds sought their livelihood. He was a man often applied to for his perceptive advice and infallibly fair judgement; one who by all appearances could have no causes for regret and called the world at his feet.

He squeezed his eyes shut. No causes for regret... except one. It was nothing, really. Not something that should have had any lasting importance. After all, he could not be the first man who had been rejected by a woman. As far as he knew, the consequence was not fatal. There were times, though, when he felt like it ought to be.

Was it the natural state of affairs that he should still, several times a day, fail to remember to breathe? How long had it been? His mind calculated the answer before he was aware it had asked the question. Three months, twelve days, and four hours. Just over a quarter of a year since his heart had found the courage to beat once more, and then had been promptly crushed for its audacity.

He turned his hat awkwardly in his hands, unconsciously brushing the nap smooth as he did so. His eyes blurred. Why was he still standing there? He had paid his tribute, made his annual salute to the man who had sired him and set him upon this course. Nothing else was owed his sense of justice. For the first time in many years, however, he wished he could have asked that man one single question.

The natural question— *Why?*—had long since been canvassed to exhaustion. Nothing remained there but heartache and misery. No, the question he would have asked today was far less profound, but a great deal more practical-and it was one for which he felt sure the man in that cold ground might have once had the answer. *What is a man to do with a broken heart?*

Yes, surely George Thornton would have known, for Hannah Stewart had not been the first woman to catch his father's eye. That first, a London heiress, had been far above the humble reach of George Thornton—even more so than his own remarkable mother.

Perhaps that was the answer. Margaret Hale was not the only woman on earth. His father had found another to admire, and even love, had he not? Though George Thornton's final act had been the ultimate betrayal, he remained convinced that his father's heart had at one time been healed, and at the hands of a woman.

He himself had never paid heed to women, obsessed as he had always been with the all-consuming demands of his life. Never once had he felt the lack—or at least it had not been such a nagging torment that he had not been able to overlook it in favour of his ambition.

Then, something rather extraordinary had occurred. A fire had sparked out of nowhere, a flicker of that aspect of manhood long neglected. Man, after all, was not made only to labour, to produce, and then to expire. He was shaped for life, to search beyond himself and to seek his peace in relationship. He was made to find an answer to his masculine singularity in the form of a complement to himself—an opposite, yet in the greatest paradox known to humanity, a perfect match. Love.

The word flashed through his consciousness, triggering an agonized shudder in his soul. *I admit it!* He gritted his teeth, refusing to allow his emotions to display over his features for the world to see. *Aye, I confess. Yes, I loved her!* No, that would not do; not if he were fully honest. *I love her still.* There was no recourse but to clench his eyes shut again.

The insignificant spark had blazed to a raging inferno in the blink of an eye. He had been wholly unprepared for the awesome ferocity of that emotion. How had he even been capable of it? Rigid control had been the order of his life. One glance from a haughty young woman and all had ruptured. Despite himself, he could not help feeling that the heavens were laughing at him. Fool that he was, he had thought he had the world in his palm, when in truth he barely clung to his pathetic self-discipline.

His father had certainly had the right of it in this one point. There were other women on the planet—women who would receive him. Others would not fling his heart back in his face as though it were the vilest of refuse! There must be yet a woman out there who would not despise him… whose very presence would ignite the long-dead embers of his soul. Surely there was… there had to be another whose every word would inspire him… whose every touch had the power to scorch him to his very marrow. There… there *must* be another woman somewhere the equal of Margaret Hale. And perhaps there was, but never for him.

His eyes were by now blinking rather rapidly. John Thornton never wept. Never. Not even when his father's body had been lowered forever out of sight. Not even when his broken mother had turned to the boy for all that the man had lacked. Never did sorrow dim his eyes. Right now, however, he was grateful for the soft drops of rain just beginning to fall. It would spare any awkward explanations as to why the Master of Marlborough Mills suddenly required a handkerchief for his face.

Margaret Hale shifted her pitifully small bundle of letters under the crook of her arm as she manipulated her father's heavy umbrella. He had insisted that she take it today, citing his fears for a coming storm. She had complied more out of a desire to cheer and comfort him than any actual fear of the weather. Of course it would rain. It was Milton! It rained nine months of the year here, though not always heavily enough to justify an umbrella. Most of the town's residents did without one of the ungainly contraptions unless the rain picked up some real vehemence, which it just might do today.

Most of the poorer residents, she corrected herself. The more well-to-do tradesmen's wives and daughters who did not own carriages nearly always kept one near, but Margaret had developed something of a sense of independent competence. She was proud of her newfound ability to cope nearly as well as those who did not possess her resources. The weather was of little concern to her these days.

Of great concern, however, was one particular letter in her clutch. She had been waiting anxiously for many days, calculating and recalculating the length of time it ought to take before it could arrive. Her heart had leapt into her throat when she had claimed that day's mail at the office, and she had promptly trod a direct path out of the city so she might have the privacy she required to read it.

Glancing about, she made her way to a small bench along the path where she could separate out the much-coveted correspondence and break the seal. Her eager gaze flew over the opening script, slowing in sorrowful denial as it continued, and halting in abject mourning at its close. She dropped the missive to her lap.

So, that was it. There would be no reprieve, no pardon which would allow her brother to return to his homeland in safety once more. He was in Spain to stay. She bit her lip, refusing to cry. Her poor father! How he had counted on that hope, that one chance that his son might return! An unbidden sob pierced her and she felt convicted of her guilt. It was she who had planted that false hope there. Her father had told her it was a futile exercise before she had begun, but naively she had pressed onward, insisting that the world must bend to her wishes.

Her hand stretched out, her fingers curled into a tense little vise to snatch up the letter and crumple it along with her broken dreams. Clenching her fist, she stopped herself. Frederick's letters were now to become all the more precious, as they were apparently the only contact she would ever have with him again. Heartbreaking as this particular specimen was, it would take its place of honour in her mother's old box of memories.

Oh, Mother! She swallowed hard, that shooting pain returning to her heart. At least Maria Hale had seen her son that one last time, and would nevermore mourn his absence. Her father, on the other hand—bruised and jaded from the loss of his wife—still lingered half his days in a dreamy stupor. Once or twice even of late she had heard him speaking as if her mother still sat across the table from him. Perhaps, she mused, it would be best not to share with him the contents of this recent letter right away.

Margaret had, in the last months, grown startlingly adept at burying her own sorrows. She could not afford to show them, not at home. It was only here, far away from all humanity, where she could slowly piece out her troubles; giving them full examination as was their due, and then carefully packing them away again for perusal at a later date.

Her father... no, he should not hear of this just yet. He was not yet strong enough to learn that he would never see his son again. Let him cherish that hope a little longer, if it gave him pleasure.

The other letters in her stack—two of them, to be exact—were meaningless by comparison. One was from Edith and the other was from Mr Bell. Both would be admired and savoured in their proper time, but the dry comfort of her father's study would do for their examination. Tucking the paper stack into a fold of her cloak, she gathered the umbrella once more and began her return home. The few sparse droplets which had begun to sprinkle down as she read Frederick's letter had multiplied in number and in force. Adjusting her umbrella to account for the wind blowing the water back into her face, she set out with long strides for home once more.

There was scarcely a soul about, as she had chosen the rather melancholy route of her walk specifically for the privacy it offered. Thus it was with no little surprise that she made out a tall black figure as she crested a small knoll. The man was standing stock still, only about twenty paces from the path on which she walked. His back was turned, but there was no possible way anyone in Milton—least of all she—could fail to recognize his towering figure. She froze. Mr Thornton. He was the last person whose notice she wished to attract just now.

He gave no indication that he had heard her approach, standing as he was with his bare head lowered. Perhaps if she moved to the sparse grass off the path and stepped very softly, she might hurry out of sight before he could turn from whatever held his interest. What was it?

Curiosity took her, and she craned her neck momentarily to see what had captivated him. He was not the kind of man to waste time in one attitude. It must be something of some marked distinction to command his attention so.

An abrupt chill washed over her when she realized what it had to be. She suddenly did not need or even wish to see the actual object, standing silently just beyond him. There was only one possible explanation for Mr Thornton to pause so reverently in a graveyard, hatless in a pouring rain. Catching her breath, she redoubled her wish to escape as quickly and discreetly as possible. No man would desire a witness to his grief....

That last thought arrested her even as she gathered herself to move away. It had little occurred to her that the enigmatic, powerful man who held sway over half of Milton might yet grieve the father he had lost as a child. For her, the loss of a parent was still raw and fresh. His sorrow could hardly compare, seasoned as it had been with the passing of time.

And yet, if that were the case, what would compel him now to bear such a pitiable sentinel? He stood in only his suit coat, as if the cold rain threatened little further distress for him as he rendered his duty. Intrigued by this notion, she forgot her attempts at escape. Instead she merely stood as silently as he, watching and marveling and wondering what he could be about.

She was still rooted thus when, a moment later, he slowly turned, his eyes down until they encountered her feet on the path. His head jerked up as if he had been shocked. He said not a word, merely stared, dumbfounded, as she gazed quizzically back. Her open, honest expression searched his, and shame filtered into her conscience. The man before her was a man broken and heart sore, and one who no doubt had felt assured of solitude as he explored his pain.

She pressed her mouth firmly, dropping her eyes from his and swallowing. For the first time, she began to feel a trickle of compassion for him. Almost the first time.

Slowly, and not quite knowing what she intended, she took a deep breath and a bold step in his direction. He drew himself back slightly, almost as a frightened animal. She stopped, watching him uncertainly. At her hesitation, he visibly forced himself to an easier posture. Blinking, she took another step, and then another.

There, this was not so bad. Another step, and then a few more. She was within arm's reach now, and with great trepidation, she turned her face up to his. Still, neither had spoken.

Propriety insisted that he ought to greet her by name, and that she should respond in kind, but what would be the point? It was useless to claim they had not acknowledged one another. Indeed, the shock of her sudden appearance and the memory of all that had passed between them reflected in every fiber of his being.

What more could they say to wipe out the misery of their past several encounters? Nothing, Margaret concluded. All she could offer him was basic human civility; what she would offer and what was owed to any other creature.

With that resolve, she deliberately extended the umbrella to him, her manner gently insistent. Surprise flashing in his eyes, he responded in the only way he could. He took it.

He stared rudely, in mute amazement, no doubt appalled at her lack of deference for his privacy. She took another long, trembling breath. It was too late to withdraw gracefully now.

All at once, the carefully ingrained manners of a gentleman reasserted themselves. He replaced his hat, shifted the umbrella and offered his arm, silently inviting her to share in its shelter. With a miniscule nod, she nervously accepted. Her gloved fingers hovered over his drenched coat sleeve until she gingerly touched them down, sealing their uneasy truce.

She found herself standing uncomfortably close to the most bewildering man she had ever encountered. *What on earth have I just done?* She closed her eyes, clenching her teeth. *Given him another reason to doubt my modesty, that is what I have just done!*

She blinked the drops from her briefly exposed lashes and discovered that she was looking directly at his chest, where a very soggy handkerchief dangled uselessly from his breast pocket. Bravely she raised her eyes to meet his face, which was also thoroughly drenched from the rain. He, too, was blinking rather rapidly as more droplets trickled in stubborn rivulets down from his hair.

Still without a word, she held out her own handkerchief to him. It seemed only the right thing to do, she reasoned. No matter how tempestuous their relationship had been, she could not simply walk away from another person whose pain was so obviously raw.

She dropped her gaze again discreetly as he hesitantly accepted the article from her, and so she was unable to witness with what feeling he received it. She was the intruder upon his solitude, and though she found it within her power to offer some simple comfort, she would never betray his vulnerability or seek to encroach more deeply where she was not welcomed.

"Thank you, Miss Hale." At last the first words were uttered. Succinct, but sufficient.

She dipped her head in acknowledgement. "You are welcome, Mr Thornton," she murmured softly.

Mr Thornton stared at the top of her head, reaching just to his shoulder. Those glorious eyes would not look up at him again.

They had been the first thing he had noticed about Margaret Hale. She had from the very beginning met his gaze freely, with a refreshing frankness, and idiot that he was, he had looked right back.

Now, even that tenuous connection had been severed. Of course it had. He disgusted her by the gritty realities of his life. The very force of character and willingness to labour which had borne him to his position—placing him at the pinnacle of Milton society—had sullied and defiled him in her scornful eyes, locking him forever out of that coveted place in her company.

Yet, here she was. *Why must she torment me?* He had looked to this day's homage as a temporary escape from the regrets haunting him. To get away from his thoughts of her, and every room of his house where she had once set her foot, and from each street corner where he had ever caught fleeting glances of her; if only for an hour to retreat from those memories, that had been his hope. Despite his efforts, here she had found him out in the most unavoidable of ways.

What could she have been thinking to stop? Would that she had simply walked on, pretending quite properly not to have taken notice of his presence or posture! Not Margret Hale. *Oh, no,* he thought bitterly. *Never she.* She would think to offer some paltry succour to her fellow man, claiming to owe it to her own sense of feminine dignity.

That was, after all, what had once led him on to the agonizing folly which even now he longed to forget. There was a righteousness about her, compelling her to extend her gentle touch in refuge and defence to anyone in need. Yes, anyone—even if that particular one was a man she detested.

He glued an iron gaze to the top of her hat brim, daring her to look up at him again. He could not decide whom he despised more—her for avoiding his eyes, or himself for desiring the fleeting contact. Her head had tipped fractionally, and he intuitively determined the trajectory of her gaze. He tilted his own chin back to the flat stone over his shoulder. She absorbed the cold script in silence, then the corner of his eye caught movement as that hat brim finally lifted.

Her clear eyes studied him, boring into his very thoughts as she held him breathless in her grasp. She needed no snare or noose. He was helpless and utterly at her mercy. Those expressive eyes spoke volumes of her empathy without resorting to words. She, so familiar with grief herself, looked into his brokenness and acknowledged their shared bond.

If that were only the sum total of the pain he carried! *Curse her! I don't want her pity!* She thought she understood. She knew nothing of it! She could not know how this moment, sharing the same space and the same air with her, was equal parts anguish and ecstasy to him.

He stared back unflinchingly, refusing to allow her to know the full measure of the emotions drowning him. After a moment of uncomfortable silence, she dropped her eyes.

"Excuse me, I beg you, sir." Her voice was scarcely audible. "I have been too long from home." Her fingers, still resting lightly on his forearm, lifted and broke their faint connection. She began to withdraw herself.

"This is yours," he stopped her, moving to return the umbrella.

She shook her head slightly, beginning to protest. She would not easily take what she had previously offered to him, though the rules of civility absolutely demanded the item's return. He sighed. "May I see you home then, Miss Hale?"

Her eyes flashed back to his. She clearly wished to deny this as well. Exactly as he would expect. She had made it plain enough before that she never voluntarily sought his company... yet, had she not done just that? He firmed his resolve. She had been more than forthright with him in the past. She ought to bear a little of the same from him.

"Miss Hale, I thank you for sharing the shelter of your umbrella, but if we are to part company you must take it back. I need hardly be reminded that you do not think me a gentleman, but I cannot suffer a lady to leave with me her protection from the elements."

Her eyes flared indignantly. "I meant no insult, sir! I only wished to offer... I at least have a warm coat. You look very cold, sir."

His determined hand, thrust toward her, dipped somewhat at the unexpected concern in her voice. His tone softened. "And much do I appreciate your offer, but one of us must be so. It is my own lack of foresight which brought me out thus." He firmly pushed the contested article back to her.

She glanced disinterestedly at the handle of her father's umbrella, then back to his face. To take it would be to admit that he was in the right, and that, he knew, she was not pleased to confess. She lifted her chin. "Mr Thornton, I would be grateful if you could see me home."

THE RAIN INCREASED. THE only way to comfortably walk together under their small shield was for Margaret to tuck her arm under his, avoiding his steady gaze as she did so. She kept her eyes forward and on the path.

Neither knew of anything appropriate to say. She would not relive the discomfort of that little scene in the cemetery by bringing the subject up again, even in the form of an offered consolation.

He, however, was busily admiring her light and easy movement as she walked beside him. No stranger to exertion was she! Her flushed cheeks glowed with radiant health and her steps were firm and untiring. He repressed a little sigh of aggrieved pleasure as he watched her striding next to him, falling neatly into step at his side. This singular event would live long in his memories, but was destined never to be repeated. More was the pity.

After some moments, he had cause to steer her gently around a large puddle in their path. If it was all the thrill to be afforded him, he would exult in her easy responsiveness to his guiding touch. If only he could think of something to say!

Sighing again, he tried to resign himself to the awkward silence. He would go to his solitary chamber that night having been in her sweet, torturous presence this day, and that, at least, was something in which he could take a small measure of perverse satisfaction.

"May I ask, sir," she ventured, breaking the silence at last, "how does your mother today?" That, she hoped, would be a safe and civil few words they could exchange.

He hesitated before replying. "She never comes with me," was his blunt response.

Her eyes swept up to his in surprise. "Excuse me?"

"To the grave. She never comes."

Her gaze returned to the path. "I see, sir." Her forehead creased. Not such a safe topic after all.

He bit his upper lip. "Forgive me, Miss Hale, I fear you find me somewhat agitated at present."

She considered silently a moment. Though she had been unwilling to return to the melancholy setting in which she had found him, he appeared not to have left it yet. "You come often, then?"

"Only once a year." He studied her reaction, wondering if he were causing her much unease. "I gather you must come more often?"

She flicked a pained expression up to him. "It is a good place to be alone," she answered softly.

He thinned his lips and nodded in wordless commiseration. That was a longing he could understand. In the absence of a true companion of the heart, there were times when the next best thing was complete solitude.

Did she come here for the same reasons as he? Surely her grief over her mother was still fresh, but did she yearn for a shoulder to lean upon in her sorrow? *She found one once,* he remembered bitterly. *Where is that fool now?* Some vengeful spirit hoped viciously that she had been spurned and rejected by the one she had turned to in favour of himself. *Perhaps she does know some measure of what I feel!*

Even as the thoughts were born he angrily shoved them away. He had made his decision, and he made it again every day. He would not despise her for loving another instead of himself. How could he, when the mere sound of her voice took his breath away? He felt like some wandering, homeless knight of old, who devoted his unrequited fealty to a distant and unattainable Lady Fair. That was what she was, was she not? Always holding his undying allegiance, occasionally dropping her errant devotee a token, but otherwise completely beyond his reach.

They had walked on several more paces during his reticent musings. Her musical voice, an even alto, floated to him again, though her face remained turned away. "Why does your mother never come?"

He stared briefly, wondering if she were simply making polite conversation or if she truly wanted to know the answer. He recklessly decided in favour of the latter. After all, what did it matter if he gave offence? It was not as though relations between them could grow any worse. "She does not acknowledge my father. He is never mentioned in our home. She wishes to forget... a good many things, Miss Hale."

His voice had been so soft, so devoid of his recent brittleness, that it caused her to look him full in the face and half draw to a halt. She opened her mouth as if to reply, then, sucking in a deep breath, closed it and looked away again. He wondered at her reaction. The mere death of a parent or spouse would not normally engender such a response as his mother's, but Margaret seemed to take it in stride, as though she knew more than he had once told her.

"Father made some mention of the matter to me," she confessed after a moment, as if she could read his thoughts. She halted her strides and looked up to his face again, those green eyes offering her whole sympathy, and perhaps even a speck of contrition. "I am very sorry, Mr Thornton."

A reluctant smile softened his lined mouth for a moment. "Thank you, Miss Hale." He paused. Did he dare say more? "And if I may, I would also thank you for your company. It has been most welcome to me just now."

Those bright eyes flashed again. She fixed him with a careful expression, tilting her head ever so slightly. "I had thought, Mr Thornton, that we had declared our mutual dissatisfaction with our acquaintance. Was I mistaken? If so," she forged ahead before he could interrupt, her ears turning pink, "I might receive your thanks with complaisance... with goodwill."

"I..." he tried to respond, and broke off, his throat suddenly quite dry. Was she trying to ask forgiveness or extend it? "I do remember words to that effect, Miss Hale, but have since had sufficient time to regret them."

She focused her gaze intently, in the most unmaidenly attitude he could imagine. *Bewitching.* She reminded him of some of the toughest negotiators he had ever encountered as they prepared to unbendingly broker high-stakes transactions.

"I realize, Mr Thornton, that you have reason to despise me, and I accept your censure if I must. Know, however, that in light of more recent events, I consider my own judgement of yourself to have been somewhat in error."

His heart lurched. She did not regret...? Could she? "In error?" he croaked.

"I... I abused your good name when I spoke with Mr Higgins. I spoke prematurely, and I owe you an apology. You are very noble to have taken him on after everything, and I ought to have said as much sooner."

His hopeful breath left him. So, that was all. He began walking again, drawing her reluctantly along. "Think nothing of it, Miss Hale. I was in need of experienced hands, and so far I have no regrets in his employment." He unconsciously quickened his pace, not noticing that she had to lengthen her strides considerably to keep up.

"Also, Mr Thornton..." she tugged his arm, dragging him again to a grudging halt. He faced her unwillingly, waiting as she battled for whatever shocking statement was next to come forth. "As I may not have another opportunity," she took a trembling breath, "I must beg to offer you my gratitude in one other matter."

His eyes narrowed, his tones hardened as he brushed her hand from his arm. "I said before that *no thanks* were necessary!"

Her rosy lips puckered in annoyance. "Then in that, I suppose we are even! We, neither of us, are able to accept the other's gratitude! There can really be no reason for us to go on walking together, Mr Thornton. I will bid you good-day!"

She shrugged her arms further up inside her cape, out of the cold rain, and marched off, squaring her shoulders. His face crumpled in bewilderment. *Aggravating woman!* Contrary, exasperating, obstinate, provoking female! *Magnificent.*

He caught up to her in a few quick strides, his jaw set. He could be just as stubborn! Without speaking, he paced beside her, holding the umbrella awkwardly aloft so that she might still reap the benefits of its shelter without forcing either of them to endure physical contact.

She ignored him, her eyes fixed ahead and her sculpted cheek muscles twitching as she walked on without slowing. She really had quite a ground-covering stride for a young lady. *Idiot. Stop looking!*

It was in this manner that they gained the outskirts of Margaret's neighborhood. Anyone with eyes could detect some spat had taken place between the unlikely pair, and Margaret at last halted. "This is ridiculous, Mr Thornton! I offer you a choice. Allow me to have my say, or let us part company!"

He tightened his grip on the umbrella. Neither seemed a safe option. "I yield to the lady's pleasure," he answered stiffly.

"Very well." Her tone was clipped, irritated, and not at all grateful. "I would thank you, Mr Thornton, for your actions to prevent damage to my reputation. It was most unlooked for, I assure you. Yet my thanks are not primarily concerned with myself. Had an inquest taken place, another would have been compromised, and I speak of the sort of injury which is far more serious than a mere slight to my honour." She narrowed those brilliant eyes, daring him to respond.

Oh, how her words galled his raw feelings! This was why he had not wanted to hear what she had to say. He had somehow done a service for that reprobate, that scoundrel who put her at risk! His very dignity as a man rankled by the association.

"I suppose I am to say now that you are welcome!" he returned icily, his voice threateningly lowered so that she had to strain to make out his words. "You *are* welcome for your own sake, and for your father's. The gentleman, if he can be such, I take no notice of. I wonder at the kind of man who would cower behind a woman!"

He glared right back at her, his tall, powerful figure squaring off in the middle of a public street during a rainstorm with a mere slip of a woman. Had he been able to see himself in that moment, he would have been horrified, but blinded and baffled as he was, all he could see was the livid woman seething before him.

"You know nothing of the matter!" she lashed out hotly.

"Nor do I wish to! Are we finished here, Miss Hale?"

"One thing more, if you please sir!" She clenched her little gloved hands into fists, her eyes blazing with righteous indignation.

He bit back his temper. Awareness of his surroundings was slowly registering, and John Thornton had never in his life raised his voice to a lady. He locked his jaw. "Proceed, Miss Hale," he growled between his teeth.

Her form, rigid and potent with the fury of a moment ago, withdrew somewhat as her face softened. She had not expected him to relent. "Simply this, sir. Had you never considered that my mother may have had those cherished loved ones who would risk the very gravest of consequences, simply that they might see her once more?"

His mouth gaped. What could she be speaking of? "I have not the pleasure of understanding you, Miss Hale."

"Nor, I fancy, will I be able to enlighten you further. I only demand of your justice that you allow the possibility of... of other explanations for what you believed yourself to have witnessed. We both know of my failings regarding that event, and you have been good enough to keep the matter to yourself. I am not afraid of my shame—I quite deserve it—but you have shown yourself to be a man of the very highest honour in this business, Mr Thornton. I feel I owe you what explanation is within my power to offer without compromising another. Things are not as they likely appear to you. I am in your debt, Mr Thornton."

He stared dumbly, not realizing that his hand had begun to slacken and the heavy umbrella tilted rakishly to the side. Both of them stood once more unprotected from the rain. That blinding flash of her ire had spent itself, and she was looking back at him almost beseechingly, begging him to accept her explanations.

He blinked and swallowed, making some effort to command himself. "Come, Miss Hale," he murmured huskily. "I promised to see you to your door." Her petite frame relaxed somewhat, and she meekly accepted his escort once more.

"John! How pleased I am to see you!" Mr Hale's gentle voice surprised him through the door as Miss Hale offered her cool parting civilities.

Mr Thornton tore his longing eyes from her downturned face to greet his friend. "Mr Hale," he nodded in acknowledgement.

The father turned his curious gaze on his daughter. "Margaret?"

"Mr Thornton was good enough to walk me home, Father." She removed the drenched cape from her shoulders, hanging it to drip dry. With an uncomfortable little dip of her head, she bid Thornton her farewell and stepped behind her father.

"Oh! Well, that is indeed good of you, John! I thank you."

He offered his friend a tight smile. "Miss Hale is being modest. She happened upon me at a time when I had forgotten my own umbrella, and she spared me the discomfort of a return trip without it. I am most grateful for her thoughtfulness." He searched her face until she raised hesitant eyes to his. Her features flickered, but he could not discern the meaning. Well, if that was to be all he could expect in response... "Excuse me, Mr Hale, Miss Hale. I have appointments to keep."

He removed himself from the top step but Miss Hale's exclamation froze him. "Wait!" she cried. She extended that much-debated object once more, pressing it firmly upon him. "You must not go without. I fear the rain shall become quite fierce, and you have three miles yet to walk."

He shook his head politely. "Thank you, Miss Hale, but doubtlessly you will have need of it."

"Well, as to that, John, Margaret rarely carries it at all, except at my behest," Mr Hale smiled kindly. "You are most welcome to it. I should hate to see you take cold, John. We have not seen you much lately, I do hope you have not been ill! I was hoping you will still be able to read tomorrow—if you are not too busy, that is."

Mr Thornton relented, aware that the pair of them had determined that he should take the blasted thing and there would be no escaping without it. "I did intend to keep our appointment. I am sorry I have not been able to come for the last few weeks." He flicked a meaningful glance at Margaret. "If it is agreeable, then, I shall return this to you on the morrow."

"Of course, John! Do come a little early if you can," Mr Hale peeked hesitantly to his daughter, requesting her endorsement of the invitation. "Well, you know, we are always here, and we would be happy for you to take tea with us later as well, if it suits. I only mean, do not worry on that account. You are always most welcome, John."

He shook his head, both grieved and grateful that he could not accept. "I am afraid I have guests of my own tomorrow evening."

"Oh," Mr Hale's face fell a little. "Well... well, we shall still be most glad for you to come in the afternoon, will we not Margaret? Do get dry as soon as you can, John. Will you give Mrs Thornton our good wishes? She has been very kind to us. We were so honoured when she called on Margaret... well, good day, John." Mr Hale's hopeful smile beamed; his pleasure in anticipating his good friend's call the next day, and his disappointment that it would be cut short, causing him to bumble quite a deal more than was his wont.

Margaret had observed it too. Thornton glanced at her and noted her faintly worried expression. It smoothed almost immediately as her eyes met his once more. She parted from him in complete civility—not offering her hand, as she had done once or twice before, but not shunning him either.

"Good day Mr Hale, and Miss Hale." He tipped his hat, and took his tormented self out of her presence.

WILL JOHN AND MARGARET learn to let go of their pride and reach for the one person who can understand them? Keep reading *Northern Rain* to find out!

Acknowledgments

Had my family any notion of what I had been up to this past year of writing *No Such Thing As Luck*, I have no doubt they would all be immensely delighted to see all of my distractedness finally bearing fruit. However, being an intensely private person where my writing is concerned, instead they all probably just believe I am touched in the head. Regardless, they have been my constant inspiration and support, without which I could not have finished a single chapter.

To my husband: If I ever allow you to read this, you will feel like you are looking in a mirror. You have treated me like your queen since the day we met, and I am humbled and grateful to call you my love.

And to my Lord: For always guiding my footsteps.

NOTE ON SECOND EDITION

I also owe my profound gratitude to Janet Taylor of JT Originals and *More Agreeably Engaged*.

It was Janet's enjoyment of this book in 2015 which not only inspired a friendship, but introduced me to a world of other authors and lovers of N&S. I am proud to present the new cover, which is the original creation of Janet and her son Jeff.

Thank you, my dear friend, for pouring your heart into this project and for taking me under your wing.

****NC, 2017*

Made in the USA
Las Vegas, NV
23 March 2025